BROWSING COLLECTION
14-DAY CHECKOUT
No Holds • No Renewals

Brooklyn
Crime
Novel

Also by Jonathan Lethem

NOVELS

The Arrest

The Feral Detective

Gun, with Occasional Music

Amnesia Moon

As She Climbed Across the Table

Girl in Landscape

Motherless Brooklyn

The Fortress of Solitude

You Don't Love Me Yet

Chronic City

Dissident Gardens

A Gambler's Anatomy

NOVELLAS

This Shape We're In

SHORT STORY COLLECTIONS

The Wall of the Sky, the Wall of the Eye

Kafka Americana (with Carter Scholz)

Men and Cartoons

How We Got Insipid

Lucky Alan and Other Stories

NONFICTION

The Disappointment Artist

The Ecstasy of Influence

Fear of Music

They Live

More Alive and Less Lonely

Brooklyn Crime Novel

Jonathan Lethem

ecco
An Imprint of HarperCollinsPublishers

BROOKLYN CRIME NOVEL. Copyright © 2023 by Jonathan Lethem. All rights reserved. Printed in the United States of America. No part of this book may be used or reproduced in any manner whatsoever without written permission except in the case of brief quotations embodied in critical articles and reviews. For information, address HarperCollins Publishers, 195 Broadway, New York, NY 10007.

HarperCollins books may be purchased for educational, business, or sales promotional use. For information, please email the Special Markets Department at SPsales@harpercollins.com.

Ecco® and HarperCollins® are trademarks of HarperCollins Publishers.

FIRST EDITION

Designed by Alison Bloomer

Library of Congress Cataloging-in-Publication Data has been applied for.

ISBN 978-0-06-293882-4

23 24 25 26 27 LBC 5 4 3 2 1

FOR LYNN NOTTAGE

CONTENTS

I. Everybody Gets Robbed 1

II. The Case Against Boerum 73

III. Locked-Out Memories 117

IV. The Dance 231

V. Brooklyn Crime Novel 321

VI. No Music 349

ACKNOWLEDGMENTS 375

I.
Everybody Gets Robbed

"IT WOULD BE FOOLISH TO SAY that all renovation areas are safe or that once renovation begins an area is magically transformed into a crime-free haven . . . If you are concerned about crime in an area, don't just take one person's word about it. Go over to the precinct house and see what the police have to say about your block and the surrounding area. Ask people on the block who are living there now. Former residents usually give the least reliable information.

It can almost categorically be said that neighborhoods that have a lot of renovation activity do become safer, either through private patrols or through pressure upon policemen or just because more people are on the streets. The pioneer in an emerging area like Crown Heights will find bargain prices for a number of reasons, and a higher crime rate is a key one."

—JOY AND PAUL WILKES,
You Don't Have to Be Rich to Own a Brownstone

WHEN WE announced our production plans for "THE CASE AGAINST BROOKLYN" . . . the startling expose of cop-bookie corruption . . . we expected gangsters, hoodlums, and merchants of violence to give it the lead-pipe treatment. We expected threats and worse from the gunmen of Gowanus.

But we never expected reasonable citizens to challenge the free screen. We never dreamed that important citizens of Brooklyn would have "ordered" us not to show this picture in the Borough of Brooklyn. But we have been told to stay out . . . or else!

We think the citizens of Brooklyn want to learn the truth. We think that you will side with "THE CASE AGAINST BROOKLYN".

—ADVERTISEMENT,
The Brooklyn Daily Eagle, June 6, 1958

"MANHATTAN KEEPS on makin it/Brooklyn keeps on takin it"

—BOOGIE DOWN PRODUCTIONS,
"The Bridge Is Over"

1.

Quarters, Part 1

(1978)

A first story. The start of our inquiry.

Two white boys, in a second-floor apartment above a storefront on Court Street, between Schermerhorn and Livingston streets.

The boys, both fourteen, gleefully labor at something captured in the teeth of a small, table-mounted vise. They labor at this thing with a hacksaw. The tool, the vise, the whole tabletop workshop, belongs to the divorced father of one of the boys, a man who lives alone in this apartment except during those days when his son visits. The father works as a therapist but aspires to make jewelry. Hence the vise, the hacksaw. The father is absent this morning.

THE STOREFRONT BELOW the apartment features an Italian restaurant called The Queen. A small dining room with red plush curtains, eight or ten tables crowded together. This place has a reputation among some as a throwback, a place for "fine dining" of a sort cherished only by probable mobsters, or by nostalgists for a version of Brooklyn that is already, by this point, quaint. Though hardly vanished.

Mobsters may also be nostalgists. Probably so, in many cases.

The restaurant's proprietors own the building. It's to them the father pays his rent. The Queen also has a twin, The Queen Pizzeria. A thriving slice joint, two addresses away. Wedged between the two, the tablecloth Queen and the pizza-counter Queen, is a mid-sized pornographic movie theater. The proprietors of the pornographic movie theater pay rent to the owners of the storefronts on either side of it, the pizzeria and the tablecloth restaurant. Two of these businesses, the porn movies, the slice joint, are required to keep the third—the table-cloth restaurant—afloat.

A slice of pizza costs fifty cents.

A subway token costs fifty cents.

Hmmm. Is this some golden law of affiliation? The city an oblique, untranslatable system? Or might the sole religion here be the price of things?

Let's return to the boys. What's the thing in the vise?

The vise holds a coin. A U.S. twenty-five cent piece, a Washington Quarter dated 1968, from the Denver mint. The therapist-jeweler's son wields the hacksaw. He runs it diligently in its groove, until the quarter is cut in half. The boys grin, sharing a nerve-wired, chortling delight. The vise is loosened, just long enough to turn the half-quarter in its grip, then tightened again. The hacksaw is applied anew. The slim blade rips through, halving the half-coin. The other boy seizes up the result for scrutiny. All that's left is Washington's proud forehead and nose and the letters LIB. The boys have made a quarter-quarter.

The two fresh quarter-quarters are moved to the table, where we see them now added to the results of this afternoon's industry: a pile of ruined coins. Nearly all twenty-five cent pieces, some halved, some quartered. A couple of nickels, too, have been sawn in half. Dimes? Too small. Pennies, not worth the trouble. The room is sharp with the scent of hot metal, of microscopic shreds of coin.

They are doing this superbly pointless thing off the back end of a sleepover. It's ten in the morning. The two boys are caught like flies in the web of the summer between eighth and ninth grades, the shift to high school, a great confusion of dispersal from these particular streets into the city at large.

Everything will be nothing like it was ever again.

They scoop the ruined coins into their palms, and pour them into their pants pockets, until the pockets bulge. The energy between the boys is high and delighted. Yet this is a delight in something craven. They're sly with self-regard. Sure, they're vandals—this is established fact. They've been known to write graffiti on the city's surfaces. On trains, when they're courageous. More often brick walls, metal doors, commercial vehicles. They've egged the Court Street bus at night, from the windows of this same apartment (divorced dad being not much for tallying his egg supply). What are they hoping to prove by destroying the coins?

The boys move through the apartment door, which is triple locked, including by a bar lock that braces at an angle to the floor, and down the back stairwell, heading for the street.

CHAPTER 17 of the U.S. Legal Code covers "Mutilation, diminution, and falsification of coins. 332. Debasement of coins; alteration of official scales, or embezzlement of metals."

The boys are committing a crime, then.

Are they likely to be arrested for it?

Not too likely.

In the world of these white boys, television cops are more present than the real thing. *Dragnet*, *Adam-12*, *Kojak*, cornpone fucking *McCloud*.

No television cops are going to screech up in a black-and-white and bust them for mutilation of currency.

The boys cross Atlantic, along Court Street, in the direction of the Italian neighborhood, their old school, the projects, Cobble Hill Park. All we know for certain is that though several dollars' worth of quarters jangle between their two loaded pockets, these may no longer be offered for purchase of a subway token or a slice of pizza. They ruined their money! What gives?

2.
Nobody Knows
(forever)

This is a story about what nobody knows.

It's set in a place nobody doesn't think they know. Yet nobody knows anything about this place, and they never did.

Maybe I exaggerate.

Still, not many can be bothered to know. Not, for instance that Malcolm X's family was hidden, in the hours and days immediately following his assassination, in a safe house on the corner of Dean and Nevins streets. Nobody knows this. Or they forgot.

Equally, they forgot that Willie Sutton was apprehended on the corner of Pacific and Third. He's the one who when asked "Why do you rob banks?" replied "Because that's where the money is."

Nobody knows this anymore if they ever did.

Nobody knows that Isaac Asimov lived in 213 Dean Street for a year in the 1940s. To care, you'd have to be a nerd. Even then, how would you find this out? Guy wrote four hundred books; you read fifty of them. You'd walk right past.

Nobody knows H. P. Lovecraft, the paranoid racist, lived at 169 Clinton, corner of State Street. Lived there in abject misery, cowering within his terror of the Other. *"The population is a hopeless tangle and enigma; Syrian, Spanish, Italian, and negro elements impinging upon one another, and fragments of Scandinavian and American belts lying not far distant. It is a babel of sound and filth, and sends out strange cries to answer the lapping of oily waves at its grimy piers and the monstrous organ litanies of the harbour whistles."*

Geddouddahere, you!

We don't need your type around here.

And five minutes after he goes, Brooklyn wipes its hands of him.

This is that kind of place. A babel of sound and filth, but it's *our* babel of sound and filth, and the rubble of what's in front of you today is too much to sort through, never mind what weirdness just packed up and went.

Example: a row house at 246 Dean collapsed. This was one of four anomalous wood-frames on that block, likely not a good idea to squeeze them into the sequence of brownstones. Rain squeezed between, at the roof line, at the splice. The brick of the brownstone didn't care; it grew moss. The wooden structure secretly absorbed the moisture. It sagged and rotted, and by the time they noticed, there was nothing they could do about it.

Once it fell, it was cheaper to bury the ruin in the earth of its own footprint, and the backyard. So, when the eventual hippie renovators acquire the lot, along with the brownstone beside it, the one with the mossy brickwork, they're astounded to find a mountain of lathe and plaster and shattered bathroom tile and marble mantelpiece just mingled in the soil there. They've intended to plant a garden, but good luck. It's like the earth just opened and chewed up and half swallowed the house. It's like a bombsite.

Why, in these blocks of brick and stone, the strange four wooden A-frames jammed into the sequence? Who lived there? Why did it fall? How was the decision made to entomb it in place? Nobody knows, nobody cares. Around here we call that *off-street parking*.

Nobody knows what was here five minutes ago, just before they got here, let alone a hundred years.

Nobody cares that nobody knows.

In this place that used to be, in a time the city was synonymous with crime, nobody ever got arrested for forgetting.

3.
No Name White Boys
(generally)

Why don't the white boys with the ruined coins have names?

They don't need names.

On these streets, in this Brooklyn Crime Novel, there's simply too many of these white boys. Some will reappear, and some won't. It doesn't matter. In this inquiry, we're taking a wider view.

Here's a tip: among the white boys, keep an eye on the spoiled boy and the millionaire's son, when they come along.

Also the younger brother, who'll appear in the next story.

And that Black boy too, here, coming along the street just now:

4.
Hockey Warriors

(1976)

A Black boy and three white boys walk carrying hockey sticks down Dean Street, westward, across Smith Street. Then, at Court Street, as Dean jogs and changes its name to Amity, they move into Cobble Hill. From there they turn south, down Clinton Street, toward Carroll Gardens, the Italian neighborhood.

Two of the three white boys are thirteen. The third, an eleven-year-old, another white boy, is a younger brother.

The younger brother is, frankly, a compromise recruit. They need him to flesh out a team of four. They've got a date for a game of street hockey, with an established all-Italian group who await them on Henry Street.

The younger brother needed some persuading, because—hockey? *Street* hockey?

But his older brother rarely rounds him up for anything anymore. He likes that it can still happen. His older brother and his friends, they said they needed him.

So, street hockey. Sure.

None of these three white boys is Italian. With the Black boy, they all live on Dean Street.

If they're non-Italian, are they something else? Sure, a muddle. Indistinct fallen WASP, half Jew, hippie, whatever. None with an identification to rival that of the Italians.

They're Brownstoner boys.

The Black kid is ten months older, one grade of public school, and a million significances ahead of even the oldest of the three white kids, those he now leads into the strange turf of Carroll Gardens for this ostensible street hockey throwdown.

Do any of these four boys know how to play hockey—even street hockey, in sneakers? Barely.

The Black kid is their best hope, on account of confidence, kineticism, his excellence at street games generally.

The younger brother, on the other hand, is likely to be useless. He'll need continuous buoying even to carry on competing, as he needs continuous buoying on this journey into the unfamiliar neighborhood. This younger brother, he might even be worse than dead weight. But to show up with fewer than four players is to default the challenge.

In any case, this is a quixotic group. The Italian boys are going to kick their asses. There's a kind of glory in knowing and not-knowing what they've gotten themselves into. It's somewhat incredible they even managed to find four hockey sticks—blades splintered, bound everywhere with electrical tape—with which to represent their hopeless cause.

On the corner of Kane Street, they divert one block farther west, walking past the quiet schoolyard of P.S. 29, to reach Henry Street. It's a Saturday afternoon in early May. Now fall back, let these boys veer into the honeyed light that leans now over the rooftops and seeps through the canopy of leaves, that ripples itself across ornate brownstone cornices. Let them be out of sight for an instant, let them go unescorted into this day's fate. It's the truer truth. Nobody sees them, not just yet.

A check against lyricism. Keep the light, let alone the honeyed light, from your eyes. Just the facts, man—no painterly effects. We're here to enumerate crimes. Or perhaps, to distinguish not-crimes, the exception, from against an overall criminal background. We're not out collecting light on faces, or light through leaves on cornices. The city's a grid of schematics. Let's try to put some pins in the map. No need to pin butterflies. No butterflies, no buttery light.

We'll follow the boys' lead in this: Tend your secrets, tuck away your secret excesses. If, say, there's any special allure or romance between any two of these four Dean Street boys, it's at present strictly maintained behind this afternoon's martial façade. Four bodies marching, sticks on shoulders. A sight, so far unseen.

AT THE CORNER of Henry and President, the four are met by four others. A day of fours. These aren't their designated opponents, those
presumably waiting another six blocks farther down the street. These
are four *other* Italian guys, sitting on street-corner chairs, outside an
unmarked social club, a tiny storefront with windows painted black.
We're speaking here, of course, of local recognitions, these aren't Italians in the national sense, maybe none have ever been to Italy, maybe
one has a Puerto Rican mom shamefully unmentioned, but come
on, yougoddabekidding, weknowwhatwemeanhere, this is an Italian
neighborhood and there's a self-concept, a clarity here that might
nearly be a relief in contrast to the weird muddle of the four boys with
sticks. The Italians range in age from fourteen, the same age as the
Black kid, to one who might be a twenty-year-old trying to pass, in his
bomber jacket and penny loafers. He's certainly got a pencil moustache formed of something much harder than peach fuzz. At the sight
of the Dean Street boys, the four rise and stand, beaming slouchy
insolent astonishment at what's arrayed itself before them.

"You got to be kidding me."

"What?"

"What kind of thing is this walking down the street? What am I
looking at here?"

"We've got a game."

"You're going nowhere like that with sticks. Now turn around and
don't make me articulate it twice."

"We got a game, c'mon."

"A game he says. I'll make a game out of you. You'll be gaming on
your ass and crying for your ma and she'll be saying what's the matter
and you'll be saying I don't know what happened I accidentally fell on
my ass in a game."

"He'll game your mother." A second voice, to clarify what's been
explained.

The youngest Italian reaches out and latches his fingers on the
stick of one of the Dean Street boys, who doesn't let go so easily.
There's a moment of tug of war, then the oldest and tallest Italian, the
pencil moustache, slaps the younger Italian's hand away.

"We're doing you a favor."

"We're meeting Vinnie," says the Black kid. "They're waiting for us."

"Where? Who?"

The game's set for the quietest block in Carroll Gardens, Summit Street, behind the parish of Sacred Hearts of Jesus and Mary & St. Stephen, none of which would bear mentioning even if it were on the tip of the tongue, which it isn't. "Vincent."

"Who?"

"Vincent, Vinnie."

For any signs the Italians show, Vinnie might be someone's younger brother, might be someone's worst enemy or a dog from Mars.

"What are you doing hanging out with these guys?" Pencil moustache addresses this to the Black kid. "What are you trying to accomplish? This don't make sense."

"Street hockey."

"What even is this?" The questions widen to some implicit ontological ground, to fundamental matters of being. "What am I looking at? Someone say because I don't understand."

"Just let us pass."

"What even are you? You, tell me. Are you Jewish? Does anyone even know what I'm looking at?"

Another echo of clarification: "Does your mother know?"

"C'mon."

"He says c'mon. You're lucky we don't break all those sticks across our knees. Where'd you even get those? Triangles? McCrory's? They shouldn't be selling that to you, it's irresponsible in a case like yours. What is that, doctor's tape? You got your stick in a sling?"

"Duck tape."

"If I know one thing, *that ain't duck tape.*"

For no clear reason, this is a laugh line for the Italians, a bust-up. The mood is so suddenly bright and infectious that the Dean Street boys smile too, and chuckle in confused relief. Then, as if laughter is a signal that the exchange has obtained its result, the pencil moustache says, "No seriously get out of here. You ain't crossing this street. Go home before we kill you with your duck tape sticks you agglomeration of nothing."

The other Italians chime in:

"Mother nothing."

"We'll fuck her with the stick."

"Go. Now. Get out of my eyes."

The Dean Street boys know when they're routed. They retreat up Henry, jostled in confusion. At Kane the Black boy says, "This way! We'll go down on Columbia Heights and cut around. Kane Street cuts through!"

One white boy agrees eagerly, another doesn't. "Forget it, you saw those guys, they'll kill us." The younger brother is wide-eyed, maybe traumatized by the encounter on the corner.

"We can't forfeit. Vinnie and his boys are waiting."

"It's too late." Time does seem to be ticking away, the sun a blobby bomb arcing to hide itself in rooftops.

"Let's go, my brothers, let's go!" The Black kid's leadership is irrepressible. They move west, a nervous pod, but acting as one. That is, until coming to the neighborhood's deforming limit, the Brooklyn-Queens Expressway. In this place, rather than lancing overhead, the Expressway is carved as a savage moat into the natural grid of the Brooklyn streets. A roaring trench of cars and gray pollution so chunky you feel it catch in your teeth.

The little brother balks, not wanting to cross the highway. Abandoning the cover of the tree-lined streets had been more than he'd bargained for. This, now, feels like falling off the earth's edge. "Let's go back."

The older brother turns on him. "Back? We're right here! We have to make the game!"

The Black kid's more consoling. "They can't see us, man, don't worry." He gestures with his stick, full of animation. "Listen, we'll stay on Hicks but cut down the other side of the highway, they won't see us. It cuts right back across the BQE at Sackett and Union, there's no way, they can't cover both streets, too lazy anyway to get off their motherfucking milk crates minute after we was gone."

His savvy and expressiveness, the flow of street names, the relentless invocation of the word *cut* and *cuts*. All are for the moment irresistible, even to the younger kid whose eyeballs are not-secretly swimming in tears. Nobody corrects their leader to say it was chairs on the sidewalk slate, not milk crates. They cross the highway and creep southward along Hicks.

But the Italian squad, against all hope and likelihood, have located a pointless motivation in the dead of the afternoon. They're up off their chairs. They too know the BQE street bridges at Sackett and Union, which are after all only a single block apart. They wait, then jump and point and sock fist in palm as if expecting a fly ball.

"Run!"

The Dean Street boys flee toward the waterfront, down Sackett, and reach Columbia Heights. After an instant—one in which the group is in peril of disintegration, two heading north, two south—they fall in again, helplessly really, behind the Black kid. Improbably, he's emboldened, moving south, deeper into the strange turf, still adamant they won't blow this game.

YOUNGER BROTHER'S CRYING now. Is this Red Hook? He doesn't know. He didn't ever wish to go to Red Hook, let alone on this day, with no guide except the crazily fearless Black kid. The name Red Hook was always disturbing to him. Suggestive, as with other unvisited place names, of a journey into an unwelcome past. As if Red Hook ought to have been severed from Brooklyn's mainland by now, amputated, to float off to sea.

And to journey there carrying sticks? Couldn't they at least abandon them?

The younger brother is isolated within the group by his role as younger brother. He's bracketed on the sidewalk, kept in a protective cordon as if under quarantine. Perhaps his tears, his irrational copious weeping, might be infectious. Perhaps he cries on all their behalves, the secret everybody knows.

It is only two months before the worst thing that will happen to the younger brother.

Maybe he's crying because he feels it coming. That worst day, in June, he won't cry as he did this day, just crossing the BQE, into the unknown territory of Red Hook. He won't cry at all.

You can't always make sense of these things. You can't always predict when you'll cry.

SO, THEY WANDER. Is there an appointment still for keeping? Any chance in hell that Vincent's team of four haven't thrown up their hands, gone off into other activities? Claimed victory, if they'd even troubled to remember the challenge?

The Dean Street contingent are far from home. Perhaps they always were. How long will they persist? Will they engage the older Italian four again, or perhaps even some other unforeseen thing, as they inch and edge their way along the blocks, probing back in the direction of a street hockey rendezvous, one diminishingly likely to occur?

Tune in again to this same sad channel.

5.
C., Part 1
(a snapshot)

What is it that this Black kid sees in them, his white friends?

Or is it something he wants from them?

Or wants them to see in, or want from, *him*?

What is it that drives him to offer his leadership to the white boys of Dean Street—in hockey, of all things—or to teach them to properly throw a Spaldeen off a stoop, or flick a skully cap across the pavement, or boost a soda from the rear of a bodega? He even feels he needs to teach them to walk down the street properly, not to be cran-ing their necks around backward every five steps telegraphing suscep-tibility for all to see. He teaches them every trick in the book—every trick in the book of his body.

Years before *magical negro* was a notion you could only deplore and deride, certainly nothing ever to admit you'd consented to re-semble, this one Black kid from Dean Street had found himself cast in the part, for every taker in a five-block radius.

WHAT DOES IT take to get a name around here anyway? Call him C.

Now restate the question. What is it that C. sees in them?

The answer may not be about something he sees in them, the white boys, at all. Sure, he sees them. But he *feels* their parents. Their parents, and his mom. C., he's a parental tuning fork. He didn't ask for this power. Like most powers, it's a curse as much as a gift.

C. hears the parents when they speak, and when they don't. But his awareness of the white parents comes later. First, inescapably, comes his attunement to his own mother.

His mother, unlike his father, is from the islands. Haitian. She works as a nurse at Brooklyn Hospital, in Fort Greene Park, and brings home stories of horror from the emergency room. Specifically, the filthy condition of the white children's underwear when they appear with broken limbs from the playgrounds. The private school children from Brooklyn Heights, most of all. The richer, the filthier.

"You treat them like anyone else," she says, about the white peo-ple, practically before he can know what she is talking about. "They hardly know any better."

(C.'s father, who is from Bushwick, keeps it much simpler. "Don't let them get you in trouble. Don't let them get you mixed up with the cops. Because be assured the cops will be bringing you in, not them white boys.")

His mother's philosophy comes at him from all sides. It blurts from nowhere. She'd be cooking him eggs. Teaching him to knot his bowtie for church, a thing he never did get exactly right. Her thoughts floated out like banners:

"You have to teach them who you are. Don't figure they already know."

She will begin with some assertion plainly dubious to him, but never mind. For her, it is gospel: "It's your neighborhood. You treat them like a guest in your house."

Or: "Introduce yourself, look in their eyes. You call the parents Mister or Missus so-and-so."

Or: "You see the dirt under the fingernails on that boy? Don't those people even know how to wash a child?"

Or: "You walk that boy to school, and you walk him back to the block after, I don't care if you never speak one word the whole way."

Among the many things his instincts commanded he protect the white children from, C. will think ruefully, so many years later, is the ferocious judgment of his mother.

She glances at him, as they step out on their way to church, sees his eyeballs sliding sideways to inventory the morning street and says: "They don't even know how to *play* right."

It's like she knows before he knows what he'll be doing later that afternoon. The bowtie tossed aside—somewhere, he's still got a cigar-box of the things—to run outside and cajole some misshapen clump of white boys of different ages and capacities into a fair facsimile of a stickball game. Based on—what? What did he know that they didn't? C. based it all on some black-and-white footage of Willie Mays in a Harlem street, marking distances with the manholes, picking who's up first by every kid grabbing the stick until someone lands on top.

To hell with eeny meeny miny moe, you'd be deaf not to hear the echo lurking in that shit.

Like his mother knows what he'll be doing before he knows, or maybe like she's making it happen.

Maybe the answer is that simple, to the question of C.'s tenure as the white boys' champion and protector: his mother made him do it.

6.
Screamer

(1975–82)

Hoyt Street, between Dean and Pacific, in an eyesore house with a crumbling face, its ineptly painted brick flaking, through a third-story window, she appears routinely: the Screamer. Some kind of nightmare Rapunzel, white girl, crazy, banished upstairs. She looks out at the street and she screams. Indecipherable, unpredictable, and fucking loud!

Who at?

Anyone passing.

Sometimes no one, just exhortations of crazy right into the blue sky, the Catholic hospital's mute windows.

Increasingly, at the boys who come to egg her on.

The white boys and the Black boys and the Puerto Ricans (some of whom we should note are Dominicans, but the white boys don't grasp this distinction). The Screamer's block forms a kind of haven, a neutral zone. The situation's a kind of universal solvent, an ingredient that galvanizes anyone who's been hailed by her zany bolts from the clouds.

For the boys, it begins to seem a sexual thing, though no one wants to think about that. The joke about the Polish stripper: *put it all on!* Go ahead, try it, bellow your stand-up routine up at her. Like trying to roof a Spaldeen, harder than it looks. All wit is lost on the Screamer. She'll outlast you.

Hoyt Street, passage to the A train, out of the Gowanus Houses projects, gauntlet of uneasy new commuters, path of eerie hospital run by resident nuns in row houses worth future zillions. But the Screamer owns this one block, by dint of the total law of aggression.

This is a time of sirens, the firehouse on State Street roaring the southward streets, Nevins and Hoyt, deep into Gowanus to confront the burning third-floor walk-ups, the Wyckoff Gardens incinerator fires, the god-only-knows Mafia-incinerated warehouses and funeral homes, sometimes perhaps to extinguish the burning chemical slick floating atop the Canal.

Time of outcries ignored, shrieks through upper windows generally, moaning of all-night bodies sleeping it off on Atlantic Avenue sidewalks or in boarded storefront doorways.

Copious musics pour through open parlor windows, interlacing on the street with what blares from car windows, merengue and Jackson 5, Harold Melvin and the Blue Notes, maybe scraps of Funkadelic or Pink Floyd.

Money, it's a hit!

But this is a realm of dead spots too, weird gulfs and valleys in the sonic sphere, often not a single car sludges past on a given afternoon between the passing of two Dean Street buses half an hour apart.

In any case there's nothing like the Screamer, an avant-gardist like John Cage or La Monte Young. She's pre-punk!

Either nobody or a hundred people have ever called the cops on the Screamer, each possibility equally plausible and pointless. What are the cops going to do, tell her family to tell her to quit? You think they haven't tried that?

Decades later, it's a test, are you really of the precinct and vintage you claim? Yeah? You know Dean Street, Pacific, Bond? You remember Buggy's grocery, corner of Bond Street? Sure. Or maybe. Remind me. You remember the Local Level? Didn't think so, because it was a place that made no sense. You remember Ziad's? Good sandwiches there.

But do you remember the Screamer?

Those who do are like Masons, sharing the secret sign. In a divided land, there was one clarion, the horn of the huntress. The boys knew it, unmistakable.

Maybe the crime is to remember?

The Screamer screams still.

7.
Speaking of the Police
(1971–82)

On a sweltering summer day in 1971, a seven-year-old white boy
from Dean Street is bitten by a stray dog on the west side of Nevins
Street, near the fish market. What's the seven-year-old doing wandering around that corner? Who knows. These are free-range city kids.
Nobody's told him not to approach a stray dog. He likes dogs.

The dog draws blood, the kid outcries. The dog—a cringing, tail-
tucked, pitiable thing—trots across Nevins and shelters in an open
garage. The kid—a cringing, hand-cradling, pitiable thing—scurries
around the corner to home. Parent appears, concerned to identify the
dog. Does it have an owner? Is it foaming at the mouth?

Police are summoned by phone, by two different neighbors. Police from two precincts, the 78th and 77th, appear. The two pairs of
cops arrive more or less at the same time, which is not particularly
quickly on this tar-melted afternoon in this unpromising sector. For a
rabid dog? It's a miracle they've come at all, let alone in duplicate. Yet
once here, faced with the prospect of fishing the growling mutt from
the back of the garage, then to deliver it to some pound or veterinarian
for inspection as the parents are demanding, then to be faced with the
resultant paperwork, both sets of cops consider their options.

Exactly where was the kid bitten? Here in front of the fish shop?
This side of Nevins? That's the 77th Precinct. Where is the dog holed?
Across the street? That's the 78th. While parents and neighbors stand
incredulous, the two sets of cops begin squabbling over whose juris-
diction is in play here—site of incident, or the fugitive mutt's garage?
Each wanting to foist the effort onto the other.

That's one celebrated police story. It's like a local version of
O. Henry or a Norman Rockwell painting, except with more blood, a
possibly rabid dog, a turpentine-rag stinking garage that seems ready
to burst into black smoking flames at any instant, and, since this is

Nevins Street, thruway to the Wyckoff Gardens houses, a whole lot of people walking past shaking their heads saying "Who the *fuck* called the fuzz?" and "Look at they stupid-ass police all afraid of some dirty old dog."

Other tales might be more private, in circulation among small orbits of the kids of the neighborhood.

That one day a black-and-white pulled up on Bergen without warning or explanation in broad daylight and snapped two Black kids' homemade skateboards, nothing but roller skates stuck on a board, in two over their knees. Snapped them in half for no reason and tossed them in the gutter, then drove off, not even troubling to laugh.

That on those blistering afternoons when someone—older brother or uncle with a wrench?—wrestled open a fire hydrant valve to let the street's kids cavort in the gush of water, and to direct it at themselves and through the open windows of unsuspecting cars with a tin can open at both ends, the cops would eventually pull up and scatter the activity and tighten the valve. But this was an action as natural as a crocodile scattering flamingos at a watering hole in a Disney nature film. Nothing personal in it, and funny enough to see the cops roll up sleeves and get their shoes soaked in the gutter's flood that it was almost worth it just for that.

Or that once a cop car was seen parked on the time-lost block of 5th Street off 2nd Ave., that microcosmic industrial wasteland trapped between two forks of the Gowanus Canal, the backs of the heads of two cops visible through its rear window, the blue-and-white Plymouth Fury gently rocking up and down on its chassis. The story originates with an older brother though all the Dean Street boys brandish it as their own. The story's a prematurely jaded one, yet as is frequently the case with the boys also features a demure omission, such that some younger kids don't even know the exact point of the story while telling it themselves.

Twin hooker blow jobs? There's no room in the back of the police car.

Jacking off?

Jacking each other off? Let speculation cease.

More than anything, though, the spirit of the police dwells in the city metal scrap reclamation yard under the Brooklyn Bridge, a place easily broken into through curled cyclone fencing for any boyish vultures wishing to pick over the remains. Here's a kit for making a city, the infrastructure of undead authority: dented decrepit file cabinets, junked street signs, uprooted parking meters, all stacked like Lego or Lincoln Logs or that dumb erector set in the basement your dad gave up trying to spur interest in. Why play with miniatures when the real shit's stacked up, free if you have the will to drag it away? Here, miraculously, are whole crapped-out chunks of police cars, the bumpers, the cages dividing front seats from back. The actual doors of old black-and-whites, with the antique emblem. Shortwave radio rigs unbolted from dashboards.

The boys go to this pile to clamber and dream. Rarely drag anything away in the end, despite dreams of dead parking meter heads stuffed with dimes if only you could crack them open.

Too fucking heavy.

Reassembling these shards into a stable idea of "police" seems about as likely as making sense of the alternate-side-of-the-street parking rules everyone complains of. For that matter, the cops who pass along Dean Street in their cars might be about like those street-cleaning vehicles the parking dance is ostensibly to make room for: laughable bulky devices, dirty themselves, moving dirt around pointlessly, then passing by.

Police just an epiphenomenon of a city that's written off this whole zone. The way the banks red-lined it, the way the EPA zoned it industrial despite the humans living there, the way you could pull the lever in a firebox on the corner and never know whether it threw a signal to the firehouse or whether they just had better things to do. The Screamer is the only mayor of where you live.

This writing off frees the white boys to write cops off in turn. These '70s police, they're hardly fear-strikers. Not *militarized*, at least none that any of the boys have yet laid eyes on. More like cultivators of silly sideburns and moustaches, lazy-looking men ill fit for their jobs. Baretta and Columbo have more to do with the boys' day-to-day lives than these uniformed fools. Easy to dodge if you have white skin and even the slightest gift for deference. The cops drive off and then you can make jack off motions to their departing car.

Most, but not all, of the white kids can summon, when needed, the slightest deference.

Not one of the Black kids can summon, when needed, white skin.

So, do the Black boys of Dean Street carry a different sense? If so, it is a thing maintained, during collective street play, in silence within their bodies.

8.
Jews in Projects
(196?–198?)

There are Jewish families, at least two of them, living in Wyckoff Gardens. Why is it that this feels almost too intimate to speak of? They're right there, hiding in plain sight, though it feels they shouldn't be. Once gone, it will be as though they were never there.

One is a robust family of six, the two boys and two girls all with bright pink cheeks, which is to say, everything screams wrong here. They've moved what seems an entire suburban home, including a matching five-piece living room set, into one of the largest units, in Building 3, facing out on Wyckoff. So at least, when another white Dean Street boy visits, he doesn't have to navigate the project's inner courtyards. Nonetheless, the older brother walks the younger one's friend home along Nevins to Dean on those occasions when he chances to visit. It's just a courtesy, obvious and chagrining to all.

The youngest has at age twelve still never been to Manhattan. Not to his knowledge. Sheer astonishment to some of the kids he plays with since, as they point out, it's a mere three subway stops away. Their friend shrugs, he's not resistant to their suggestion. He very much hopes someday to go, but the occasion hasn't arisen. His is a Brooklyn-facing family, cousins all scattered through Midwood and beyond. Relatives believing them, incidentally, insane to live where they do. Indeed, when they abandon the Wyckoff Gardens apartment it is to settle ten crucial stops along the F line, at Avenue N.

The other family? Parents and one girl. Younger family. These are Jewish hippies, with a more ideological footing in this place—the parents met in CORE, on a bus on the Newark to Arkansas freedom ride. They know Manhattan well, schlep to Chinatown frequently, and to Bleecker Street for jazz, still reenacting their life before the kid came along.

Relatives believing them, incidentally, insane to live where they do.

(Divorce will come for both these couples before the '70s are through, but that's hardly to do with the housing projects, nor being Jewish, more like a craze sweeping over this generation of young parents, leaving only exceptional survivors, outliers.)

What are we cataloging here? Are Jews in Wyckoff Gardens a mystery or merely anomalous, awkward to recall? Clues, or red herrings?

9.
Incompetent Shoplifter of *Heavy Metal* Magazine
(1977)

A white kid in a hole-in-the-wall Puerto Rican magazine-and-candy shop on Bergen off Smith Street, behind the F train stop, place the size of a closet.

He may well only have ducked in here to avoid some kind of trouble sensed on the street, real or imagined. Another kid he wished to avoid, one requiring more than just crossing the street in the middle of the block. Never should have stayed late at the after-school art class, what was he thinking? The floods of kids exiting the building are his only hiding place, he rides them to safer waters of Dean and Hoyt, beyond.

So, pretend to browse a minute or two, but now what's this thing, a glossy comic with a crazy logo, some kind of international underground magazine with the weight and sheen of a copy of *Playboy*? What the hell? With airbrushed paintings of breasts?

Just one single copy, a mistaken delivery or an alternate-reality artifact plopped into this world from another.

The woman at the counter might be like one of those stony cafeteria presences, deadened to the boy's presence by weariness. Maybe this is the day of his long-dreamed-of invisibility! Idiotic assumption, he's the only body in the space. But with useless slyness, the boy pushes the outrageous magazine up under his shirt and ducks for the door. Only makes it one step across the jamb before she's out behind him, pinching his arm in a claw-like hold. They're the same height, which doesn't make her big, but doesn't make him un-small.

Boosting, lifting, stealing, it is the done thing. The boy's been on the back end of this certainty long enough, coughing up pocket change, bus pass, a wristwatch, pride and morale on a regular basis. In this absconded zone, you take what you want, everyone knows this. Apparently, everyone short of this one incredulous Puerto Rican lady demanding not only the magazine back but as well petitioning of him some kind of explanation or apology with her look. The white boy shrugs.

She's talking fast but in Puerto Rican which is, let's admit it, plain lucky for him.

It means any chance that notice of his pathetic gambit will cross into the world of his parents or the other Dean Street boys is significantly shrunken. Plus, he's granted an excuse, or he feels himself to be, for his wholly mute departure.

Even in the coils of his shame he's slavering over the lost object. What chance he'll ever lay eyes on a second copy of the outlandish thing? What's going to happen to it?

Cheeks burning, the white boy slinks away on the sidewalk. Maybe he can send a worldlier friend back to try again. Or a team of two, in some ruse of diversion? The shop is awfully tiny. Two white boys in a scripted commotion would be like the Marx Brothers steerage routine in there. He never should have been so impulsive, the magazine was like a drug on his senses, a call from an impossible planet.

Send a friend to steal it for him, but how to hide it from the friend?

Or maybe buy it, but that means facing the lady. That magazine's gonna go up in smoke.

He's just no good at this at all.

In a world of crime, the failed criminal.

10.
Gentrification
(b. 1964)

The word exists but was not always there. When did they first hear it? Does it name anything certain?

A disaster area, an instability in somebody's desires?

The word, destined later to be glued to these years as a painting is glued into a frame, is already in the air—if they listen. Was the word covered in shame and confusion from the beginning, like an accusing epithet painted on the doorstep of their days?

The Dean Street boys prefer to stick to what they can see and feel.

To the extent the boys grasp this word, it doesn't split them in half. You can be anti-gentrification, sure. That's if your parents explain it completely enough before you throw your cereal bowl in the sink and tie sneakers and get out the front door. But just because your family's *anti-* doesn't mean anyone would ever consent they're playing on the other team. Likely you never met a racist or a Nazi or even someone who voted for Nixon either. We're all good people here.

Another reason the whole gentrification thing seems a little foggy, a little theoretical, maybe, is take a glance around this sector with your own bare eyes.

11.
Working on a Building
(1981)

Two white boys, on the third floor of a half-gutted row house on Wyckoff Street, without ventilators or dust masks, protected only by thick canvas work gloves, otherwise in T-shirts and jeans, ripping lathe and plaster out of the ruined interior wall of a former rooming house. They've been hired by one of their dads, who bought the condemned house and the one next door to it, in equally ruinous condition, for a song.

No fathers working in banks, but maybe some traffic with bankers? Subject for further investigation.

But this isn't gentrification, no. This is a thing you do with your hands. Unless you can trick a couple of teenage boys to do it. Renovation, a material concern. Sweat equity and a hands-dirty summer job. A few bucks in your pocket, representing future LPs scored at Bleecker Bob's. Camaraderie of two newly grown and fearless bodies ready to walk a street they've cowered down—fearless particularly today, in possession of a claw hammer and crowbar.

The smashed guts of buildings everywhere testify to this voracious process. Mountains of such plaster and lathe and elements of corroded plumbing, hauled down stoops in buckets to—if the block's lucky—a hired dumpster. If not, someone's shoving it into metal garbage cans and praying the city's truck operators will haul it off. Window frames and shattered doors, edges jagged with teeth of cracked lead paint, all piled in empty lots, or used to make backyard divisions where no one wants to shell out for cyclone.

Rusted window–sash weights stacked in triangular piles like unexploded ordnance in some black-and-white battlefield photo.

Kids always think they might swordfight with those things until you lift one and it half drags your arm from its socket.

Italian maestros of the plaster ceiling and marble fireplace, brownstone-alchemists, called out of the crypts of the past, or maybe just a neighborhood three subway stops away, to perform artisanal miracles on buildings likely last maintained by their grandfathers.

One day, you see a row house that's all cinder-block windows, flat-faced and bald of cornice, brownstone lintels long dissolved in the acid rain. Next day you look up, guys are standing on its roof with a pulley with a new cast-iron cornice dangling over the block's daily traffic, it's a miracle nobody's killed.

They still make those things! Can I get the number of the guys who put yours on?

Try. If he picks up the phone, he'll say he's backed up a year and a half, he'll put you on a list.

Gotta visit in person and slip him some twenties, that's how it's done out there.

But let's bear down on those two lads laboring in the swirling motes of the shattered third story rooms in the shell of the house on Wyckoff. What a pit. It's a miracle they didn't plunge through the floorboards, or collapse the staircase, which is entirely missing its newel post, so the banister just sways free, no help in securing your ascent. Everything's lathered in dust, white and gray, and that's a mercy where it covers brown spots, evaporated pools of let's hope it was coffee or a can of beans, not blood or shit. The premise that the rooming houses were to be rehabbed as a target for the next wave of Brownstoners seems thin. Could this building ever have been as grand as those on Dean Street, or Pacific, let alone the gold coasts of Clinton Street or Pierrepont? Where did all the marble and plaster go? Why aren't the parlor windows ten feet tall like on Dean? The tin ceilings appear to have been here forever, even if the linoleum was slapped on in angry layers over the subsequent decades.

What if Brownstone Brooklyn is salted with fakes to begin with? False fronts, a Potemkin village?

Maybe the dad that hired them is off his gourd, thinking anyone wants to live here.

Maybe all the good ones are gone, and the whole proposition that this so-called gentrification can gain traction is like a Ponzi scheme or chain letter, one that's collapsed from indifference. Its devisers left holding the debt or obligation, with no takers foolish enough to come on board behind them.

Someone else's problem. These boys are dreaming on a shorter horizon, planning to rinse the plaster from their hair and meet a couple of Saint Ann's girls on the Promenade, girls who've suggested they might be lured to the 8th Street Playhouse for a showing of *Pink Flamingos,* though there's a party beforehand they half-already know will probably be too good to leave. West Village railroad apartment of another abdicated single parent, manifold rooms with doors for make-out hopes. Somebody said somebody's bringing LSD, which they've yet to dare sample.

For now, they're sure wishing they'd brought a transistor radio.

One boy crowbars apart an interior wall, cracking lathe struts down to the floor. The muscle-y part of this work is fun at least—they're destructors. Heigh-ho, heigh-ho, they're unleashed, licensed to assault the old realm for a change, instead of revering it, the rows of brass lamps at the antique shops on Atlantic, the dress-up shit.

Now, a discovery. Inside the wall, a cache of pulp magazines has been hidden, for however many years, bound in string. The wall-destructor fishes out this glum treasure.

Four issues of *Sexology.* A digest-sized, all black-and-white crypto-scientific prurient "health" magazine from the early '40s, the bundle thrills and horrifies the nervous systems of the two white boys on first contact, and second contact, and beyond—its power might be inexhaustible. An unwished but irresistible avenue into the murky fact of sexual lives preceding any they want to consider (that's to say, their own). *Sexology* evokes sinister appetites predating the glossy full-color sensorium of Bob Guccione's Vaseline-smeared lens. This might be grandad's porn.

Every photo a Victorian postcard seen through X-ray specs. Every diagram like the moldiest science textbook illustration you'd ever defaced in grade school. Every advertised sexual device more or less resembling a hot-water bottle.

They've dropped hammer and crowbar and removed gloves, sitting legs crossed on the vile floor to better savor this dusty horror. One plays avid, the other averse. They could as easily swap roles—they just need a way to sort their interior poles of attraction and dismay.

"Holy fuck."

"This is so great. Bedroom Tragedies. When Midgets Marry Normals. Trial Marriage Among Polynesians—Illustrated!"

"I need bleach for my eyes."

"No, wait, Can Humans and Animals Crossbreed?"

"Oh, shit, what's a gonadectomy?"

"No, no, check *this* out, the Public Universal Friend, it's a Quaker transvestite. The P.U.F.!"

"Don't tell my dad."

"Are you kidding? Don't tell a soul. I'm going to collage the fuck out of these, make the greatest posters for Matthew's band. Never tell *anyone* where it came from."

"No way."

The treasure's salted away in a backpack.

The cache of pulps is a vortex of human meanings for them to contemplate, though mostly they'll demur. It's too much. Instead, they'll scissor the pages to bits, make the aforementioned collage posters for their friends' bands. Even so doing they'll avoid the direst pages, favoring drawings over photos, mechanical-looking antiquated sex aid devices over the anthropological and medical imagery.

The fact of the magazines, and the location of their hiding place, also points in the direction of another mystery the two white boys are inclined to avoid: that of the men of the rooming houses. Their neighborhood's immediate prehistory, which lies evident and unspoken, uncomprehended, all around them.

The men in grease-soiled fedoras and wearing suit pants and undershirts and with hotplates in their rooms, living six or ten to a row house, in one of these future *restored* brownstones, these Cinderella buildings. Men of bewildering races, histories and vices, ex-shipyard, ex-Marine, ex–sales-traveler, ex-gambler, ex-manager of undesirable vaudeville acts, reputed Sterno and formaldehyde drinker, fumbler-away of some small family concern, he who'd sworn to send money back to the old country and didn't and fell silent, Italians, Polish,

Portuguese, Dominican, Cubans, Black-from-South, Black-from-Islands, Africans, Mohawk—*Mohawk?*—and more, men like a converging point of dereliction, all distinction erased, men of no fates whatsoever.

12.
Smudge, Part 1
(1989)

Black man walks into a glasses shop on Atlantic Avenue.

Outside, rain falls. At the door a cardboard box waits for umbrellas.

Not so many people walk through this door. We remain in the long valley between the invention of this neighborhood and the acceptance of the proposition as a done deal. The triumphalist phase is decades away. Was this gentrification premature?

The white-coated opticians turn as the door chimes.

"You're back."

"Damn right I'm back." The Black man wipes his feet, jogs forward. He wears a baseball cap, and his glasses.

The optician doesn't move. "You don't need to use language." He sold him these glasses yesterday. One hundred dollars, cash, not out of a wallet.

The customer bounces from one foot to another. He pushes his chin forward, hands by his side. "Look. Same damn thing."

The optician grunts and moves to look. "A smudge."

"*Scratched,*" says the customer. "Same as the last pair. If you can't fix the problem why'd you sell me the damn glasses?"

"A smudge. Clean it off. Here."

The customer ducks. "Don't fool with me. Can't clean it off. They're already messed up. Like the old ones."

"Let me see."

"Where's the doctor? I want to talk to the doctor."

"That's my associate. He's not a doctor. Let me see."

"*You're* not the doctor, man." The customer dances away.

"We're the same," says the optician. "We make glasses."

The second optician comes out of the back, and the customer grins. "There's the man I want to see!"

The second takes it in. "Something wrong with the glasses?"

"Same as yesterday. Look." He strips his glasses with his right hand and offers them to the second optician.

"First of all, remove with two hands, like I showed you." The second optician pinches the glasses at the hinges, demonstrating. He raises them to his own face.

"You touched them. That's the problem."

"No."

"That's fingerprints."

"Damn, doctor man. I'll show you the old ones. You can't even fix the problem."

"The problem is you touched them. Here." The second optician dips the glasses in a shallow bath of cleanser, dries them with a chamois cloth. The customer bobs forward, trying to see.

"What do you, scratch at your eyes all the time?" says the first optician, smiling now.

"Shut up." The customer finger-points. "You're not my doctor on this."

"Nobody is," said the first optician. "You don't need a doctor. You need to keep your hands from your eyes."

"Shut up."

The second optician glares at the first. He hands the glasses over. "Let me see you put them on."

The customer bends his head and lifts the glasses to his face.

"Wait a minute, I couldn't see," says the first optician. "The bill of your cap was in the way."

"Put them on again," says the second.

"Same thing." The customer shakes his head. He pulls off the glasses, again with one hand. "Look. Still there. Little scratches."

The first optician steps up close. "You smudged it again. When I couldn't see. It's how you put them on."

"I call that a *permanent* smudge. I paid a hundred dollars. Might as well kept the old ones." He thrusts the glasses at the first optician.

"They're just dirty. Your hands are dirty."

The customer raises his eyebrows. "That's *weak,* doctor man. I come in here show you a pair of glasses with scratches, I'm looking for *help*. You tell me I need new glasses. Now *these* ones got a permanent smudge, you tell me I got dirty hands. These the glasses you sold me, my man."

"Your old pair, you had them, what, ten years? The hinges were shot, the nosepiece was gone. The lens touched your cheek. The glasses I sold you are fine. You have to break some habits."

"Habits!"

"He's a clown. We should've thrown him out yesterday."

"Instead, you took my *money,*" says the customer. "Good enough for you yesterday. You couldn't see *Black* for all the green yesterday. Now I look Black to you. Now I'm a clown."

"You think we need your hundred dollars?"

"We'll make you right," says the second, ignoring his partner. "Sit down, let me look at the fit."

It's a good optometrist-bad optometrist routine. Now the glasses, the proof, are in enemy hands.

"Shit, doctor man. What you know about my *habits*?"

"Okay." The second optician's voice is soothing. "I just want to see you put them on. Naturally, like you would. Don't push them into your face. They won't fall off." He offers the glasses, then pulls them back. "Take off your hat." The customer removes his hat. "Here you go. Nice and easy."

The customer stuffs the hat in his ass pocket, then raises the glasses with two trembling hands.

WE DON'T ALL see things the same way, through the same lenses— yeah, sure, we get it. It's a metaphor, if not an outright allegory.

But not for these three men! For them it's a material issue, one hundred dollars and a matter of professional pride. They'll solve it *today,* if it takes all day. It's raining. They've got nothing better to do.

13.
Mr. Clean's Windshield & Junkie Stadium, Part 1
(1977)

A white boy, thirteen, throws a ball in the street in front of a Dean Street rooming house. One of the last rooming houses on his block, or anywhere between Nevins Street and Court, where Dean Street dissolves into Amity Street.

The boy throws not a Spaldeen, for once, but a real baseball, fresh bought at Triangle Sports and hard as a stone. He stands alone on the block this early Sunday morning, daring the day, the Dean Street bus, the kids who might intrude or even try to steal his mitt, to dislodge from him his right to stand on a manhole cover pretending to be Jerry Grote smothering pop-ups. Whipping the ball skyward with an under-handed lunge to create the facsimile of a towering foul, the boy loses it in the sun and finds it again in his mitt's webbing, each catch a miracle. Less you think about it, easier it is.

Once or twice drifting with eyes only for the ball in its dazzling backdrop he meanders into a parked car to make the catch, should take it as a warning but fails to.

The ball is always in the glove, the flings go higher, his delight reckless, until the seventeenth or seventeenth million throw, which bullets unstoppably downward in the exact center not of the boy's mitt but of the windshield of Mr. Clean's 1968 Dodge Dart Swinger, black with a white top, coolest car on the block easily. With audible authority the baseball spiderweb-craters the windshield.

Mr. Clean lives in the rooming house, or rather he lives on the stoop of the rooming house, when he isn't actually physically in connection with his car, which he rag shines with obsessive regularity. In truth, it is the only car the boy has ever actually seen cleaned outside of a television program about the suburbs.

Mr. Clean is called Mr. Clean by the kids of Dean Street, but also, confusingly, by the adults. The derivation seems to oscillate among various possible causes. He cleans his car. His head is bald, like the Mr. Clean of the "lemon-refreshed" solvent widely advertised on television, though it is usually covered in a Cuban-style straw fedora. He dresses nattily, with ironed creases in his knee-high shorts, his matching striped socks aligned high on his calves.

The boy has also heard Mr. Clean referred to as a "white Cuban." The man's own name, when he acknowledges it, which he does with a kind of odd merriment, comes out as "Mr. Kling," or perhaps "Mr. Klang." There's a chance that is simply, somehow, his actual name.

Mr. Clean half doesn't speak English. The boy half understands the half that Mr. Clean speaks.

But Mr. Clean is miraculously not present for the splintering of his windshield. Today is one of those dead days, the block a machine for devouring sound and time. The boy furtively retrieves his baseball from where it has rolled into the gutter—evidence now—and, seeking to make himself invisible, slides hushed down the slates, to his home.

14.
Lies
(whenever and wherever lies appear)

Mr. Clean lives in a rooming house but has a car?

Can we square this with "men like a converging point of dereliction, all distinction erased, men of no fates whatsoever"?

Mr. Clean lives in a rooming house and is chipper and merry and may be one of the better-dressed men on the block. Everyone knows him and admires his comportment and car. There is nothing *erased* in his *distinction*.

Generalizations, then, may betray the spirit of our inquiry here. Let's lay off the romantic flourishes, the rhetoric of memory. Mr. Clean calls these out as lies, simply by strolling without reluctance nor any exaggerated sense of injury down Dean Street half an hour later to ring the bell of the boy's house, to speak with the dad who appears there.

These guys know and like each other just fine.

15.
Mr. Clean's Windshield & Junkie Stadium, Part 2
(1977)

The boy finds himself called downstairs to meet on the top of the stoop with his father and Mr. Clean. The day appears not to have progressed an inch, air barely whirring in the leaves, the sidewalks entombed in Sunday's light. How is it that so much can have happened? The baseball and mitt reside in the milk crate in his closet, as if the boy had never stepped outside.

"Were you going to say something?"

"I was looking for you, actually."

"Nice try. I was in the parlor."

"Must have walked right past."

Mr. Clean smiles. He mimes catching a baseball. Mimes missing it, widens his eyes.

"Mr. Clean is being very nice about it, but we're paying for the windshield."

"It's okay," says Mr. Clean. "My cousin fix it good, fifty dollars."

"That's very nice," repeats the dad. "We'll certainly cover that. I'll cover that and he'll work it off his allowance. What do you say?"

Mr. Clean grins.

"Sorry."

"Baseball," says Mr. Clean. "Yankee Stadium." Not exactly how he pronounces it, but the point is unmistakable. In case it isn't, Mr.

Clean puts his hand on the boy's shoulder and says it again: "Yankee Stadium." The boy nods in agreement to he knows not what, exactly. Like many Puerto Ricans Mr. Clean likely prefers the Yankees to the underdog Mets, except isn't Mr. Clean Cuban? Also, right, beware generalizations. Well, anyhow, Mr. Clean seems to prefer the Yankees. The Yankees in three years stole Catfish Hunter and Reggie Jackson from the Oakland A's. Meanwhile the Mets traded Seaver to the Reds. A number of fickle boys have had their loyalties tested—others, wholly diverted.

The next time the boy sees the car, the windshield is fixed, looks immaculate. Nine more weekends with no allowance, only one scratched off the list. The boys tries not to wonder whether Mr. Clean has gotten a bargain or even somehow made bank on the deal. But that's impossible, isn't it?

Two weeks later Saturday morning his dad slips him a five after all, saying it's for concessions. Concessions? You know, hot dogs, peanuts, whatever. Mr. Clean pulls up at their house and his dad tells the boy to get on his shoes and maybe he wants his mitt for catching a foul? Mr. Clean is taking the boy to a game at Yankee Stadium. Bleacher seats, sure, but that's a tough ticket this Reggie Jackson August. Mr. Clean lets him in the front seat, drives them up the FDR. They make what small talk they can, each nibbling around the edge of the language barrier until it's pointless. But he's all smiles.

Dad trusts Mr. Clean on the day outing, like they're old best friends. Who knew?

Mr. Clean has a friend with a private padlocked lot a few blocks from the stadium. He parks and he and the boy walk into the throngs. The place is impressive, the boy has to admit, just this density and aroma of masculine history, the teeming smoky bars all pressed up to the foot of the stadium, the unchildish souvenir shops. Shea Stadium is somehow more like a visit to the Coney Island Aquarium or Battery Park by comparison. Mr. Clean makes the boy wait outside a bar with a long open window where he can keep an eye on him while he socks back a shot of something and talks with a couple of friends in Spanish—Mr. Clean has friends everywhere.

Reggie Jackson hits a home run into the bleacher seats that day, but nowhere near their seats. Yankees win, of course. Afterward, one more shot for Mr. Clean at the bar with the wide-open windows, while the boy waits in the swirling street, the riders jamming like reverse lemmings up to the elevated tracks. Then Mr. Clean delivers him home at top speed. The boy opens the door of the Dodge Dart and moves onto the sidewalk.

"Thank you, Mr. Clean."

"Is good Yankee baseball."

The boy has left his Mets allegiance unremarked all afternoon.

"Yes."

"Good," says Mr. Clean. It is as if some compact is concluded, a sequence ordained without the boy's knowing by the breaking of the windshield. They never go to a ballgame again, and Mr. Clean, seated at his usual perch on the rooming house stoop, perhaps alert to the embarrassment now at his command, never requires of the boy any special acknowledgment. He does offer a nod and a smile so concise no teeth are shown, but this is the same smile he typically provides to the local kids upon eye contact, familiar from before the incident of the windshield and the voyage to the Stadium. It conveys no demand of reciprocation.

The boy is too chagrined ever to ask his father whether, or in what sense, Mr. Clean's name *is* actually Mr. Clean. Or perhaps leaving this unasked reflects something cursory in the boy, some loathness to grasp the entirety of his situation.

Within two years Mr. Clean is gone from the block.

16.
Silences
(whenever and wherever silences appear)

Any given kid passing along a length of sidewalk may feel at some point that they're warping through, dissolving like an incompletely beamed-in passenger on the Starship Enterprise. Too visible, in a screaming panic at the deep molecular level, a problem or emergency in human shape.

And then again intangible, invisible, a fog.

Maybe not just kids. Maybe the street does this to the humans of all ages. Hell, maybe it does it to the dogs. Go ask them if you want.

Yet certain matters fall into wells of silence without necessarily being *lies*. The street in this case functioning as a kind of valley or vacancy, a gulf. The street may seem to swallow knowledge about itself, to render certain things unsayable.

A land of negation. A neighborhood called Boredom Hell.

Perhaps the street really is an impossible object. A figure like a tesseract or Klein bottle, something that folds upon itself. Is the street larger on the inside than on the outside? Sort of. Maybe it is even more like a thing which has no outside, a thing which encloses its only possible observer. Like a memory bank floating through space with no body attached.

Yet we're only talking of a city street. People live here for crissakes. Get off your high horse.

For, just when it seems defined by silence and indeterminacy, the sounds erupt. Bodies in juxtaposition, multiple musics fighting for primacy, those same damn fire trucks as if they're driving in circles, someone shouting somebody's name or "Drop the keys down, wrap 'em in a sock!" audible for three blocks around. The Screamer is by no means the only screamer around this place. Here is the noise that makes the silence necessary. The hypersensory clangor that numbs thought.

Or maybe something is being avoided.

Is the silence a constructed thing? Likely if some number of minds work to erase something, they could render it impossible to speak of or recall, except as a kind of explosion. Convulsive but incoherent.

This silence, then, may be that of memories stored not in the mind but exported, for the safety of all concerned, into free space. Into distant orbit, where the only risk remaining is that they might collide with other junk like themselves.

17.
How Much for the Dog?
(1979)

Among that which has consented to fall into the well of silence, there are—still? always?—prostitutes standing on the corner of Nevins and Pacific. Where in daytime the P.S. 38 grade school kids course over the curb, somehow this. The sole place sex is for sale every night, ten, fifteen years into the Brownstoner era. Big rig trucks, coming off the Verrazzano Bridge after crossing Pennsylvania and Jersey, divert here from 3rd and 4th avenues. Phone calls to the police sometimes trigger a cosmetic sweep of the corner for a night or two, but they're always back. Better find a way to keep it in a mind's eye blind spot.

The boy walking his dog, seven at night on a November evening where it's already dark out, promised he'd do it all afternoon and shirked, now they're holding him to it, and pick up the poop too, that's the new regimen—the boy is white, and twelve years old.

Resents the hell out of the chore but he isn't fearful because the dog makes him bold. Half German shepherd, half something, somebody said Weimaraner but that can't be a real thing, what's a Weimaraner? He isn't fearful because the Black kids he doesn't know, the ones he doesn't play with, always back away, saying stuff like, "Dang, looks like a *wolf* dog!" The boy says nothing, wouldn't know where to begin, but the dog clears a field of operation when he's got it out on a leash.

Goes up Nevins because the dog's already walking funny and his parents won't see if he doesn't pick up the poop on Nevins. The empty plastic bag he'll stuff in someone's garbage can when he rounds to tree-veiled Pacific.

What tonight inspires the boy to break the deal of silence, the deal of two worlds passing through each other, as if on separate axes?

Did she call out to him first, out of a blip of boredom?

That's how he recollects it. Because what else could have emboldened him? "Hey, little white boy, where you going?"

His witticism, a rupture in the field. Did he forge this quip on the spot, or had he cultivated it in the back of his mind for days, daring himself to try it out? By the time he brags of the line at school the next morning, it's like he's quoting a movie he once saw.

18.
Brazen Head
Wheeze, Part 1
(2019)

The bar called the Brazen Head sits on Atlantic Avenue between Court and Boerum Place, near the odd juncture where the Brooklyn Bridge outlets the flow of returning taxicabs to split in three directions upon bashing into Atlantic. The crossroads where Cobble Hill and Boerum Hill, those renovator's or developer's fictions, divide from Brooklyn Heights, with its somewhat better-historicized neighborhood name and boundaries.

A stone's throw, too, from the unspeakable morass of Borough Hall, the Albee Square Mall, the old Dime Savings Bank that somehow resembles the Jefferson Monument, Flatbush slicing through anarchically, Metrotech, all of it thronged with ascending tangle of skyscrapers, all dotted with presences like Chipotle and GameStop and Banana Republic, confusions the Brownstoner imagination aches to deny.

Aches now, and for what has to be admitted is a long yesteryear too.

An uneasy axis, then, but the Brazen Head shores against these confusions. A pub, with square paned windows and a timeless raised-wooden sign. A neighborhood joint, with chicken wings and darts but also a terrific array of single malts. A degree of texture not excluding those possibly dropping in for the first time. Affectations minimal. Nothing cloistered in the vibe here.

That said, occupying prime real estate at the bar is the Brazen Head Wheeze. A figure bent around the pint he's been nursing for hours—or is it that he's drained a series of them? Is he drunk? The Wheeze's wire-frame spectacles support two different densities of glass, one eye magnified to a watery enormity if you're ever caught in his gaze direct. Balding with a ponytail, never exactly a terrific look. And muttering—can it really be a rant about everyone staring at their cellphones? Has he really just bitched about "yuppies," that antique slur?—in a steady monotone. Time might seem to bend or slow around the Wheeze. At least the bar's regulars give him space, and newcomers follow suit, by a preconscious instinct.

The bartender's attentive, though. She seems fond. And all adore the bartender here, she's salt of the earth. Likely in her early thirties but appears timeless, an anchor of authenticity. So, her approval is a reassurance—perhaps the Wheeze is a sort of ornament, a bar pet. His monologue's pointed at the bartender, even when she necessarily moves away to serve others. This is preferable to believing he's talking to himself, even if it's a kind of filibuster.

Before he was the Brazen Head Wheeze, he was the Hank's Saloon Wheeze. And before that he was the Brooklyn Inn Wheeze.

Now, though, he's laid a trap. Despite anyone in the vicinity likely swearing not to be enmeshed, a pair of young listeners lean in. The Wheeze has made his play.

"Sorry, what?" says one of the listeners, a woman. This is just a third date. She's still amused, aloft, susceptible.

"I saw you noticed, not many do. The building's shape, I mean." The Wheeze motions with his flattened hand, bending his wrist to carve two non-parallel strokes, as though slicing an invisible pie. "The bar's wedge-shaped, few bother to wonder why."

"Wow," says the man, leaning in to join. Not that anyone young and beautiful would be jealously triggered by the Wheeze's attentions— he just wants to be part of whatever she's found interesting. "It really is. I never thought about it."

"Palimpsest of the Pre-history of the Borough," declaims the

Wheeze, whose superpower is that he can Vocalize Capital Letters. "You're seeing traces, if you know how to read them."

In fact, the building is anomalous, now that they bring it into focus. One side square, the other slanted, making a wedge. Any urge to dismiss the Wheeze runs up against their curiosity.

"What, did some old trolley track run along here?" guesses the man. "Was this building a depot?"

Wheeze shuts his eyes, sighs a galactic disappointment. "*Trolley depot.*" He pulls out a single cigarette from where it's apparently been resting in his pocket, doesn't light it since smoking isn't allowed. It's a cold night out there. "Go back to the Land of Make-Believe. Give my regards to King Friday."

"There *were* trolleys here," said the man defensively.

Wheeze doesn't trouble to credit what they all know perfectly well. Instead, he examines his cigarette, places it carefully behind his ear, says, "you know Red Hook Lane?"

Red Hook? A neighborhood not plainly accessible or in view, divided from Brownstone Brooklyn by the Brooklyn-Queens Expressway but as well by some aura of historical trauma. That's the feeling evoked in the listening couple, at least. Red Hook is too far, it's where you don't want to have to go for parties. Yet perhaps it is also colorful, like the Wheeze himself. If only they could get free of this conversation.

"Sure," jokes the man. "Red Hook Lane, where the Mafia bury the bodies."

"You're standing on it, you dolt."

"Sorry?"

"Red Hook Lane. Native trail, running slantwise through the street grid. There's just one solitary block with the name on the sign." The Wheeze tips his chin toward Borough Hall. "Between Livingston and Fulton, barely more than an alley now. Same angle as that wall." Wheeze takes a pull on his pint. Then pronounces the single word "*residue.*" Like postage due, or mortgage due.

"Native trail?" The Wheeze's interlocutors have to give it up: this not-terribly-old-but-old Brooklyn type seemingly does know where the bodies are buried. Really, though, they'd have preferred a Mafia tale. The drag part of any American story is the name of the tribe whose stolen land was required to enact it in the first place. Yet this fellow's surely about to supply it.

"Canarsee Indians."

"Canarsie, like out near Queens. Isn't that, like, where Ralph Kramden lives?"

"It's a native name, dumbass."

"That isn't necessary."

"Red Hook Lane ran from the Heights down to the bay, when this was all farmland, and before, when it was woods. Nowadays it's one block, making a straight shot to the dumpsters behind *Metrotech*." The Wheeze stretches this word, and brings the last syllable down like *severed-neck*, or *street-cred-check*. "George Washington's army hid in the trees, picking off redcoats. *Right. Along. Here.*" Wheeze trains an imaginary rifle, then strafes the slanted wall that represents the vanished Red Hook Lane, crossing across the eyeline of the man, pausing there for a bull's-eye at the bridge of his nose. "Exactly in the spot you gentrifuckers chose for tonight's Tinder hookup." He moves his cigarette from his ear to his pocket again.

"We met before tonight," says the woman. Not too defensively, not denying Tinder.

"*Ill met by backlight,*" quips the Wheeze, but the couple has moved on from this terrifically annoying person, deeper into the wedge-shaped bar. Their psychic space seals easily against the Wheeze's impingement. On the one hand, sure, local color. On the other, the fellow seemed possibly just an inch from pointedly grabbing his crotch, spitting in someone's face, or simply farting.

Darts thump into tired cork. Conversation bubbles. Other couples and small groups enter to dent and sometimes rupture the Wheeze's space, this evening only just underway. An evening he's chosen to endure here, to ride out in plain sight of all he abhors, shoulders hunched against Wild Cherry's "Play That Funky Music" playing yet again on the jukebox. No one to blame but himself.

The Wheeze hails the bartender. Not turning her back, she lofts one finger, indicating she'll first finish swabbing and restacking the pint glasses in the drainer by her sink. The Wheeze begins talking at her anyway, something about *tattooed gluppies*, how, not content to destroy coffee and pizza, they'd now ruined even chocolate bars—had she tasted one lately?

19.
The Case Against Brooklyn
(deep file)

Consider, fine people of the jury, the possibility that it is just a fucked-up place.

Call for the prosecution the blighted Gowanus Canal, that causeway of black mayonnaise, a Superfund site.

This place may be in its essence always Breukelen, the Broken Lands.

Crooklyn.

The famous Battle, George Washington's disaster, a retreat to nowhere. He ceded the city to the redcoats.

The election to consolidate to Greater New York, the election that stole Brooklyn's autonomy, cinched by fewer than three hundred votes out of a hundred thousand. The election, surely stolen.

"John O'Connor was shot and killed yesterday afternoon at 4 o'clock at the corner of Hoyt and Butler, Brooklyn, in plain view of a number of people who were passing by. O'Connor, who lived at 145 Butler street, was standing in front of the saloon of Patrick Galligan when Catatelo Campilell, a barber, fired a shot at him from the door of his shop. News of the shooting quickly reached O'Connor's house, and his wife ran into the saloon in time to lift her husband's head to her lap just as he expired. She grew hysterical and was conveyed to her home." (*Brooklyn Daily Eagle*, 1899)

"A short time later Harold Seaman, sought for some time as the slayer of Dominick Caporelli, who was killed when he resisted beer garden bandits at 127 Adams St., staggered into Cumberland Hospital with a bullet in his abdomen." (*Eagle*, 1934)

"A U.S. Senator was identified today as a frequenter of a 'house of degradation' in Brooklyn which was used by Nazi spies to obtain military information. In an affidavit made in the Raymond St. Jail, Gustave Beekman, convicted operator of the house, named the Senator . . . Beekman was convicted yesterday by a jury of 12 men on a morals charge in connection with the orgies in Beekman's three-story house at 329 Pacific St., Brooklyn . . . probably the most sensational allegation was that the Senator was on good terms with a man described by authorities as 'one of Hitler's chief espionage agents in this country,' a mysterious Mr. E. This Mister E. and other Germans repeatedly lured sailors and soldiers to Beekman's house and there, in the midst of wining and dining, obtained military secrets from them." (*New York Post*, 1942)

"Let's refinish our floors before Christmas. It's really a very simple process. All you need is a strong back, a floor sanding machine, an edger, a handscraper, a hammer and countersinker for the 2,000 nails in each room, several hundred gallons of poly-eurethane and the ability to walk on the ceiling. It also helps if you can leave the dogs, cats and children somewhere, like in the street . . ." ("Lookout on Cobble Hill" column, *Brooklyn Heights Press*, 1970)

"Detectives who questioned hundreds of people in two buildings in the Gowanus Houses said that many residents heard the victim's screams. But they said that no one called the police until after the fatal shots were fired . . . they likened the case to the 1964 slaying in 'Queens of Catherine (Kitty) Genovese, whose screams were heard by 36 witnesses who failed to call the police." (*New York Times*, 1984)

Etcetera.

Call for the prosecution the Ulano solvent factory on Bergen Street near Nevins, spewing out cancer at a rate that earns a listing as one of the top U.S. polluters of the 1970s.

Call for the prosecution the Canarsie Indians.

20.
The Dean Street Boys
(Boerum Hill era)

In truth, the Dean Street boys, Black, white, and brown, don't all live on Dean Street. And they don't call themselves the Dean Street boys— like some gang. A gang is nearly the exact opposite of what they are.

Some live on Bergen Street. Some on Pacific. Some on the lonely blocks of Cobble Hill. That kid with the jeweler-psychiatrist dad is on Court Street, north of Atlantic—technically, Brooklyn Heights. (Nobody, talking of Brooklyn Heights, would have meant *that* block.)

Some of them attend the public schools, some others attend Friends or Packer or Saint Ann's.

Nevertheless, they lived and played in particular ways.

They came into consciousness in a distinct time and place. Later they'd find evidence, deep inside their bodies, of how they'd been formed by certain arguments that time and place was having about itself.

Names aren't withheld to protect the innocent, but because they'll be no help. *Dean Street boys* is enough, at least for now.

Are there girls?

Of course. Some of these boys have sisters. There's even a house on Dean Street with *only* sisters in it. Cryptic place.

The girls move around the edges of the mind-world of the boys. If only this inquiry could make contact with them, they might help us know what the boys cannot.

We'll give it a shot. Try to rise out of ourselves. Anything that might help.

The aim of all our efforts is to locate that evidence lodged inside the bodies of the Dean Street boys. Use it, to name the signature crimes of the moment.

To use what we know to know more than we know.

Our challenge is to make meaningful distinctions. Not to take one thing for another just because they're similar.

Yet our greater challenge may be that the Dean Street boys sometimes exchange properties, one with another.

21.
Deeper into White Childhood
(Boerum Hill era)

Before there was a neighborhood, there was a street. Before the street, a house.

Not everything that happens to the white boys begins the day they are shucked out of their front doors, into sight of one another, into the perplexities of the landscape.

(And nothing that happens to white boys happens *only* to white boys.)

They've got adults to contend with, or the absence thereof.

Adults or no adults, childhood's a dream space, ruled in this era by the dizzy abjectitudes of television.

The Electric Company, Green Acres, The Monkees, Batman.

The Hollywood Squares.

And that's just before dinner.

The parent-world bears a whiff of decayed opulence, headlined by the space program, the sexual revolution, Vietnam, the Beatles, civil rights, plus whatever fantastic personal horizons they were forced to relinquish to begin caring for *you*.

We'll call the sixties a draw.

The formerly great city may have cried uncle even earlier.

The institution of parenting is itself in a mixed state, one of collapse, abdication, reinvention. The parents might identify with you more than you identify with yourself, who can say?

This will surely involve crimes. Terrible things will happen to and be done by some of these children.

Yet the parents are not monsters.

General statements can take us no further at this time.

22.
The Spoiled Boy
(1975)

Here's a specific thing: a new white boy moved into a floor-through apartment on Dean Street.

The new boy is only spotted here and there, nobody knows his name, nobody seems curious. He might be a little younger than most of these guys, who are now ten or eleven. Then again, some kids are older or younger than they look. On a given day any number of younger brothers are swept in the flow, nobody's checking credentials here. He'd be like a younger brother with no older brother if he came around.

He doesn't.

Word goes from a couple of the moms, though, suggesting someone ought to do something. The word playdate is at this point unknown, the operation is subliminal if it happens at all.

A couple of Dean Street boys go around, a combined group, for strength in numbers, also just to show what's possible around here. Someone may or may not have rung a doorbell. Someone exhibits a baseball card or a Duncan Imperial yo-yo or a Spaldeen or a skully cap. Most likely all of these are circulating at some point.

The boy's mom, however, won't leave the stoop.

Nothing can really happen in this situation. Even when the boy is down on the slates, nominally playing with what's been brandished, a Spaldeen or whatever, and making curious sounds from his mouth, he's also glancing back up at the mom.

This more or less brands the new boy as useless. It is as if he knows it and therefore has to say something idiotic, something to draw chafing rebuttal.

"What's your name?"

"I said it already."

"Yeah, but nobody heard."

He shrugs. "Not my fault."

"Are you ten or nine?"

He glances back at his mom again.

"You want to come down the block?" They need to move him away so they can begin their teaching.

The new kid again shrugs.

"Can you catch? Do you want to get in a game?"

"I can catch better than you, but I don't want to."

"Better than who? Him?"

Another glance. The new boy's mom stands, like she might come down here.

"Forget it. You flip cards? I'm calling him Mr. Magoo. You flip cards, Magoo?"

"What?"

"Baseball cards? You got a collection?"

"In my room."

"You don't want anybody to get it, am I right?"

Shrugs. Of course, every kid's thinking: What *else* has he got up in that room?

"But if you learn to flip, you can *build* it, Magoo. Take mine off me, make me shit my pants. I'll show you how."

Shrugs. There's a get-it-over-with air pervading his whole presentation, like he already tried to tell them it's useless. A couple of boys move away soonest, the ones with something better to do than contemplate the oddity. Others like probing the sore spot. Finally, in immense perversity someone shoves the new boy, right there in sight of his mother. He lands on his ass and cries and the mom sweeps down like she was always destined to. The situation, exhausted before it began, can only be a relief to end.

That evening the Dean Street boy whose mom made the distinct campaign for something to happen asks, how did it go? Did he come out and play? Well, sort of. What's that mean, sort of? The boy sees no option except painting the picture: the new boy couldn't be pried from his mother, or maybe it was vice versa. What this boy has no words to express is how a basic precondition for childhood at all is to be loosed, secret, away from sight and supervision, out on the street for wild and uncanny durations.

This boy's mother gets it. "That's what they call spoiling a child." She shakes her head.

"He's *spoiled*?" The boy has heard this word. Perhaps his mother used it with his father, expressing what not to do: *Don't spoil him.* The word sounds grievously final. Which in this case provides relief, if he won't be required to persist in the unworkable. Plus, he'll have an explanation to offer the other boys he unfortunately dragged over there: turns out that kid's spoiled. That's what spoiled looks like, we finally know.

Also, seriously, what else has he got up in that room?

23.
Interracial
(the old dream)

We can probably discern—we'd have to be blind and deaf not to notice—that the group who arrived at the stoop to audition the play potential of the spoiled boy is mixed.

A mixed gathering. A mixed bag.

Crazy and mixed up. Mongrel. Motley.

Is it this peculiarity of the neighborhood that inaugurates the spoiled boy's mother's vigilance?

Let's allow better of her than that. No idea what's in that woman's head.

But this is a thing that's not so usual, a thing deserving a look.

When the Black kids from around Dean Street fall in with groups from other neighborhoods, a situation that happens frequently on graffiti runs, or when one of the Black kids sorts out into a less-integrated high school outside the precinct, they're faced with wonderment:

"Dang, what's going *on* with that?" Their only option, to plead ignorance. It was just like that around there, nobody knew different.

In Brownsville you might never meet a white person who isn't a figure of authority. Teacher, housing agency, cop. The doctor who fits you with the Department of Health eyeglasses. Elsewhere, one pretty cool white kid might get swept up and sheltered. "Leave him alone, he's my man, he's cool." Yet the neighborhood was Black. You'd walk the pavement unconfused.

Equally clear, those streets the Irish or Italians chested around with unembarrassed idiocy, still aping *West Side Story*. In those zones there might dwell the token whiteboy's photonegative: that one cool Black dude or Puerto Rican, who'd forged his passage among the whites, at the expense of absorbing a relentless stream of characterizations. "You're all right, Chico, not like them other so-and-sos." Well, my name isn't Chico, but never mind.

The format's grim coherence didn't prevail on Dean Street. You just couldn't say what was what.

Hemmed by the projects and the Fulton Mall.

In reach of the ungraspable Heights.

Even walk to Manhattan if you felt like it.

Stick-up boys work Hoyt and Schermerhorn on same principle as Willie Sutton robbing banks: It's where the money is. Where the poverty and the money go to try and change places.

Legacies, palimpsests, these may be some fault or instability on these blocks: the nearness of the shipyards, sailors mixing in the bars on Atlantic, going AWOL to vanish into those rooming houses, men from Trinidad and Tobago, the Mohawks . . .

The white boys here made no sense to begin with, these Jew, Fallen-Wasp, Hippie, Communist, Artist-made creatures. In kindergarten, they actually *do* hold hands and sing "Kumbaya." Parental idealism casts the white boys into a dreamworld. What incredible luck that just a minute before you came along, we solved all these conundrums thanks to civil rights, reefer and jazz appreciation, now go out on the street and play.

Everybody's shaking their heads over the situation, the first minute they step free of the sweet dream of indifference, of undifference.

If you were sorting boyhood on Dean Street into epochs you might call the first the false oasis. I am you and you are me and we are all together!

Then, abruptly, not.

But, okay, so: say mixed. To be interracial, you have to be racial at all, and we're not.

Damn word sounds like *racist,* just like *epidermis* sounds sexual, just like you can't convince me there isn't something a little off about *homo sapiens*.

We're mixed here, that's all.

Okay, so how mixed? To what extent mixed?

The streets, a lot. The schools, a little. The families? The actual people? Just a few. Some in their houses, some in their actual bodies. He's got a white dad and those three have a white mom and in this house, they adopted the Black kids. Over here, the Triple Axel: mixed parents, then they fostered the teenage white one, who's fucking trouble, he's like a self-appointed mixing cop, having come from one of those million other territories that just don't get how it works around here.

Fascinating, you say?

You're making me uncomfortable.

Interracial? Don't name it, for fuck's sake. Just another feature that shifts overnight from you didn't notice to you might preemptively punch yourself in the face for speaking it aloud.

24.
Instrumentalization of Difference
(1978)

Then again, there is some sly superpower here, the way the children—these are children, remember!—instrumentalize difference. That's to say, they are acknowledging what they are not acknowledging.

We could cite any number of examples, good criminal examples, involving elaborate schemes of distraction for shoplifting. The several Black graffiti writers with large coats stirring a panic among the employees in the paint department of McCrory's basement, but who leave without incriminating themselves, indeed, without touching a single item. Meanwhile the one white kid, a collaborator who has slipped into the store discreetly and separately from his Black friends, is loading twelve cans of Krylon into his voluminous backpack.

Candy is often boosted in the same manner.

Later, LPs, from the new Tower Records in Manhattan.

Let's feature instead the simple uncriminal poignancy of two Catholic school girls, best friends, wearing identical costumes as if painted by Norman Rockwell, and burdened by the layers and by their own textbook-laden backpacks, slugging home miserable in 95-degree heat along 6th Avenue.

They come to a pizzeria and eye the gushing purple and orange drink in the elevated rectangular tanks, waiting to be tapped for the price of a fifty cents, small. Alas, neither of them has fifty cents! Francesca Dallaglio "borrowed" their pocket change from them at recess, in order to buy herself some cigarettes.

Home is still five blocks away, for both the Black girl and the white girl.

"Let's ask him for a cup of water," suggests the Black girl. The white girl nods. "You do it," says the Black girl. The white girl nods. The Black girl waits outside in the sun.

25.
They Are Lovers
(1977–?)

Let's glance at another pair. A Black boy and a white boy. Another instance of the interracial. This pair, this instance, is hiding.

Partly it's hiding in plain sight, likely nearly everything does. They walk down the street together, bounce Spaldeens off stoops, purchase baseball cards at the bodega, and play games involving one or two or three or ten others—Skully, Running Bases, Stickball, Ringolevio. They mix into groups, mixing their mixedness with the generally mixed, hiding themselves in the general mixedupitude.

Yet these two are mixed and mixed-up in a different special way of their own: They are lovers.

How is this possible?

Long quiet afternoons, tall houses with two or three or even four levels of possible distance from a basement entrance to the dusty fourth floor, free-range child-rearing policies that cover not only the lives of the children on the street but within the tall houses.

You could, say, return home by way of the disused stoop entrance, at the parlor level, instead of crashing and cavorting through the usual under-stoop basement gate looking for a snack, exasperating one's parent, then on into the backyard for noisy games. One could, in other words, *sneak into one's own house.* In such instance, a responsible grown-up in the basement kitchen wouldn't necessarily even know whether it was the life in the street or the life of the upper floors of one's own property which parental license, parental distraction, had left unpatrolled.

You could perhaps fiddle with your best friend's dick for untold hours.

Such things happen. This happened. It just happened!

But *lovers?*

They'd never use that word themselves in a million years, and it is only from this distant vantage, glimpsed in this reverse telescope as barely visible figures, squiggles moving through days, weeks, years as if in a sped-up nature film, that the word becomes inevitable: of course they're lovers. They practice love.

Technically, first, they practice self-love. In the same room.

And before that, they practice drawing superhuman comic book characters, ones they made up. And they draw their characters' girlfriends, who are also superhuman, particularly in the chestal area, so to speak. Actually, it's quite difficult to draw women with chests larger than the bosoms of the superhuman men, but they somehow manage to do it. *Actually*-actually, it's quite difficult to draw women at all. These two fail. The wretched drawings become painful to consider almost seconds after they're completed.

Yet somehow the failed drawings have a magic power over the bodies of those who've drawn them.

All of this is a kind of miracle.

So, self-love. Then love. Sustained and tender, there is no other word for it. Not that they're looking for one.

26.
Board Games of Empire
(1977–81)

In the same span, here's another pair. Two white boys. They find an altogether different use for vast unsupervised afternoons, for hours in the empty upstairs of a four-story brownstone.

No, they have not discovered each other's penises. They are not lovers. They are living a life of the mind.

The house bears description. The parlor floor is among the most lusciously restored, its plaster scrollwork ceiling intact, the marble fireplace too—perhaps this is a home in which these were never ruined to begin with. The floorboards, the original wide planks, are luminous. The house is one of the rare ones that features elaborate internal shutters on the high parlor windows, and they are mostly sealed, against the chaos of the street, the sirens, the voice of the Screamer. Built-in bookshelves, full with hardcovers, but not for show. This is a working library, or was. The father's a philosopher, a scholar of Hume, with several studies to his name. A man of multifarious capacities, the Hume philosopher also restored much of this house himself, applying polyurethane to the floorboards at a great cost of self-poisoning, also great endurance by his family, forbidden as they were from entering certain rooms for weeks lest they create a sticky footprint. A man of multifarious appetites, he ran away a year ago with his department secretary.

He may come back, he may not.

The mom squirrels herself with the telephone and a pack of cigarettes in the rear basement kitchen. Also, when the weather invites, on the back patio, the wide flagstones laid two years earlier by her cursing husband, possibly former husband, at terrific expense to his lower back.

Big sister flew the coop; age seventeen, she's already out every night at Max's Kansas City.

The son's inherited the elegant parlor and, apart from when his mother climbs the stairs, bombed on scotch, to collapse in the master bedroom, the upper three-quarters of the building belong solely to him.

His father's Hume and Graham Greene and George Orwell and Kurt Vonnegut, his father's mammoth manual typewriter, looming like a tombstone, his father's framed French poster of Humphrey Bogart in *Le Faucon Maltais,* his father's Dave Brubeck and Lenny Bruce LPs, his and his father's expensive shelf of board games, assembled over a decade of Christmases.

(Elsewhere on this street, you could find multiple families, maybe seven, ten, twelve humans, occupying the same four stories.)

His father educated him first, in the years he can barely remember, in the elementals: chess, backgammon, even an antiquated English checkers game called Nine Men's Morris. On from there into a delirious affair—first the father, then the son—with the 3M Bookshelf series: Acquire, a mergers and acquisitions game, also Twixt, Executive Decision, Feudal. After that point, there was no turning back. History beckoned, in the form of the Avalon Hill war games, with their meticulous re-creations of specific battles, their hexagonal-celled maps, their uncubical dice, their tactical epics, hours of winnowing and attrition. PanzerBlitz! Richtofen's War! Tobruk! 1776! Starship Troopers! This is what real war was like.

Then his dad was gone.

The boy needed to school another in the arts.

A candidate was close at hand.

They were both students at The Packer Collegiate Institute, on Joralemon. This other, this elected companion, he was an at-school acquaintance. A chess club opponent. Worthy. He only had to be enticed to the parlor. A Cobble Hill kid, he was already halfway there, since he had to cross Atlantic, out of the sanctum of the Heights, every single day to walk home.

It wasn't impossible to thread a path to the house, on Bergen between Bond and Nevins. The companion had only had to be shown it was possible.

Because no fucking way were these game materials leaving the safe harbor of the father's parlor.

Once imported into the parlor, the companion was rapidly worked up to adequacy, trained into a satisfyingly defeatable opponent at each of the games in turn, until, like the son had done with the father, they'd mastered the shelves. The paper maps, the hexagons, the dice, the sharpened pencils, the personalized World War I biplanes, one German, one English, each trailing histories of kills, each somehow magically immune to elimination by the other.

They were halfway through exhausting the shelf, a project of three, four, five months' diligence.

For Christmas, one planned to request Caesar: Battle of Alesia, the other Fortress Europa.

If you closed the shutters, it was quite a lot like you didn't live in the neighborhood at all.

27.
First Participations
(forever)

For one, a white boy, it is the bus pass he is meant to use to board the B63, to ride out of Boerum Hill into Carroll Gardens each day for school. The cardboard passes are issued in neat little packets, each page a different color for a different month, for the ease of the driver's catching an expired pass at a glance. They're torn from the booklet along a perforated line, a satisfying little rip. A boy's first identification card? Not really, since it isn't actually personalized. But sized for a wallet holder, like a license or credit card. Living in a front pants pocket, the pass may retain its rigid corners for a few days. Thereafter it softens and rounds, warmed to by skin heat, like a beloved baseball card.

Once he became the quarry, chosen by a certain Puerto Rican teenager, this boy never again keeps a pass long enough to find it worn to that chamois-like softness. Let alone to have it tatter in the waning days of the month, to need cellophane tape repair to make it to the changeover. Instead, he's begun handing the bus pass over within the first day or two. His tormentor waiting like a toll collector at a certain street corner, one cleared of witnesses or interveners by that magical process of vacancy, the attunement of other children to the risk of joining in his misfortune. First or second or third day of each month, clockwork.

Ironically, the mistake is *not* riding the bus. Walking home on a pleasant day, too much juice in his body to stand with backpack at the bus stop on Union, the white boy legs it. Thus, he obtains the thief's attention, coming across Smith Street. The upshot, he now has to walk home, and to school as well, while pretending in sarcastic humiliation to prefer it. Sure, I've still got my bus pass, dad, I just choose to walk. I'm that kid, who just *likes* leaving half an hour early.

When at last, some sleet-raining day, he confesses the plight to his father, and in outrage his father demands the chance to meet him at the bell, to walk with him to find and confront this nemesis, well, we know where this goes. A white father walking with injured dignity, jaw upraised, ignominious victim in tow, this pair is easily spotted for miles around, they're klaxon-loud even in glum silence. Not a chance in the world the father's patrol will turn up a result, and it doesn't. This white boy is Big Bird and the older Puerto Rican boy the Snuffleupagus, that creature Who Will Not Be Seen. The next day, the ceremony resumes. The white boy is relieved of the pass. The half-empty booklet sits on his dresser just daring him to tear out the next month's offering.

FOR ANOTHER KID, the first is a bike.

Actually, this is a common story: bikes. Nothing distinctive in a bike.

A coat. Also common.

Socks, less so, but it is recorded that it happened once.

For another, a package of Hostess CupCakes. Weird place to start, with food.

A Frisbee.

A yellow plastic G.I. Joe Adventure Team vehicle.

Hot Wheels. Or did the kid who brought these to the pavement merely lose them? A group of kids works pretty hard to convince him that's the story. You lost them, man. We saw you. Raced them right into the storm drain, you were groping around, why you trying to blame it on somebody else?

One kid can't recall a first, only a kind of cascade or abyss in memory. An infinite regress.

These participations, for some they are the first whisper of a thing we'll call *the dance.*

FOR THIS OTHER kid, a Black Dean Street boy, the first is a baseball mitt. Black kids are eligible for participations too.

A lefty glove, Willie Davis's autograph branded into the leather strap. Boy wants to play shortstop, his father needed to explain why there were no left-handed Gold Glove winners in the infield aside from first base, and why you didn't want a first baseman's glove. So, Willie Davis.

The boy is encouraged by his father to try it out with a group of kids playing something resembling baseball, albeit on a field of concrete, in the P.S. 38 schoolyard. Within minutes he's invited up to bat and asked to lend the mitt to a left-handed kid who wants to play the distant outfield. Though the boy is sickly nervous to relinquish it from his hand, this feeling is not yet rooted in any experience. Rather it is felt as an intimation, stemming from an excess of love for the fresh object. (Later it will feel to him that this aura, his excess love, is precisely what attracts the loss.) The glove instantly and mysteriously exits the scene. The boy returns home in tears. This story has an anomalous finish: the father goes to the schoolyard and cannily offers a fiver for anyone returning the glove, no questions asked. After a moment of conference, someone climbs to an accessible shed-roof, above eye level. There the glove's been flung. The item goes home with the father. For now, newly shimmering with disturbance, it is returned to the boy's dresser top.

Smart father.

We'll visit these two again.

28.
C., Part 2
(a snapshot, continued)

Does C. feel he lives in Boerum Hill, or Gowanus, or South Brooklyn? Or what?

We can try to guess what he knows.

He knows, at least, that he is a Dean Street kid. He knows this because his mother joins the Block Association.

And C., recall, is his mother's tuning fork. She hums, he vibrates.

But this is decades before secret parent texting. Parent e-mail groups, these don't exist.

So, like any other kid in this era, C. is auditor to a lot of phone calls—to a lot of *half* phone calls, that is. You puzzle out the other side, like solving a standardized test by seeing what the questions imply about the answers. Or like certain comedy routines involving phone calls, rampant in this era, Bob Newhart, Lily Tomlin. The comedy of pauses. Or the words "you don't say . . . you don't say . . . YOU DON'T SAY!" pronounced with different emphasis.

("What did he want?" "He didn't say.")

C. is a great student of television comedy, the mild ribaldry of Flip Wilson and Carol Burnett and Sonny & Cher but also the sitcoms, the households of *Maude* and *Good Times* and *All in the Family* and *The Jeffersons*, the weird interpenetration of the white worlds by the Black, the spinning-off of one from the other.

C. monitors the Block Association phone calls in particular. How his mother sounds on the phone and again after she hangs up. "They think I'm supposed to explain to them why some hoodlums from Gowanus Houses want to pull down their new trees," she says, around the lighting of a consolation cigarette. She metes these out two or three a week, invariably after talking to some white people. "Like I'm in charge of those jackass boys." Then, noticing him watching, she stubs it out. "You know who's stripping those trees?"

"No."

"Don't let me catch you."

C. would never dream of hurting the trees. Why not? By this time, he's become a rapt observer of the changes to the block. He tabulates the process, the physical fact of the transformation of the buildings themselves. He is unashamed in his admiration for the repointed brick. He's amazed by the persistence of new owners who trouble to replace the shattered sidewalk slate with fresh slabs of gray stone rather than mere poured concrete: these are people who want to live neither in the present nor the future, but in a cleaned-up dream of the past. He's fascinated at the sight of a moving van, or the return of the truck full of Italian ceiling plaster specialists, or the other Italians who will hoist a gleaming black new cornice and attach it to the roof in one afternoon—something's always happening now. C. feels enmeshed in the drama of the block's becoming.

It is in this phase of his mother's involvement with the Association, the phone calls, and also the meetings to which he is sometimes dragged, that his field of vision expands. His vision of the street and his place in it, beyond his mother's wishes both for him to flourish and to be justified.

His vision begins to widen. Perhaps this marks the onset of C.'s sensitivity to the muddled-up desires of the white parents themselves.

At five years old he'd already felt his antennae vibrate to their delight when he plays with their kids. As he ages, nine, ten, eleven, then begins the leakage of their actual notions into his mind. Audible whether they moronically pronounce these within his hearing or only emanate them at close range.

They might say:

"What a little gentleman."

Or: "Hey, slap me five!"

Or: "I *know* you know what I'm talking about. See, he knows, oh yeah, he knows."

Or: "You two keep up the good work."

Or they might unpack this thought a bit further, and say: "See *this*, the sight of *this*, you have no idea, this is everything we fought for when we marched."

Or: "You like that? You can keep it if you like, we'll buy another one."

Or: "It's remarkable, you just go anywhere you want, don't you? Is there a kid in this neighborhood you don't know? And am I crazy, or was that you I passed in the P.S. 38 schoolyard, playing basketball with . . . a bunch of . . . your other friends. I mean, those older kids. You know what I mean."

Or: "Where's your father?"

When C. wins over a new set of white parents he sees them transform, like phases of the moon. He can watch as their initial fears, their uptight self-loathing reservations, melt off into fond relief.

Their relief is in thinking that this street—this one mad block of it in particular—where all the kids mix and you don't know what's what, a scene so alluring, so threatening to the white mind—this street is going to be okay for their child.

Whew.

Their children will be ennobled by a Black friend.

Whatever that means.

Their children be cooler with a Black friend, and so will their parents.

Whatever, whatever, whatever.

Their children will also be safer with a Black friend.

Of this, there's no doubt.

And he, C., he can deliver the goods.

WAIT. IS C. the only Black kid around?

Obviously not. Not even on the block. Plenty others.

There was, for instance, the one who only came out and played ball. Didn't care who with, but barely talked about anything. Certainly never accepted an invite into a white kid's house. That kid, he drew a strict line.

THEN THERE WAS the one drawing no line at all, who had his secret afternoons upstairs with his white friend, the two of them all misty and dewy with each other and thinking it wasn't screamingly plain.

Plain, at least to C.'s eyes. He didn't wish to have noticed but did. Damn, that's a mess. Somebody's parent is going to walk in on that before long.

Want no part, see no evil, say no more.

THEN THERE'S THAT Black boy whose first participation is with the Willie Davis baseball glove. This one is a subject of study. C. has given him a nickname.

C. calls him the Slipper. Not only because on Saturday mornings this kid has been seen on his stoop in his pajamas and slippers, just looking out, neither inside his house nor out on the street.

But because the Slipper tends to slip away. Perhaps too, in some way C. cannot exactly quantify, because he also slips *between*.

What is to account for this property of slippage? Is it because though he's Black, the Slipper goes to Brooklyn Friends School? Is it because his parents are divorced, and he moved to the block with his father? Is it because father is an actor and was on a Hertz commercial with Joe Namath? Is it because he is left-handed?

In C.'s view, it is simply that nothing sticks to him. For instance, in the matter of the glove, C. once overhears some girls telling the Slipper that they heard anyone could get a free five dollars out of him just by taking his baseball glove.

The Slipper only shrugs. "My dad says some people have less than you and want what you have."

The Slipper plays with anyone from time to time, but unlike C. he isn't saddled with the results, with the residue. He slips away.

SO, PLENTY. ON C.'s own block alone, these other three Black boys. More, really, if you count the younger ones, coming up from behind. Not to mention the girls. Yet C. has recognized his special role as the ambassador, the solver, the involver.

If it were a white neighborhood, the role wouldn't have existed.

For sure, C. could only have charted all this years later, it would never have occurred to him at the time. But he absorbed it into his senses.

If it wasn't a white neighborhood, does that mean it was a Black neighborhood? No, not that either, though the relentless hodgepodge included plenty Black, yes. Also plenty P.R. and Dominican. The projects were buttoned up tight around the neighborhood's ass end. Arabs on Atlantic Avenue, buying up buildings while no one was looking. The Italian factor bracketing on the Carroll and Cobble side, the ancient polack couples, the Mohawk residue, the weird drunk men about who the last thing that mattered was that many happened to be forgotten varietals of white.

Then all these Brownstoners and their children.

Mostly their children went to the private schools, but a few not. A few were sent, luckless beacons, to P.S. 38, P.S. 261, I.S. 293. It was these white boys, above all, who'd become C.'s special appointment. Is the acceptance of his appointment wholly altruistic?

It is not.

In the benign invasion of their homes, the charging through the basement-level kitchens in order to get to the backyards, the raiding of the freezers for the Tupperware frozen juice pops, or just in the awkward conversations when he is invited to stand in the parlor while someone races to tie on their shoes for school, C. is permitted to see inside the white houses. To find out whether they are like the houses on television shows, or whether the television lied.

Would the houses, for instance, be secretly full of outright bellowing racists like Archie Bunker?

Not that, no.

Sometimes full of weird cooking smells, sometimes other weird smells. A lot of hippie shit, candles, even in otherwise not apparently hippie families.

Sometimes the belongings look alluring, major stereos and record collections, or collections of other things, seashells or, once, antique pistols. There is in general a lot of collecting.

Sometimes the interiors are startlingly un-soft, ceilings busted out and walls all squared-off and white, like they want to make their houses look like a bank. Much more often there is the smell of solvent and varnish, of layers of paint removed and replaced with layers of gloss, a foolish pursuit if ever C.'s seen one.

The fathers with their gloss brushes and solvent are, C. is confident, as high on fumes as any bag huffer. Their eyes spin with it.

In the end, there isn't so much that can be said about the insides of the houses in general except, in direct opposition to the outsides, that they are seemingly without exception violently *unfinished*.

This almost seems a law of the Brownstoners' world: finish the exterior immediately, then take a thousand years to complete the inside. Subject your children to life in a construction zone.

That the insides don't match the outsides, that's one thing.

Another thing: that moving through the insides of the houses, C. feels the electrical buzz of the white parents' unstinting attention.

29.
What About Those Girls?
(just outside the frame)

Right, there are girls too.

Black girls, white girls, Puerto Rican.

Would any of them, an older sister of a white boy, ever take on a protective burden in the manner of C.?

Girls of all kinds might have problems all their own.

The special overall historical circumstance of womankind being just one place such speculation would need to begin. Let's say a girl— not just a white girl, but any of them—might have been pushed out-doors at a young age to go play with the kids on the block. Shooed down the stoop. Look, kids! Go meet someone, go play. If they can, you can.

It happened to be that on Dean Street the boys of all kinds signifi-cantly outnumbered the girls.

A girl might be absorbed into the false oasis just as easily as a boy, for a day or a week or a month. Yet it was a certainty they'd be ex-pelled from it much sooner. The boys had the privilege of being bliss-fully ignorant for a longer time, since long even before the difference between Black and white and Puerto Rican was articulated, expelling the boys from the Oasis, henceforth, another difference would be articulated.

That's to say, the boys were always pointing out to a girl that a girl was a girl, not a boy. So, you can play with us, maybe. If you do, you will be a girl who plays with the boys. The Oasis persisted, but the girls found themselves placed at a special angle to it. Lodged in parenthesis.

And a girl probably wouldn't be cast in certain roles.

You might, say, be one of the mob of runners in Running Bases, screaming in delight as you blobbed between the two safe bases, but you'd be less likely to be one of the two fielders with the gloves and the ball.

So, you could get tagged out but not tag others out.

There was pleasure being in that blob of runners, it was a good place to hide and scream all at once, to be a body among bodies, mostly the younger boys as the oldest and most athletic hogged the gloves for themselves. But you were as old as the older boys and you actually knew how to throw a little and it might be nice to be one of the taggers-out.

It was also true one of those older boys, the taggers-out, had begun singling you out for tagging while conspicuously letting all the younger boys in the blob leak through to safety at the base. As if he had some special grudge or interest in tagging only you.

As a result of this special grudge or interest, one day you'd say nah to being waved into the game. Then either find your way back up your stoop or group yourself with the girls doing Double Dutch with a rope and either try to figure out that sport (which was actually quite a lot harder than throwing a damn ball) or sit and just watch and chant along under your breath, memorizing the routines.

And the Oasis split now, into a Boy Oasis and a Girl Oasis. So maybe, for the boys, girls had been the dry run, the first skirmish with the dividing power of *other*.

PROTECT THOSE FOOLS?

First of all, unlike them, you are capable of getting it on the street from both girls *and* boys.

Second of all, you've got parts of your body to protect from laughing plunder, not just a dollar in your pocket and a five hidden in your sock.

Third of all, if the curse they've inflicted when not paying you an excess of attention is to pay none at all, why wouldn't you use invisibility for what it's good for?

Case in point is the morning one white Dean Street girl is running late for the group of white boys she always walked to Brooklyn Friends School in the company of. For protection, so-called.

Each parent having armed the kid with mugging money as they scoot them out the door at the appointed hour.

That arrangement made—how? Did the parents consult? Or arrive at this each independently?

(They likely consulted.)

(We will investigate this question of mugging money in due time.)

So: this girl is running late. Her mother, annoyed at her dawdling, informs her that the group, which includes her older brother, is leaving without her. She'll get what she deserves, have to walk to school alone.

Implicit in this is *face-street-perils-without-the-boys.*

She gets out the door ten minutes later, to follow the usual route. Walking alone, she's pretty fast, compared to the bozo boys. She's crossing Jay Street when she sees the group, her brother and the others in that crowd. The Dean Street boys stand immobilized while their pockets are frisked, the near daily ritual.

What do we think the mugging money is for, after all?

It is for handing over when mugged.

She stops, invisible a half block from them, and watches it unfold. Doesn't take long.

Today she has an extra dollar in her pocket, thanks to said invisibility.

She is an independent discoverer of the fact that in this situation a lone girl may slip between the traces when a boy or a pair or group might as well be a walking dollar sign. A sign in parkas and backpacks that may as well be outlined in neon.

From that morning onward after exiting her house with her brother, the girl excuses herself from the group and takes a separate route to school. This is a technique for converting the mugging money into an after-school candy or pizza fund, and makes the least recompense, really, she thinks, for her troubles.

NOPE, PROTECT YOURSELF. No one else will. Gather methods.

Some of these remorselessly pragmatic.

Another girl making use of an invisible-watching occasion: she's on Dean's sidewalk in broad daylight when a twelve- or thirteen-year-old boy, no way he's older, zips past, skirting her like a traffic cone, to snag the purse of a grown white woman walking ahead. He collects the purse in stride and vanishes around the corner of Bond Street.

The takeaway here is the girl never wears anything except cross-body bags.

Another usage the girls of all colors will know, once they're old enough to come home from a subway stop after dark: the open bodega as the savior and protector, the open bodega as the safe harbor. Ducking into Sammy's on the route back to Dean Street from Hoyt-Schermerhorn. Into Ziad's if exiting the F train stop at Bergen. There to wait out the predatory footsteps of somebody following you from the station. You'd weld yourself to a route that included a few open, bright-lit bodegas, no mind if it was an extra block or two out of your way. Practically marry that one bodega man who'd not only nod knowingly and let you idle in the back near the humming refrigerated cases of Yoo-hoo and Manhattan Special, but seize up his baseball bat from behind the counter and stand visible at his door, like some look-out barkeep in a western.

OUR ACCOUNT IS bankrupt in this respect: it can't afford too much more than these scraps, these glances. As the Dean Street boys find themselves helpless even to adequately witness, let alone valiantly protect—ha!—the girls in their midst, this investigation meets its helpless limit here. The girls would need a proper book, an entire book. Let this one at least assent that it has enlisted them in a cause not their own.

Let this one say it knows that even to *mention* the valor of the bodega men with their open doors and their brandished bats wounds the boys, wounds them in the tiresome region of their remorseful thwarted masculinity, would be to make the story about them again, always about the boys and their weakness and failure, their voluminous shame.

So, don't.

30.
The Slipper Carries Mugging Money
(1975–79)

You can slip out of some things, and then again not others.

A price for being so very often on his own as he moves on these streets, streets still new to him despite the uncanny self-possession which seems to be his inheritance, is that the Slipper gets robbed.

Anybody can be robbed. It happens all the time. Corralled by two or three others. Pockets frisked, head dipped in a headlock at the least sign of resistance. You can only run sometimes. Slippage meets its limit.

The Slipper's dad eases him into the logic of their new street: carry a little something for your fellow man.

Carry the rest in your sock.

A nice, easeful phrase, isn't it? *Your fellow man.*

Slipper, taking the cue, wears this bifurcated cash on his person with relative equanimity. Relative being a relative term, of course. Relative to not being robbed at all? No. But relative to taking being robbed personally. Relative to thinking such sunlit mess-arounds are required to sink deep into your nervous system, into your psyche. No. Not for the Slipper.

NEVERTHELESS, NO ONE can be looking forward to such encounters, in the silenced afternoons, five steps from the bodega, at the gate of the vacant lot, in the island of the crosswalk of Boerum Place across from St. Vincent's Home for Boys, whether by Italians or Puerto Ricans or those Black kids who have placed you, by dint of your sneakers or hair, or by whatever deeper radar, outside recognition, outside affiliation—no one can be looking forward to the helpless adrenaline-quickened, heart-sunk encounters during which one hands over one's mugging money.

No matter the satisfaction at what remains in the sock or the sole of the shoe, no one could be so perverse as to be looking forward to that.

The Slipper takes no pleasure in being robbed.

Yet he copes. Keeps it together. He has a way of slipping within himself when he needs it. Training his eye on some far-glimpsed horizon.

31.
First Whisper of the Dance
(ongoing)

Anybody can get robbed. Everybody gets robbed. So, is getting robbed the dance?

Not exactly. Though the regularity and routine, the employment of the mugging money, is a prerequisite.

Yet not just anyone will be swept into the dance. Not the Slipper. It's not for him, though he'll know plenty about it.

Everything in this matter is nerve shreddingly specific.

We'll get there.

II.
The Case Against Boerum

"WITH THE WONDERFUL BLESSING OF hindsight (or, in some cases, culpable ignorance) it looks so easy. What you do is, you take a declining neighborhood, move into it, fix up the premises, and encourage other, like-minded souls to do the same. Hey, presto, a rejuvenated neighborhood or a gentrified one, take your pick.

Although a lot of incredible flapdoodle has been written on the subject, it wasn't that simple. Nor was it, as certain ageing hippies would have us believe, an act of dark and sinister cunning—unless, of course, one prefers limitless vistas of vacant lots begreened with the first tender shoots of ailanthus pushing their way up through the rubble. I know some people find this hard to believe, but buildings don't repair themselves; it is one of God's many shocking oversights."

—L. J. DAVIS,
Phoenix Newspaper editorial

"SO I went to this meeting. It was in the house of a writer, a cat who gets his kicks out of having six working fireplaces (half of which he had to discover under old wallboard, scraping, tearing with his fingernails like a man escaping from a high-security cellblock) . . . we all agreed—in our beards and boots and clean jeans and wash-and-wear work shirts—that the gentry on the block had flubbed it . . . But what to do? Invite squatters to live in the vacant buildings! Start a free school in the basement! Make the parking signs bilingual! Get a giant speaker and alternate rock and Latin music on the weekends! Get St. Anselm's Mercy Hospital to do abortions! (Half the women in the room would volunteer to have one if that would help.) Push the pushers to another block! Take down the backyard fences! Have a block party whose theme will be Discover Thy Neighbor! (Since you will all be ultimately ripped off together). . . . We passed around a joint to signify our accession to our three radical points that night . . . we had vowed as homeowners—most of us having been pushed by the Misfortunes of Economic Realities into borrowing down payments from our capitalist parents, who loved to see us crawl into that hateful bag— not to charge our tenants more than three hundred dollars a month, if we could help it, letting conscience be our guide. We had decided to have a multiethnic Street Fair complete with police barricades to close it off even to the rest of George Street, thus indicating true inner-block solidarity (as opposed to intra-block, which comes later). We would find a cause to use the money for at our second meeting, when we could fight about how many people could relate to flower boxes, how many to gas lamps . . ."

—ROSELLEN BROWN,
Why I Quit the Gowanus Liberation Front

32.
Lovecraft Basement, Part 1
(1983)

White kid walks into an antiquarian bookstore.

That September pretty much every other white kid he knows is off to college, either a year earlier or just now. A few maybe opted for colleges in the city, NYU, Brooklyn, Hunter, a couple even stuck in their childhood bedrooms for a semester or two, but seem gone nonetheless into new lives elsewhere. And anyhow are none of his former friends. That's how they feel now, former. Like in his way he'd been rehearsing to be the one who stayed, dropping out of Brooklyn Tech and who even knew the difference? They'd stopped hanging out on Dean Street years before. Nobody left but a few younger siblings he'd assessed and dismissed as uninteresting in any regard.

A howling sense of a neighborhood never your own but now left to you, dumped in your lap to prowl and ponder alone. At nineteen, he finds he can practically turn in his radar, no longer needs his street sense. He's grown too strapping, too broad shouldered, to be a part of the dance any longer. It's his size, yes, but also perhaps his shaggy, round-shouldered style of looming down the blocks, so that he appears as if on a mission, or maybe headed for a stool at the bar of the Doray Tavern. It felt almost lonely, becoming so untouchable. What's wrong with my money? I've got a dollar in my pocket, come say hello!

In high school, even before dropping out, he'd taken his first job in a used bookstore and lost interest in nearly anything else. The little walk-down on Henry Street was a sad labor of love, he'd hung around the place fifteen or twenty times before the middle-aged guy, a classic antiquarian misanthrope, even grunted acknowledgment that he featured a return customer. One who not only browsed, but purchased, and purchased interesting stuff. When the kid offered to work, the guy first few times tried to brush him off, but the kid persisted. One day the guy was simply worn down, or abruptly glimpsed the chance to escape the inevitably empty shop for a few jaunts to the diner on Montague where he afternoon drank with his misanthrope friends.

"What are you, out of school at three?"

"I could be here earlier on Wednesdays."

"Come after school twice a week, you pick, not Fridays. Three is fine. Five bucks an hour's all I can manage."

"I'll take it half in books."

"No stealing. I catch you stealing from me, I'll call the police, I'm not kidding."

"Okay."

"I'm kidding. You'll steal books from me, I know you will. I stole from every store I worked at."

The guy was a bewildering mess, but there the kid was, installed at the helm of a shop, instructed to price the books in pencil out of a formula based on listings in *Books In Print*, two massive volumes he braced on his knees while sitting on a stool behind the counter, infinity of titles he learned like a bible. This guy's store didn't actually feature the dusty layers that most turned the kid on, like in the place on Fourth Avenue in Manhattan and the four moldering outlets he'd found in the neighborhood, the ancient shops on Jay Street and Livingston and Flatbush. Behind each of those stores lay a secret warehouse; if you inquired for a particular book they'd always say come back in a week, I'll have it. And half the time they would. This was the realm the kid craved, the deep archive, the books behind the books anyone knew existed.

But those men were too much older, all cigars and phlegm. Every fifth word polack spic and beyond. They appeared webbed like figures in a painting and they hectored the kid from their shops with laughter when he offered to work. Between guffaws, they harangued him about experience. They called it *busting his cherry*, a thing he should have accomplished before he came bothering them. They suggested he could pay *them* if he wished to hang around. He could open his own store.

Whereas, this guy? This guy sort of seemed to need the kid. So, he'd bust his cherry here. In the college of New York antiquarian bookselling, he'd start at the bottom. At a store less like a real business than like somebody's private library ventilated hopefully to the indifferent street. Every book was on view, the kid doubted there were any left in the guy's apartment. On those rare days when something sold, you'd turn a book face out to fill the gap until someone else walked in with a box to sell. The guy liked Beat poets and writers twenty or fifty years from vogue, A. E. Coppard, J. B. Priestley, C. P. Snow, he might stock a whole shop solely with novelists with two initials if the kid didn't protect him from buying yet another copy of *The Go-Between*.

In six months, the guy was asking him to come five afternoons a week, in order that five afternoons a week he could go drinking at the place on Montague. In a year he was out of business.

They put in a dry cleaner joint, and within a month you'd never have known the shop had existed.

Yet the guy had known a few things, told a few tales. One was the legend of the Lovecraft Basement. The guy, it turned out, had done his own apprenticeship, on Jay Street, on Flatbush, on Fourth in Manhattan. Though he'd never seen it himself, as a younger man he'd been chasing the legend: a basement full of the books and papers sold out of H. P. Lovecraft's Clinton Street apartment when the old rat had fled back to Portsmouth. One of the old Brooklyn booksellers was sitting on the hoard, paralyzed by the myth of its worth, the risk of being fleeced. The guy had been hunting it, and had it narrowed, he thought, to the two ancient shops on Jay Street.

What were the odds this was true?

The holy grail. The kid would have to take a run at it himself.

He'd been stealing, as predicted, from boredom. He was good at spotting the oddity among the common, as if by some perverse nerve. He'd steadily gleaned a stash of the off-kilter items, stuff that interested you because in all your days in the trade you'd never come across it before. Left alone to clerk at the guy's counter, not only as seller but also buyer, he'd simply acquired certain material as it came across on offer. Paid out of his own pocket, if he was nervous about how little was in the till. The bulk of these items the proprietor never even laid eyes on, let alone shelved. They went straight home with the kid.

Now, the collegians gone, he's ferried a box with eight or ten of these enigmas and returned to the shops on Jay Street. The two storefronts were just three addresses apart. Truly, they'd grown by familiar animosity into a single entity, many afternoons the proprietor of one wandered over to the other for some spiky banter in lieu of any action from customers. They were together this day.

But which shop possessed the Lovecraft Basement? It couldn't be both. Maybe he'd get a job in one and tunnel through to the basement of the other.

The kid, nineteen now, stacks the box up onto the counter with maximum nonchalance.

"It's the gunslinger," cracks the keeper of the other shop. "What do they call you, the vellum kid?"

"He's been working in the Heights," says the other. They know everything, somehow. "At that poof's store."

Poof? All this time, the kid hadn't considered it. In an instant he knows it's true, and a partition falls in his worldview. A gay guy could be less than groomed and vain, why not? A gay guy could be a schlub with a bookstore.

Meanwhile, these men are revolting. Yet they are also the Keepers of the True Flame. This circle will have to be squared at some other point in time.

"I guess he's back around looking for work," says one to the other. "You gonna ask the vellum kid for a resume? You gonna give him a test? What's the only good Britannica? I mean, relative to the shit that is the others."

"The eleventh edition," says the kid.

"See, I told you, kid broke his cherry. You want a job?"

Now our hero executes his big play. "Nope, I'm just scouting now."

"Oh, you're scouting?" The proprietor puts his nose over the box on his counter. "There's a living in that?"

"Maybe."

The two booksellers pass goods back and forth, talking a language of squints and eyebrow-furrows, of cigar chews. "Where'd you come by this?" The designated bait has arrived in the proprietor's hands, a ribbon-sewn first of Henry Miller's and Michael Fraenkel's *Hamlet*. Pages uncut. "This in that fruit's stock?"

"No, he sold the remains to Strand. The lot."

"Fuck the Strand. I'll give you forty bucks for this box."

"Let's keep it to individual items. I'd take forty for just the Miller."

"Oh, you might consent to take forty for just the Miller?" This in a mincing voice.

"Let's go one book at a time."

The proprietor paws deeper into the box.

"You got other buyers? You came to us first?"

"There's a law that says I have to come to you first?"

The proprietor grunts. "You still want to work?"

"Maybe later, I'll try this for a while."

The proprietor grunts. "Sixty for the box."

The kid collects the Miller and the other books that have left the box, hoists it again. "I'll do better piecemeal. I'll come back around with anything left over."

He's got them right where he wants them.

33.
Quarters, Part 2
(1978)

The two white fourteen-year-olds with their pockets loaded with destroyed coins—let's check in on their journey. They now idle at the doors of the Rex movie theater, examining a poster for Charles Bronson's *Breakout*, half of a Bronson double feature they've been wondering if they'd like to check out. Their legendary Black friend, not seen around Dean Street lately, was reputedly seen by another kid coming out of the Bronson flicks last week. The first showing, though, is hours away still.

Anyway, they've sawed all their quarters in half. Maybe one of them has a dollar wrapped around his ankle, concealed by his tube sock, a dollar he's hoarded and left unmentioned? Better keep the secret for now. The hidden dollar is Schrodinger's Cat, a thing neither dead nor alive so long as it remains in its place, just as this day features a million possibilities so long as they opt for none of them. Bored, unharassed, the boys take a turn down Butler, past their former school. Former, that is, as of five weeks ago, it's just barely in the rearview mirror, though already it appears like an alien citadel, a ruin from *Land of the Lost*. They move toward the Gowanus Houses projects.

A girl they both like, named Cherelle, former schoolmate in the building they're passing, lives on Hoyt between Degraw and Douglas. Cherelle's Black-not-Black in the hazy schema of the two white boys. Neither are clear on the fact she's Trinidadian. This shouldn't be a hard fact to grasp, but the nature of the boys' admiration, the awesome spell of Cherelle's beauty, has dictated years of keeping her obscured in the mighty denial engines of their forebrains. Now that they're no longer schoolmates with the daily privilege of basking in ostensible mutual indifference, the white boys have, with the paradoxical certainty of casino gamblers seeing the sun come up on an all-night losing streak, determined that Cherelle is likely to give them a whole lot of her time and attention just for coming around to say hello.

Cherelle's older brother is a famous graffiti artist, Phraze. Phraze has been reputed to carry a joint at all times, and to get younger kids high if they run into him on the street. This account is in all likelihood based, like the policemen in the jiggling car, on a single occurrence. Therefore, it is stuck in their heads, a mythic song of possibility. More concretely, Phraze departed the neighborhood in the middle of his teenage years, is rarely seen hereabouts. His trajectory is one the white boys would like to emulate and may in fact attain, though in an entirely different way.

The hope of some conjunction of Cherelle, Phraze, Phraze's older friends, or any comparable group they've envisioned on Cherelle's legendarily busy stoop, all makes an intoxicant now, as they approach Hoyt Street.

Yet no luck, the whole scene's a zero. Cherelle's younger brother is there alone, dinging a Spaldeen off the front step, trying to calculate the angle that will propel it upward and across the street. The younger brother speaks to the visitors only in shrugs.

They've temporarily forgotten about the gimmicked quarters in their pockets. Now they temporarily remember them, long enough just to show one off to the younger kid, without explanation. Their reward, another shrug.

Everything might be temporary with these guys. They edge away along the sun-heating slates, then up past the Gowanus Houses, falling silent, daring something to happen. The boys seem to blur and vibrate as they walk. Any given stretch of sidewalk might bring up self-remorse and shame, as if the street was recollecting them on its own dime, against their wishes.

Like the corner of Bergen they now avoid, that one where three years earlier one of the two in great hilarity shoved a paper bag full of rotting maggot-covered French fries toward the other and accidentally smeared his face, causing them both to go home crying.

The mental dance of disaffiliation as they pass the house of a kid they still go to school with yet no longer greet when they see him passing. Making themselves strangers to someone whose mom once fixed them plates of Fig Newtons and glasses of lemonade in a backyard.

There's something positively watery about these two. Are they even qualified to be characters in a story?

Some afternoons seem to go on for years.

34.
Everybody's Stereos and the Cops Don't Care
(1973–74)

There's a B&E gang operating on Dean Street and they have a methodology that can't be beat. It drives everyone crazy. Everybody knows what they're doing and even where they're keeping the stuff and no one seems to be able to stop them.

Breaking & Entering, of course.

When the Brownstoners started fixing up these houses they threw a lot of iron up, fast. Iron bars on the parlor windows, iron gates on the doorways beneath the stoop, the entrances to the basement level apartments. Reason being that which is widely and regretfully understood: this is a place with plentiful poverty, and with a wide streak of defiant and prideful robbing or burgling of anything that wasn't bolted down. Smash-and-grab car radio prying, backyard prowling, fire escape scampering, as well of course as raw frontal mugging and cowardly snatching. One dad had his wallet fished from his back pocket as he stood waiting to buy a token at the Hoyt-Schermerhorn stop, within twenty feet of the central station of the transit police. There's a reason the savvy bodegas seal themselves firmly behind roll-down gates on a nightly basis.

The Italian welders, masters of the authentic or at least authentic-appearing ironwork, appear on the block regularly to apply the heavy gates to the new-renovated houses. Kids are admonished not to look directly at the hot center spitting sparks as the Italians apply the cutting torch to the metal, though it's hard not to. The admonition passes from kid down to kid, each of whom sees the other sneaking a look. That spark's a drug.

But forget it. This B&E crew have broken the code. They have an answer for the gates. Like something out of an all-Black remake of *Oliver!*, they've got a kid small enough to hoist over the top of the basement-door grates. He wriggles through, climbs down the inside of the metalwork, and unlocks it to let in his crew. Or, upstairs, boldly climbing off the stoop in what must be plain view, to squirm between two bars of the parlor-window gates that have been ratcheted wide with a car jack.

Next day, everyone walking by agrees: they sure used a car jack on those window bars. That kid sure is a skinny bastard, to get through that gap, dang. Shaking their head. Seems like a hundred neighbors, Black, white, and P.R., dozens you never met before, just happen to wander in front the next day.

Victims could be excused wondering: Where were you the night before? Didn't anybody see anything? How is everybody so positive of what nobody saw?

But for greater indignity, consider this: everyone seems completely sure about where all the stolen stereos and televisions have been stashed: an apartment, less than a block away. At least they're sitting there temporarily, on their way to some quick cash resale in another quadrant. The apartment in question is on Dean between Nevins and Third, a third-floor place, nobody answers the bell. Residence or at least warehousing space of the presumed Black Fagin of this gang.

Every fresh victim calls the cops but the cops don't seem to care. They say they've got no inkling of this thing everybody knows with such certainty. Sure does look like they used a car jack on those window bars, yup!

Recall that Nevins is a boundary between two precincts, as well as a secret limit in the Dean Street boys' sense of their province and sanctuary. East of Nevins is an all-bets-are-off block.

Isn't anybody going to *do* anything? Soon every stereo in the neighborhood is going to be up in that dude's apartment.

The Italians with the welding torch, secret winners in this game. They come back and install reinforcing crossbars on the parlor windows, removing the car-jack method from the equation.

Then they add a decorative starburst of pointed metal spikes over the basement gates. Try wriggling over that, my young friend!

No, now you'll have to go to the next block down, and steal someone else's stereo.

35.
The Yo-Yo Gang
(1975)

There are less subtle operations. There are the guys who simply tie a rope to their bumper and the other end to the basement-level window grate and end up ripping the window frame out of a house on

Dean, near Hoyt Street. This occurs midsummer, midday, the parties in question having ascertained no one was home, and also spotting a television and clock radio sitting in plain sight of the window. Broad daylight. A witness at the bus stop says they claimed to him they'd forgotten their house keys.

The Screamer is aroused by the calamitous noise and goes off for the rest of that day, long into the night.

Cops explain in an atmosphere of humorous recognition, yeah, this right here is the work of the Yo-Yo Gang. White guys, reputedly Irish guys, from Jersey City, that's the legend anyhow. Total impunity, the price of choosing to live in such a ridiculous place and own a television. Price of moving in here in the first place.

Cops themselves standing there retailing this perspective, shaking their heads at the damage. Whole window frame, shit. You need not only a carpenter and glazier but also an ironworker and a bricklayer, after the Yo-Yo Gang hits. You'd have been luckier to get cleaned out by the kids who squirm over or through. No big deal hammering the car-jacked bars back into place. Or leave them as they are, advertising that you probably don't have a television at the moment.

36.
A Word About the Brownstoners
(1964–78)

This is their name for themselves, that's the first thing to say. The name covers a maelstrom of confusion.

Later they'll be given credit or blame for guile, foresight, calculation. Townhouses they purchased in 1967 for eighteen or twenty-one grand, then slowly refurbished, they turned over during the first peak in the mid-aughts for a cool three or five million. Seeing this, it's hard not to understand them as a deliberate engine of displacement and pillage. Hell, they brag of it themselves. Those for whom it worked out. They need no sympathy from us, or anyone.

Yet at the start these are weirdos, lacking a compass, a plan, a consensus. Often at one another's throats.

The banks and police, both think they are fucking batshit. This will be true for ten years, fifteen, more.

They are from Idaho, Manhattan, Pittsburgh, France. Anywhere but Brooklyn. They have no grasp of where they've come to.

Obsessed with conjuring provenances, they are known to dress in Victorian costume for photographs on the street, embarrassing passersby.

(The costumes may be more appropriate now that we see these people from afar, with their arcane notions that the slow restoration of a building could be conjugated with the wreckage of their lives, inner and outer, in this time when all provenance was crumbling. Their sense of which portion of what they understood about life they felt they had to brandish, and which to repress. Victorian in a way.)

There are graduate students, there are radical organizers, there are Quakers, there are painters and novelists, there are younger gays spilling over from Brooklyn Heights to populate Pacific Street. There are renters who despise their new landlords as bourgeois.

They form associations and counter associations.

They plant trees along the curbs, many, though not all survive. The trees are destroyed by passing trucks and buses. Teenagers also bend the fledglings until they snap. The Brownstoners sometimes attempt to protect the new trees with, you guessed it, expensive ironwork gates.

They plant community gardens in vacant lots.

They fill inexpensively rented storefronts on Atlantic with inchoate hippie boutiques selling very little in particular. In one, someone opens a puppet theater.

They strip painted sections of marble with solvents that take all the skin off their hands for two weeks.

They take *National Lampoon, The National Guardian, The New*

Republic, Mother Jones, Ms., Scientific American, Ebony, Playboy, and *TV Guide.*

They have consciousness-raising groups.

They have affairs with each other.

Every single one of them has tried pot. Or at least been handed a joint. Okay, maybe not the old lady.

A brownstone is decorated with anachronistic brass gas-fired lamps on posts. Five more such gas-fired lamps appear before the trend is snuffed by word of mouth.

A brownstone is painted top-to-bottom with purple-to-pink rainbow stripes, including the cornice, hardly any easier on the eyes than a subway train bombed with graffiti. How did they even get up there to do that?

A bomb explodes in a parlor, sending the windows raining out onto the street.

Somebody goes to prison for hashish smuggling.

They are raising children, and they are children.

The banks and police are right enough. They are batshit.

37.
If Things the Screamer Screamed Were a Greatest-Hits Album
(compiled)

SIDE ONE:

1. "They Don't Like You"

2. "You Want to Call the Police, Go Ahead"

3. "I Said I Don't Want to Eat Now"

4. "Everybody's Puerto Rican on My Block Except Me"

5. "You're Looking at Her Ass, I See You"

6. "Some People Got Killed"

7. "It Isn't Even Funny"

SIDE TWO:

1. "People Are Liars"

2. "I Heard They Incinerate Bodies at Holy Family"

3. "You Can't Come Upstairs to Shit"

4. "Where Are They Going? To Hell"

5. "I Am Very Tired"

6. "That Lady Pretends She's Nice"

7. "They Don't Like You (Slight Return)"

38.
Brazen Head Wheeze, Part 2
(2019)

He's bad tonight, issuing a poison vibe to every quadrant of the wedge-shaped room, even the bartender steers a berth. But this guy, tall, maybe thirty-five, in a jean jacket, a straw cowboy hat, and bushy muttonchops, waltzes into the teeth of the Wheeze's subvocal monologue, and grins.

"You're my guy."

The Wheeze halts, long enough to assess. "I'm no one's guy."

"I know you."

"Nobody resembling you does."

"You're hurting my feelings, brother. You almost electrocuted me. Flung a half-full pint on me when I played bass with The Pall Mallrats at Hank's Saloon. We did five nights in October, remember? You kept your back to the stage. You were glued to your chair. You're a legend."

"That's what they call you right before the guillotine drops. Why, if I kept my back to the stage, do you think I poured a beer on you?"

"Last night of the stand, we made up a ditty about you on the spot, folks were clapping along. You had your head on the bar, thought you were passed out. Then pow! You struck like a fucking *mongoose*, man. Mad props, bro."

"I might remember now."

"Let me buy you a beer."

"I'll pour it on myself just to make you go away."

"Seriously, no hard feelings. I owe you one. You're an apparition of better nights in better bars. This neighborhood sucks donkey now."

"Sucks now. In reference to when, he asked."

"Before all the money came in. Dean Street is like millionaire's row, all the fucking movie stars." Muttonchops waves his hand, indicating their immediate environs. "I mean, use your eyes, it's like an episode of *Friends*."

"Friends, Packer, Saint Ann's," mutters the Wheeze, who's begun sliding back into himself.

Yet Muttonchops won't let him. He's located some compass of authenticity to which he yearns to align. "No shit, I dated a Saint Ann's girl once."

"Good for you."

"Seriously, she was a hot mess. Grew up right around here, never left. I met her at Hank's, come to think of it."

"Did she tell you what stood there before?"

"What you mean?"

"*Hank's Saloon*, Joel McCrea. The building stood before you and your cowboy outfit turned up. She tell you the secret?"

"What secret?"

"The Doray Tavern, Where Good Friends Meet."

"Do-Re-Mi Tavern? What the fuck, man?"

"Indian bar, before you moronic dude-ranch-dressing jackalopes appeared. You stand on the sacred burial grounds, and you don't even know it."

Some are difficult to insult. They believe themselves the protagonist in any given situation. The white man with muttonchops is one of these. He has a cleft in his chin, hence the design of his facial hair. Who'd be so stupid as to cultivate a beard over a cleft that deep and good? The cleft has opened doors. Muttonchop gets what he wants, usually, and scarcely notices when he doesn't.

Tonight, he's concluded that he and the Brazen Head Wheeze are allied, against anyone who fails to recall the profound authenticity of Hank's Saloon, of a halcyon time five years earlier. Allied against the other denizens of this bar, against anyone who'd mistake this version of Brooklyn for anything but a pale residue. He places his arm around the bony shoulders of the Wheeze while raising his other arm. He half drains his Brooklyn Lager in a gulp. "You know what I love about you, brother?"

The Wheeze, though undesiring of this man's love, has had a few too many. He lacks the means to fashion his contempt into a spear sharp enough to pierce Muttonchop's armor of vanity. He would content himself not to be caressed, not to feel the weight of the muscular and hairy forearm now tickling his ear. Yet even in this simple wish the Wheeze may find himself thwarted. They're going to get drunk together tonight. Will Muttonchop ever grasp that he is not remotely liked? Hard to say.

"I'm terrified to learn."

"You make as little fucking sense as anyone I ever met."

39.
Doray Tavern
(193?–2000)

Let's step in. Muttonchops has a point. As the Wheeze drinks he grows incomprehensible, and he wasn't starting from a strong position in the first place. Let him enjoy the free beers while we try to clarify. Indian bar? Sacred burial grounds? Has this to do with the Wheeze's earlier obsession—the phantom street called Red Hook Lane, and the Canarsee Tribe? No.

Different Indians.

Mohawk Indians. The Doray Tavern was a Mohawk Indian bar.

The Kanien'kehá:ka, or People of the Flint. One of the five original members of the Iroquois Confederacy, the Keepers of the Eastern Door. Widely referred to as the Mohawk.

The Doray Tavern, now a lost name. The name of the dive bar occupying the corner of Atlantic and Third Avenues, same place where later the lamented Hank's Saloon stood. In fact, while the name changed, service was nearly continuous. The owners who redubbed it Hank's didn't renovate much. Only the words Doray Tavern were effaced, along with the slogan in white letters on the black exterior: "Where Good Friends Meet." Replaced with painted yellow and orange flames. Inside, for anyone bothering to notice, the ironworker's union stickers remained on the mirror behind the bar.

Mohawk ironworkers built skyscrapers. That meant they lived in New York City. They came from Canada to work on the skyscrapers, and landed here, in the region later to be dubbed Boerum Hill.

They had to live somewhere.

Little Caughnawaga, their nickname for this place. Does the name constitute another claim on these streets? Perhaps something less than a claim. Nobody would have called it that unless they were part of it. Just a community's name for itself. The tribal people who drove from Quebec to labor on skyscrapers and who, drawn to this part of Brooklyn by the presence of their union local office on Atlantic Avenue, filled the cheap, placid brownstone blocks with hundreds of families. And, for the younger men, or those whose wives didn't want to leave Canada, there were the rooming houses. Mr. Clean lived with some of these men. The men who drank at the Doray and other Mohawk bars. For decades, a church on State gave services in their native tongue.

Like many forgotten things, Little Caughnawaga is strewn around hiding in plain sight, after the forgetting's mostly accomplished.

Still, it's too much history. Surplus contradictions to hold in your head. Say it with me: fuggedaboudit.

Or remember, if you want to be like the Wheeze.

40.
Skateboard Hostage
(1978)

Two white boys and two Black boys all trying to master fresh skateboards in a neighborhood bereft of hill.

Three-quarters of this group were also part of the street hockey unit, last seen wandering on the far side of the Brooklyn Queens Expressway. The two brothers, and C. The younger brother's shot up in stature and viability, generally, since that hockey expedition. Details of which lay entombed in time and silence.

The fourth boy today is the one C. calls the Slipper. He's slipped outside and into their company with his usual knack. Like he's always been there, and perhaps he always has.

The skateboard craze has hit Dean Street but it's still propositional. There's a healthy dose of bluffing involved. (The key to mostly anything being pretending your first time isn't.) The two brothers, for instance, have conducted a series of subway pilgrimages to Paragon Sports, to gaze at the skateboard counter in the back room. There, serious Manhattan riders hand over untold cash for fresh Gullwing Split-Axle trucks and Kryptonics polyurethane wheels they'll ratchet-wrench onto hand glossed slalom style decks, in the process lounging around the buying area throwing a lot of sardonic smirks at anyone venturing a dumb question.

These boys don't. Their interest at the Paragon counter is strictly dreaming, and they float through the place as invisible eyeballs, bereft of any pretense of joining this party. They don't have the cash, the ratchet tools, the knowhow. Nor, if they look in their souls, the commitment. Maybe somehow, someday, they'll vault to this level.

Not now. The boards they're auditioning today on Dean Street's uneven pavement, and in the middle of the street when the traffic's quiet, are ready-mades, sold in one piece at Triangle Sports on Flatbush, or in the basement of McCrory's. Clattery-ass plastic wheels, inflexible molded-plastic boards in garish solid colors, bearings locked in casings, inaccessible to tools or oiling, so they rattle like beans in a jar. These boards are nothing you'd be seen riding if anyone here had any knowledge otherwise—like, say, the knowledge the brothers gained on their window-shopping voyage.

Who knows who among them has visited Paragon? They all keep mum, protecting one another's ignorance. So long as they're just the four of them, falling off onto their asses every five kicks down the pot-holed street, and cracking up laughing attempting tricks nobody here on Dean Street's qualified to teach or assess, they're skatekids, sure enough. A conspiracy of ignorance, like four guys wearing rejects who agree to act as if they've never even heard Nikes or Pumas existed.

"I did it, three-sixty flip!"

"You didn't do shit!"

"You weren't looking, man. I did it, wait up, watch, I'll do it again."

Seeking anything smooth or ramp-like they resort to the drive-through entrance of the Catholic Hospital until the nuns kick them out, stand glaring making sure they don't return. The boys fling the nuns the finger and head back to their base block. They resume curb-clattering, bouncing off of parked cars.

By long habit these boys instinctively hew to the block's center. There's a good front yard there, paved flat, forming a sort of home base. The abandoned house, a couple of numbers away, with its gateless yard and cinderblock-flush windows, if you're looking for a flat face for bounding a Spaldeen off. A monitoring Black dad often sits cross armed in the yard with his bigass dog, rarely actively involved in any dispute yet a solid passive deterrent to whatever. Most simply, the distance from Nevins or Bond, the vents to the projects, to downtown, the Hoyt-Schermerhorn subway station. The middle of the block is leaf covered, spacious, theirs.

Today the last thing on their minds is any vulnerability. Their limbs are stretching, shoulders too. A couple of these guys are just off to high school, fresh domains, and the energy of their self-reinvention feels it should apply even back here, on the very slate-shattered main-stage of their childish fear. Fear is that thing they've outgrown. Did they trouble to conceal the skateboards as they crossed Bond, coming back from the hospital? They did not.

Besides, they are that perfect thing, a balanced quartet. Two Black, two white, exemplars of the oasis. It should make them invulnerable, unquestionable.

So, next thing, as though by axiom, the four are swarmed.

One push from behind, little brother is off his wheels, on his ass. The others turn to see, shouting "oh, shit, look out," and before they understand what's unfolding, they've had their boards jerked away by a springy group up from the projects. Five guys who obviously followed them up around the corner from Bond Street, and are now hightailing with, incredibly enough, all four skateboards in arms, toward Nevins. Like some kind of blitz play, and the leaf-blotted light of their sanctuary served to keep them obscured until the last instant.

"Get 'em!"

C., Dean Street's leader if they want to be honest, is chasing the lead thieves, booking hard in the direction of the corner bodega, before they round to Nevins Street. The other three, the two brothers and the Slipper, are slower out of the gate, but running too. And here's a target, unexpectedly: while the four with the stolen boards are nearly out of sight, running last in their pack, empty-handed yet slowest, is a young, scrappy, skinny Black boy. A younger brother. He likely tagged along, and they told him he could stick with them but he damn better be ready to run.

He failed. He's fallen way behind his group, and stumbled. Now the older of the two brothers throws his arms around him and, amazingly, converts him to a captive.

Meanwhile the four with their skateboards are around the corner

of Nevins, and C. too. The pursuit has petered out for the three remaining Dean Street boys—the brothers and the Slipper. They lack
the will to turn that corner, into uncontrollable situations. They're flat
footed, exhausted somehow, while the thieves are lightning, running
like their lives depended on it.

The skateboards are gone.

They're holding a hostage.

The three Dean Street boys feel inflamed and defiant. Also, stupid. Who'd ever brandished new stuff on the block, mitts, bikes,
radios, whatever, without calculating these odds? Yet they'd done it
today. Imagined themselves immune.

"Damn, let me go!"

"Hold him!"

What's it worth that they've captured the weakling, the weak link,
from the pillaging army? The two brothers have the boy's arms pinned,
one with a knee in his back, bringing him to kneel on the manhole
cover. Little kid's going nowhere unless they release him.

"Hold him for what?" says the Slipper. "They're gone." He's already eyeing the exit from this unsavory scene. It's as though he never
had a skateboard in the first place, was just passing through.

"Make him tell us where they live," the younger brother says,
pointlessly. They all know where he lives, just like everybody knows
which apartment the stereos are in. He lives in the projects.

"They'll have to come back for him–" This too dies in the air.
They won't come back for him. Or if they did, the white boy captors
wouldn't want to know in what numbers. The situation is rousing and
abject at once. They've exchanged four brand-new cheap-ass skateboards for something they'd never wanted, a Black hostage, a kid,
maybe nine or ten. He's no commodity unless as a souvenir of an
instant they're already conspiring to shrug off, employing well-worn
systems of shame and self-loathing.

"Later," mumbles the Slipper, and he slips off toward his own
home, like stepping through a stage's heavy curtain.

The Slipper, understandably, sees no margin in being a Black
Dean Street boy pitched in direct conflict with Black kids from the

projects. It's not for him. He leaves the two white brothers holding their captive.

"I kill you fucking motherfuckers," cries the captive in his high childish voice, his face on the sidewalk now. Why in heaven won't some parent come stop this from happening? Same reason they've never stopped any of it, ever: the street is a laboratory of unseeing, a secret shuttered theater, midnight at noon.

The two white brothers seem to drift in free space, their moral compass having gone around the corner of Nevins after the thieves. That's to say C., who frequently makes sense of their entire reality, but won't easily solve this one. They've managed to drag C. into their own shame: he actually got himself robbed, out of sheer association with the misfit group! Of course, C.'s also booking righteously in pursuit of his skateboard. Which, should he retrieve it, will only make this scene more pathetic. There's exactly zero possibility he'll come back with all four skateboards—as likely he'd return with a girlfriend for each of them. The sole coherent action possible here is the one that already occurred: The sublime theft, five runners washing over them like a wave. What's left is residue. Seafoam. Every second that ticks with this poor kid pinned only deepens their revulsion.

"You *know* they coming back with a gun, you dying."

The brothers will let him go, yes. No other possibility. Their bodies conclude it before their minds or mouths find gear. The little hostage springs loose screaming taunts back as he flings his arms running. Then it's the two of them standing there, no skateboards, no sign of either C. or the Slipper, the whole day vacuumed of all possibilities. No option, except residing in their insane failure ever to navigate one second of the epic wrongness of their childhoods, which won't so easily end.

Fuck it, those skateboards sucked anyway. The streets are too irregular. No conceivable improvement on the pairing of those stiff wheels and the lumpy terrain. Their ankles already hurt. Their asses. They required no new mechanisms for falling on their asses to begin with. Where are they going to go even if they rewound every mistake today? Better pretend there never were skateboards. Be relieved of the fiction that you're anything like regular children, even the ones in Manhattan.

41.
Kill You?
(really?)

He said *kill you*. He said *dying*. Do boys really want to kill each other?

As the saying goes—Is the Pope Catholic?

In their inmost animal selves, they want to kill each other with regularity. Of course they do.

Do they also sometimes want to fuck each other? Or to transform into each other?

As the saying goes—Does a bear shit in the woods?

But do they ever actually try to *do* these things?

As the saying goes—Does the Pope shit in the woods?

Which is to say that we've arrived at a more interesting and specific question.

42.
Boerum Hill
(b. 1964)

But, first, wait, what did you say about the hill? That there *is* no hill?

There's no hill in Boerum Hill.

It wasn't called that until it was. Somebody thought it up. It sounded better than Gowanus, South Brooklyn, Not-the-Heights, Cripplebush, Fucktown.

The name, the word, comes from somewhere?

Sure—somewhere.

It might make you think of the Boer War. South Africa.

Okay, right: Dutch stuff. We know about this. Stuyvesant, Haarlem, New Amsterdam.

So, Dutch?

Henry Boerum. Among the old Long Island names is that of Boerum, a name which the citizens of Brooklyn have perpetuated in Boerum Street and Boerum Place. The emigrant of the family was a Hollander, and his descendants, for many generations, have been landed proprietors on the Island. His father, Jacob Boerum, married Adrianna Remsen, a daughter of William Remsen, at the Wallabout. They had eight children, Henry being next to the youngest, born April 8, 1793. He passed the days of his boyhood on his father's farm, and during the idle winter months, availed himself of the limited educational advantages afforded by the public schools of his time and locality . . . On November 21, 1827, he married Susan Rapelje, a daughter of Folkert Rapelje, at Cripplebush, of the well-known family of that name, which has been prominently identified with Long Island almost from the date of its first settlement. May 1, 1828, he purchased from the executors of the estate of Folkert Rapelje sixty-two acres of land, being a part of the old Rapelje farm, at Cripplebush, for the sum of $7,000 . . . His life was a busy one from boyhood, and terminated May 8, 1868. In a quiet way he did much good, was instrumental in developing a now important part of the city, and left the impress of his business capacity and high commercial honor on the times in which he lived. He was a friend and companion of the leading Brooklynites of the period during his manhood and his name is inseparably linked with that part of the city within the borders of which he lived and died.

I copied that out of an old book, *History of Kings County*. The Wheeze showed it to me. Resembling a hundred-year-old bible or dictionary, the book was heavy, tattered, a relic. The binding was rotten, and I offered to have it replaced, but the Wheeze only laughed.

"I found it for five bucks in a junk shop," he said. "You could spend two hundred dollars on a new binding. No one cares."

"That's Boerum?"

He shrugged. "The old lady made it up. She pulled it out of her ass. There is no hill. She just liked the sound."

"But these are his sixty-two acres, right?"

"I wouldn't want to bet on that. She drew a rectangle. East of Smith Street, because you don't want to tangle with Smith Street. South of Schermerhorn, because fuck downtown, Fulton, all that crap. North of Wyckoff, because the projects. Close the drawbridge at Nevins, for god's sake. It's a fantasy. She made it up."

Henry Boerum's a red herring, then? A MacGuffin? There's not only no Hill, there's no Boerum in these parts. It's a vacancy wrapped around an enigma, a nothing sandwich. It might make you think of Lewis Carroll's *The Hunting of the Snark*:

"They hunted till darkness came on, but they found
Not a button, or feather, or mark,
By which they could tell that they stood on the ground
Where the Baker had met with the Snark.

In the midst of the word he was trying to say,
In the midst of his laughter and glee,
He had softly and suddenly vanished away—
For the Snark *was* a Boerum, you see."

43.

The Case Against Boerum

(21st century style)

But no, it's worse than a nothing.

The old lady had a shining rectangle in her mind, a sacred space. State Street to Nevins to Bergen to Smith (no more than that inside her protectorate, at the start!). A totally imaginary thing, yet shining in her mind.

It needed a name.

She came *this* close to calling it Sycamore Hill.

But she went to the history books, went and found Boerum.

And Boerum, it turns out, is a slaveholder name.

You can trust the Wheeze on this. He has the receipts. Or you could look it up, read it in cold type. From the 1790 United States Census, Kings County Register:

John Boerum. Free White Males of 16 Years and Upwards, 1. Free White Females, Including Heads of Households, 3. All Other Free Persons, 1. Slaves, 2.

Nicholas Boerum. Free White Males of 16 Years and Upwards, 3. Free White Males Under 16 Years, 1. Free White Females, Including Heads of Households, 1. Slaves, 3.

(Martin Boerum, congratulations—you held no slaves!)

Why, old lady, why?

The answer, surely, is antiquarianism. The more imaginary an American thing, like that shining rectangle in the old lady's mind, the deeper the ache to drape it in the bunting of provenances, lineage, Victorian frills.

44.
The Block Association
(1970s-style)

Excuse me, but the boys could be forgiven for wondering of the block associations: What exactly the fuck are they for?

The white people trying to get the unwhite people interested in something without ever it seems being able to specify what.

And failing, largely.

This seems more or less an open declaration that they're living in two different worlds: the world that simply *is*, and doesn't need any help in associating with itself, and the one that is a construction of papery wishes and dreams. The boys are sometimes enlisted in the distribution of leaflets enjoining people to come to gatherings to discuss things like *Attracting a Cinderella Project to the Block, Pro and Con.*

These frankly pointless goings-on would seem to have zippo to do with crime, except the parents always make certain to drop a number of the invitations off at the far-distant precinct houses. A way of saying to the cops, we exist. We're improving this block. It deserves your attention. Sometimes, incredibly, a cop even attends a meeting.

Hurry, guard the donuts!

Feeble joke, but he really did eat four.

On one block, the association actually organizes for block-watching evenings, where the white boys are enlisted to stand out on the stoops in shifts in the dark, looking out for crime.

Are they given fake badges, or toy handcuffs, or nunchucks? No. They're given whistles.

Whistles.

Thank god this isn't Dean Street. They'd never be able to walk down the street again, in dark or daylight.

Then there is the fiasco of the block party. Traditionally, at the block party, certain neighbors with grills sell hamburgers from their stoop. This is a tradition that has taken care of itself at all previous naturally occurring block parties, the ones in which the Association had no hand. This year, members of the association attempt in the name of fairness to dictate the price of the hamburgers on the block.

Had it been just the prices, grumbling would have ensued, but maybe no more than grumbling.

However, the Association takes it further. In order to be certain that the cost as well as the price of the burgers is fair, it is proposed that all agree on a certain poundage of ground beef that will constitute a standard for the burgers on the block. Before you know it, a Black woman is yelling *you think I need a white lady to tell me how to make a* HAMBURGER? *What kind of bullshit is this now?*

Of all the times for the never addressed to break out into view. Of all the topics to be the fuse. The amount of ground beef in a burger patty.

You never know.

There is only one thing that a block association is clearly for. On this we can agree.

Trees.

45.
Awkward Metaphors
(Brownstoner Era)

That's the second time we've alluded to a "Cinderella" project. What gives?

It's a real thing. Mostly forgotten now. Brooklyn Union Gas sprinkled grants around Brooklyn, often up to ten grand, to those who'd agree to spruce up the façade of a formerly abandoned row house. Seemingly no catch, except you had to put up a big sign for a specified duration, advertising the renovation as sponsored by the energy company. They'd even number them: "Cinderella Project Number Seven." Or whatever the number.

Cinderella, get it?

Neglected, beautiful, grateful for the makeover.

Except what does that mean—that, like Cinderella's stepsisters, other, uglier buildings deserved to be neglected?

Or that at the toll of midnight the Cinderella Project brownstone was destined to revert to decrepitude?

Awkward at best.

Here's another one: in 1972, brownstone Brooklyn got a newspaper of its own. A dedicated local alternative to the cursory attention provided by the city dailies, or even the *Village Voice*. Run out of a storefront on Atlantic near Bond. Scrappy little thing. Called *The Phoenix*.

Bird rising from the ashes.

Maybe awkward.

Another term, prevalent at the time, urban pioneer. The Brownstoners are "urban pioneers" or "settlers." You can even find references to Conestoga wagons if you're into microfiche work, like the Wheeze. A metaphor which maybe, if you take the historical perspective, implies more than it means to concerning attitudes toward the existing environs. It casts Black and Puerto Rican people as Indians. Also, given that Boerum Hill has a population of Mohawks, it cast Indians as Indians.

Let's just go ahead and say super awkward.

Everybody just sort of tiptoed away from those particular usages.

Not crimes though. We've got an amendment for that. You can say a whole lot worse.

Move on.

46.
Who the Parents Are Likely and Unlikely to Meet at Parties
(1970)

At their first cocktail party, these young white parents, the newest arrivals, those appearing interesting and interested enough to be invited—which figures in the prehistory of this mythic neighborhood are they likely and unlikely to meet?

This party would be held in a parlor of one of the newly renovated, or glamorously, incompletely renovated houses on Dean Street, or State Street, or Pacific, or Bergen. Or maybe one of the short blocks of Bond or Hoyt, but this is less plausible.

Not Nevins. And not the block of the Screamer.

It might be in the parlor, or on a warm night, it might be at the basement level, doors open to the back patio, though this carries with it the risk of mosquitoes, or the sound of firecrackers or music from a Caribbean island, or the scent of marijuana smoke.

Then again, this party, if it spills into the backyard, might provide its own marijuana smoke. Most likely, if it goes long enough, it will. That's one of the reasons to accept the invitation. Who are the heads in the neighborhood? You know there's gotta be heads among them. They can't talk about plaster ceilings and brass fittings and marble fireplaces all fucking day.

Or maybe you'd have to be a head to be *able* to talk about it all day.

Don't embarrass yourself, baby. Wait until someone offers.

FOR THE RECORD, they will get high that night, deep in the backyard's depths, beneath a fig tree. (Figs are all over Brooklyn's backyards, sprouted from cuttings brought over on boats, fifty or seventy-five years earlier by immigrants from Italy.)

This is the sort of evening that these two have in mind when, decades later, learning from a friend that said friend's son had, on selling his internet startup, purchased an eight million dollar brownstone on Dean Street, they let drop, "you know, we met the people who started that gentrification. I mean, really, the first ones."

In making this boast, they feel conflicted. They're distancing themselves, absolutely, from a scene and situation they were, after all, only passing through. Gentrification is a scandal and a disaster. It is also an object of wonder, when enacted on this legendary scale. Having been equipped with the political lexicon, these two have concluded that they were always firmly against it.

They're renters, have never been anything else. They bailed on the apartment on Wyckoff after three break-ins—to hell with fire escapes, just tear the stupid things down!—and lucked into a rent-controlled floor-through on Hudson Street where the boys had to share a large bedroom through high school. You don't surrender a rent-controlled place in New York City. That's how the middle class survives in a place like this.

Their sons, they're not in this Brooklyn Crime Novel. The parents moved them back to Manhattan. This man and this woman are barely characters in this book, really. Don't get too interested in them. But they do *remember*. This talk has them strangely agitated.

They were always against gentrification.

They also missed out.

Eight million dollars.

"Those houses were selling for fifteen, twenty thousand at that point!" she cries now.

"Of course, they were practically condemned properties," he reminds her.

"They weren't condemned. They had people living in them. They just needed work."

"It was a joke," he says. "You couldn't get a bank to give you a mortgage. The fire department wouldn't put them out if they caught fire. They wouldn't *come*."

"People banded together," she says. "They stuck it out."

"They made a killing."

"They were crazy."

"They were crazy fools." On this they agree.

"It was terrible there," he says. "It was, you can't imagine. Another world."

"Your mother would have given us the loan herself," she says. "But you wouldn't ask her."

BUT WHAT IS it they mean when they say they met the people who started the gentrification? Who is it they remember? Who would they have met? Did they really meet those who shaped the neighborhood, that night?

Would they, for instance, have met a "blockbuster"?

Absolutely not.

Hold up, hold up. What's a blockbuster and why wouldn't they have met one?

Blockbusters came along much earlier. Blockbusters seeded the

ground, laid down some of the preconditions for the invention of Boerum Hill. Blockbusters were predatory real estate operators, the cyni-
cal handmaidens of white flight.

Whether the blockbusters believed themselves racists isn't important. (We aren't meeting one in any case.) Blockbusters were open
exploiters of the racism of others. They installed a handful of Black
families on a block, or took advantage of Black families happening to
arrive.

They sowed rumors of crime and drug addiction and of further
Black families arriving soon. Then bought up houses on the cheap,
from the white homeowners they'd panicked.

Such cartoon villainy. Imagine basing your whole enterprise on
race panic. Who would do such a thing?

No one would call themselves a blockbuster.

Or at least not outside of some dusty den of iniquity. Maybe a private back room of an Irish bar. Like something from a Damon Runyon
vision of Olde New York.

Not the purview of our inquiry, really. We aren't even confident
that blockbusters still existed in 1970, the year this couple lived on
Wyckoff Street.

Anyway, no blockbuster would attend a party like this one.

Around here, the scourge of blockbusting was mostly forgotten. It
had worked too well to be much recalled.

SO, DID THEY mean they had met a "redliner"?

It's weird to imagine that anyone would *identify* as a redliner.
Meaning a banker who redlined. One who refused, on the basis of
race or other factors, to issue mortgages for a neighborhood like North
Gowanus.

Yet bankers exist. Some actual human beings were responsible
for those decisions. Some of the new husbands in the neighborhood
might even have worked in banks. Maybe some young banker present
that evening had been associate to a decision to refuse a mortgage

to one of their own neighbors, here in the fledgling Boerum Hill. It's possible.

The young banker in question sure would have kept his trap shut, if so.

No. The couple that left Wyckoff Street, they didn't mean that they'd met a redliner.

DO THEY MEAN that they'd met the old lady?

The founder, the neighborhood-namer herself?

Not a chance. She's alone in her giant house. Her cocktail party days, whenever those might have been, are behind her.

She's probably asleep.

It might make all these younger people nervous if she appeared, like having some weird god walk among them.

DID THEY MEET a real estate broker? It's a sort of pointless question. Probably they did meet one, in a technical sense. It isn't that hard to get a license. Some of the early arrivers here, in order to combat the effects of the banks' redlining, and the city's neglect, and the unfortunate zoning, got licenses. They did this simply so they could show houses that no one else was willing to show.

But they weren't in it for a career. The point was to strengthen the Brownstoner ranks. When the professional brokers grew interested in the neighborhood, these amateurs largely quit the field.

There may be some at this party who'll get heavy into speculation, but that's not the tenor of things, at least not yet. Everyone's renovating by hand. They're literally showing off injuries to their hands, comparing notes on splinters, thumbnails split by hammers, jeans eaten through by paint thinner. They also compare notes on crime, fire, the unresponsiveness of the civic authorities, the corruptness of the established contracting firms.

They're giddy with debt and high on self-inflicted disaster. No professional real estate broker would go within a mile of such talk.

DID THEY MEET a "displacer"?

A more interesting question. It has a sort of philosophical quotient. Or maybe I mean ontological. Or Archimedean? The problem of volume displacement is associated with the Archimedes Principle. I should look it up.

To meet a displacer, they might not need to have attended the party, they might only have had to look in the mirror.

People rarely think this way.

Still, the matter of who lived in your home before you, and on what terms they departed the premises, is a deep one, if you permit it to gain your attention.

THIS COMPENDIUM IS surely tipping into absurdity. Did this couple meet gentrificationists? Pioneers? Settlers? They did, of course. And they *were* them, too. In a way. They were weak pioneers. The type who would have been eaten by the Donner Party.

The question is who do they mean, when they claim to have stared the gentrification of Boerum Hill in its newborn face?

They mean their own landlord.

They weren't intending to party with their landlord. This woman didn't go to the trouble of ringing up her mother-in-law and asking her to babysit tonight, in order to hang out with their own landlord.

But they should have figured, because he is that kind of guy. A little bit everywhere in this neighborhood these days. A tall, garrulous, muttonchops-wearing guy with, yes, perpetual plaster-globs in the fine hairs of his forearms. A little too interested, a little too solicitous always, if you ask the father, of his wife. But then maybe he's just like that, it's nothing personal, she points out. Look at how he flirts with you too, and with the boys, and with the sullen men on the stoops who seem not to reciprocate. In fact, they can be heard muttering behind their landlord's back, they seem distinctly leery of him.

Maybe they know something. This comes out a little more petulant than the father might have intended.

He just comes on a little strong, darling.

What is it with these fucking hippie Victorians? I mean, mutton-chops?

Darling. She takes his arm.

Truth is, if they recall that night honestly, they're grateful their landlord is there. It isn't as easy to break into the insular Brownstoner scene as one might have imagined, not without having purchased a building. In his tall garrulous flirtatious way, he brings them around the party and introduces them here and there. "Heh heh heh I shouldn't let you talk to these people," he says on making one set of introductions. "Because you're heh heh heh gonna find out what I paid for the building, and you'll want a heh heh heh break on your rent." And then he is the one who takes them into the deepest part of the backyard beneath the fig tree and reveals a nicely rolled and pristine joint. Yes, it is their landlord who gets them high this night.

"So, what *did* you pay for the building?"

"Less than you can possibly imagine. But I shouldn't heh heh heh tell you this or I'll lose my coolest tenants, but it isn't too late for you two heh heh heh. I mean, prices went up but there's still plenty of good material for a song."

"Don't worry, we're not buyers."

"You want another hit of this? Heh heh heh you're smart to lay out for a minute, actually. It's strong stuff. Listen, I'm serious, you're throwing your money away not that I mind heh heh heh. But I could point you to some material."

"I—we prefer to stay uhhhh modular." Now the father is annoyed with himself, knowing he's offered a term that is wrong for what he means and only doing so in the effort to keep up with the pretentious euphemistic use of the word *material*. "Anyway, it's not like we're sitting on a down payment."

"Barely need a down payment if you go a little deeper in, forget Pacific and Dean, think about something a little closer to the heh heh heh projects. One of the side streets can be a good move. Don't overlook the side streets. Hoyt, baby, Hoyt."

HOYT BABY HOYT. That stood as the epitaph on this particular thought at the time. As the father recalls it, anyhow. It wasn't as if they ever seriously discussed going to his mother for a down payment. It wasn't as if they ever seriously discussed buying in the neighborhood at all, not at the time. Only later was he made to feel he'd missed something.

Well in fact he *did* once take one dreamy walk down Hoyt, staring at the facades between Wyckoff and Atlantic and trying to guess which were in the possession of the older owners who might be inclined to sell, but it was interrupted by a strange teenage girl who shouted down at him from the top story of one of the most decrepit of the houses.

"ARE YOU LOOKING FOR YOUR PENIS?"

THIS NIGHT, THOUGH, the stoned conversation under the fig tree shifts, from whether or not the parents ought to buy, to the topic of their landlord's own soul journey. How it was that he acquired his little kingdom on Wyckoff Street.

"Thing no one tells you about is that you gotta move them out to move 'em in. There's heh heh heh a few different ways to go about it, but nobody says a thing, it isn't like there's a handbook."

"Move who out?"

"The heh heh occupants man."

The mother wanders off now, seeming to lose interest. To the father's relief, for the moment. She's spotted an acquaintance, perhaps? Yet the father feels the price for the sharing of the marijuana is that he should stay and listen, at least a while longer, to his landlord's reflections.

"Your building wasn't empty when you bought it, you mean."

"You can pay 'em to move, but it isn't cheap."

"Did you pay them?"

"First few. Sooner or later though, you're gonna have to get serious and evict. Even that takes six months unless you get lucky. Court grants time to relocate, that kind of thing."

"Did you evict people from our—building?" The landlord owns three buildings on Wyckoff, two attached, one across the street. The father doesn't want to say *apartment*. Doesn't necessarily need to know with such exactitude.

Likely sensing the father's queasiness, the landlord obfuscates. "I had to evict a few on Wyckoff heh heh sure, get mixed up about which from where." He relights his joint. "You want to know the funny thing, bunch of 'em still live there, I mean on the block. They just bounced a couple of doors down. Doesn't seem to have done them any harm."

"You mean like the people on the stoops? The people you wave to?"

The landlord grins. "Couple of 'em."

"They used to live in your buildings?"

The landlord shrugs.

"They don't mind?"

"There's been some heh heh heh heh heh heh let's say give and take."

"What did they—take?"

The landlord grins. "One night they set my car on fire. Right there in front of where you're living, man. Went up like a fucking bonfire, like some kind of Celtic ritual. Nobody put it out, either."

"Are you serious?"

"Of course I'm serious. Gotta hand it to them, they know how to heh heh heh get something out of their system."

"What did you do about it?"

"What do you mean what did I do about it? I bought a new car."

47.
The Spoiled Boy Has Got Something Going
(1976)

Go figure, barely months after his arrival, the spoiled boy has got something going in that little concrete square of a yard. The kids are mostly younger than him in the new throng there. Some have that talent, for playing down, agewise. Of course, that's based on a guess, as if anyone among the Dean Street crowd is certain of the spoiled boy's exact age, which they aren't. His dad is missing so who can say how tall he's meant to be. Maybe he's a secret giant, and the key to his sullenness is that he's really more a baby. Maybe his dad's a secret giant covered in tattoos.

Anyhow, the kids are younger that gather there, and no restriction on color. Anyone plays who wants. A couple of Black girls follow their younger brother to the spoiled kid's yard, and a Puerto Rican boy comes around too. No one can get the Black girls to put down their jump rope and give you the time of day, so what's the spoiled boy got? Everybody's younger brother, the little Puerto Rican and the two Black girls: he's whispering them secrets, apparently, or feeding them from some secret stash of candy, maybe. Well, he's got *something* going there.

The Dean Street boys try not to notice how much fun's being had. There's chalk, and Spaldeens from time to time. Nobody's making especially much sense, not one single game seems to have a coherent rule to it, and sometimes the Black girls are on the sidewalk across the street doing Double Dutch—of course they are. Yet they're still in the orbit, still glued to the spoiled boy's address.

The mother peeking out the window might as well be a cat on a sill for all the notice they give. She's worn them down with her vigilance, which deters nothing since she never actually seems to budge. She might be a cardboard cutout.

The activities in the spoiled boy's yard are a throwback to the phase where nobody notices what color anybody else is or what the name for the color might be. The false oasis. The scene makes the Dean Street boys remember this thing that's peeling away from their lives even as they speak, but nobody ever speaks of it.

That everyone once played together with no notice of the question whatsoever.

That time is now gone.

Certain affiliations got laid down within the dream. These

affiliations may be individually sustainable—it would be pretty to think so! Like the presence of their cool Black friend, their protector. There are some other lines that got permanently crossed, people hanging out in mixtures of total impunity, taking up one another's talk or walk, going into each other's houses and accepting a plate of cookies or a pitcher of lemonade.

This inspires fascination in some quarters, in others a shrug: look at those crazy kids. Yet elsewhere, it may be scandalous, or politically inspiring. There was that day someone's drifting grandmother came looming along over a skully game and said, "*Look* at you," and she meant a Black kid and a white one together, and they knew it, but the boy whose grandmother it was, the white one, said, "What?" while the other, the Black kid, just looked away.

"You two playing together."

They couldn't speak to say how wrong it was. It might be the stupidest day on earth, that this grandmother pointed it out like they'd accomplished something on her behalf, like they were making a display in favor of some cause or concept.

Yet now it is gone. They are only two or three years older than the spoiled boy and the others in the spoiled boy's yard. Yet they'll never again dwell in that place from which they were expelled. No matter that it is this street, their own, under their feet: they walk there expelled. Banished from some realm.

The action in the spoiled boy's stupid square of concrete makes them know it.

48.
The Slipper, Meanwhile
(1976)

The Slipper, meanwhile, has got something going of his own: a brand-new skateboard, the real kind, like what the two brothers merely window-shopped in Manhattan. A hand-glossed slalom-style deck with Gullwing trucks and Kryptonics wheels. What the fuck?

The skateboard is spotted going in and out of his father's car. The skateboard is never exhibited in action, nor are the Dean Street boys invited to inspect it. The polyurethane wheels never dip to the slate of the sidewalk nor the asphalt of the street.

For that is just the way he Slips.

He isn't rich, but he isn't poor. There was that TV ad for Hertz, starring the Slipper's dad and Joe Namath. The Slipper's grandmother reputedly sends him money on his birthday.

It is entirely possible that the day of the skateboard hostage was the one misstep of the Slipper's whole life on planet earth. It is entirely possible that he'll never play with those particular white boys again.

Yet no hard feelings. He's always willing to flash a smile and slap you five as he goes slipping past.

Maybe the Slipper just senses things about to go down. For you or in general. A bad year coming, or maybe a whole lot of bad years.

Maybe the Slipper knows the truth about this book, which the rest of us will have to read to find out.

49.
Guy on Corner of Atlantic and Nevins
(1974)

There is a guy on the corner of Atlantic and Nevins. Curled up on himself, lying on the curb, in a jacket coated black with filth, his face concealed from view by his position and your reluctance, let's be real about this, to get any closer.

He's nearer to the street than the buildings.

There's a small liquor store on that corner, barely more than a corridor of plastic barrier through which you push some dollars and are handed something from the wall, some midsize bottle of something. Hard not to draw a line from that door to this guy in his place on the curb.

Not that he's going in and out, or doing anything that would involve movement to prove he's not dead.

Is he dead? Has anyone checked?

Isn't it some kind of collective crime that he's still there and nobody even knows? Can it be that nobody's made a call? He's in plain sight.

Is it weeks? Or months? Or merely days? It feels like months that he's there.

Is it a crime against the sensibility of a person's brain that they might have to stare at him every single day on their way to the Nevins IRT?

Is it a crime that we are forced to recall him, half a century later?

50.
We
(nervous)

This pronoun, it grows increasingly nervous.

The pronoun may wish to apologize to anyone whom it makes nervous as well.

Or at least disambiguate itself.

Is this "we" meant to enclose the readers of the book in a kind of intersubjective cloud: anyone still reading at this point? The "stakeholders," shall we say, in the project of turning the pages of the book?

Or is it a more archly ironic "we"—the investigative unit, the enumerators of crimes?

(You're not abandoning our survey of crimes, now, are you?)

(Is there a monster at the end of this book?)

51.
We

(joke, cf. *Mad Magazine*, 1958)

"The Lone Ranger and Tonto are watching a horde of Indian braves bear down on them in full battle fury. 'Looks like we're in trouble, Tonto,' says the Lone Ranger to his pal. 'What you mean "we," white man?' Tonto responds."

III.
Locked-Out Memories

"PERHAPS THE BIGGEST DISADVANTAGE TO owning a brownstone
is the City of New York. The city, which gets so much of
its charm and vitality from brownstones and the people
who restore and live in them, couldn't care less about
brownstones. Just to see what would happen, the other day
I called the Housing and Development Administration and
ask an operative there what city programs were of benefit to
brownstone owners.

The operative was flabbergasted . . . he wasn't
really sure, because the city did very little thinking about
brownstones per se. The city didn't even know how many
there were (neither does anyone else). 'It's not a legal
term,' the fellow said. 'It's really a fictional designation.' I
strongly disagree with this last. If there is anything that
is non-fictional, it's living in and working on a New York
brownstone."

—JOY AND PAUL WILKES,
You Don't Have to Be Rich to Own a Brownstone

"**PROSPECT PARK** is filled with longhairs and sideburns, expensive dogs with exotic names, dungarees, brilliantly colored clothes and antediluvian furs and plastic, expensive-kite fliers and slackjawed Frisbee levitators . . . There are festivals and rallies now. Everyone gets stoned and groovy and enunciates love. There are block festivals, exotic foods, handmade jewelry and Saturday Sweeps and, dig it, CULTURAL EVENTS, poetry readings, filmings, block associations, Reform Democrats, Women's Lib, sex and rent-saving communes—even revolutionary soviets . . . Our local tribes of hitters pause in their wars of mutual annihilation to look around. New people pass their watchposts on the stoops and in the bars. An ancestral stoop, in fact, becomes someone else's property. A new breed of shaman passes by, bearing strange magical symbols . . . a chunk of stained-glass window, a piece of loot from 1880 . . . Why do those crazies pick through discards in the areaways that yield some thirties Victrola that they greet with ritual squeals of delight? They will bear it off to do magic with sandpaper and varnishes . . . Dignity is inextricably wound up with space. Space, like time, is money. Money spent buys someone else's space, time and dignity. And after all, what's so unreasonable about wanting to live among your own kind, people who speak the same kind of language and flash the same kind of signs? People you can drop in to see for talk and grass and hash and consolation and even sex. You don't make a block association or an omelet without breaking a few eggs . . . The street kids look hungrily after the children of the middle class. They tried love and togetherness for a while, but that's fallen apart. There are a few beatings: a few ripoffs. Patrols of junkies infiltrate slowly from the surrounding perimeters. One has to run a gantlet of thieves when you get off the train late at night at Grand Army Plaza. Someone gets stomped or shot every night. The people of Park Slope retreat indoors."

—Sol Yurick, *New York Times*, June 11, 1972

52.
Millionaire

(1977)

A millionaire is moving onto Dean Street. So go the whispers among the boys. Never mind nobody knows what a millionaire is, or that any number of their parents or friends' parents or grandparents might have more in the bank than these boys realize. They know not from zeros, from trusts. They know from *Gilligan's Island* and the Monopoly board.

Some kid's overheard the gossip, maybe a parent who's involved with the Boerum Hill Association. Their intel gleaned from one of the realtor's offices on Atlantic Avenue (those offices and the Association being often pretty hard to distinguish). This guy bought cash, one of the already brick-repointed houses. He's not renting out the basement apartment, but hired a carpenter to knock out the stairwell in the back, make the lower floors into a double-high parlor. Two months of renovation before the people appear, unlike everyone else living amid their own plaster dust, shifting their own buckets of joint compound back and forth to the dumpster at the curb.

Someone said million. Maybe the buyer said this himself. Feel it in your mouth, *million, million*.

Millionaire!

One day the contractors evaporate, and a moving van unloads and fills the place in hours. The moving guys are savvy, Jews from Borough Park. They post one firm sentry at the back of the truck so nothing walked off in the hands of the many interested passersby and lingering gawkers.

There is no top hat, no monocle.

He does not speak like Thurston Howell III.

Though it is not waxed and curled at the ends, there is a moustache, thick, curling over his upper lip. Tiny round wire-frame glasses, like John Lennon's. He's tall, and his hair goes behind his ears, almost to his rounded shoulders.

There is, however, a BMW. Copper colored.

Can this car and Mr. Clean's actually coexist on the block? Two such radically divergent visions of mouthwatering wheels?

That car won't last a night, they're betting.

The millionaire isn't alone. There's also a wife—secret, unseen—and a boy. The boy shares his father's height already, and his loping gait.

Leave it to C. to make first contact. He and the millionaire's son sit talking on the stoop for half an hour. Afterward, the report comes: the new kid will attend the local public school, which must be some kind of galactic joke or error. Though maybe this millionaire's son's height will protect him. His height, along with the aura of the absurd, that same aura which, it soon appears, seems to shield the BMW from attack, night after night. If a millionaire comes, then this is where a millionaire lives, unharmed. A self-ratifying proposition.

Have they misunderstood the whole premise of their childhood?

Local white dads, too, seem both aroused and on the back foot, concerning the millionaire's house. They're thinking like their sons: I've got to get inside that place and see what the hell's going on.

53.
Smudge, Part 2
(1989)

Outside, the rain still falls. In the back of the shop on Atlantic Avenue the customer, the Black man, places his glasses on his face and emphatically lowers his hands, like he's gentling an invisible baby. The second of the two Irish opticians brings his own face close. For a moment the two men are still, breathing together. The intimacy calms the customer. He's getting his due, possibly even his money's worth.

Then the second optician sees it. "Wait a minute. They're still smudged."

"I told you!"

"He touched them again," says the first of the two opticians, the cynic. He's been leaning back, waiting for this moment. "I told you, he puts his thumb on the lens."

"You touched them again," says the second optician.

"You watched me! You saw! I didn't touch them!"

The second optician shakes his head, crestfallen. "I don't understand how it happened."

"Simple, he touched them."

"Liar! You watched me."

"What do you think? They smudged themselves?"

"I want my money back."

"Look, it's not going to do any good. You're screwing up your glasses yourself. It's going to be the same wherever you go."

"It's the fit."

"What are you saying, fit?" interrupts the first optician.

"You think they're touching your cheek?"

"That's right. My cheek."

"Show me where," says the first, leaning in.

"For chrissake, don't make him put his hands up there." The opticians trade places now, the fierce, the abiding. Only the customer is unperturbed, true to himself. He moves his hand with slow drama, like a magician. The opticians press close to see.

"It's my *cheek*," reminds the customer.

"Maybe your last ones touched you there," says the second optician. "Your nosepiece was all worn down. These don't touch."

"I feel it."

"No, you don't. You're used to touching yourself there, putting your fingers in. Like a phantom limb. That's why I say *habits*."

"You don't know," says the customer, with a Buddhist calm. "Now you got to give me my money back."

"We'll see about that," says the second optician grimly. He plucks the glasses from the customer's face.

"Give him his money," says the first to the second. "Get him out of here."

"No. He'll sit here all night if he has to," says the second. "He's putting his fingers on them."

"I got all the time in the world," says the customer happily.
The rain falls. Some afternoons seem to go on for years.

54.
Premature Gentrification, Atlantic Avenue and Thereabouts
(1968–90)

The antiques shops are the least of it, though many will fail. They're anchored by the need to refurbish the brownstone parlors with mantelpiece clocks, with fireplace tools, with standing mirrors and rocking chairs. And enough of them cluster, like rafts lashed for survival, to form some kind of viable ongoing concept.

Some will remain for fifty years, more.

Many of the antiques dealers are clever enough to buy the buildings. They'll make their fortune decades later renting to restaurants, bakeries, boutiques, toy stores.

So, okay, antiques. They do okay.

A children's bookshop, on the block between Boerum and Court, in 1979. (Is it in the same wedge-shaped space that will become the Brazen Head bar? Nice try, but let's be real.)

Those two opticians, the Park Slope Irish guys, with their glasses shop? They should have set up on 7th Avenue or Montague Street, shouldn't have cheaped on the rent. Two years on the corner of Hoyt, then gone.

The used bookstore that briefly shimmers into visibility on the block between Nevins and Third—that's a true mirage.

A row of galleries. On the Brooklyn Heights side, between Henry and Hicks. Four or five of them huddled for strength, like the antiques shops. 1975 or 1976, it starts. This is interesting! They're anti-commercial, curated and managed by the artists themselves. Collectives, that's the word.

They coordinate the nights of their openings, put out wine and cheese. Wine and cheese—what are they going to put out, a mug full of rolled joints?

The artists, their families, a few friends, throng from doorway to doorway on a summer night, it's a memorable party.

Gone.

The French restaurant, Hubert's. Bergen and Hoyt, past site of the King's Pawn, future site of the Brooklyn Inn. The renovation's sublime, a long dark wooden bar, high tin ceilings, corner windows. They get a write-up in the *Times* ("A Continental Touch, in Brooklyn"). This is good, this is a thing!

For a little while. Then it graduates to Manhattan.

Something else arrives, in another corner storefront on Bergen. Who knows exactly what to call it except what it calls itself, "The Local Level." Hippies, organizers, a yoga class, a Spanish class.

Hey, if it was worth doing, if it brought some joy or opened some eyes, then maybe it's fine that within a year of its vanishing it is hard to remember it was there at all.

The anomaly, the counterexample: the batik shop, specializing in T-shirts with alligators whose tails wrap around over one shoulder, which lasts forever.

Then there's this: A small upscale delicatessen on Atlantic near Bond, a couple of doors from the Berk Trade School for Automechanics, with a glass case full of upscale meats and cheeses for weighing out by the quarter pound or customizing in handmade sandwiches on portions of crosscut baguette. Three different kinds of pâté—three!— which most weeks become brittle and need to be thrown out. Shelves full of imported cookies, small bottles of balsamic, a dozen items that would fly off the shelves twenty years later, here a sculpture in dust.

The shop is staffed almost exclusively by young and skinny gays from the enclave on Pacific, renters all, louche slouching presences who reward the indomitable optimist shop owner likely only ten or fifteen years older by calling him a "fat old queen" behind his back, while eating their own weight in Roquefort and smoked salmon every day.

The shopkeeper also likes to have one of the Dean Street boys on staff, a link to the Brownstoners, thinking he'll lure the families in for some expensive shopping.

Is premature gentrification a crime?

Outward appearances make this place enough like a bodega—the metal slicer atop the glass counter, the scent of to-go coffee slowly charring in its pot—that the street does wander in, largely only to be bewildered at the prices. On lunch breaks, the students at Berk Trade come in and try to order a "hammoncheese" and are stymied by the question "Black Forest or Bayonne?" One of these guys persistently taps the glass to indicate the pâté forestier and says, "howabout a meat sandwich, with a lotta mustard? Put it on a roll, man."

"That sounds good," says the Dean Street boy at the counter, who improvises a price for this unlisted item—a meat sandwich!—one that will not scare the Berk School student out of his shoes or make steam issue from his ears like a cartoon character, a price that surely represents a steep loss for the shop owner, and he makes the sandwich for the guy, and then he makes one for himself, and it *is* good.

55.
Everybody Knows
(in the time before certainty disintegrates)

Everybody knows you go walking around Carroll Street and Fourth Avenue, you get your ass kicked. Those guys at the Italian social club will hit you in the head with a garbage can. You'd have to be stupid.

Everybody knows that house where they renovated around the one rooming house guy who wouldn't take the buyout and they got tired of waiting for him. He's got that one room on the second floor. You see him looking out the window from a room that's just hanging in space in the middle of their parlor duplex.

Everybody knows they found a body in a dumpster.

Everybody knows that one kid's mother is crazy and it is like a force field around him, because she beat up a kid who took his bike.

Everybody knows R. carries a gun, because he shows it around, and it might or might not be just a piece of a gun, you can see right through the handle to the palm of his hand, little better than a carving of a gun or a piece of paper with the word "gun" on it. And still again, R. carries a gun.

R. is willing to carry a gun.

Everybody knows R. is scared of that one kid's mother.

Everybody knows that that one kid's dad is a fruit.

Everybody knows that one kid's dad is a famous actor who was in a commercial with Joe Namath and also was on a subway platform in the background of one scene in *The French Connection*. He's just waiting for his big break.

Everybody knows that when that white ponytailed dude who hangs out at the community center was in Vietnam, he punched a guy in the throat and killed him in one blow. That's why nobody messes with him now.

Everybody knows that, though he looks like John Lennon, the millionaire was in the C.I.A. and that's why he's got a BMW.

Everybody knows that when you're in the C.I.A. you're never really out, you're just between assignments, or maybe you tried to quit, and someday they're going to come and kill you.

If you were trying to quit the C.I.A., Dean Street might be a good place to hide since the dapper French or German hit man who tried to come get you might get mugged and have his Walther and silencer used on him by the muggers, or be chased off by a rabid stray dog. You might be saved and never know it. These comically fitting scenarios are easy to envision.

Everybody knows that the white people are all rich unless they live in the projects. Everybody knows that the ones who don't send their kids to Packer or Friends or Saint Ann's must hate their kids. They hide their money.

Everybody knows that one Black kid plays with the white kids because his mom was white.

Everybody knows that Puerto Rican teenager is going to jail.

Everybody knows when he goes, his family is selling that house.

Everybody knows they're related to the family that runs the bodega but they don't talk to them anymore because of drugs.

The mom got hooked.

If you get hooked, you eat the bark off a tree. It was on *Dragnet*.

The boy cried. Everybody saw.

Everybody knows that the system of territories is beyond understanding, you can barely read the language of one block. But if you walk with the right kid on a given block, it doesn't matter. They're territorial erasers, they block the system's operation.

Conversely, everybody knows not to walk home with that one particular kid. Somebody's dad, in a moment of indiscretion that may also have been one of incalculable cruelty dubbed him "muggable Theo." Muggable Theo makes it all too easy, since all he does is walk glancing back over his shoulder. He's jittery. He practically mugs himself.

It's cruelty, maybe, because everybody knows that two kids together are a target, they're begging for it, doesn't matter who the two are. Two are the ideal partner in the dance.

Then again, maybe some are just beyond help.

Everybody knows that one alone has options, one alone is a subterranean operator. (This is what that Dean Street girl discovered, the morning when she watched her brother and his friends get taken to the dance.) You'd think that one alone would be more vulnerable, but you'd be wrong. One alone can cross the street. One alone can duck into a bodega and hide back near the soda case for an hour if needed, with no apology or embarrassment to some other who'll accuse them of overreacting. One alone can break into a run at a moment's notice, and without having abandoned and betrayed another left behind.

One alone can be frisked or even preemptively hand it over and never be faced with another in whom to bury the shame.

Three is a puzzle, one is a subterranean operator, and two are just a dance partner sashaying out onto the floor.

A Black kid with one white kid is a peculiarity.

A white kid with two Black kids is a conundrum.

Most days a white kid can get a Black kid across Court Street safe. A couple of Black kids can get a white kid across Smith Street safe on most days, depending on the white kid.

Everybody knows that nothing anybody knows counts if you meet an actual gang or crew. Too many of any one kind is easily mistaken for a gang or a crew and so sometimes ironically some mixing or breaking into threes is a recommended approach.

Everybody knows that the mayor is a racist.

Everybody knows that Son of Sam is a racist.

Everybody knows that the I.S. 293 math teacher is a racist. The after-school math club is a white kid's club.

Also, someone saw him on the promenade late at night so he's a fruit.

Mr. Sweetner, on the other hand, always touches his moustache when the big Black girls come into the science lab. He twists it like he's winding a clock.

Everybody knows no white teacher lives within ten miles of where they teach.

Everybody knows things they wouldn't say.

Everybody knows the "record store" on Nevins sells drugs.

Everybody knows the cops know.

Everybody knows that one kid's mom ran away or died or is about to come back.

Everybody knows that that one kid's mom fucks. She hires baby-sitters and comes back at three in the morning. The babysitter reads her journal, and it says she fucks three different guys in one night.

Everybody knows that kid who claims he fucked the Screamer is full of shit.

Everybody knows that kid's parents blow dope in the backyard and stink up the whole block and blame it on the Puerto Ricans.

Everybody knows it is beyond useless, a mistake of incalculable implications, to involve your parents in what goes on in the streets.

Everybody knows you get robbed, mugged, jumped, whatever you want to call it, by kids everybody knows, knows the name of, sees the next day in school. You might even know their mom.

56.
Queer Enclave
(1960-something to 1990-something)

Back up: what does it mean to say that Pacific Street is gay, or queer? One block especially? Is there proof? Might there be some misunderstanding?

The shipyards at the end of Atlantic have a legacy. Brooklyn Heights, sure. That's enshrined. Truman Capote, Jane Bowles, James Purdy. (Everybody Knows.)

Away from the Heights, those who arrive for the cheap rent in Boerum Hill mix with another queer Brooklyn, the Black and Latino lives less enshrined. Some on the down-low, some pretty damn flamboyant.

Forty years later, as it happens, a history of "Queer Brooklyn" is written. The book quits in 1969, in Brooklyn Heights.

This is somehow typical. We've encountered this before. These particular streets, these particular years, they're a kind of impossible object. They slip from study.

So, put a pin in it. Queer Pacific? Does this really exist?

Hard to give evidence. Is this zone slop-over from Brooklyn Heights, or Christopher Street, young men drawn here from provinces? Something to do with Atlantic's antiques shops? The polymorphous hippies? How does a block become a haven? A friend tells a friend tells a friend.

It's all of this, and none.

Can we give it a name without making something too simple?

Queer men and women live here in this time. The men who staff the premature sandwich boutique on Atlantic, as well as some of that sandwich boutique's few regulars—most of them, though it is brutal to say it, likely soon dead from AIDS. Top-to-bottom house parties are thrown, unfamous art is created and left to rot in basement storage, somebody gets murdered scoring drugs on Hoyt and Warren, somebody gets his dead boyfriend's money left to him by a bereaved family in Wisconsin, uses it to buy up a cheap building with two rentals, stays fifty years, more, and is the last vestige.

Only who knows he is a vestige of something? Just one old rich gay guy.

Living alone.

Even the new queer couples who come here now to begin families and find this old guy something of a pill, sitting out on his stoop shooting arrows of ancient distrust with his eyes, they don't have the faintest idea.

57.
Walked In On
(1980)

While we're here, what about those two in their secret afternoons, the Black kid and white kid who are lovers?

C. had made a dire forecast. Was it correct? Was someone destined to walk in on them? A parent?

In fact, yes.

Not because they were too quiet for too long, behind closed doors, but for the opposite reason. They made too much noise. They made what is technically termed a *goddamn racket*.

Clothes not all the way off, but not all the way on, either. They'd been in their crazy space for an hour or more, playing 45s on a little portable player, listening to Bill Withers and Doris Troy and Blue Magic and other imperishable forgotten songs from the one kid's father's dusty collection, nothing to do anymore with the music on WBLS or in the streets, just a wonderland of their own. Bounding around in their underwear, crazy, just crazy, from the wonderful touching of each other's penises. They're making up nonsense syllables to sing along with lyrics in the verses they don't know.

What are they going to do—cuddle? Spoon? They're fifteen-year-old boys.

Three years ago, they not only collected baseball cards, they chewed all the gum from the pack. Three years from now, they'll be doing a little too much cocaine, nothing they can't handle though, off a copy of *Thriller*, at an after-hours club in a loft in a piano factory in Hell's Kitchen, the conversion of which represents the start of the gentrification destined to transform that neighborhood into something called "Clinton."

Today, they're in the between of those selves, the very middle of the middle of the middle of everything they sense and feel, and nothing sounds better than grabassing around the one kid's room, jumping on and off his too small kid's bed, trying to harmonize with the exultant mopery of Blue Magic's "Sideshow."—*so let the SIDEshow begin, STEP right on in, CAN'T afford to pass it by, GUARanteed to make you cry*—

And in strides the one kid's dad, not even rattling the doorhandle for warning. He spares barely an instant inspecting the scene. A glance takes in all he needs to know.

"Sideshow's dead right, you couple of freaks."

"Sorry."

"I told you I don't care how loud you play the goddamn music, but your bouncing on the ceiling has *got* to stop. About to break the goddamn house."

"Sorry."

"Hell, man. Even a *cat* can be sorry." This elliptical remark freezes them in an instant of silence. When the father resumes, it is in an ever-so-slightly gentler tone. "I don't *give* a good goddamn what you get up to behind closed doors, just don't knock down the house on my watch. You want to bust a hole in the floor go do it at *his* house. I don't want to answer to either your mothers, you hear me?"

"Yes, sir."

"Don't sir me in your underwear." The father laughs. "Sir Fruits of the Loom, goddamn."

The boys stare wide-eyed as the father goes chuckling backward through the doorway.

Our inquiry, might it reasonably exit this room with the father? Might it conclude here for the time being?

Let's do leave the boys where they are, one whispering reassurance to the other that it really is okay, that the father isn't going to tell. Adjusting the volume on the portable record player.

Rather than concluding, however, let's consider the father, just an instant more. What enables him to convey, all at once, such blunt annoyance, and such kindness?

For, to be sure, there was kindness here.

The puzzle has an answer. This particular father has been on a path of queer self-discovery, of queer self-amplification. He's been on this path for some time now, since even before joining up with the mother of his son, to whom he is devoted. Lately, the journey has carried him through some pretty funky parties on Pacific Street. It has brought him into a dalliance with one of the countermen at the premature gentrification sandwich shop. It has led him, even, on certain nights, to Manhattan's Hudson River Drive, to the bars along Manhattan's periphery, and farther, to the fabulous and notorious parked tractor trailer trucks parked at the waterfront.

It will eventually cost him his life.

But not for some time. He'll be one of those the drugs keep alive, on oxygen, in a diminished, almost twilight state, for decades. He'll be a survivor of those first years, the years of slaughter. He'll be watched over by his wife and son.

But let's not dwell on this. It's too much for now.

Not so fast, you say. What makes his wife, the boy's mother, willing to accompany the father on this journey? Is it so simple as that we should pity her this devotion, view it as a sacrifice?

We'd best not assume. She might be into women.

There are mysteries in the way people live.

Let's stick to the moment: the father walking in. Can it be possible that what we have here is an instance of not just a good-enough father, but of pure perfect parenting? Well, maybe that's a reach. He's pretty curt. He has some fun at their expense. Yet maybe that's what makes it so perfect. There's nothing in what he's seen, his words seem to say, that's worth making such a big deal over. It's just a matter of *quit making that goddamn racket*. The father's remarks—curt, unsurprised, aggravated, affectionate—restore the two lovers out of the catastrophe of themselves, into the ordinary, into the everyday.

Of course, to grant this, one would have to grant a world in which an adult calling a child a *freak* could be seen as fond. As opposed to damaging. As opposed to cruel.

Such a world either did or didn't once exist. You decide.

In any case, it's possible that what we've discovered here is, at least, neutral. That what we have before us is an uncrime.

Of what relevance to our inquiry? Hard to say.

Onward.

58.
Milt the Vigilante
(1975)

No block is just one thing or another. Right in the middle of Queer Pacific, for instance, is Milt the Vigilante.

As with the boys, zones coexist and float, cities passing through cities unseen.

Milt makes 'em all nervous, though, the ones he collars, the ones he enlists, the ones who are forced to sit still for his diatribes and insinuations.

Milt's house is the one with the Garden State Brickface and Stucco exterior, the one featuring irregular dun and gray and ochre colored "stone" mosaic. To make it extra painful, this exterior is newly applied. Maybe if the Brownstoners had gotten there a year or two sooner, they'd have somehow talked him out of it for the sake of continuity with the houses they're restoring to repointed brick and resurfaced brownstone glamor . . . sure, it's a nice thought. Dream on.

Milt's aged parents live in the upstairs and Milt occupies the basement apartment.

Awful lot of time spent moving garbage cans around to no apparent purpose.

Wearing New York Mets batting gloves.

Satin shorts.

Who is it that Milt collars; who is it that he enlists? Not the young homosexuals. Not the renters of various non-white extractions, no. Milt collars and enlists the Brownstoners, the new white families. Parents and children, both.

Indeed, Milt commits a really troublesome amount of energy to making himself familiar to the kids on his block, as if he is a big child himself. Every halfway-responsible parent will feel it is their duty to work their way into a conversation with Milt, to screen for the standard unmentionable awfulness. But no. On this point they find themselves assuaged. Yet, alas, now here they are, talking across Milt's low concrete fence, paying for their parental due diligence. Lending their polite unwilling attention to Milt's monologue. Adding themselves to Milt's collection.

When Milt tells you about an argument he gets in, invariably you begin taking the other person's side. Milt will retail everything he knows about the block, and it is horrible and at the same time strangely vague. A fog, a catalogue of inexact horrors, of suspected rogues, of scurrilous accounts of why someone you never heard of had to pack up and leave overnight and also, just wait for this, that Someone Else who couldn't be named was *in on it too*.

Milt sees *trouble all around.*

But mostly Milt believes it is a *good block.*

It just has to be protected from the *you know what.* Which is why he *always looks out.* Because he is *looking out for the you know what.*

And when such things happen, *Milt knows what to do.*

And now you're standing here with him nodding along.

The danger from Milt is not to your children, but to your morale, your sensibility, your belief in this place you've come to.

One day, for instance, you might wake up to Milt ringing your doorbell at one A.M., and when you open it, he's proudly brandishing the remains of a box leaf honeysuckle you laboriously planted in daylight.

"Chased those little cocksuckers two blocks," he chest-heaves. Then plops the root-torn thing at your feet and slumps, theatrically supporting himself, hands on knees. "Got your plant back."

"What . . . what did they want with my . . . plant?" Can this be real? Can Milt have uprooted the honeysuckle *himself?*

"They hate what we're building here, Mr. S. They destroy just for the fuck of it."

"I see. Well, thank you."

"Don't thank me. I positively live for this shit."

At the next occurrence, you're denied the luxury of imagining that Milt has engineered evidence of the necessity of his vigil over the block. This time something was stolen right from your hands, in broad daylight. Milt couldn't have engineered the scene, though he also couldn't have scripted it any better. He couldn't—no. You're not that paranoid, or if you are, you save it for Nixon, not for some dumb local guy, not for Milt who happens to be your block's vigilante.

You'd walked to Court Street, to the pharmacy there, to pick up a supply of your son's allergy medication, a large bottle of blue pills. Returning to Pacific, you're apprehended, again, yes, by Milt, with some urgent incomprehensible crapola concerning alternate-side parking. Standing, again, yes, on either side of his low concrete fence. How much of your life and spirit can he winnow away with such stuff? Fiddling with the package, you remove the white paper sack and ball it and shoot—swish!—into Milt's open garbage can. Almost at that instant a passing body snatches the plastic bottle of pills from your hands—from your one hand, where it foolishly dangled behind you as you shot the wadded paper.

What the fuck? My son's allergy medication?

The runner is halfway to the corner of Nevins before you've recovered your wits, but Milt is sprinting in hot pursuit, and reaching into the rear waistband of his short-shorts for—can it be?—a gigantic kitchen knife? Does he carry it at all times?

You run to follow, wanting only for this disaster to be as unreal as it feels. Forced to root for the sprinter ahead, the one with the pills, not the one with the knife. Though, if only the thief would drop them, it would save aggravation. For god's sake, allergy pills, what does he think he's stolen?

Perhaps it's about what he can pretend he's stolen, to represent to some buyer, some next sucker.

Or maybe it was just a shiny object in the hand of a white man.

Are only idiotic things stolen in the vicinity of Milt the Vigilante? There's no way to credit him with arranging this happening, no. But it nonetheless feels like a manifestation of Milt's reality field, his world of crooked priorities, absurd grudges, inane crimes.

You run, knowing you'll never catch Milt, who will never catch the runner ahead. Knowing that when you collapse, lungs burning, hands on knees for support, you'll have Milt's respect and commiseration to look forward to.

Milt the Vigilante is not a liar, but things he says are not and cannot be the truth of this neighborhood. He's a wild loner, unaffiliated, insane.

The unrepeatable words that come out of his mouth, not the truth.

His view of his neighbors, despite his boundless regard for you and your *lovely better half,* to whom you are going to have to explain the absence of the allergy medication, is not, cannot be, the truth.

Your fear is not that Milt tells truth.

Your fear is that Milt *is* the truth.

59.
Communes, Day Care Center, Food Co-op, Etc.
(1960-something to 1990-something)

No block is just one thing or another. If we're saying *not-just-this* and *not-just-that,* preferring instead to widen the aperture and let it all in, to tabulate the clutter defining this place (or making it incommensurate with all definitions), let's notice that this block that forms the heart of Queer Boerum, the same block patrolled by Vigilante Milt, also makes room for one of this neighborhood's five or six communes.

If the rooming houses or those filled with multiple families depopulate when they're picked up by Brownstoners, the communes are a check against this trend. In some, communists, hippies, and NYU students live twelve or fifteen to a house.

Some of these communes feature a revolving door, they have turnover like a youth hostel. Others are more stolid, organized around the core of a family or older couple who operate like den parents, or resident advisors in a dorm. Some have themes, are built ideologically from the ground up—here's a Maoist brownstone, there a Quaker one, here's one full of international peace protestors. Others are themed more inadvertently: hashish and smack, for instance. Or: That beautiful guy who sleeps with anything. Or: The one with the hairy men. You might expect the inadvertently themed to dissolve more quickly than, say, the Maoist. Makes sense if you had to bet. Then again, some less hidebound aggregations show an ability to adapt. Some slug along for decades, until the hairy men are bald.

They built a day care center on the corner of Nevins and Atlantic. Before becoming a taken-for-granted eyesore it was a monument to years of advocacy and feminist struggle, protests at the Municipal Building on Chambers Street.

Like the Jews in the projects, like the scattering of white kids sent not to Brooklyn Friends or Saint Ann's but to the public schools, there are white people who send their kids proudly the day it opens. Kumbaya, my friend!

A few.

For a while.

Subject for further investigation.

Within a few months, the local food co-op, which has been floating, running out of the Colony-South Brooklyn Houses office and various open parking lots, finds a home in the basement of the Nevins Day Care Center.

Did I mention the Colony-South Brooklyn Houses? I think I just did. Place for Social Services, on Dean Street. The halfway house, on Nevins? The youth center, on Atlantic and Bond? The parole office, on Nevins and Schermerhorn? That all of this is shadowed by the presence of a large fucking jail, right there? Did I forget to mention the large fucking jail?

The world is exhausting.

60.
Brooklyn House of Detention
(b. 1956)

Let's not avert our gaze. Maybe, given our appetite for crime, we ought to find stomach enough for a glance at the jail.

The Brooklyn House of Detention. 275 Atlantic Avenue. A jail for those awaiting trial at the neighboring courthouse. But also, less well understood, a penitentiary for short-term sentences, minor drug bids, small-time robberies. The Brooklyn House of D. perches at the throat of Boerum Hill, the chokepoint where traffic evacuates to the Bridge.

Take me to the bridge, and step on it!

Brooklyn's own Rikers Island. Though not, if there's any confusion, on an actual island. It squats there, enigma to consider or, mostly, to not consider. Fogged glass bricks so you can't see inside, and tomb-like silence emanating from the thing's façade. Maybe a few scraped cries descending from the rooftop recreation cages, eleven stories up. Yet largely the building's a cipher, a monolith. Unlike the monoliths plopped down by Kubrick's aliens, it emits no signal, spurs no evolutionary leaps in those nearby.

By those with a stake in the concept called "Boerum Hill," the jail is islanded in the mind.

The moat is the traffic, moving in pulses, on Atlantic Avenue, and Boerum Place, and Smith Street. The moat is the silence of the shadowed block of State Street, the canyon's passage backed by the Central Court Building. Who'd walk the block where they might be crossing from jail to court?

Supposed to be an underground tunnel, but still. You wanna go east to west? Get from Boerum Hill to Brooklyn Heights? Walk on Schermerhorn instead. Walk on Pacific or Dean, cross at Court Street.

The moat is denial.

Steer your feet to another block, steer your mind around the monolith of despair in your midst.

The zone is islanded in unnameability, on a block that is no clear part of any neighborhood. The off-white bland rectangular tower aligns easily with the dullness of the housing projects, of the low drab bureaucracies lining Flatbush, in the time even before Metrotech and Pierrepont Plaza. All the unBrooklynish municipal crapola a Brownstoner's eye tends to flinch from just on architectural grounds.

All you need do is ignore a cluster of bail bondsmen in hundred-year-old storefronts on the south side of Atlantic, interspersed with the bicycle shop, and the scuba gear place on the corner of Smith. Whatever. They're picturesque. Better than boarded-up storefronts. Maybe.

The Atlantic Avenue bail bondsmen: another local professional the parents are unlikely to meet at neighborhood parties.

Then again, if you want to go the route of undenial, look no further than the "From Behind Prison Walls" letters column, a regular feature in *The Amsterdam News*. Here, an excerpt from the issue of November 10, 1973:

Dear Editor: Is it at all possible for you to place an ad in your paper for me? I would love to correspond with any mature minded woman capable of understanding the need of human relationships under isolated conditions . . . (name redacted) 7LB9, Brooklyn House of Detention, 275 Atlantic Avenue, Brooklyn, N.Y.

Or another:

To All Black People: I hope a good state of mind and a desire to unite is in your minds and hearts. And now I greet my brothers and sisters by saying a word that we all know, "peace" . . . I want to survive and I will fight to survive. I want to live the life of a man. I don't want stardom. I want a life of happiness and peace with my people . . . I am young and in jail facing bank robbery charges and I know what happens to Blacks that rap or become aware of their Blackness but I must let my people know that another brother is ready.
P.S. Amsterdam News I would like our people to hear my words.
(name redacted) Brooklyn House of Detention, Brooklyn, N.Y.

The Wheeze sends me these things with no explanation, enigmas from yellowed newspapers, material dug out of old basements and storerooms. He clips them by hand and stuffs them into hand-addressed envelopes that arrive by U.S. mail. I don't know how to make him stop.

61.
Conundrum of Absolutes
(1813, 1857, 1956, 1813, 1973–80, forever)

But wait, what's this? In the shadow of the towering jail, rows of painted wooden benches in a high-ceilinged room, rows of silent human beings seated on long cushions, heads bowed or not bowed, eyes shut or not shut, all in silence.

Then one among them stands. He grips the bench back before him with both hands. He sighs deeply. Other bodies creak in their seats. Those not directly facing the risen man adjust their positions and organize their attention and readiness, making small exhalations in reply to his. This man will shortly speak into the expectant air. But no hurry.

These are Quakers.

Quakers?

The ones who believe in no pastor, no reverend, no intermediary between persons and The Light.

Out of their silence, anyone speaks if moved.

It isn't them, really. It's The Light that's moving their mouths.

Speaking in tongues, but in a staid, Northernly fashion.

They're elderly and middle-aged, a few in their twenties and thirties. Not a thousand percent white. Dressed plainly, that's how the Quakers do it. Some of the men may wear a jacket, but no tie. Most are in sweaters or flannel. No showing off on a Sunday morning, unless it is a modestly brocaded vest.

The meeting room of the Brooklyn Monthly Meeting of the Religious Society of Friends, that's the full name. They've gathered in this room to enact their Sunday services for a century. More.

This red brick meetinghouse, with its austere, high-ceiling grace, its twenty-foot high square-paned windows, its ancient benches, dates to 1857, no joke. It's older than Gage & Tollner, the oldest restaurant in Brooklyn, that other celebrated survivor a few blocks away. Just a decade younger than Borough Hall, also nearby. They're swimmers in time, these buildings. But swimmers drowning in the scale and mediocrity of the architectural nullities that have risen since. The county courthouses, the headquarters of the MTA, the Board of Education.

The jail.

"From my place on the bench," the man begins. He pauses to gather himself, and let others adjust to the shock of his voice, his fallible words, violating the perfectly articulate silence. So long as Quakers never speak, they never disagree. The art of thinking the best of those who rise to deliver a message, that's the higher task. "From my place here, the two tall windows present a conundrum, a conundrum of absolutes. Here"—the man needn't gesture, and doesn't, no one needs to glance to know he means the left window—"nothing but this gray monotonous wall, cement and glass bricks, filling the view to all four corners. The cells where men sit in degradation. At the bottom edge, my view is met with barb wire."

This flourish isn't precisely an exaggeration: the top of the wall separating the Meetinghouse property from the car lot that squeezes between the Quaker property and the House of Detention does feature a curl of razor wire, unmercifully close to the Meeting Room's elegant windows. But the wire was placed there not by the jailers, but by the owners of the car lot, to keep anyone from climbing over and stealing a car. Still, it makes a good visual foreground rhyme with the jail.

The man turns his head, just barely, toward the window on the right. "Here, open sky, to the sea. Not even a rooftop is visible. Occasionally a distant sea gull."

This, too, is accurate enough. In fact, the horizon in that direction might open all the way to Sheepshead Bay. Though more likely if the man is seeing gulls these hover above that man-made industrial wasteway, the Gowanus Canal.

"What sense can one's heart make here, confronted with these two views? On the one hand, such utter sorrow. Such constriction and unfreedom, such a flat rebuttal of human hope, of the dignity of all living beings, our Peaceable Kingdom. To entomb a living man in a cell. Deny him all life."

The man's voice trembles, slightly. Yet to suggest he's moved by his own words would be unkind. This is the Quaking. He's unsure he's a vessel worthy to bear the import rising through him. Then he locates the strength. His eyes move to the window on the right.

"Conversely, the opening to the infinite. The sky of possibility, sheer dizzying height, humbling unconstriction. The unseen power beneath which each one of us here is free, at the conclusion of this gathering, to walk. Yet the men in the jail do not taste it."

At a poetry reading, listeners faced with such a juncture, such a pause, are often heard to commit a certain "mooing" sound. These Quakers, though steeped in silence, in an ethos of non-exhibitionism, might nearly be tempted to "moo" today. In one or two, an intake of breath is at least audible.

"What I ask, in the presence of our collected Light, is whether we are meant to reconcile these opposed absolutes, to somehow stitch them in our sight? Or are we merely to learn to bear to abide, to give witness? This morning I do not know the answer."

The speaker sits.

THOUGH THE JAIL wasn't there when they designed those twin high windows, of course, the histories of this Quaker Meetinghouse and the Brooklyn House of Detention are intertwined in ways perhaps not obvious.

They opened the jail in 1957. Couldn't pick a better time to plop it down. The thick of the borough's decline, the blockbusting era. At that point the Brownstoners, those sublime Not-In-My-Backyardists, would have been no more than a gleam in Jane Jacobs's eye.

But a jail isn't built overnight. Planning for this construction dated to the late '40s.

In fact, preservationist sentiment held sway in where they plopped it down. The City Planning Commission originally placed the jail on Schermerhorn. It would have required the demolition of the Meetinghouse.

You heard right. No Meetinghouse. Just a jail.

This was a plan in 1947.

Jane Jacobs's book was published in 1961.

The notorious demolition of the old Pennsylvania Station, generally credited with waking up the urban preservation movement in New York City, was less than two years later. Announced in '62, begun in '63.

At Penn Station there was a protest, a hundred or more people with signs, August 2nd, 1962. And a petition, signed by names like Philip Johnson, Eleanor Roosevelt, Norman Mailer, and Jane Jacobs.

They're still talking about it, the quixotic attempt to spare Penn Station. How it spurred a movement.

On January 16, 1948, two hundred Brooklynites marched on Borough Hall in protest of the planned demolition of the Quaker Meetinghouse. The Citizens Union of Brooklyn declared opposition. Petitions flew, though none signed by Jane Jacobs, who was then working for the U.S. State Department. Norman Mailer? He was on Pierrepont Street, checking proofs of *The Naked and the Dead*.

In 1948 Mayor O'Dwyer agreed to relocate the jail plan to Atlantic Avenue.

The victory, forgotten. Maybe even by the Quakers themselves, by the time this guy stands up and offers the image of the barb wire and sea gulls.

If you want to be remembered, protest in Manhattan. Only the dead know Brooklyn.

QUAKERS AND JAIL? More than just these two buildings shoved up against each other, the two are braided in time.

Quaker prison advocacy goes back to England. In 1813, a Quaker named Elizabeth Fry inaugurated reforms to the dreaded Newgate Prison. Fry fought for separation of women from men. She inspected convict ships launching for Australia.

Quakers in Pennsylvania invented modern solitary confinement, at the East Pennsylvania Penitentiary. To sit in silent contemplation is a good thing, right?

Maybe too much of a good thing.

Quakers thought better of it. Elizabeth Fry herself tried to unmake the error.

Here, Schermerhorn Street, 1973, the Brooklyn Quakers start something called the Newgate Program.

The children of women visiting prisoners idle on the sidewalk, sometimes playing in the traffic on Atlantic Avenue. The kids enduring long waits for visits, the kids not allowed inside. The Brooklyn Quakers step in, offer daycare. They welcome the strays into the Meetinghouse, run art classes, fix meals.

Newgate takes pictures of the kids to give the prisoners for their cells.

Deliberate Byzantine protocols notwithstanding.

With no funding from the Department of Corrections. The guards dig Newgate. The Warden, not so much.

The program lasts six years, then is worn down by non-cooperation or worse. Corrections starts shifting city short-termers upstate, a new strategy to break community bonds, ostensible criminal networks, drug smuggling, gangs.

Putting visiting families, if they've got the endurance, on Greyhound buses out of Port Authority.

Too many Brooklyn House of D. parole hearings had begun to feature prisoners brandishing Newgate Program photographs of their children, working on art projects at round tables in the Quaker rec room, alongside the white children of the Quakers who run the daycare. The kids together looking awfully orderly, looking awfully cute. Too many appeals to judges in the courthouse feature public defenders reading Newgate Program spurred correspondences between incarcerees and their families.

The jail is meant to be a wall, a brick. Its doings, opaque.

Sorry, Elizabeth Fry, but enough is enough.

STILL, AS LONG as Newgate lasts, and however entirely the accomplishment has been effaced and forgotten, it accomplishes some things.

One effect is that a handful of the volunteers' kids are dragged along for after-school activities. Childcare is childcare, hey. If you had the kind of parents who'd volunteer for the Newgate Program, you'd learned you had to follow them to all kinds of things, including Quaker Sunday School to begin with. Organizing meetings, demonstrations, block cleaning or tree planting parties, vacant lot gardening initiatives.

So, now one of the Dean Street boys finds himself sitting in the basement of the Meetinghouse. The exact same place he loses an hour every Sunday morning, only this time it's on a weekday afternoon. A bonus round.

Doing arts and crafts with the kids of the mothers visiting the men in the jail.

It's not that big a deal. Few of these kids demonstrate a whole lot of talkativity to begin with, and especially not on the subject of their fathers, the situation that has caused them to be candidates for the Newgate Program to begin with. As in the minds of the adults, the jail goes islanded in the minds of the children. Instead, somebody proffers a rolled-up comic book, panels read to death by a thousand eyes before yours. Another kid's pocket disgorges a Duncan Imperial and they don't know how to walk the dog, so you show them. Nothing so great or terrible can happen in such a circumstance. As the Dean Street boy and a thousand others like him have proven, any given set of children can sit around a table in too-small chairs in a bland institutional setting and ignore a mildly patronizing lesson in cutting out a fingers-and-thumbprint Thanksgiving turkey from construction paper. An hour goes by, somebody's picked up, somebody's dropped off, all aspirations for this day, whatever those might have been, are worn to dullness by the after-school light angling through dust motes through the basement's half windows. You're more or less just missing the pre-dinner roster of *Gilligan's Island* and *I Dream of Jeannie* reruns on WPIX.

Institutional boredom as the solvent for wild differences between those shoved together at the table.

Nevertheless, there they are. Together, eye to eye, who wouldn't have likely been otherwise.

What this amounts to? Hard to say.

62.
Locked-Out Memories, Part 1
(wherever and whenever these occur)

Say a guy walks down a block he's walked down for fifty years and all he feels are what he calls locked-out memories.

Locked-out memories are the thing where you stand at the door or the gate or the stoop of a building that once was yours—I don't mean you owned it, for heaven's sake, nor even that you necessarily lived there, only that you were once permitted entry and are no more, for reasons we can get into if you insist upon it, but for now just take my word for it—and you can no longer enter. Can only glance at the windows.

And the memory is inside.

And you are locked out.

The memory is too. It is stuck in the air outside the window. Or stuck in your skull and crying for release.

Locked-in memory, maybe he should call it.

Someone else bought the building. This is an easy one. Your friend lived there and doesn't anymore. Hasn't in this present century.

The new people with their kids look happy coming out of their house to their car, but you are staring at them a little too long.

Or a more baseline condition. The building was, not yours exactly, but your parents'. They sold it.

So, maybe somebody possibly including yourself or a member of your family died or cried or fucked or discovered what cocaine was in the rooms and now cannot go into the rooms anymore. This happens all over the place, and now it has happened to you. Not to be excessively hardboiled about the thing.

In other instances, it was a bodega and now it is a pediatrician's office, or was a bookstore and now it is a dry cleaner's or a realtor's office. *Big fucking deal.*

You can walk down a given street and think that was X's house and I was inside, and this was Y's house and I was inside, and this was Z's house and I was inside, and now I walk by. Get over it, etc. Get over yourself.

Then there are some enigmas, some locked-out memories, which perhaps reach into the body of the man walking past the building in a slightly different way.

The daycare center on Atlantic and Nevins is one of those.

A blank edifice, he knows, to all who pass. In its dullness, invisible. But not to him.

The man was one of the scattering of white children placed there as a boy—in fact, he was there the day the place opened.

He remembers four things. Maybe five. Maybe twenty.

Wiffle ball on the roof. He pitched.

Graham crackers.

A packet of salt he pocketed, and which taught him that though a little salt on a fingertip tasted good, a packet of salt shaken into your mouth entire was a quick lesson in diminishing returns, in less is more.

A portable record player with a 45 of The Jackson 5's "Dancing Machine" played on it every minute of every day, except he also remembers a 45 of Mary Hopkin's "Those Were the Days" being played on the same device.

The salt, the two different 45s, the rooftop pitching. These are the easy ones, the gimmes. They flutter around a main event from which they attempt, and fail, to distract. The main event is a locked-out memory which describes itself, enters into conversation with the body of the man, each time he walks past the building, each time he goes anywhere near it. He does not volunteer himself to this memory. He has no language with which to conjure a reply, with which to elaborate his side of the conversation. The locked-out memory is indifferent to the man's non-participation. It describes itself as abundantly, as fulsomely, as if it were enshrined in the pages of a family photo album, as if he had a digitally transferred Super 8 film to share with his friends, to say *look, that was me!*

It is this: that there was a girl he liked. Alondra Martinez.

The man, the boy, he would have been seven or eight years old.

What can he say about Alondra? That she was—nice? Nice to him? That he remembers the feeling of his *like* for her? Like, the word then, for what he felt. Like, the feeling the boy savored in confusion.

And that one day, when Alondra had left to walk home to State Street, and he'd still been there, in that fourth-floor room his entry to which he can no longer conceive, but at whose window he can gaze, from the street, if he chooses, if he allows himself—he'd still been there, one of the last kids. Not yet picked up. While others had gone, including Alondra, who'd left with her backpack, to cross Atlantic and return home to her family's apartment on State Street. And, as the B63 bus flew across the Nevins intersection, too full to take on further passengers, accelerating past a bus stop full of aggrieved would-be riders, Alondra had been destroyed.

Had the boy been looking out the window overlooking Atlantic, as he possibly recalls it, and seen Alondra struck? Likely not. Not the moment of impact, no. Imagination places him there by the logic of his horror, but also his sense that this memory belongs to him, that Alondra, her life, its robbery, was specially to do with him. Other children, more likely, called him to the window. Before the Peruvian woman who watched over them—the things he recalls!—hurried them from the window.

Alondra was taken to Brooklyn Hospital. Lived a few days in a coma, but with a demolished brain. Died, perhaps mercifully. Mercifully—this was how the Peruvian woman, in gentleness, suggested the boy understand it.

Salt, pitching, "Dancing Machine," Alondra Martinez in the roadway before a stopped B63 bus, her form barely glimpsed in the circle of those who'd rushed to help what wasn't helpable.

None of this and all of this is his.

Three years and a million developments later, he'd meet Pietro Martinez in 6th grade, at the I.S. 293 Annex, in gym class, and know he was the younger brother.

Never spoke a word to Pietro, never alluded to any connection.

What's the special problem here? What is it in this locked-out memory that destroys the man's capacity to name?

It's that Alondra Martinez died inside the time before the boy knew that he didn't belong in the Nevins Day Care Center. Or, perhaps, that the Nevins Day Care Center didn't belong to him. She died before the world corrected this mistake for him, before the boy was stolen from the realm we've elsewhere identified as the false oasis.

By the time of the gym class when he sees her brother, the boy's already a million years past any world where he'd have known Alondra or her brother from anyone else. In fact, already by that point, he walks past Nevins Day Care like the building might fall on him and kill him with its secret knowledge.

After two or three decades of it not falling, not killing him, he begins to be able not to hurry past. He no longer glances up at the fourth-floor window through which he gazed upon Alondra's ruined body. He no longer gazes at the crosswalk where she lay.

You get good enough at disclaiming, and one day you realize it doesn't take any effort at all. In fact, it's all done for you.

It's a wonder they let a man walk down the same street for fifty years without explaining this to him in advance.

So, what's he going to do? Walk through the tiny lobby, enter the tiny elevator, its dinged stainless steel walls layered with scratchiti that might date back to the last time he rode up in it, fifty years back, tags by kids he knew and still sees on the block and doesn't talk to anymore, mostly doesn't even say hello, and ask to see the fourth-floor room? What's he going to say? *I didn't used to be white?*

This may be our first clear introduction to this form of memory torture: to have no claim on what claims you.

63.
Claim and Disclaim
(joke)

Q: Claim and Disclaim are sitting on a fence. Claim falls off. Who's left?

A: I have no idea what you're talking about. I never saw any fence. This has nothing to do with me. I'm not from around here. You've got me confused with someone else.

64.
The Parents Are Hiding Something, and They Contradict Themselves
(1976, 1977)

The parents are hiding something, and they're not very good at it. Whatever this thing is, it makes them contradict themselves.

It makes them upset. They're hiding it maybe from themselves. They're arguing about it.

This moment comes like a sort of sickness over the Brownstoner families. Afterward, like an event occurring during a fever, it will seem difficult to recollect. In many cases impossible.

Whatever it is, though, they're not talking about it directly, they're not talking about it with the kids, they're not clear they want to hear more.

The parents talk about it on the phone, but not in the usual leaky way. One kid's mom reverts to Yiddish to speak of it to her own mother. This is not a usual thing. The kid whose mom spoke Yiddish didn't even know this was possible.

Nevertheless, some of the kids overhear some portion of it. This was always going to happen.

Or it trickles down to them in the form of oblique and crazy warnings. Something involving a knife. Something involving someone's balls. Exaggerations, they think. Surely these are exaggerations.

And the parents contradict themselves, particularly on the question of how to conduct the dance.

"If someone pushes you around, you have to stick up for yourself. Fight back, scream bloody murder."

Scream? Only the Screamer screams. You've been raised to the opposite reaction: muteness, passivity, mummification. "I thought you said to just hand it over. You gave me an extra dollar specifically for mugging money."

"I'm telling you now to fight like your life depends on it."

"You don't understand—" But the kids stop before they begin. The parents have never understood. Why should they suddenly understand now, when they are burning up the phone lines with their feverish calls?

One kid takes this new consultation seriously and comes home bloodied and weeping from the schoolyard and his mother actually seems exultant, like he ought to be congratulated.

"You got in a fight."

"Yeah, mom, I guess, if you want to call it that. I ended up with my face ground into the concrete."

"It only matters that you fought back."

"If you say so."

In the time of this hidden thing the parents grow easily enraged. It only deepens the general resolve in the kids that the parents shouldn't be asked to handle being told what goes on in the streets.

We've seen a really crazy parent or two in our time. The mom who heard about the bicycle and charged down Nevins Street toward the projects carrying a baseball bat. The serial precinct house caller. The dad who couldn't believe the bus pass was being stolen on the first of every month and so went to walk his kid home from school, as if actually likely to meet the kid who was taking it.

Such parents are a ticking time bomb.

And this new task of hiding the whatever-it-is is making the parents too crazy, *collectively*. It's bad for the general prospects for every kid living in this place, day to day, hour to hour. It's amusing enough to have a Milt the Vigilante in your neighborhood. But no one wants Milt the Vigilante to suddenly become your parents. All of this makes the kids want to calm the parents down, and calm themselves down, and not to think about it.

So, the kids end up hiding something too. They hide that they know the parents are hiding something. They hide that they're helping the parents to hide what they are hiding.

Years later, when they are grown adults, the kids will be left to intuit the presence of this thing. To search it out in the rooms of their recollection, an object described predominantly by its quality of having been hidden, a shape around an omission. Some do this only in whispers. The matter remains charged, radioactive. Some may manage to dig evidence out of old newspaper archives. Even then, those of the former children with parents still living hesitate to mention it to them. It continues to hurt the parents too much. And they're old. If they couldn't handle it then, why now?

65.
The Street Is the Real Life
(gnomic)

But the children have been hiding something all along. In a way, they're hiding the very center of their knowledge.

Things happen on the street that are beyond explanation to the parents.

Some of these children are stoical, some are braggarts, some are open wounds. Some are eloquent, in their way.

Yet eventually it overtakes even the most eloquent, the eagerest to share, to be known: the parents are never going to *get it*, not really. What goes on out of doors. What a dance actually feels like. The words actually spoken, and what is meant, that meaning rustling around beneath the words of the street.

And so, for all their difference, all the varieties of experience, it is a general condition that the children know that the street, for all its uneasiness, for all its unsafety, is the real life and the real life is beyond explanation.

The consolations of the hearth? If they are consolations—we shouldn't suppose that each child has access to anything like consolations—these are a falsehood. The street is the truth, and the children have quit, one after another, trying to explain it to the parents.

Silence prevails.

This general condition means that, even after the discrediting of the false oasis—after their expungement—the children share something, each with one another, each with the all. Nemesis, friend, unrecognizable shape down the block you cross the street in preference not to discover—doesn't matter. You're still, in a way, *together* out there.

Close.

In relation.

66.
Inside the Millionaire's House
(1977)

Breaking news from the Dean Street boys:

They're inside!

Of course, C. has to do the liaison work. What is it with a gaggle of perfectly functional white boys, that in the absence of parental matchmaking they need their Black friend to introduce them to a new kid resembling themselves? What gives, with this reluctance to understand the simple use of a doorbell, or their own viability with a boy who could basically be mistaken for them in a lineup? But nobody's mom is in, say, a consciousness raising group with the millionaire's wife. No parent knows the millionaire from some other time and place, no one's managed to run into the new people at the premature French restaurant or the premature sandwich shop. So, it's left to C., again. At some point this really is something we'll need to take a look at.

But let's take a look at the millionaire's house first. Having been introduced by their Black friend, the white boys have tumbled inside, in a bunch, like puppies. It's the kid equivalent of one of those nosy neighbor renovation tours the Brownstoners are always subjecting themselves to, then bitching about when they think the kids aren't listening.

The finished state of the place is a kind of wonder. With its knocked-out basement level and fresh Sheetrock, and the scandalous removal of the plaster ornament and the marble mantel, the two story parlor resembles the interior of a gallery. But the house is messy, already, with no butler or maid trailing around to pick up, as in, say, a movie about some eccentric possessing a fortune. And this millionaire, this dad-unlike-their-dads—though they can't yet specify how—is eccentric by definition. He's eccentric for coming here.

This dad's got a record collection which includes, unlike those in their own houses, many new albums. Albums by the very latest groups! And he appears to actually play them. Also, unlike their own dads and moms, who often just seem too tired to do something like play a record. As if that took so much energy.

The mom? She's invisible, behind some kind of scrim they can't quite figure out. Maybe this is one of those crypto divorces, cohabitation dangling by a thread. The boys have seen it before.

The dad greets the little parade coming through like it's been thrown in his honor. His grinning moustache is beginning to remind them of Gomez from *The Addams Family*.

"You boys like Steely Dan?"

"Uhhhhh . . ."

"'Kid Charlemagne'? 'Doctor Wu'? *C'mon.*"

"Uhhhhhhhhhh—"

"Are you with me, Dr. Wu? Are you really just a shadow of a man that I once knew?"

"UHHHHHHHHHHHHHHHHHHHHHHH—"

But before the needle drops, before their fascination can prosper, the Dean Street boys are swept upstairs, to the boy's rooms. They tromp up the stairs, which still feature the old banister, the old newel post, the first sign that things might be different in the upper regions of the household. Though the millionaire's son is as breezy, as welcoming, as his father had been on their way through the parlor.

Upstairs, another scene entirely. The renovation stopped at the basement and parlor. These rooms are still full of the old molding on the window and door frames, the old ornament, the tin ceilings and marble. The molding's freshly painted, sure, but blobby, formless, nobody scraped it, must be the seventeenth paint layer, just like in their own houses. The bathroom's got the old black and white checker tile, cracked and stained in the familiar way. What kind of millionaire can't be bothered to renovate the upper floors? Doesn't he care about his kid?

On the other hand, the millionaire's son has a Farrah Fawcett poster, a *Star Trek* calendar, a British Special Forces issue Ibberson gravity knife, a Visible Man, folders of Kennedy half-dollars complete from 1964 including years with actual silver content, a chemistry set with reputed bomb-making potential, a gyroscope, a poker chip dispenser, a Telecaster with a Pignose amp, and a long box of *Fantastic Four* comics in boards and plastic. Granted, not all of this appears to be treasured anymore. Nor should it all be, at thirteen. The Visible Man bears conspicuous signs of neglect, with missing intestines and a Sharpie-drawn dick-and-balls. But still. The millionaire's son has cool stuff. A few of the Dean Street boys might possess a few such cherry items themselves, though not an entire curatorial wing.

What really distinguishes the millionaire's son, though, is a cavalier attitude. He gifts his belongings at the drop of a hat. The gyroscope, you like that? Take it, it's yours! The kid also suggests they bring stuff down to the street, specifically the gravity knife. Of this, the Dean Street boys try to dissuade him. Perhaps the millionaire's son isn't entirely clear about certain things. As if anyone is.

The millionaire's son notices one of his guests hefting The Visible Man. "Why don't we set it on fire," he suggests.

"Hell yes, but what about your parents?"

He shrugs. "Sparkle and Rabbit wouldn't have anything to say about it." *Sparkle and Rabbit?* Seeing their double take, the millionaire's son clarifies. "That's just what I prefer to call them."

Maybe the Dean Street boys once met a kid who called their parents by their first names. Maybe they've attempted it themselves. But nicknames?

After persuading him the front stoop isn't the place for the experiment, the Dean Street boys follow the millionaire's son into the backyard, which is still an ailanthus thicket, a total nest for rats. There they set the plastic model ablaze. It only feebly half melts, half chars, stinking wildly. Soon they're out of matches. Still, their nerve for chaos is tingling.

More. As they pass through on their way back upstairs, the millionaire's son gestures at the refrigerator, and practically stage whispers: the freezer is full of marijuana. "Rabbit doesn't keep track," the millionaire's son says.

"You smoke it?"

Another shrug. "Not anymore. I'm taking a break. But you can if you want. We just have to wait until they pass out."

Not anymore!

Pass out!

Just one quadrant of this archive of treasures is off limits. The millionaire's son has a glass-fronted bookcase, three stacked front-lifting shelves full of plastic-wrapped hardcovers, novels by George MacDonald Fraser, Patrick O'Brian, Tom Sharpe, Eric Ambler. "Hands off," he says, casually icy when one of his guests gets too near. "Those are first editions."

"First whats?"

"I collect historical and espionage novels of a certain stripe."

Of a certain stripe? Maybe it's the son who'll stun them by suddenly producing a monocle and top hat from among his holdings. To reveal himself as the true millionaire, in the sense of the cartoon man on the Monopoly board, or Thurston Howell III. Maybe he's some sort of boy genius inventor, or boy king of an island nation, one who keeps the fake parents downstairs—Sparkle and Rabbit, previously underemployed character actors—for protective coloration.

Except he also is just a white kid too dumb not to walk around Dean Street with a gravity knife brandished in full view. If it wasn't taken off you in thirty seconds, it would have attracted the otherwise negligent police like catnip.

"So, where are you from?" they ask. Because the whole atmosphere of not-from-here is wailing from the boy like a siren.

"We lived in Montreal, and San Rafael, and Lyon." He rolls his eyes upward as if mentally tabulating. "And my aunt's place on Deer Isle. I guess that's it."

"Yeah, but where did you come from?"

"Sparkle and Rabbit stayed out on Fire Island while they renovated this place. I spent three sessions at Androscoggin, which, believe me, was three too many."

They shake their heads. Not one single word from his mouth makes the remotest bit of sense. "Yeah," they say again. "But where are you *from?*"

The millionaire's son manages to look sly and helpless at the same time, and says nothing, as if sharing in their wonderment at himself. A kid who is not a boy inventor nor a boy king but is, perhaps, a genius of incoherence, of anarchic possibility. He grins at them, then, and it is as if they share a collective thought balloon, while Steely Dan's counterfeit reggae "Haitian Divorce" bleeds up through the floorboards—Rabbit must have gotten excited and flipped up the volume—and in the collective thought balloon are the words *what the hell is going to happen when this kid hits the Street?*

67.
Shoplifting as Skill Acquisition

(an underlying premise)

Well, the first thing that happens, one bare week before the start of school, is this: C. rallies the millionaire's son for a jaunt off the block completely, a tour of the wider ambit.

Is this what you were expecting?

No? Not the Dean Street boys either.

If anything, they might have figured that with that case full of first editions, military adventure stories, whatever they are, the millionaire's son might glide right over the fact of the city, end up in the parlor on Bergen Street, playing eighteen-sided dice games with those two from Packer Collegiate.

But no. Remember he's destined for public school.

Some things are just plain confusing.

C. and the millionaire's son go for one of those daydream runs, touch all the bases. First, under the bridge, to the city metal scrapyard, to ogle the puzzle of cop cars. If you dragged off enough pieces you could assemble one yourself. Then back by way of the waterfront, underneath the Promenade, all the way to the hospital before they curl back toward the neighborhood. They visit Cobble Hill Park, placid in its box of carriage houses, all the white moms, but quiet enough today that C. pulls out a fat drippy marker and tags the dolphin statue, then hands the implement over to the millionaire's son. He's got no tag? Not a big deal, just don't write your full name and phone number. Anything else is cool. No? Some other time, if you feel like it.

They cut loose of the park, head up Court Street, across Atlantic. Here's Queen pizzeria, where they snag a couple of slices, fresh and hot in greasy wax paper. Which, after scarfing the pizza, they slap onto a stationery shop's plate glass window and scoot away chortling. Next, under the jail's shadow they cross Boerum Place, onto Livingston. Dip into the basement entrances of first McCrory's, then Korvette, for a brisk introduction to the basics of shoplifting.

Shoplifting? How can this be necessary? Is there something they want at McCrory's or Korvette? Something the millionaire's son couldn't afford? No. Nothing here really entices them. They'll make their selections based on ease-of-operation, palm a few junky items which may end in the trash before they're back on the block. Some dumb Hot Wheels cars, stuff they'd bored of playing with at age seven or eight, if they'd ever cared about at all. A Duncan Imperial, a thing which they might have two or three of in a drawer somewhere already. A pack of striped tube socks, which C. will stuff up under his shirt to make false tits, trying to crack his new friend up, and succeeding, for a minute. These stores suck, basically. Perhaps nobody stops them stealing because nobody wants this stuff to begin with. Unserious about graffiti, they've got no motivation today to tackle the highly guarded spray paint rack in the hardware area, nor to pit themselves against the superior security staff at the more fabulous Abraham & Straus.

This little run is something else, then. But what? Ritual? Initiation? Test? Showing off? It has the air of an intensive tutorial, as C. schools the millionaire's son in the "instrumentalization of difference" trick: see how they follow me through the store? See how they leave you alone? See how you therefore can grab all the shit you want and feel justified, since you're proving they're racists?

It's like math. A thing that you can't explain aloud, you have to diagram it on the chalkboard. Even after it's proved, you can't put it in words. Show me again! The answer always comes out the same, that's the remarkable thing.

THERE'S AN ELEMENT even more basic, though, regarding shoplifting. Let's zoom out, away from these two. Peculiar though they may seem.

The thing about shoplifting—boosting—is there's barely one kid who *doesn't*. Boy, girl, Black, white, P.R., doesn't matter, it comes with the territory. Even the incompetent ones, the one-timers, they feel differently afterward. Whole areas inside them exfoliate, stir into activity. The first day they go into a store with criminal intent, that's the day they've gotten separation, the day they've achieved liftoff. Because this is a criminal world. You wouldn't want to be on just one end of it, would you? Always the victim, never the perp? Recipient of the memo, taker of the call, unable to shout back?

No.

Shoplifting is skill acquisition. You might need it for later, a basic life art. Best to get these things under your belt.

It might pretty much always begin with candy. At a candy store, or bodega. Pity the bodegas. What chance did they have, needing to guard a glass-fronted soda case in the rear, itself wedged behind narrow, loaded aisles, while also keeping your eye on the candy bars stacked right there at the register, far too near the door. Does snatch-and-run count? Of course it does! Hell, even stealing coins from your parent's dressing table in order to *purchase* candy counts as a kind of participation. It makes a start at least. Not everyone is ready for stealing from strangers, some need to practice on a parent or sibling.

Fulton, Flatbush, Smith Street, Vanderbilt Avenue. Hooper's Store on Sesame Street, whatever. You steal because it's there: candy, soda, comic books, baseball cards, cigarettes, beer. Tampons, rubbers, horny goat weed, even before you knew what any of that stuff was for.

Girls make the shift to lipstick and eyeliner and L'eggs Sheer Energy pretty naturally.

Two or three Black girls and one white girl? That's a team to confound Sherlock Holmes. Send them into Fort Knox, they'll emerge with the gold.

Smartasses steal pieces of the city from itself. Pry hubcaps off cars on a shady street, not because there's some resale destination, but just to put in your room for your parent to do a double take. Advertising from the subway, easily popped out of its frame. Whole subway car full of riders just shaking their heads at you, but what are they going to do, protect a subway advertisement?

All this goes without saying. It's taken for granted. You try it in pairs, usually. Pairs—at least. That poor incompetent kid, sticky-fingering the *Heavy Metal* magazine all by himself, what was he thinking? Boosting is an art one kid graduates the next into, sometimes you pass along a good blind-angled spot and a useful target in a spirit of pure altruism. Just passing it down along the line, to a younger who'll appreciate it.

A good example: that box of Charleston Chews, right there. The largest candy bar known to our human species, Charleston Chews, truthfully, are like eating dried turds that threaten to pull out each and every one of your fillings. Yet here they are, too easily sleeved to ignore, begging for it. Reveal one of those, secreted in your sleeve a few steps from the door of the bodega, it's like a magic trick! Now, too bad, you have to eat it. No, really, I insist. I stole it for you.

No one ever finished a Charleston Chew. It's technically impossible to choke it down.

From candy, boosting continues its association with things you'd never eat in your own house, appetites to make parents weep. One white kid, for instance, develops an addiction to cans of Chef Boyardee ravioli in meat sauce, easily palmed into a winter parka. He pillages these from the corner bodega, where who on earth would ever suspect him? White, plus nowhere near the candy or soda. At home he wolfs it with a fork straight from the can, then takes the evidence straight to the garbage cans in his front yard.

For some, boosting may become an enterprise, a ladder into other types of theft. For the graffiti writers, it's a credibility issue. Pearl Paint on Canal Street, that's where the good stuff hides. The war with a shop like that is as much a dimension of your culture as knowing who the king of the A train is, or the right way to hold a can of Krylon to make a non-drippy period on an exclamation mark. In pursuit of such higher targets, you might become an innovator of some device or gimmick, like the structured backpack: appearing full but actually cavernously empty. Or extra pockets sewn into a coat lining. Or elaborate methodologies of distraction, such as having a friend telephone and report an intruder on the roof or at the back entrance, in order to pull an avid security guard off the floor.

Hell, who knows, at this rate you might someday be drawn into a real crime story. You might rob a bank!

Before you boost at least a little something, you might not even really qualify as from Brooklyn. You're just waiting around to see, and unincidentally getting robbed in the meanwhile. You might have chosen to pay for that candy, after all, if a kid hadn't relieved you of your dollar a block earlier.

Or maybe you've got the dollar secured in your sock, in which case it really isn't advisable to drag it out and wave it around. Everything points in the same inevitable direction.

So just grab it, he can't see you from here. I'll meet you outside.

68.
C., Part 3
(a snapshot in retrospect)

For C., at a distance of decades, the names of the white boys are a blur. The white fog. He never was great with the names, one reason he handed out so many nicknames, a mnemonic device. Can they really have been all named for apostles or Beatles? Peter, Simon, Matthew, Luke, George, John, Paul? What are the odds? Not recalling their names, this might be a more agreeable sensation than recalling them. It suggests a slackening of the power of those days over his consciousness.

How often are the white boys of Dean Street thinking of him?

Never? Always?

Either answer might stick in his craw.

Yet always, plummeting through these involuntary recollections, there's more.

There's this: names aside, he *does* often recall them individually. That some of them, with their daft collections, shelf rows of replica Adam West Batman toys still in their original cellophane-windowed boxes or paperback reprint collections of *Mad*; with their tales of vacations and summer camp, their sports paraphernalia they didn't know how to use; with their arch and inept retellings of their parents' smutty jokes that they don't even quite understand; and the others, the hippie kids, in a big house no one can afford to renovate and with the hair and fingernails that make C.'s mother shake her head, and so penniless they sometimes even sponge off him, a Black person, for the price of a bottle of Yoo-hoo; and all of them most of all with their renewable innocence about the street, their endless injured dignity at the fact of being robbed, at those things they didn't mention and so imagined that no one knew; he saw them, and their parents too, and he sometimes, somewhat, really loved them. He really did. Even if their names are unavailable to his tongue. They reached into him. They moved him, the fools.

Code-switch, intersectional, co-dependent, a dozen other names presented themselves to his awareness decades too late to illuminate the confused life C.'s body lived in those days as a Dean Street boy.

WE NEED TO go deeper into our postulates here, risk guessing more.

Again: what is it C. sees in them?

Years later, he's still capable of posing this question to himself. What was he trying to prove? Most days, all such questions are lost in a swirl of good and bad days, just living the life appointed to him, often consisting of its own replenishing fog of white people. Many of whom evoke versions of the Dean Street boys, a few that jump out at first as false recognitions, so he nearly greets them as familiars. He catches himself in this error and marvels at the readiness of his impulse to reassure—hey, I'm harmless, I'm your friend! An impulse which, ironically, its recipient might only be likely to read as some form of sinister intention.

C.'s readiness to salve the whiteboy insecurities is an uneconomical part of himself, a vestige worth nothing.

But there's more to it, even, than that.

By the time he was twelve, thirteen, fourteen, and street routines had begun to evolve beyond skully and stickball and stoopball, more in the direction of skateboards and nunchucks, vandalism and pilferage, and C. had been hanging out with his white friends and his Black friends for years already, on Dean Street and on Bergen and Pacific and on the Heights Promenade and in the Wyckoff Gardens Houses and the Gowanus Houses and the Walt Whitman Houses courtyards, and using in each realm his special talents to ingratiate himself to his friends' parents, too, to get inside all their houses and say a polite *ma'am* to somebody's mother like he was trained to do, thus enabling him to conduct his serial investigations, C. felt he was the only person alive who knew *everything* about this place. He was stretched like a bridge across worlds.

By that time, too, the false oasis had ruptured like a soap bubble.

A floater over rooftops, one which, just when it seemed it might be destined to float forever, pops.

Could the older white kids, the more experienced white kids, protect the younger ones, and the newcomers? No.

Sure, there's a couple of cooler white dudes who've launched themselves successfully into the realm of graffiti on the strength of artistic talent and the willingness to make nighttime train yard runs, and so have joined that unique system of status and affiliations. But that was in itself a form of graduation from the locality, from Dean Street. The day those white boys got cool, they were gone.

Sure, there were residual stickball games, already taking on a tinge of nostalgia. Those weren't going to help the Brownstoner kids on the day the stickball game graduates into something rougher.

The Brownstoner offspring, that motley crowd that wasn't Carroll Street Italian or Park Slope Italian or Park Slope Irish. That crowd that didn't have a carful of cousins with baseball bats at their backs. Instead, a dad in wire rim glasses. Or not even that, just a neighbor looking out, some old Mohawk lady sitting out on her stoop, shaking her fist, permanently outraged at the disquiet of the dance going down.

It was up to C.

C., the one destined to be able to tell those fools apart, to know and be known by their parents.

Also, to represent them, justify them, to the kids from the projects.

To those poorer kids, Black dudes like himself but also some Puerto Ricans who lived in the projects or in the apartment buildings on Warren and Wyckoff. Those who'd never crossed the line to begin with, who'd never played in the false oasis. Those who scorned the white boys, even if they didn't shake them down.

They'd say: "Dang, man, what you doing with all them white people?"

Or: "I can't even tell one from another, they're like bedbugs to me. You collecting them like some kind of Pied Piper."

Or: "You horny for his *mama?* Is that what you doing all up in theys house?"

Or: "I feel sorry for you, boy. Don't you know what they say behind your back?"

Or: "If you wasn't walking with that kid, he'd be dead hamburger. Homies snatch the pants off his ass."

Or: "If you gonna teach him how to run, you better teach him how to walk first."

Or: "How much they got to pay you to be they friend?"

How to reply to such provocations? C. didn't offer rebuttals or explanations. He shrugged them off. Made funny faces, verbal mime gestures, for displacement of the burden of being himself into collective social comedy. C. was just That Guy. Crazy that way, crazy for the white boys. He had no excuse, it was his thing.

There wasn't one single day that he wasn't aware he spent copious afternoons with dudes who'd turn around and prey on the Dean Street boys the moment they were left unprotected.

Unprotected by the likes of him.

But he couldn't be everywhere at once.

ALL OF THIS is to be clear on one point: that when C. arrives that day, to take the millionaire's son on a shoplifting run, it is in the cause of a *civilizing* project, above all. Even if he has no particular inclination toward criminal matters himself. C. schools him because he's taking pity, and taking care. If the white boys who've lived here for ten years can still manage to be so ill-fitted for their world, then this new arrival has no advantages at all, and upon start of the school year is sure to be besieged. Boosting is about skill acquisition, and also about accultura-tion. There is no time to waste.

69.
A Half Block Behind Them, the Slipper
(1977)

It so happens that on this campaign of boosting C. has led the million-aire's son to the traffic triangle at the intersection of Fourth Avenue, Atlantic Avenue, and Flatbush, there to practice rolling a comic book into one's jacket when the newsstand vendor's back is turned—and that on the block of Atlantic between Third and Fourth, they are with-out their knowledge being sighted by the Slipper.

The Slipper has just come from the Times Plaza Station of the post office, located on that same block. He notices C. and the mil-lionaire's son through the window and sacrifices his place on line at the P.O. to Slip outside and follow them.

What's his interest here?

He likes to follow C. as a study, for sure. C.'s persistence in attach-ing to the various white boys, so unlike the Slipper's own propensities.

And the Slipper has never seen this particular white boy before, though he's heard the buzz about the millionaire. It isn't hard to put it together.

Past the gaggle of derelict men at the doorway of the Times Plaza Hotel, past the darkened windows of the Doray Tavern, the Slipper trails the other two boys, unseen.

He scopes them entering the newsstand on the traffic island. When he sees them begin to browse at the rack of comic books, the

Slipper's attention is satisfied. He returns to the post office and takes a place at the end of the line, to wait his turn.

What's he doing at the post office?

The Slipper is getting a money order. He likes to purchase things from catalogues, without having to consult his father.

What kinds of things?

We can't know yet. We haven't peeked inside his secret room.

A different order of acquisition than a comic book, that much is for certain.

70.
Those Who Cannot Be Helped

(subliminal)

Deep in the collective brain of the Dean Street boys is a sense that some kids just can't be helped. For many, this is a blurred suspicion. Not named, but felt. A fear. Perhaps it is even themselves.

The kids in question, white or not, are mostly boys. That they are beyond help is less a judgment, a moral assessment, than a kind of triage. You just can't let it bother you, that's the point.

The ones who can't be helped might be younger brothers with older siblings too strange or helpless themselves to offer any protection or guidance.

Or younger ones with no older siblings at all.

But being young doesn't mean you can't be helped. There are young kids who've got it all together, who can make it work. They've been watching. By the time it counts, when they are thrust out of the place where everything is so deceivingly in accord, they're ready. They've got tools. An attitude, a stratagem.

The ones who can't be helped are the others. Those about whom you can only shrug.

If all of this is seeming a bit abstract, let's take an example:

The spoiled boy.

Look at him there. (C. always does his best not to. He averts his eyes from that which he doesn't want to take on.)

First, put aside, though it's difficult, the spoiled boy's mom. The way her own nonviability is leaking all over the poor kid.

Some things just can't be blamed on a parent. The spoiled boy is profligate with error, says too much, makes wild boasts, weeps and shrieks at the drop of a hat, joins groups in which he is nakedly unwelcome, asks dumb questions, shows off valuable toys. But wait, you say—his yard is full! The little children have flocked to him, they understand his awkward language.

I thought he was killing it.

Nope. The kids who pick up the can't-be-helped vibe, they don't stick. They steal his toys and make mock of him behind his back. The crowd there from day to day is too young to matter, the scene a mirage. The spoiled boy's present popularity is contingent on a dumb misunderstanding. Some who come to his yard to play don't even learn his name. Most crucially, when graduation day comes, that is to say when it is time to experiment with a taste of shoplifting or graffiti, nobody will enlist him, nobody will even glance twice.

Wolves will circle this one.

Stay away, if you know what's good for you.

71.
Having a Nemesis
(subliminal)

Another thing that happens but goes unnamed: some guys, every once in a while, pick up a nemesis.

This is a different condition than the can't-be-helped.

The can't-be-helped are the ignominious. No one, for instance, would bother to make themselves a nemesis to the spoiled boy.

A nemesis requires stature in its target. Often a nemesis appears precisely when its target is on the cusp of aging out of the dance altogether. One day, a certain person is taller, takes up a little more space, or his voice drops. Or perhaps it happens on the day he gets a first stylish haircut, or a certain new jacket.

At that moment, a nemesis may appear.

The nemesis has to be a little threatened by his target. And a little aroused.

Other times, a nemesis is created by a story told on the street. If you are inclined to be a nemesis, you may overhear a legend or claim about some other kid, one which forms a grain of irritation, like that around which a pearl forms inside an oyster. In this case, the pearl of enmity. Of obsession.

Or a nemesis may be formed in the act of witnessing something directly. They may catch sight of someone who seems to scribble outside the lines. A kid who projects a frenetic or fearless manner of walking down the street, of simply existing. Someone who seems to deny the right order of things.

Someone who just doesn't sit right.

By logic, this could be a newcomer. Someone who never got the memo. Say, the millionaire's son.

Everyone else turns from such a scene, made uncomfortable by the exaggeration of the dance into something truly personal. Something intimate, even. It's a drag for all concerned. A nemesis and their chosen object form an accursed pair.

So, without consultation, without conscious intention, kids on either side of the formation pretend it isn't happening. Friends of the nemesis. Friends of the nemesis's object. This worsens everything, of course.

The nemesis and his foil plummet through a vacuum together, beyond rescue.

When all is said and done, a can't-be-helped is just one kid.

A nemesis coupling is more than twice as bad.

C., being a creature of the middle spaces, a secret emissary between the white children of Dean Street and the children of the

Gowanus Houses, may be specially challenged in his desire to turn his attention away from such a scene.

We'll see if he can.

72.
The Funny Muggings
(1976, 1974, 1991)

Things are getting heavy, we need some comic relief.

Everybody loves the Funny Muggings!

(They also help delay having to try to describe or understand the dance.)

Here are three of our favorites.

The Pizza Mugging. Two white boys walk up to the outdoor pass-through window of a pizzeria on Smith Street. One of them has the price of a slice in his hand, exact change, the only money on his person. (The other one may or may not have a dollar in his sock.) Just as he claps the coins on the counter, a pair of Black boys walk up and target them. A typical dance in the making, all the elements one hundred percent generic.

You would think the pizza man would be an element in a story like this one, but you'd be wrong. It is as if the boys are invisible where they stand on the street, all four, the Black and the white. It is as if the coins have clapped themselves onto the counter from thin air.

"Gimme that."

Today, for whatever reason, a grain of resistance or incomprehension, or some mingled element containing both resistance and incomprehension, rises up in the prospective victim. "What?" he asks, faking innocence. He pushes the coins farther inside, across the pass-through sill. "One slice," he says to the pizza man.

"The money," says the older and taller of the two Black boys. He turns to his companion, the younger and smaller Black boy. "Take it off him." This element, of coaching, of indoctrination of a younger by an elder, is also generic to the dance. They've all been here before.

Yet before intervention is possible, the coins are exchanged for a slice. As perfectly generic as the incident had promised to be, before this turn. The wax paper, already greasy. The slightly spilling cheese, the single singed bubble of dough in the rippled perfection of the crust. It looks delicious. I want one now. I could eat one of these every day of my life.

The white boy claims the slice from the pass-through counter. The mute indifferent pizza man having already turned from the scene, as if it were a view onto a street containing no persons whatsoever.

"Gimme that," says the larger of the two Black boys to the white boy who holds the slice, still intact, still, perhaps, too hot to bite.

"What?" says the white boy again, suppressing a smile. He even reaches for the shaker of garlic salt, and rains it on the slice. His companion, it should be said, stands paralyzed. He'd have handed over the money, the pizza, his shirt.

"The slice, man, you know what I'm talking about," says the older. Then turning again to his apprentice, says, "Take it off him." At this exact moment, the pizza-possessor raises the drooping tip to his teeth. And bites.

"Stop!" commands the older. He's trying to keep this game alive. This dance gone wrong. "Don't bite that, man." To his ward: "Take it off him, man."

The smaller's expression is sickened and helpless. He'd rather be anywhere but here. "He ate it, man."

"I'm saying take it! And STOP EATING IT, MAN." The white boy has taken another bite. Now he grins openly. Folds the cooling slice, which as always causes a tiny trickle of orange oil to sluice off the bitten edge, there to drip to the sidewalk unless one has been incautious and held it directly over one's new Converse High Tops. He bites again at the doubled slice. It is amazing, always, how fast a slice of pizza can be devoured if one is in a hurry.

"*Damn*, man."

"He's eating it," restates the younger and smaller, trying to find purchase on this situation, to unwind it in time. He never wanted to be here in the first place.

"I told you not to do that," says the older, in disgust. "You stupid motherfucker." Or the emphasis here may be different: "You *stupid*, motherfucker."

The white boy just grins, while his own counterpart and sidekick stares at him in astonishment. This was possible?

The older Black boy continues to present an exaggerated tableau of irritation and disappointment. He turns and beckons to his younger—friend? Cousin? Intern? "C'mon." This whole day, this whole world, inadequate to his demands, his orchestration.

He should have brought a knife. That would have made them pay attention.

I don't feel like you're laughing.

Let me try again: The Check Mugging.

A different couple of white boys are moving down the sidewalk, on Franklin Avenue. A pair of brothers this time. The two are merely puttering on a Saturday afternoon.

They've extended their range of activity, meandering eastward, across Underhill and Classon, all the way to Franklin. This jaunt has been encouraged in the younger sibling by the older, who projects a quirky indifference to the atmosphere of what is, to the younger, even in daylight a terrifying street, onto which he'd never venture alone or with one of his friends. The older has, perhaps, begun to age out of the dance, transformation of which his younger brother can only dream. Also, the older brother is studying karate. Not that he would be terribly likely to use it on the street. But still.

They're approached, not by a kid or kids their age, but by a somewhat older, shambling man, a Black guy with a wool cap in the warm weather, an ingrown beard, a trace of yellowness to his eyes. Apparently unarmed, but large enough to be intimidating.

He's really old, truly a grown man. Yet the script of the dance is lurking in the margins of this encounter. Perhaps it could be said that *two* ex-dancers are meeting here, on this street now so typically characterized by the sudden blazing vacancy of witnesses or interveners, as if neutron bombed.

Better call it a mugging, then.

And no, this will not be the debut of karate. The older brother feels this encounter can be handled otherwise. The confidence that karate imparts may be best applied in verbal maneuvering, after all.

Two aged-out veterans of the dance, and the younger brother a currently eligible participant, the sole witness to whatever will transpire. To the younger brother, it feels as though his presence has drawn the other, ensured this humiliation, as though his own older brother has already forgotten what it is to be twelve and on the street, a magnet, begging for it.

"Let me have what you got in your pocket."

"I don't have anything."

"Let me see."

The older brother reaches in and pulls out what's there: a fifteen-dollar check, a paycheck for newspaper delivery. The older brother has a paper route. This seeming vestige of some older, cornier rendition of childhood has somehow improbably made itself available to him at this time, in this place.

Time is unruly. The piling up of incommensurable realities, its signature.

"See, I don't have any money."

"What's that, then?"

"That's a check!"

"What's it worth?"

"It's worth fifteen dollars, but it's a check."

"So, give it here."

"It isn't worth anything unless you take it to the bank."

"Then let's go to the bank!"

"It's Saturday. The bank is closed."

"I'll take it to the damn bank, just give it to me or I'll kick your ass!"

The check is handed over. The check is peered at in dismay. A familiar moment, a transaction meant to align on a certain axis, has teetered. Failed its actors, on all sides. Can it be salvaged? How?

"What bank I got to go to?"

"The bank on the check. It says it right there. But it has to be signed."

"So, *sign* it, motherfucker! You're pissing me off!"

"I don't have a pen."

"*I'll* give you the damn pen." Incredibly, from the depths of his pants pockets the Black man produces a stub of pencil, and shoves it with the check back in the direction of his would-be victim, who only seems to grow more amused.

"You can't sign a check in pencil, man. You need an ink pen."

Yellow eyes grow wild with frustration. The Black man restrains the older brother with a grip on his sleeve while turning on the side-walk, to find a woman passing, a Black woman with a grocery cart. "Hey, 'scuse me, hey, you got a ink pen?"

The woman shakes her head, sorrowfully, and clatters on.

Another couple of passersby also fail to give forth.

"You'd have to have an account at the bank, you know," says the older brother. Somewhat mercilessly, it seems to me as I consider it now.

"An *account?*"

"Sure, you have to deposit the check in an account."

"Fuuuuuuuuck."

"And then it probably would need a couple of days to clear."

As reward for the adeptness of this sequence of verbal karate, the older brother is recipient of the crumpled-up check tossed in his direction. Then a quick hard open-palmed blow, one that turns his head. Days later, an unprecedented rash of pimples raises itself on the cheek and along the jaw where his flesh was traumatized by the blunt force. This is a detail one rarely hears about in the wake of a blow to the face. Slap-acne, it's a real thing, a visible shame.

But the brothers are permitted to go on their way. The check un-crumples easily enough, is ironed flat, endorsed, and deposited.

Fair enough, a semi-humorous semi-abject semi-tormenting Funny Mugging.

I realized only semi-humorous halfway through.

The last one: The Guilt-Tripped Stickup. This story brings us into the nineties. We're following a white girl now, one who's grown up, is in her mid-twenties. Working as a server at Windows on the World, to pay her tuition at Brooklyn College, to which she's returned for a teaching certificate. A public school girl, she's been teaching for several years at Saint Ann's. Which doesn't require the certificate. She's discovered a vocation, possibly, to be a real teacher, but, frankly, fuck this bogus prestige and privilege, which never actually seems to rub off on her, only rub up against her.

She wants to teach public school, which not only matters more to her but offers real career protections, class solidarity might be the word for it, as opposed to the parents of the wealthy kids, dads with groping hands, whimsical, self-besotted administrators, secret handshakes that get her most insolent students into Harvard and Princeton, her druggiest up to safe harbor at Bennington.

This girl, woman I mean, still lives on Dean Street. She's one of those who stayed. Like the bookseller looking for the Lovecraft Basement. Let's admit it now, we've got a thing for the ones who stayed. The endurers and abiders, those coming of age inside the Crime Novel.

The city's changing, but then again not. A Black man is the mayor, that's different. Racial tension has come out of hiding for the White Collective Brain, on one side the Crown Heights riots, on the other, well, Squeegee men. That scourge. Horrible how they swarm your car.

This city is hurtling toward the Abner Louima incident.

But wait, this was meant to be a funny one, let's collect ourselves.

Her Walkman is her survival mechanism for the IRT, a cassette recorded by a friend, a mix with Desmond Dekker, Penguin Cafe Orchestra, and her fave, Marine Girls. The sound of those seagulls on the beach never fails to take her away, no matter how brutal the crowd, glances of the Wall Street husbands, begging cataclysm of drummers on the platform, blackout delays beneath the river, everyone muttering except that one guy having a panic attack. The sound of those seagulls on the beach frees her to merely laugh at the yearning pressure against her ass from some guy in a suit, laugh and recall the days of the frotteur on the 42nd Street shuttle, buddy, you have no idea, you're waaaay out of your league.

Tonight's ride is over now, though, she's slogging home with no umbrella from the Nevins stop. Popping out with the reverse human waterfall up the narrowest stairs, never her favorite way back to Dean and Hoyt, but the longer walk from Borough Hall's not worth it in the rain. Past the Flatbush vendors, the carpets full of VHS tapes, the tables loaded with beads and incense and essential oils. Umbrella sellers too, but not worth it. She'll duck her head and dash.

She corners to Nevins, the darkened street, always, it seems, under shadow of scaffolding. Welcome tonight because of the downpour, but the line of morose figures huddled beneath makes it unenticing to linger. She pops from underneath to cross Schermerhorn, where the rain has chased all away except this guy in a glistening Members Only jacket rising in front of her like a specter, a baseball hat pulled over his eyes and, sure enough, grabbing her arm.

"What?" A lousy day is getting no better.

"I've got a knife."

"What?"

"A knife. Take the speakers out your damn ears, girl."

"Okay." She complies. Maybe the first mistake, what if she'd kept walking, pushed past him. Or just stood there saying what over and over again.

"I'm not fucking around," he says, when she stuffs the earpiece into her pocket, along with a handful of rain. For god's sake, let her walk home and get dry.

"Okay, you're not fucking around."

"Where's your money?"

How long has it been? Since those days of the shakedowns? The years, really, of money in the sock or the shoe, sometimes in several places, with a dollar in a pants pocket as bait for a concession. Likely they always knew there was more hidden, the single dollar was always viewed sideways, leery, barely sufficient. But surrender it, and both sides could walk away.

The boys, the fucking Dean Street boys, always acting like it was their exclusive cross to bear. The days of the toll, the street tax on being short and white and unaccompanied by a good tough angry-faced friend who'd scare the shit out of them before they crossed the street to assess you. *They* might even cross the street to avoid the stare down. Sure, the boys endured the hazing longer, mainly because they stayed shorter longer. You grew tall and grew tits and swapped out the predictable ritual for things far worse.

Suddenly, standing here in the dark and wet on the vacated corner of Nevins and Schermerhorn she revisits an unwelcome memory. The night when that fucking guy she'd known forever, all the way back to P.S. 29, and whom she dated for about five minutes—less than that—mock-stalked her from the subway. Just to see if he could terrify her. Just to claim some of the street power for himself, at her expense. It was on this exact corner when, wheeling to face what she thought was a pursuer, she discovered, instead, that asshole, flashing a sick grin at his trick. In drawing on this enraging recollection, she locates her response to the man standing before her in the rain. "I have to see the knife."

Now it is his turn to say "what?"

"You're not taking anything off me unless it's real."

Her pockets are loaded with cash, of course, tips from Windows. She folded the night's take into her pants and split it in two when the first wad of singles and fives got too big. Not one lone dollar reserved for a sock or in any other fashion concealed.

"Fucking shit," complains her mugger, but he palms forth a short dagger of some kind. It looks like a letter opener, actually, but he seems to have kept up his side of the bargain.

"What are you complaining about? It's you who's got us standing out in the rain. So, what do you want?"

"Money. Give me your money, all of it."

Money, right. Should she begin singing the Flying Lizards version to him? Instead, she hears herself say, "no way all of it, this is my rent. You can't fucking have it. Tell me what you need and what it's for."

"I don't got to tell you shit, lady."

"I'm not a lady. We probably went to the same fucking high school." She's letting it run away with her: the confluence of this fool, the rain, and her day, enraging in all respects. The wild size of the folding money bulging her pockets, if only he knew. It makes her feel crazy. If she turned her pockets out the bills would bloom and scatter and soak. If she took out a wad, she could peel off a few, like some kind of street hustler, a seller of stolen goods or a three-card monte dealer, but this guy would surely try to grab the chunk. At least it's two chunks. Despite the usual monstrous risk—his body could overpower hers—her crazy feeling writes a script, one in which she imagines she might say or do anything.

What pops out is a guilt trip harangue. "I just didn't need this today, I really didn't need this. I know you don't give two shits but I had a day from hell, really, do you know what time I had to get up to make it to class? Subway fucking stopped because of an incident investigation and they sent a local, doors open and you should have seen it."

"Seen what?"

"Sardines, they're stuffed like sardines, already barely fit. Everybody from the first train stands there just moaning, like how the fuck are we supposed to fit. I had to wait for three more trains."

"Nobody told you to live in New York."

"I was born here, you bozo. But you wouldn't know about rush hour, because you don't have anywhere urgent to go, just helping yourself to my paycheck." Maybe this is the wrong approach, maybe she should talk to him in the manner indoctrinated by her Windows on the World manager, who explained that their service training was "European" style, who said *none of that Suzy-American-hi-how-are-ya with our customers.*

So, she backs off a degree. "Sorry," she says. "I don't mean anything. Just I had a hell day, you have no idea. I got soaked and dried off three times, and now you're making me stand here. What do you need, tell me what you need and what for and I'll give you some of my rent money, some of the money I earned by standing on my unsteady pins, standing on my aching dogs—"

She's reverting to salt-of-the-earth-Irish-mom crap stolen from her Park Slope friend Gina's mother in sixth grade, stuff she and Gina used to quote in punk rock hilarity, but now it's pouring from her with weird sincerity, next thing you know she'll mention her nonexistent varicose veins—"serving frat boy Wall Street dudes a twenty-dollar cheeseburger. It's them you should rob, but you found me, my lucky day. So, help yourself to my money. Just tell me how much and what for, because you're *not* taking it all."

"Woman, shut up." He's been chastened from calling her *lady*.

"Where do you live? With your parents? They told you to come out here?"

"Okay. Damn."

"I was out pounding the streets all day, ma, just looking for a job, but then this nice *woman* spontaneously gave me all her hard-earned tips from Window on the Frigging World."

"You don't got to be like that."

"No, I take all my showers outside. I enjoy this. Just get around to telling me how much of my money you want when the mood strikes."

"I don't need your goddamn money." He slaps her hand away in disgust, as though it hadn't been him grabbing her arm all this time but the reverse.

He's moving down the street now, away to—what? A next and quieter victim? Repentance of his ways? Maybe he'll go through the doors of the nearest church. Yeah, right. She feels the urge to chase him, there's a craziness in her now that wants to chase him and hand him one of the wads, push it on him. It's half in each pocket, approximately. Approximately enough. She could have spared half, that was her calculation all along, to get him off his rhythm so he wouldn't frisk her pockets and find them both. But half is his, by rights, she thinks. He should have gotten something for his effort, that was the deal.

The deal?

She watches him walk off, her tongue stilled now.

73.
Brazen Head
Wheeze, Part 3
(2019)

Was the Wheeze ever part of a Funny Mugging?

We thought you'd never ask!

Tonight, he performs his old parlor trick. He collars young couples and asks whether they live in the neighborhood. If they are so unlucky as to mention Dean Street, he demands their address. Not just anyone consents to play. Who is this old creep? Would he follow them home?

"What are you afraid of? What's your street number?"

Often enough he bullies it out of them. Then he smacks his lips, raises a knowing finger, tries to corral the bartender's attention. After a dramatized interval, between hacking sounds that might be throat-clearing, might be the sound of a man dying, he repeats the street number, screws up his mouth, and declares, "Your landlord is _____."

And is right.

He's memorized the owners, house by house, for a three-block stretch. I've never seen it fail. Maybe he's had to mutter his way out of a stumper or two, but he never guesses wrong. You see their eyes widen, wondering what's encircled them. Has he been stalking them all along? Was this the reveal, the jump scare, the moment the undead creature erupts from the sacred burial grounds on which they've innocently staked their futures?

Why didn't they take their parents' advice and stick to the Upper East Side? It's cheaper there anyway!

Tonight's victim looks more incensed than afraid, actually. A square-jawed type who's bristling at the Wheeze's lip-licking proximity to his girlfriend, so I'm inclined to wade in and distract them, before any escalation. The Wheeze is never one to back down in the face of a recent arrival.

By his standard of course everyone's a recent arrival.

Even he's a recent arrival. He speaks for the dead.

He might really be the ghoul of this young couple's worst dreams, or maybe just their worst possible night out for a pint and some darts in a smoke-free bar. They might have little notion how much I've spared them when I divert him with my question. "Hey, you remember the pizza mugging?"

The Wheeze turns reluctantly from his quarry. "Ehhhhh, sure."

"You got one of those?"

"Got one of those what?"

"Were you ever jumped, I don't know, for food?"

He looks as though he wants to spit in my eye. "I once gave a derelict a fresh bucket of KFC I'd just bought on Flatbush." He spoke slowly, meting out the syllables. "I feel pretty certain he was one of Henry Miller's childhood friends. I'd like to claim it was an exalted gesture but really, once he'd pawed the first drumstick with his snotty hobo gloves, I lost my appetite."

"Not so much getting mugged *per se*," I point out.

"Yeaaaaaaaaah, maybe I'm not as turned on by that whole thing as you are."

"What's that supposed to mean?"

"Just get over it already."

"You're a fine one to talk!"

"I only tell those stories because you're always asking." The Wheeze's dry tone makes it clear I'm the one who should feel humiliated. "So, you were a bullied child. We all were. Don't make a furshlugginer religion of it, like that writer." This, the only way the Wheeze will ever refer to him: *that writer*. He means that Dean Street boy, who lived among us, and wrote a novel. "You know the crime nobody talks about? What whatsisname did."

"Who?"

"Whatsisname. The Revenger Kid. You remember. We all thought his dad was a millionaire."

"Ah."

"Somebody should write a fucking novel about *that*."

74.
Millionaire's Son Meets Board Games of Empire

(1978)

The two in the parlor with the Board Games of Empire? At some point, they crave witnesses. They want someone who can testify to the conquests they've enjoyed, the powers they've attained, the territories they've claimed.

What's the point of refighting Field Commander Rommel's war in the desert so scrupulously that you're pretty certain you could have reversed the outcome of the actual siege of Tobruk if given Major General Hendrik Klopper's ear, when there's nobody but you and your counterpart to affirm the triumph?

All this time holding themselves aloof and superior, deeming nobody worthy of their time, and they might just be a tree falling in a forest unseen.

The millionaire's son is a kid they're adequately curious about.

The millionaire's son has been heard quipping in the language of the British Navy: "flog you with my cat-o-nine-tails," and "codswollop, sir, I call it codswollop," and so forth. Though the Napoleonic era isn't the boys' preferred historical realm, this behavior suggests at least a susceptibility to their bodies of expertise.

Plus, as a new arrival to the neighborhood, the millionaire's son might not have had his opinion of the two of them poisoned by rumor.

Not yet.

Probably not yet.

At the very least, he's certain never to have *personally* witnessed them being humiliated in some street encounter, since they've removed themselves from that scene for a while now.

Their brand of aloof and sardonic authority might really cut some ice with him. It's worth a try.

So, one day at a neutral site, a backyard party of the Block Association where their mothers have each dragged them to endure an otherwise all-adult mingle, nothing to eat but squares of cheese and Triscuits, the first boy, the one who has become the proprietor of his dad's parlor and the magical shelf of board games, sidles up.

"You've come to the attention of a couple of us who gather on certain afternoons to, ahem, play at the pieces." He speaks with the lofty air of a king lowering a sword to the armored shoulder of some squire, designating him for knighthood. It occurs to him even as he does so that of course their moms have each dragged them there in precisely this hope, that they'll resort to making friends. But whatever.

The millionaire's son seems unflappable. His tone is instantly arch, in some kind of mid-Atlantic accent as if quoting from a movie, which perhaps he actually is:

"Excuse me, sir, but I don't think I've had the pleasure."

The board game proprietor and the millionaire's son exchange names. The proprietor mentions his friend and companion, the Cobble Hill kid.

The millionaire's son, in turn, drops C.'s name. Based on the evidence of his own block, he's thinking that that kid is some kind of gold standard, a human passport into Brooklyn childhood.

But no. It seems to displease his listener here. The proprietor of board games winces. *How unfortunate,* he appears to be thinking, *that the locals should have gotten to him first.* Though there is that kid they all wish to meet, the Slipper . . . but that is too esoteric a wish, and he doesn't even ask.

Instead, the proprietor of board games says, "That kind of company is fine, so far as it goes. He'd hardly have the patience for our type of pursuit, which combines a fascination with authentic military history with a ghoulish appetite for carnage."

"Cool." He gives a shrug of pleasure, as if sliding into a fitting new costume.

"Maybe some afternoon you'd like to pay a visit, and enter the lair of imagination." Left implicit in this is: enter the lair, and exit that vale of idiocy and humiliation which is the street.

A certain day of the week is proposed and accepted.

"If you have any existing combatant profiles, bring them along, of course. I warn you, most of ours are levelled up pretty far."

"Sure." The millionaire's son has no idea what the other one is talking about.

"I hear you're going to I.S. 293," says the proprietor of board games. "Tough draw. We both attend Packer Collegiate."

The millionaire's son shrugs. Again, he may know nothing of what's at stake here, but he's unbothered. "Ever try boosting?" he counters, a new conversational gambit.

"Eh, no." The proprietor of board games may or may not recognize this word, but the context is completely off, so he's hedged his bet.

"Local sport."

"I guess."

"With the help of some youths, I boosted a forty-ounce of malt liquor," the millionaire's son says, and pretends to shudder. "Vile concoction, but it made for an amusing pastime."

"Never tried it myself."

"Maybe I'll bring along some of Sparkle's Kahlúa." The millionaire's son tips his head to indicate his mother, who's currently enduring inspection by several other moms in the rear of the backyard, beneath the trellis. "That's a little more drinkable. She'll never notice it missing, probably think she's done some sleep-tippling."

"I . . . don't know about that," blurts the proprietor, unable to contrive anything better. This conversation has landed outside his *Snappy Answers to Stupid Questions* paradigm. The millionaire's son had seemed so much like a prospect, like one of them. Instead, he presents a blur of arrows pointing in random directions. The proprietor wonders what he's gotten himself and his friend into.

"Speaking of which, I have to go," says the millionaire's son. "Sparkle made me promise to tug on her sleeve. She has trouble extricating herself from parties."

"Oh, okay."

"See you at the Battle of Aqaba, muthafucka."

"*Lawrence of Arabia?*"

"*Seven Pillars of Wisdom,* Rabbit's favorite book. He read the entire thing to me when I was five."

With this maximally bewildering send-off, he's gone.

ON THE APPOINTED day, he's there at the top of the stoop, ringing the bell, no apparent Kahlúa in tow.

"So, this is the lair, then?" he says, coming in.

"Uh, yes." The proprietor recalls idiotically offering that word.

"I'm here for the historical throwdown, or whatever it's called."

Introductions are made. Or, really, formalized, since the two have each awkwardly shared the millionaire's son's company once or twice already, at adult occasions like the Association backyard. They lead him to the board game cabinet, the holy shelves. "We have a few recommendations, but see what grabs your eye."

The millionaire's son shrugs. "Nah, you pick." He drifts immediately to a semi-forbidden zone, the vanished father's music collection, in the built-in shelves that also house the stereo.

"What have we got here?"

"Just my dad's records."

"Let's see." He begins browsing, before objections can be raised. "Well, pretty much all hopeless garbage," he muses insolently. Then his hands pluck out an item of interest, a gatefold double LP, something psychedelically ugly, in hot pink. "But this, this, this is worth the whole collection. This is the motherfucking shit right here. *Trout Mask Replica.* Here we have ourselves a soundtrack."

The choice is especially irksome to the proprietor, since he's ninety-five percent sure this record isn't one of his father's, but in fact belonged to his cool older sister, and was filed here by his mother, in error.

The millionaire's son widens the gatefold and runs his finger through a residue there. He pulls a Sherlock Holmes face. "I'm pretty sure someone cleaned pot in this record."

Yes, definitely his sister's album.

"Highly appropriate, get it?" says the millionaire's son.

It's obvious he can't be prevented from opening the dust-layered turntable and playing the record. Still, the proprietor does his best to keep their eyes set on the larger goal. "If it's all the same to you, why don't we play Richtofen's War?"

"Biplanes? Far out."

"Of course, our aces have a great number of kills under their belt, so you may find them . . . formidable."

"What the hell, muthafuckas, let's give it a go."

The game is removed from the shelf; the board, with its wide hexagonal sky, unfurled. The dice made ready. The denizens of the parlor, the proprietor and his Cobble Hill friend, place their veteran planes in the field, far from the immediate action for now. They're playing the English side, while the millionaire's son has agreed to play as a German. It's World War I—they weren't Nazis, after all. Not yet.

The two patiently ease the millionaire's son up to an acceptable level of operation by bringing a few helpless non-player English aces into his airspace. In this way, they'll give him something to shoot down before the scheduled slaughter—their slaughter, that is, of the neophyte's plane.

The dice perform as they ought to. The millionaire's son obligingly, and boringly, mops up the non-player planes. He's got the hang of this thing, easy.

Now he rotates his plane and soars along the hexagonal grid, in the direction of the proprietor's plane.

"I'm attacking you."

"You're not quite in range."

"As soon as I am."

"I'm an Ace. With the bonuses I've accumulated you'll find my Sopwith Snipe is virtually impregnable."

The proprietor has selected the Snipe in order to disguise any sentimental lineage to Snoopy and his Sopwith Camel. Which is to say that the sentimental lineage is strong.

The millionaire's son grins. "Attack!" He counts off the hexes and pulls up directly behind the Snipe. They've lazily allowed him to drop to their altitude, certain that the insulation of their large Accumulated Damage Counters will prove sufficient against any fire.

"You probably don't want to come so close to my rear guns. If I'm given the chance to return fire, it could be costly."

The millionaire's son lowers his register. "Attack muthafucka attack."

"Okay, you can stop saying that now. Just roll. I'll defend."

The millionaire's son scoops up the die, and rolls an instantaneous natural twelve.

"Oh, that's awkward. At that range I've taken six points of damage. Impressive, I'll admit. Now prepare to accept return fire."

"What's that asterisk there?"

"Where?" The proprietor may or may not be playing dumb at this moment. He ought to know there's an asterisk on the natural twelve.

The millionaire's son pokes at the box, at the Target Damage Table.

The boy from Cobble Hill leans in helpfully. "He's right, you know. He gets to roll from the Critical Hit Table on a twelve at that range."

"Ah, right."

"I roll again, right?"

"You roll again."

Another twelve. What odds?

"What's it say?"

"TWELVE. PILOT KILLED. AIRCRAFT SHOT DOWN."

"Too bad, I win."

"He killed you."

"The dice," says the proprietor, gasping a little for breath. "You . . . picked them up . . . and then dropped them again . . ."

"No, I rolled them good."

"You—"

"Look, they're two feet from my hand, from where I let them go, for fuck's sake."

The proprietor turns white. He know this is true: the dice rolled. His protest is going nowhere.

The boy from Cobble Hill says "you don't understand."

"I think I understand pretty well. I shot down his plane, right?"

"No, but you don't understand. He's been building up that Ace for months."

"The bigger they are, the harder they fall."

The proprietor relocates his tongue. "I—you shouldn't have been able to do that. It was a *severely* lucky shot."

"Of course it was lucky. They're dice. Don't worry, you can pretend I didn't kill your guy, I won't tell anyone. I don't care."

The proprietor flips rather desperately through the rule book, one he already knows like the back of his hand. His sense of order has been disturbed by the exhibition of superhuman luck. Perhaps this is what's meant to occur in an encounter with a millionaire. Yet how can the sword-thrust of inequity be at once so piercing and so half-assed? Head bent, he fingers his fallen Sopwith Snipe, just a punched-out square of cardboard. Yet he'll build it back up, pad himself with kills, reacquire all the bonuses. He swears he will.

He dredges up a defiant phrase in quotation from one of his father's preferred movies, *Scaramouche*, *The Four Feathers*, *The Corsican Brothers*: "Sir, I demand satisfaction." Pronounced aloud, this sounds more words spoken by some outraged four-star general playing opposite Groucho Marx in *Duck Soup*.

"Satisfaction! I can't get no, though I try try try try try try try—"

"Seriously. Let's play again. I'll fly a virgin craft. You'll never get so lucky twice." Though earnest in the desire to reclaim the field of battle, the proprietor has already begun to suspect they'll never invite this kid back to the sacred parlor, even before the reply comes:

"The game is boring. Let's play some records and jump around. Where's the liquor cabinet?"

75.
Is the House for the Children?
(a questionnaire)

If the house isn't a house, but an apartment, or an apartment in a housing project—or if it is a house, but the house holds persons numbering six persons or more, if a family includes cousins or aunts or uncles, elderly parents—never mind. This questionnaire will not apply.

However. Should two parents occupy a brownstone from top to bottom, whether it is a three- or four-story brownstone, and they bring with them one child, or two, or even three or four, then this questionnaire may aid in clarification of a certain concern. It is a concern lurking undescribed in the minds of the children, those who visit one another's homes, whether just once or regularly. The millionaire's home raises this question, certainly. Also the parlor housing the Board Games of Empire.

The parlor—start there. Is it a showpiece, or an adult's sanctum? Is it out of bounds, or not, for the children? (The case of Board Games of Empire shows it may be a vacated sanctum.)

1. Entrances. Are both the entrances in use? The large doors at the top of the stoop and the gate tucked in beneath it? Is one designated for the children so that they may pass unseen? If so, is that a gift to them, or a requirement that they navigate exit and entry unguided? Will they be asked where they are going? Must they seek to be handed mugging money?

2. Has a bathroom been added on the floor where the children sleep, or must they use the stairs?

3. Are the children's rooms renovated or unrenovated, in relation to the overall trajectory of the house?

4. Can fucking or fighting be heard through the walls in the rooms where the children sleep?

5. Where are the drugs and alcohol kept?

6. Is the kitchen someone's alcoholic redoubt, to be approached on tiptoe? If so, is the house renovated so that the kitchen is in the rear of the parlor level, making it an unavoidable nerve center radiating through the house? Or is it tucked at the basement? (If so, question 2, concerning entrances, may be especially relevant.)

7. The backyard. Is it a showpiece, some fussy garden, or a space allowing play? If neither, if neglected or wild, is it accessible from a stair at the parlor level, or only through the basement? These are children who may need to be able to exit their home without exiting it to the street. Not every time. Not every damn time, to have that choice, the backyard or the street. The parents or the street. The backyard, it may be essential.

76.
Changing of the Guard
(one particular day in 1979)

A broad daylight crime:

A white man stands behind the counter of a shop, his back to his own cash register, talking with a teenager. A white kid. A Dean Street kid. The man is explaining to the teenager the duties of a clerk, enlisting him onto his staff.

Meanwhile, directly behind his back, another teenager—white, Dean Street kid—rings up a small sale on the register, but waits to slam the drawer until the customer has moved out of the shop, and he's alone there, apart from the store owner and the other teenager, the new recruit. His friend.

The teenager behind the counter, after being certain to catch the eye of his friend, ostentatiously pulls a dollar bill from the drawer and shoves it into the front pocket of his jeans.

His friend, the one talking with the shop's owner, has to try to suppress a laugh.

What the hell?

Remember the premature gentrification sandwich shop? Somehow, unlike the French restaurant, it's hanging in there. Remember the Dean Street kid who worked at the counter? The one enlisted to be the token teenager, the straight vermouth in the queer martini, the liaison to the Brownstoner families? The one who made the "meat sandwich?" Well, he's had it with the job. He quit.

Honestly, he gave notice very politely. He's just tired of spending all his after-school afternoons in that place. He's worked there nearly a year.

Given the low wage the owner pays, truth be told, he wouldn't have lasted nearly so long as he did if he hadn't been stealing from the till.

Not just helping himself to bagels and lox, not just taking home chunks of cheese which he promises his parents are "extra," but actually transferring cash money from the register to his pockets, on a daily basis. What's happening here today is just an example.

He'd started small, experimenting with sliding a few ones out of the drawer. Then waiting, breath held, to see if the discrepancy emerged in the till counting at the end of the day. Nope. Nobody said anything. The owner doesn't do any spot checks of the till at the end of the afternoon shift, when the evening staff comes in, so how would it ever be pinned to the kid even if they noticed a shortage?

Maybe things are just loose. Or he's above suspicion. So, he escalates. A five, a ten, a twenty.

Maybe this isn't wise, but who said he's wise? Only shrewd. Shrewd enough to begin to think he'd better start correcting for his habit. He develops a trick. Ring up sales but slip in the VOID key right after, then hit TENDER. Voilà. The drawer springs open, and in go the dollars, untabulated. Make the change on a sale that never happened. Since a lot of the customers are the Berk Trade School guys, who grab sodas and throw down a buck or two on their hurried breaks, it isn't difficult to pad the till. Then the extra ten or twenty he scoops out when he's alone at the register shouldn't be there in the first place. It's a discrepancy, an overage, and he's making it *right*. He's balancing the books!

It's this surplus folding money in the kid's pocket that's hard to kiss farewell. Still, he quits. He leaves in such high standing that the shop owner offers him a raise. Alas, no. He already awarded himself the raise. And now he's tired of the whole operation. He has to refuse. The shop keeper then asks him whether he's got a friend he'd recommend as a successor.

Why, come to think of it, maybe he does.

Though he'd never be able to foist it off on one of his friends if he didn't let them know that the job came with a little something extra.

This day is the day he's pulled his chosen successor in for an introduction to the boss. The changing of the guards.

The shop owner drones on. He's a man with a lot of procedures. This is a real grown-up job, lots of responsibilities. Sometimes, once you're up and running, you'll have to man the counter *alone*.

Another customer comes in, and the first kid reenacts the drama. Money goes into the till. Money goes into his pocket. He waves a five around, making a little comic dance behind the back of the shop owner.

How easy this is!

His friend struggles not to laugh.

Ka-*ching*!

77.
Ice Cream Truck, Known Con Artist
(1979, the same day, two blocks away)

Another broad daylight crime:

The Mr. Softee truck is parked on Dean near Bond. A Dean Street boy—a younger brother, a Black kid—has just purchased a vanilla cone. At that moment, a man shoots another man, on the sidewalk there.

The gun is small, likely a .22-caliber pistol. The man with the gun, a taller man, shoots the other repeatedly in the body as the shot man attempts to retreat up the stoop of a rooming house, the last remaining on Dean. The man shoots from the sidewalk until the gun is emptied, then walks to Bond and turns left. His victim sags in the doorway stoop's top, moaning.

Another man appears from inside, an older man. He helps the victim to his feet, putting one arm over his shoulder, and together they walk to Hospital of the Holy Family, on Dean and Hoyt.

The boy stands with the vanilla ice cream shaking in his hand.

The boy's friend, whose father is the landlord who permits the continued existence of the rooming house, to the consternation of many others on the block—never more so than on this day—later explains to the boy the victim was a "known con artist."

Whatever that means.

Same day, same hour, two blocks away.

78.
White Kid Who Attracts Cop Attention
(1978)

Let's say there is this one white boy who attracts cop attention. What's *that* about? the block wonders.

The parents of the Black kids, in particular, shake their heads.

How does the white boy distinguish himself this way? Well, let's say standing in the middle of the street practicing his flying nunchucks and blocking the progress of the Dean Street bus.

That'll do it.

He only blocks the bus for a half minute, probably, then steps aside and with a fake-Japanese bow permits it to pass. Then raps the back bumper with the nunchucks and shouts "Hai-aaaaaaaaaaaaa!"

Few minutes later the cruiser, a white-and-blue, comes down the block, stops in the middle. Traffic so light that day anyone wanting passage can just back up all the way to Bond Street and work their way around, fuck 'em.

Kid with nunchucks standing in plain fear but also a kind of frozen admiration for what he's conjured up, an exhibition for the sleepy street, the rooming house window watchers, the Puerto Ricans on the crates in front of Rodriguez's store.

His Black friend melting onto a nearby stoop and in no provable way enmeshed or even particularly interested.

The cops not lighting their flasher or even getting out of the car with any alacrity or atmosphere of purpose. They just waltz over, smirking at the sky. One puts out his hand and the kid surrenders the mail order nunchucks.

Cop puts it over his knee, recalling the famous wanton cop-destruction of the Black kids' skateboards, for anyone familiar with the legend. Cop snaps the nunchucks apart and, sure enough, tosses them into the gutter.

Damn, maybe the same cop!

But this is a white kid!

Well, he is that one, the rare white kid who cannot summon the slightest deference.

"Don't be like that," says the cop.

"Like what?" says the kid.

Cop spreads his hands, looks up at the wall of houses, the heads sticking out of windows.

"Like this," says the cop. "You can do better."

What's he mean?

Don't be like your block?

Everyone shaking their heads. White kid drawing attention from the cops. His parents could march to the precinct and demand an explanation, so you might think. Yet seemingly some higher law of kid brandishing weaponry is in play here.

Of course, it leads nowhere. Cops drive off. Good thing they didn't frisk him and find the gravity knife.

Leads to nothing with the cops. Like it never happened.

Possibly caught the attention of a burgeoning nemesis, however.

79.
Being a Nemesis
(subliminal/1978)

What would it be like to be a nemesis? Would you know you were one? On what day does a kid decide to make himself another's worst nightmare?

No one would ever think about it like this.

The nemesis arises from a murk of impulse and injury. Of indignation. There is a world into which one is born and that world, this world, just isn't right. The not-rightness is everywhere and nowhere at once. Obvious and denied.

This wrongness carries an urgency, a call to action. If you're not going to be at the world's mercy, you'll have to bend it to your will.

The whole thing?

Impossible.

One glaring example? One little piece of the world?

A little figment, in the form of two legs, two arms, the outline of a human? A being slugging along in helpless panic on the sidewalk, or ought to be? And you can make him?

That might work.

In a way, it resembles being Batman. Not Commissioner Gordon's upright helper, the supercop. The other Batman, the neurotic avenger. The Batman no one understands, the Batman who is driven.

If you are Batman, you dwell by definition in a world of enemies. Among all these enemies, there is one who cackles at you on a special frequency. That's your Joker. You need to go and get him.

Not that any nemesis likely enunciated such stuff.

It's too existential. Too abstract. Even with the Batman comparison.

Maybe we'd better try a local example.

LET'S SAY YOUR name is Little Man.

Let's say they call you that because you're a little man, but you're not really little, man, you're big. You got left back once, a situation everyone just has to deal with. You never said *I'm little and I want to be big, leave me back.* You did not make the problem. You did not make the world. You merely move within it.

The problem of big you is one you can lend, at arbitrary moments, to another person in your vicinity. This is in no way restricted to the category of the white boy. Though few other persons give forth with quarters or sometimes even dollar bills the way the white boy tends to.

Too easy.

Alternately, at given impulsive moments you might lend the problem of your person to that pretty Black girl with her hair in two bunches. She gives forth with a satisfying wide-eyed, grim-set look. It is a twofer, since you are passing along the problem of yourself by implication to her fiercely protective younger brother.

Later that day, the brother will look at you with his volcanic look and you can say "what?"

And brush your big shoulder past.

Too easy.

You can lend the big problem of yourself passingly to the two little Puerto Rican brothers working on skully caps on the pavement. These, they are flicked like fleas from the path of your walking.

Too easy.

You are haphazard, you fall like weather. In that sense, you are not unfair.

THEN LET'S SUPPOSE that you, Little Man, find yourself confronted one day with an unsavory incongruence, in the form of a white boy.

The boy seems to Little Man to walk without proper knowledge of the sidewalk or the gutter or the street.

He doesn't cross the street at the sight of you or of groupings. He doesn't tiptoe.

Surrounding this kid is a weird field or aspect or regard. You keep hearing words like "millionaire" and "nunchucks" and "gravity knife."

He disappears and reappears in new costumes, with sudden friends, at times sings loudly in the open street.

Seeing him, it is like getting something in your eye.

You rub your eye, but that only makes it worse.

And this white kid, he's miraculously under the protectorate of C., who plays both sides, the Black kid who is untouchable and un-questionable, who always wins, who is everywhere at once.

But not really. He can't be *everywhere* at once.

And without even totally deciding to care, Little Man discovers that he is waiting for the moment when he finds the new white kid alone on a street suddenly vacant, with his Black protector occupied elsewhere, so that he can introduce him to important notions like the gutter.

And there it is! Little Man has discovered how it feels to be a nemesis, even before he has altered his trajectory in any way visible from the outside.

He sees how it can become personal.

He has acquired a darling.

THE FIRST TIME, it is played on terms not of Little Man's devising. He thinks he can just wing it.

"Hey, wait up a minute."

"Whasss goin' on, *muthafucka?*" The white boy says this merrily, like he's quoting something he doesn't understand. That's it, in fact. He's quoting something he doesn't understand. Little Man will have to make him understand. He will have to deny him this manner of speech.

"You don't call me that."

"Call you what?"

Little Man shakes his head, changes course. "I heard you got a gravity knife."

"That is correct, sir!"

"Let me see it."

"I don't happen to be carrying it on my person."

"Bring it out next time with you. Or I could check it at your house."

"No thanks."

"Why you showing it to everyone but me? You even know who I am?"

"I haven't the foggiest."

"I might have to mess you up."

"No thanks! Cheerio, old chap!"

With that, the white boy is gone. It is like their words are signals issued from divergent planets orbiting in a cosmic fog.

Little Man is going to figure out how to land on that other world. A shock, to realize he needs to plan ahead.

Next time, things will be different.

No Cheerios, no Lucky Charms, no Frosted Flakes.

THE PLAN TURNS out to consist of no more than the intention to have a plan. One afternoon, Little Man is seated on the stoop of the abandoned house, pushing some dog shit around with a length of stick. The sky is low, and the clocks are all stopped, and the brooding atmospherics of his presence seem to have cleared out a hole in the world. Then into that hole wanders the exact kid he is waiting for. Little Man can only believe it is a measure of the powers of being a nemesis, the way this happens. The whole problem of the world has shrunk down to the story of you and your darling.

"Come check this out," Little Man says lazily. Language is not the instrument he has in mind, but neither is it a hindrance any longer.

"What?"

"End of this stick, check it out."

The white boy leans in obligingly. Little Man is still back on his elbows, making a genial figure eight with the shitty stick, keeping it entrancing and hard to figure out at the same time. Maybe it is all, all, too easy. "See that?"

"What?"

"Shit," says Little Man, exactly as he paints with the stick on the face of his intended one. The moment is lavish. Nothing is hurried.

Little Man applies the dog shit to both cheeks and the chin before his astonished customer is revolted by the fresh scent and at last revolts, springs backward. Dropping his painting stick, Little Man now feels a wisdom flood into him that we might call the nemesis paradox, exemplified. If you can't bring the face to the gutter, bring the gutter to the face.

"Now you go home, wash that shit off."

Little Man shapes these words with almost compassion, but also a jurisdictional flatness, like he is a cop of this particular scene and situation. It is crafty to issue a command to do that which the commanded person is already irreversibly bound to do. No reply is required.

"You live cross the street?"

The white boy nods.

"That's what you do then, cross the street, any time you see me."

The white boy nods. Crossing, he is almost hit by the Dean Street bus.

80.
Having a Nemesis, Slight Return
(1978)

One thing a nemesis may be reasonably certain of: a target will weigh the matter of giving a report, whether to companions (if they have companions) or to parents, most carefully.

Shame is the glue binding this universe together.

A report is unlikely. Doesn't matter, though.

Because any attempt at report is likely to come out gnarled, obfuscated, rendered nearly useless. It just won't work.

Overreaction. Under reaction. Incompetent reaction. Hand wringing. More shame. These, Little Man relies upon, without even troubling to envision.

If, once in a blue moon, a Brownstoner parent has become outraged, and charged into the streets looking for their child's nemesis,
this has always gone fabulously awry.

It plays into the hands of the street.

The Brownstoner kid in question is marked forever by this terrible
decision.

All of this, Little Man relies upon, without bothering to envision
it, to work it out in his head. He just knows.

WHAT LITTLE MAN could hardly begin to envision:

His target, locked in the upstairs bathroom with the shower running for what seems to his parents to be an hour, to the point that
Sparkle and Rabbit cross the magic threshold, out of their realm,
the modernistically renovated basement-and-parlor duplex, into the
scantly renovated, more vintage floors above, where Sparkle and Rabbit never ordinarily go.

Little Man's vision would surely already fail here, at the notion of
a child possessing two floors of a brownstone for himself.

He might also have difficulty picturing the two outside the bathroom's locked door, beckoning to their child, while the father absent-
mindedly holds a drained martini glass and the mother lights and
half smokes a series of cigarettes.

Little Man would be even less likely to guess at the scene when
the door finally opens.

"Fix me one of your famous brandy old-fashioneds, Sparkle, would
you?" says the boy, in a voice meant to satirize his father's. His face,
which has been on the losing side of a war with a washcloth, appears
like a line drawing of scorn, one with red crayon scribbles covering the
cheeks and chin.

"Oh, Wonderbaby, what's the matter?"

Yes. Wonderbaby.

"Nothing, Sparkle, if you'll simply do as you're told and fix me an
old-fashioned. Everyone around here seems to have a drink in their
hand except me."

"You have other things."

"Fine, I'll go fix one for myself. I have the feeling sometimes you don't take me entirely seriously, Sparklebabydarling." He raises his hand and walks past his parents, to the staircase to his fourth-story lair.

"Now, now."

"A hair of the dog that bit me. A gin rummy ham on rye boilermaker straight, no chaser, Sparklebabypussypie." He climbs the stair halfway while delivering the words, not looking back.

"Now, now."

"Shaken not stirred. I'm telling you baby, it's the stuff that dreams are made of. I won't play the sap for you. When you're slapped, you'll take it and like it."

"Now, now."

Out of their sight now, he yells from above. "SHAKEN NOT STIRRED, MUTHAFUCKA!"

81.
Screamer and the Tree
(1981)

More comic relief:

He's old enough at fourteen, the Dean Street boy in this story, to begin earning his small allowance. His dad has sent him out front with a small bucket of foul-smelling wound paint, to treat the damaged limbs of the fledgling tree in front. The tree has been maliciously stripped by some passing tree vandals in the night, one of its lower limbs gone completely.

The kitchen stepladder his father has provided reaches only so far. The boy uses it to clamber onto the top of the spiked iron cage, perhaps five feet tall, that has been forged around the tree for protection—insufficient protection, it seems.

The daylight is dazzling, the street serene, and the boy is lost in the quiet epic of his own climb, the puzzling view from up here, another angle on Dean Street. Positive that he's alone, he's jolted by a voice from the sidewalk, a simple question.

"What are you doing?"

He glances down, and it is the Screamer, standing directly below, the first time he has ever seen her out of her house, the first time he has ever heard her speak in anything but a scream, and then he is toppling, the can of wound paint flipping backward from his hand. Even as he falls, he thinks it: *The Screamer is talking to me, holy shit!* His jeans cuff snags on the spike. He ends flipped backward across the stepladder, attached by one pants leg to the iron spike, his head just inches from the sidewalk. *He could have died* is the thinking here, but also *the Screamer is standing right there*. In fact, she steps nearer and leans over, her face inverted to his.

"Are you okay?"

82.
Quarters, Part 3
(1978)

Again, as if materialized here and there, flickering into existence, we find them. Now in Columbus Park, the two with the mutilated coins in their pockets. Empty park benches stretching the length of the massive municipal courthouse, pigeons predictably doing their encaustic work on the statue of Henry Ward Beecher. They traversed the distance between Degraw Street and this place in total mental absentia. Who knows how they managed it? Only that nothing happened on the way. Only that they're here now.

They examine a number of the clumsy graffiti tags on the base of the statue and the backs of the park benches, including their own, from former visits. They should have brought a marker, it feels now. Adding a tag or two, or writing TOY over someone else, a defining task in an indefinite world.

A single bum, asleep on the bench, hands folded in his lap. Old school, a squashed hat pulled low to his whiskers. He's getting his nap on.

"Dare you to knock off his hat."

"You do it."

"I dared you."

"Fuck you, you do it."

One finds an empty glass bottle in the bushes. He has a theory he's been working on, glass only absorbs a certain number of shocks, even the gentlest, before shattering. Lacking the word "cumulative," the principle takes astoundingly long to explain.

"Never mind, watch."

They sit together on one of the park's stone embankments and he begins tap-tap-tapping the empty, a gentle ringing. Nothing.

"It's not happening."

"Wait, just wait."

The tapping is like water dripping on a rock, like their days. The bottle's unbroken.

"You're hitting it harder just to prove the point."

"I'm speeding up. I'm hitting the same amount."

"No, it's harder."

The bottle's intact. Then, at the exact moment that his companion's vigilance wavers—always worth a scan, to see what might be coming—he strikes a firmer blow. The bottle cracks. Nothing explosively satisfying, but the thicker bottom falls off at their feet.

"See, it built up! Works every time."

"You hit harder."

"I weakened it."

"The other times didn't do anything. You just finally hit hard enough."

"I'll show you again."

"I don't care." His surveillance has proved their surroundings innocuous. This is possibly a disappointment, today. He fishes in his tube sock, brings out the sweat-misty dollar, curled to the circumference of his ankle.

"I'll give it to you if you knock off that guy's hat."

Afternoons, a lifetime. World, exhausting.

83.
Color TV
(1977)

Another story with a quarter in it. This one's not sawed in half.

White girl, Catholic school girl, thirteen, she's wandering alone at the parish fair. They hold it in the churchyard with spillover in the empty lot where the church usually rents parking to the suckers with a car too nice to park on the street around there. They lock it and chain it at night and the parish superintendent goes around a lot and nobody breaks in and steals the radios.

Somehow they've convinced all but a couple of the car parkers to clear out for the parish fair, years later she'll remember it this way, Francesca Dallaglio leaning on one of the two cars still parked there, under the ailanthus canopy, smoking a cigarette—thirteen or fourteen and smoking in front of the whole parish!—with its tip glowing in what the girl's just now noticing is the dark. Her real friends have gone home, one after the next, but she's lingering, not sure why. She'll always associate the occurrence with the parking lot instead of the churchyard, as if that site made it happen, all that energy of unstolen car radios. Francesca Dallaglio soaking up the ambient criminal potential lying around.

What can be said about Francesca Dallaglio? Is she the girl's friend or her tormentor? She was scary in kindergarten. She'll be scary on Instagram when the girl finds her a million years after, practically bursting out of an Islanders jersey, shocking teeth and same ferocious eyes drilling holes in whatever crosses their path. Now she's the sole person the girl's age. The only other girl, anyway, still at the parish fair. There might be some boys. Or some other girls, how to know, once Francesca had enclosed you in her cigarette fume trap zone of attention? Her eyes are like a prison tower spotlight in an escape film. She sees the quarter in the girl's hands. Sees it just as the girl is about to use it to buy another Italian ice, her second of the evening, just using up the free spending money before she walks home.

"What the fuck are you doing?"

"What?"

Francesca says it again, and then specifies, makes a command. "Put it on the roulette wheel."

A casino-themed parish fair, crazy, but the girl takes it for granted at the time, it's her world.

They're about to spin it again, the big final spin, and the final prize of the night is a color television. The girl hadn't even realized kids were allowed to try—they had a couple of earlier rounds for kids only, gave away a few stuffed animals and 64-color Crayola sets, crap nobody wants. Then there was one for a dinner for two at Parma Gianni's, a candle-in-the-wine-bottle joint, what kid would even want to try?

"Go on, put it down." Francesca's steered her to the verge, a place at the spinning wheel, simply by the ominous and insinuating force of her personality. "G'wan. Number 28, that's lucky."

Whatever. There's a crazy intoxication to this act of obedience. The girl steps forward and catches the eye of Brother Leo, who nods benevolently. He means to give her courage to step forward among the adults thronged there, to place her bet. He won't stop the turning until she's made her selection. He's surely not observed the connection between her and the other girl in the shadows, now grinding her cigarette butt into the lot's pavement.

Number 28 it is. Why obedience if not full obedience? She places the quarter.

Wins.

Brother Leo speaks the girl's name, grinning. "A color television, what a blessing for your family!" A murmur of congratulations, a ripple of disappointment in those around the wheel, even if they've collected some other trinket. The television was the prize. And now the night's fallen and finished and the fair's dispersing. The men to the bar on Union Street, the secret drinkers home to their secret drinks.

Tomorrow this lot will be full of cars again, and chained. The girls will be back in school.

"How—" The question takes a moment to discover itself. Though the panic, the fear, is somehow already hot behind the unformed words. "How am I going to get it home?"

"You wouldn't collect it tonight in any case," says Brother Leo. "It's to be picked up tomorrow. Bring your father."

The fear and panic is in the form of the girl shadowing her, finding her now to whisper it, "That's my fucking TV."

"What?" The girl knows before she knows. Of course, this claim would come. Of course. Though there is nothing to do but contest it with feeble logic.

"I told you to put it there. I said the number."

"It was my quarter. Brother Leo saw."

"He doesn't know. Tell him it's mine."

The girl is spared the prospect of this decision, at least for the moment: Brother Leo, the other Franciscans, are already gone from the yard. A few nuns scurry here and there, working to fold the long tables into the parish basement. Suddenly exactly zero other kids, friends, the girl's own teachers. The parish fair is a play that closes on opening night, and the stage is being struck.

"They said I won it."

"They didn't see. You were gonna eat a fucking icy before I told you."

The cooling dark, the emptying pavement, mosquitoes moving in, all's misery here. The girl sets her body to the task of the three long blocks, the journey to the safe haven of her house, a distance which suddenly stretches like a desert horizon. Francesca Dallaglio's right on her back as they exit the lot. "It's my fucking TV."

"I don't—" The girl's barely auditioned the weird windfall. The only set in her house is the giant ancient cabinet black-and-white opposite the plasticized couch. A piece of furniture. Would her parents have let her keep the small color set in her own bedroom? She's now moving it to the past-tense propositional. The color TV exists on a reality track Francesca Dallaglio's shoving her from, like shoving someone off a subway platform.

(Shove you off a subway platform? Where'd that come from? Sweet Christ, how terrifying it would be to run into Francesca Dallaglio on the subway.)

Garfield Place is empty. Under shadow cover of the London plane trees and a busted streetlamp, Francesca's free to scream it, from a point maybe only inches behind your ear, if you turned to check: "THE FUCKING TV IS MINE!!!!!" *Eternal God in whom mercy is endless and the treasury of compassion inexhaustible look kindly upon us and increase Your mercy that in difficult moments we might not despair nor become despondent.* What's Francesca Dallaglio capable of? Or rather, what isn't she? "THE FUCKING TV IS MINE TURN AROUND AND TELL ME YOU KNOW!"

"What am I supposed to do?"

Francesca Dallaglio drops to a low intimidating hiss. The curdling voice, the death-call, that must be for her a wholly voluntary mode. "Pick it up with my brother, tell them he's helping you."

Intimidation fountains from Francesca Dallaglio like rain from a storm gutter. She has five brothers, all older. Is that what makes a monster? The girl has never met them, only perhaps seen them in the fog of brutes amassed routinely around Sal's Pizza on 7th and Union. Now, she is supposed to appear in tandem with one, before the nuns and brothers, to collect Francesca Dallaglio's fucking color TV. What is it to have Francesca Dallaglio in one's life, in one's classroom? Do they ever consider the brutal price of leaving a student back to repeat a grade, a price exacted on someone else entirely unresponsible for what has enraged them?

But perhaps everyone has a tormentor, a nemesis. Someone unaccountable to the ordinary law of childhood, of Brooklyn, of school or the street. Let alone answerable to the Franciscan Brotherhood. Fortune or misfortune is only in what particular outline that tormentor will present. Francesca Dallaglio presents a startling frontality. Her demand is simple. It is merely left to the girl to address it.

"Fucking look at me and tell me you know it's my fucking TV." Francesca Dallaglio employs the low insinuating tone, though the words might as well be screamed, for there is no one to hear, no one but the girl.

"What will I tell my parents?"

"NOTHING! DON'T TELL THEM FUCKING NOTHING!"

The girl hears herself say, as though from within in a trance, "where do I meet him?"

84.
The State of Our Inquiry
(now)

It may be time to take measure of the state of our inquiry.

Once you start compiling crime it's hard to stop.

Mostly Brooklyn, sure. Boerum Hill, Cobble Hill, Park Slope. Though many of these encounters could transpire elsewhere. Bay Ridge. Maybe Sunnyside Queens, maybe Finglas in Dublin. Certain arrondissements in Paris?

We risk growing confused. We should reduce the orbit. Let distant places make their own account. We should probably stick to Dean Street, to boys.

Yet, does the story about Francesca Dallaglio suggest everyone has their nemesis, their tormentor? Some universal principle, whether between two Catholic schoolgirls or—whomever?

Is *that* the dance?

85.
Everybody Knows
About the Subway
(in the days before certainties are drowned)

Someone mentioned *pushed off a platform*?

Sure. Everybody knows about that girl. She was a violinist, went to Music & Art High School, up on St. Nicholas Avenue. They had to sew her hand back on.

We promised to address the subway. What are the things everybody knows about the subway?

That it is another world running beneath this one. That it is a neighborhood of a thousand miles, a neighborhood belonging to no one and everyone. It has its own police. The laws in the subway are actually different than aboveground.

Not actually everybody knows that it was created by the mad scientist Doctor Fiorello LaFrankenstein, who stitched together the BMT, the IRT, the IND and several other renegade outfits whose names were lost or suppressed in the experimental surgery.

For that reason, trains run on top of trains. For that reason, the system employs two different gauges of track. You can use the tunnels now connecting what used to be rival stations as a system of divination.

For that reason, there are ghost stations.

For that reason, there are tunnels to nowhere.

There are underground people who live in the tunnels who never come into the light.

About thirty or forty people touch the third rail per year. No one has ever survived. A graffiti artist tried spraying the third rail and the shock fried off his whole arm.

Everybody knows that you're not a real graffiti artist unless you steal your materials.

Everybody knows that the highest prize in a graffiti writer's arsenal is a train conductor's key.

It opens every door and every gate and neutralizes every alarm in the entire system.

The Authority only issues the key to conductors and each one is personally marked, like a dog tag. The conductor is required to fight to the death to keep it from theft.

So, clearly, if you possess a conductor's key, it is because you murdered a conductor in hand-to-hand. A kid who owns one is basically a god.

The Taking of Pelham One Two Three really happened.

An actual gang mistook the actors playing *The Warriors* for an actual gang. They killed a member of the crew because they thought they were transit police trying to bust a throwdown.

One of the actors actually killed the gang's top man and became the new leader.

You can buy slugs on Canal Street for five cents that are the same size as a token.

The tilework decorations were all created by one man, a mad genius, the Picasso of mosaic, and it is a graffiti crime to disrespect his work. The beaver mosaic at Astor Place is a joke about his wife's pussy. A Picasso is allowed such things. Right?

Everybody knows about the kid who stole the A train and took it on a joyride. He ran it better than the MTA, he hit all the lights on time, and nobody would have known the difference if he didn't get caught.

The MTA banned him for life, and he committed suicide by throwing himself on the tracks.

These are just a few things everybody knows about the subway.

86.
Looping
(1985)

Now that we are underground, let's stay a while.

Maybe it is the truth that the first realm you graduate to from your own neighborhood isn't another overground quadrant but the trains, the network, the system.

The realm of the Guardian Angels, that street gang that pulled a fast one, turned themselves inside-out into a brazen vigilante army, with their red bomber jackets and their own celebrity power couple, Curtis Sliwa and Lisa Evers. Lisa Evers is a martial arts champion and could most likely kick Sliwa's ass.

Might like to see that.

But trust me you really don't want to witness these people in action. You really don't need that in your day. Pick another car of the train, run up the platform to find one free of Angels if you have to.

The system is the realm now of *urggghhhhh must we really give him his name* Bernhard Goetz, that hideous smug nerd Charles Bronson.

The system sure is nervous.

In this realm you are confronted with the tags of your friends and enemies. Some of them fresh, still tacky, practically still dripping, so you're informed they made a bombing run without you. You're no longer eligible for such things. The day you signed up for that temp agency job you were ejected from the lively dangerous life of childhood, into the Morlockian realm of Manhattan drudgery. The great city's secret isn't secret at all: the misery of its day workers. The unromance of life as a cog in this engine of crap. Stealing your twenty-minute lunch break sitting perched on a dirty ledge in a high wind, eating a stale Gabila's knish from a hot dog cart, dripping mustard on your loafers.

Who convinced you to buy loafers? All the middle-aged men in the offices wear Nikes anyhow.

Stained suit pants and Nikes, look away.

Maybe the tags are fresh, or maybe some other days they pull a train car out of storage, and you see tags from five years ago, friends and enemies forgotten, dead affiliations, old styles of tagging, maybe you see your own tag. Old styles? Non-styles. *Wow, what a toy I was.*

Or you see the mom of some kid you babysat for, a mom you had a crazy thing for and now here's the fantasy come true, right? You're an official grown-up, you happen to meet, not-strangers on a train. You almost speak up to say hello, but she wouldn't recognize you and anyhow she's not looking so terrific just now. She looks like she's on drugs, actually.

Maybe subway means sublimation, but what's the good of a realm of sublimation if you have to bodily descend into its roiling evidence every single day to draw a paycheck?

Take for instance this one Dean Street boy—guy, man, whatever—

who never totally left the neighborhood. He took a few classes at Pace, got hooked up by a friend with this agency Manpower and now he's a permanent temp. Can we say a temporarily permanent temp? He's what he vowed he'd avoid every day through high school, a subway commuter.

The point is, this guy has got a long-standing subway practice that has now become an addiction, or an obsession: looping. He's a looper.

Looping is the name for when you change cars at every stop.

He learned to do looping as a teenager, coming home late from CBGB or some party, divided from Manhattan friends, riding those lonely A trains.

Change subway cars at every stop and no one knows where you're going. No one can follow, or at least you've made it a major pain in the ass. No one knows which stop is your actual stop.

You wander the length of one car, to the far door. Then jump out at the stop, and pop into the nearest door of the next car. Easy.

One train car per stop. As if you're looking for someone. Though actually, you're *avoiding* someone. You just don't know who.

Equivalent of crossing the street when you see someone far off on the pavement. Except if you do it on every street you walk down, no matter who's coming or if no one is. Soon you're that crazy diagonal jaywalker guy.

You can justify your looping all kinds of ways. Maybe you've become a ninja of the platform exits, you know which train car pulls up right at the stairwell you'll want to use. So, loop your way to the juncture, save a few steps, a few more seconds for a cigarette break before entering the office.

Sure, that's why you do it.

Or maybe you really think one car's going to be less crowded or smell better. You're looking for that golden chariot.

Uh-huh.

Fear, baby.

If you run, something really does follow. Keep running, you never need know what it is.

You can be the secret Curtis Sliwa or Bernhard Goetz of looping. Jostle your way through the packed cars, aggravating everyone. Loop out of the empty ones, because if you stay in an empty one it might not be empty at the next stop and then if you loop it appears you're avoiding that one particular person or persons who boarded. Go ahead, scratch that itch, loop it out, no one's doing more than shaking their heads at your idiocy. You're not going to make the cover of the *Daily News*.

Looping is no crime.

87.
Between-Car Platform Entry
(earlier)

Less furtive than looping is to move from one car to another through the doors.

Even more brazen is riding between cars, feeling the tunnel breeze.

We can fall with relief on a definite subway crime! There's even a sticker on every door, reading RIDING OR MOVING BETWEEN CARS IS PROHIBITED. Enough said.

To do it anyway is a given in this time.

The Permanent Temp kid, when he used to ride to high school in rush hour, was one who rode between. Commune with the raw tunnels while taking relief from a crowded rush-hour car. The wall of faces as you pull onto a platform, knowing not one of them is going to plow into your space when the doors open, because you're nowhere near the doors—you're between the cars.

Bound for Glory!

Part and parcel of the graffiti life. Hacking the system.

A more particular variant: never move through a train door at all. Instead, board the train from the platform directly to the space between. Stunt entry.

It takes a second to click free the gate that blocks passage. A little turn of the wrist to disengage the latch. Courage to leap the interval of free space, track visible beneath you, while holding the gate free with one hand.

Then you click it shut behind you. Voilà. Like a doorman at a fancy building.

There's no halfway. You either do it or you don't, like jumping out with a parachute. (The key to mostly anything is pretending your first time isn't.)

People die that way, sure.

Guy got his head cut off.

But it beats being Goetz.

88.
Science Fiction Paperback
(1980)

Another stupid day on the subway. By this year, so many of the kids from the neighborhood are suddenly riding out to attend high schools elsewhere, Music & Art and Art & Design, Hunter College, Dewey, Murrow. There's a kind of liberation in it, taking the subway every day at rush hour. The way the commuters not only protect you in their numbers but seem to become a kind of numbed canvas for your acting out, your lunacy.

Certain white boys who'd never misbehave in Brooklyn are feral the moment the A train hits Fulton Street, rising out of the tunnel from Brooklyn. But since they're nerds, dorks, children of the dance, they're feral *dingbats*. Few of these, for instance, have practiced graffiti in real graffiti circumstances. If they've braved carrying a marker in their pockets, it's a Sharpie. If they now whip it out, it's to draw a dick-and-balls or an anarchist *A* on a cardboard advertisement, not an actual tag on the metal surfaces of the train. Some of them have punk haircuts—*slightly* punk haircuts. Nothing that would draw too much attention on the street.

This day, one of them spots a familiar figure. In fact, a Dean Street boy. The spoiled boy.

He's squeezed between two commuters, his head sunk in a science fiction paperback. Garishly colored, the name of the author something like EDWIN L. ZARUPERNOFF just because they all have names like that. The book stands in contrast to the gray incognito of the spoiled boy's aspect. Like he's trying to be taken for a mole or a rat. Like he's trying to investigate the cheap paper's texture with his nose.

This one, this Dean Street boy has regressed, that's for sure. After the brief United Nations period, when all the younger kids flocked to his stoop.

He'd then disappeared from view for years, so far as these older boys can tell.

Something broke the spoiled boy, apparently.

And yet, he got into Music & Art by playing the tuba, practically the only one willing to drag such a thing up to Harlem for the audition, and they let him in on his willingness to puff and paw at the instrument, never mind his lack of talent.

And yet, his mother let him loose from her protectorate, to ride the A train every day to Harlem.

The sight of him disgusts these proto punks. He's too close to their own realm, their own ilk. An emblem of how they fear they once appeared, to the city, to the street.

And so now one of them dances up close to the spoiled boy in the car of the A train and says, "Hey, Evelyn Wood, slow down the *reading dynamics* a minute."

The spoiled boy makes only a sort of grunting or purring sound. He looks to be about twenty pages from the finale.

"Gripping tales, huh? Can't unpeel your eyeballs?"

And then, impulsively, the proto punk seizes the paperback, lifting it between thumb and forefinger as if handling something rank, a soiled diaper.

The commuters on either side sink deeper into their enchanted cones of subway silence. The train squeaks and shudders, vaulting 59th Street to 125th.

"Quit," mumbles the spoiled boy.

Having seized the icky prize, the proto punk has no idea what to do except escalate. The train's long breeze window is tipped open, the gap just big enough. The proto punk flips the paperback up and over the window's lip. The black rushing tunnel wind snags it, and the book is gone. It couldn't be more decisively gone if it had been beamed back up to the planet depicted on the cover.

The spoiled boy blinks up, his mouth fallen open, seeking to conjugate this event. His calf-lids raise to make hopeless appeal for just an instant, then lower.

"I'm sparing you," says the proto punk. "I read that book; the ending sucks."

Yes, in the great absolving democracy of the subway tunnel, nerd can bully nerd. A breakthrough!

89.
The Frotteur on the Shuttle
(1981)

Last subway story. Three girls whose commute together to Hunter College High School includes the 42nd Street shuttle. The shuttle is a toy train, like Mr. Rogers's trolley. It only runs between Times Square and Grand Central, back and forth all day. Always crowded.

There, the girls are dealing with a thing they don't even know the name for. Guy rides the train and looks for girls to rub up against. You can feel his dick through his pants.

Really, just one stop, the crowds pack in, the shuttle always sits there humming until it's full. Crazy how the second the doors close, he seems to find them every time. What does he do, ride the shuttle all day?

Who knows if the first time really is the first time? Maybe your thigh had to encounter it a few times to actually decipher the sensation. When she figures it out for certain, she freezes. Doors open, she looks down red-faced and stumbles out of the train with the pouring crowd.

Second time, she turns. Examines faces. The likely possessor of the offending member is bland. More young than old. Glasses of course. Prematurely thinning hair, but still productive of white flakes. By god, he might really be Goetz! But no. His hair is dark. Dark-haired dork. Her face is red again, but he's looking away too.

Third time she shouts, "quit, you perv!" The end result's not so different. There's barely a rustle of reaction before they pull into Grand Central. The shuttle's the shuttle, after all, everyone hell-bent for their destinations. Not a train anyone's admitting they *rode*. You just get through it. The guy who rides it all day. He's somebody else's problem. The three girls filter upstairs, toward their school. Just an ordinary morning.

"He got you today, huh," says one of her friends.

And then they all start laughing. It's not funny, but it's funny. "He's everyone's boyfriend eventually."

They're going to make it funny by force of will, because it's their city, because it's their lives. They're supposed to be punk rock, that's the impression they're at least trying to make on each other and themselves.

"Watch the closing doors, if the train comes to a sudden stop, be sure to grab onto the pole."

Knowing her face is still red, she nevertheless keeps the ball rolling with a line of her own. "That guy has a fear of commitment. That's why he picked the train that only goes one stop."

Next time the three see him, they pick him out ahead of time. They scramble for a different door, but of the same car. The crowd's protectively thick. He'd never be able to move through it to their end. The girls want not only to keep an eye on this guy, but let him know they've made him. They glare through the crowd. He ignores it, if he sees them at all. They start making faces. Her friend, bolder than she is, licks her lips, rolls her eyes in mock ecstasy. Nothing. He's dull, vacant, unworthy. Or maybe intent. Perhaps chafing steadily against some other butt even now. There's nothing to give it away, no ripple of disturbance. Maybe he's got a victim who likes it, who knows?

What, were they some disappointment to him perhaps?

Fuck that dude and the dandruff he rode in on.

So, next time they get into the door nearest. What's he going to do, call the cops? They don't hang by the door, but get into the middle, almost mobbing the dick-guy where he stands reaching over to the lengthwise handrail, pretending distraction, pretending to be going somewhere. Does he even recognize them?

"Catch his eyes," whispers the bold one. "I'll touch his ass."

"No way." She feels like he's overheard them already.

"Yes. Way."

"Oh fuck," says the third. "Do it."

"You too. Let's *both* touch it."

The game is changing even as they enact it. Now they want him to overhear. He's sweating, red, his nose looks like it might explode. She tracks his eyes, which are somehow all over the place like a trapped animal while attempting to maintain his signature commuter stare, like there's something a few feet outside the train he's been paid to monitor.

"No ass," comes her friend's verdict, in a stage whisper.

His jaw sags open. His eyes close.

"I mean, I can't even find it. It's like he's got no ass at all."

He swallows. His eyes open. He meets hers at last.

There's something human there amidst the utter depraved appetite and raw shame. It's like if you looked close at a fly and it had a human face. He wets his lips, but not a show of it, more like despite the sweating his lips are dry.

The shuttle stops. Now her friend is freed. "No ass!" she says loudly, to the confusion of those who've begun their surge toward the door in anticipation of its opening. "You'd be surprised how much a girl is attracted to a guy's ass," she declares, still to no one in particular. But the moment the door opens she turns to the dick-man. "You need to take up a new hobby, like mountain climbing or the Tour de France."

You'd like to think they never saw him again but in fact two or three months later, he's back, and the weird thing is they spot him and notice one another spotting him and then never say a word about it. Like some old injunction of silence has worked after all.

Years later, the three get together, and it comes up after a few drinks. Someone says, "that guy on the train. Oh. My. God." Then a shower of maniacal laughter and added remarks like "Can you believe?" and "You could try a hundred years and never explain what it was like back then," remarks which manage to add nothing at all. As though all's understood between them at a level beyond language. Though what might be the case instead is that beyond language is a distress, one indefinable except by this system, of hard-boiling memories into nostalgia. And all she knows is that once when a lover requested that she keep her eyes open, and to hold his gaze, and then afterward asked, so tenderly, so surprisingly, with no evident jealousy, when she'd first seen a man come, she'd laughed, and begun to say, "well, there was this guy on the shuttle," and then stopped herself, wondering if it were true.

90.
Smudge, Part 3

The rain tapers and they're still at it.

The customer sits, hands on knees, his body's tension stilled at some cost. The second of the two opticians, he who was previously dispassionate and flippant, is now absolute in his determination. He leans in to inspect the juncture of nosepiece and nose.

"How long are we going to keep him here?" asks the first optician.

"As long as it takes. Help me watch him. Watch his hands."

"We gotta get him out of the way, at least," says the first optician.

"Here you go, doctor-man," says the Black man. He's unfazed. His confidence is sublime.

"Keep your hands down! Let me move the chair."

They install the customer behind the counter, hands on knees, chin up, waiting. The bill of his cap juts from his back pocket. The opticians lean against the wall, inspecting him as though he were a horse on which they'd bet.

"He's gonna touch them," says the first.

"He *wants* to," says the second. "But he knows we're watching."

"You'll see," says the customer.

"Look at his hands. He can't take it, he's gotta go up there. It's like a tic, a whatchamacallit."

"*Fuck* you, motherfucker," says the Black man genially.

The door chimes. They all turn. The newcomer is white, young, in his twenties. Though perhaps only a few years younger, he seems a boy to these stolid men, a boy in a sweater.

"Can I help you find something?" says the second optician, then hisses, "Watch his hands!"

"Just browsing," says the sweater guy. Is browsing the right word for glasses?

Also, who's that Black man in the chair?

"You want to see anything, let me know."

"Okay."

The sweater guy moves along the wall of frames, searching for the expensive ones, the Japanese titanium alloy designs. Almost involuntarily, he glances back. The Black man in the chair bugs his eyes. A plea for help?

The opticians in their white coats, gold glasses, puffy hair, they evoke Nazis. Nazi doctors. Or Mafia. Yes, definitely Mafia. He's heard about this neighborhood. The dark old economic engines still humming away under the gentrifying surface.

Should he get involved?

He slides along the back wall for a better look. The Black man sits with his hands on his knees, containing himself. His keepers' gaze is locked on their prisoner. What did they say? *Watch his hands?*

"Are you okay?"

"*Fuck* you think, jackass? *Fuck* you staring at? You see something wrong with me?" The Black man gesticulates.

The second optician says, "The hands, the hands."

"What's wrong with his hands?"

"Mind your own business," says the first.

"Damn. He thinks I'm a *shoplifter*. Fucking racist motherfucker."

"I didn't—"

"*Tell* him, doctor man. I'm a paying customer."

"Sorry," says the sweater guy, moving to the door.

The three watch the sweater guy disappear.

"Now you're scaring off our clientele," says the second optician, fondly.

"Screw him," says the first. "Just browsing, you heard."

"Racist jackass got to go jumping to conclusions," says the customer, fingers bouncing on his knees.

"Let me see your hands," says the first optician.

"You got eyes!"

"I mean turn them over. Let me take a look."

The customer furrows his brow. The first optician takes the Black man's hand in his own and gently turns it over.

"You've got very rough hands. Look at your fingertips. Very rough." Second optician bends in to look. "See that? He could've scratched up his lenses with his fingers like that."

"Plastic lenses, sure. Like his old ones. Not glass."

"*If* I touched it."

"Yeah, right, *if*. We're suspending judgment."

"That's what makes you a good man. You want to do the right thing."

"That's why we're sitting here. Long as it takes."

"Don't want to go jumping to no conclusions."

"Never."

"Damn straight."

The first optician goes to the counter for a pack of cigarettes. The second optician sighs.

"You got a good man here, doctor man. I spoke too soon."

"Watch your hands," says the second optician.

"You'll watch 'em for me, boys. I know you will."

Night falls. Shops roll down their gates. Deliverymen on green bicycles fill the street. The first optician lights another cigarette and puts it in the customer's mouth for him, so the customer can keep his hands on his knees.

Who knows, they may be there still. Keeping their vigil.

91.
Eyes On Dean
(1978)

Now we know what the Slipper is doing in there.

We know because, one summer evening, out of nowhere, the Slipper lets C. up into his room. Choosing C. as his one appointed witness. It appears we all need to be seen and known, at least once, even in the existence of one so elusive and self-reliant, so nearly abstract, as the Slipper.

Maybe C. had been fishing? He'd rolled a J out of a fresh nickel bag from the pot store on Bergen, wanted a witness himself, and at that moment ran into the Slipper.

"You want to get high?"

Slipper just shook his head. "No offense, not my thing."

"What's your thing, then?"

Slipper scans peripherally for a moment, says, "I want to show you something."

Slipper's third-floor bedroom faces the backyard, ailanthus

branches grazing the brick in the sleepy breeze, the heady smell of their blossoms wafting in. No fire escape, no surprise there—these have mostly been torn down to avoid the easy break-ins. C.'s never seen another kid's room so minimized of toys or other boyish residue. It's instead like a bureaucrat's office with a neatly made daybed, the sole exception being the trophy-like picture-perfect skateboard, which has been mounted on the wall like a stuffed deer, its wheels barely scuffed. On a small wooden desk sits a ledger, its edge squared to the desk's corner, and an equally tidy pile of *Soldier of Fortune* magazines, large softcover books from the Paladin Press with titles like *How to Investigate Your Family, Friends and Enemies,* and a Lafayette catalogue of stereo and recording equipment including telephone taps and scanners.

At the window's lip, atop a low shelf built over the top of the radiator, perches an electronic kit. At first, C. takes it for some kind of wacky stereo. The kit features a handheld microphone like that in a cop car, attached by a hanging looped cord thicker than a telephone's.

"You really can't smoke in here," says the Slipper, seeing C. taking out his joint.

"I'll lean it out the window."

Slipper shakes his head nope.

"What's that?" C. asks, knowing he's meant to.

"Midland, twenty-three channel, twelve volts."

C. waits.

"CB radio," Slipper clarifies.

"Like, *breaker-breaker-one-nine?*" Everybody remembers that stupid hit song about the truckers, the *bears* and *rubber duck.* The CB radio craze had peaked a year or two before, and C. had never imagined he'd see one of the things. "You trying to avoid getting arrested for speeding in your bedroom?"

"Listen."

The Slipper clicks the thing on and begins to cycle through channels, just listening at first. For all the novelty of it, for C. the results evoke the feedback drenched squawking PA channels at school, the principal coming on after the Pledge of Allegiance and making no discernible sense through the static.

Then Slipper, head tilted in focus like a faithful dog, latches onto one voice in the chaos, and talks back. "Ten-two, Henry Street. Eyes On Dean is on your wavelength. What are you seeing out there?"

"Check, Eyes On Dean. Nothing but the usual drunks and skunks. What's showing in your quadrant?"

"Code ten-twelve. I've clocked a young man with what appears to be a marijuana cigarette, and the ladies are out on Pacific and Nevins." Slipper offers C. a sly smile.

"No police activity? I hear sirens."

"Fire trucks. Incinerator fire at Wyckoff Gardens."

"In other words, situation normal, all fucked up."

"Check, Henry Street. I hear Mr. Softee's music in your neck of the woods." C. hears it now, the tinkling, circular chime, deep in the background of the transmission.

"Fucking Puerto Rican ice cream man parks right in front of my house, I'm gonna go out there with a Louisville Slugger one of these nights."

"You heard from Promenade Patrol?"

"Fruit patrol you mean? Nothing yet tonight. Too hot for action."

"Check, Ace. Play dead, I'll be around in an hour or so. Ten four."

"Ten four."

The Slipper clicked off the device, racked the mic.

"Shit," said C. "So, you're *good buddies* with some fat Italian man in his mother's basement."

"Henry Street's just who happened to pick up. That was just a demonstration. There's an array out there." In a rare expressive gesture, Slipper fans his fingers out through the open window, suggesting the breadth of his network: Gowanus, Red Hook, Sheepshead Bay, other precincts unimaginable.

"They know you're Black?"

Slipper ignores the remark. "Bunch of jokers, really. I'm digging into a deeper layer, I just sent away for a police scanner."

"That's legal?"

"Sure, only hard to get."

"Meantime you're helping the meatball boys keep an eye on the homos on the Promenade?"

Water off a duck's back. "That isn't what I wanted to show you. Look." Slipper opened his ledger. C. looked. Each page is numbered with a three-digit code. Below, lists of dates and names.

"Go ahead." Slipper's pride has gotten the best of his discretion, if only momentarily.

C. finds his own name, and his mom's and dad's. The three numbers aren't codes. It is simpler than that. They're street addresses. Slipper has been tabulating the block—more, several blocks—in resolute, grinding detail: residents of each house, basement to top, and dates when they'd left and new names had come to replace them. Like one of those kids C. had always found inexplicable, who used a little nubby on a scorecard at the Mets game. The pages for the rooming houses are the most complex. On these many names are only placeholders: monikers like Mr. Clean, or descriptives, like SMALL-TIME CON MAN, WHITE HAT, SUEDE-FRONT SWEATER.

"I thought you might be able to help me fill in some gaps."

"I'm not so good with names," C. says. It is a helpless truth. He gives honorifics, nicknames, wherever he goes.

"Anything you see missing, just let me know."

"Sure. I'll do what I can." C. gets it. This is the secret frequency to which Slipper attunes, his horizon raised beyond worm's-eye pavement-struggles. The methods are unusual, but not unrecognizable. Control yourself, control all the adults, clock all available exits.

The question that bothers C., years later, is whether the Slipper— or should he refer to him by his chosen handle, Eyes On Dean?—had, by his methods, drawn himself into a special intimacy with the humans of their block, or insulated himself in a realm that reduced them to statistics, mere scratched marks on a page?

92.
A Ride in the Millionaire's Car
(1978)

One day one of the Dean Street boys, one of the white ones, finds himself, who knows how, going for a ride in the millionaire's car, the old scuffed copper-colored BMW. In memory this is a ride around the neighborhood—had they gone no farther than to pick up to-go food from Queen, on Court Street? Yes, it must have been. For this was one of the millionaire's eccentricities, to hop into the car at the slightest excuse. Open the moon roof, punch in an 8-track cassette.

No risk in losing a parking spot, there are plenty.

The millionaire alternates rants and raves about how the boys are missing the boat ordering a pie, the real hot ticket at Queen was the veal parmigiana submarine. Open up a bottle of cabernet and damn, kid. Life is good.

This dad is like no one else in their precinct, exactly. He's not a renovation nerd covered in plaster dust and boasting of distinctive moldings and corbels. He's not a political hippie, uptight with guilty causes. Neither is he some craven Wall Streeter or developer with a wide tie and barely plausible sideburns.

You'd call him cosmopolitan, except to the boys that's the name of a women's magazine.

More *Penthouse, High Times, National Lampoon.*

Maybe *Harvard Lampoon.*

Fear and loathing in Boerum Hill.

A sweltering day at the very end of the unrelenting summer, maybe September, even. Windows rolled down and air conditioner blasting. The passenger seat is empty. The two boys are in the back seat, not for safety's sake, but for its opposite, so that they may horse around without the restraint of a seatbelt. The millionaire's son fools with his gravity knife below the eyeline of the rearview mirror, pretending to flick it at his father's neck. Even as he does this, he's monologuing about how he spent all night out the night before on a graffiti bombing run to the Long Island Railroad yards, without his parents having the least notion he was out of the house.

The other Dean Street boy, the guest in this car, is trying to guess who might have ushered the millionaire's son on this exotic journey but he's distracted by the requirement that he follow the millionaire's son's storytelling:

"I walked in at six A.M. and there's Sparkle sitting with a glass of white wine. She wasn't waiting up for me, she was just getting her morning buzz on."

"Whoa." The other Dean Street boy spares a nervous glance at the millionaire, but he's happily singing along to his 8-track. No matter how brief his journeys, the millionaire plays his music. Today, the Rolling Stones, "Miss You." The choice is unforgettable. For, though this song has blared from radios all summer long, it is only just now, in the millionaire's car, that the Dean Street boy isolates that sleazeball boast in the lyrics—"Puerto-Rican-girls-just-dyiiiin-ta-meet-cha!"

A shudder of discomfort that welds itself to the day's shame. He'll never hear the song again without recalling this drive. Now the millionaire is singing: "whassamatterwhitchooboy, ooh ooh OOH ooh, ooh ooh ooh ooh—"

"I don't know if she even noticed I came in through the front door instead of from upstairs. But I'm covered with purple spray paint and all she says is I was thinking of making crepes for you this morning."

"Whoa."

"Then she looks me up and down and says are those your new OshKosh B'Goshes."

"Whoa."

"I said you should have seen the other guy."

The other Dean Street boy has been trying to attune to this presentation, in order to pick out the punch line he is certain is coming. He's relieved that the millionaire's son has made it so easy. He says:

"Ha."

The three humans in this millionaire's family make a vivid display of being one hundred percent inaudible to one another. Or is that just families in general?

If so, not usually advertised quite so flagrantly.

Now they corner Nevins to Bergen, working the one ways to Court Street, there to double-park this crazy car, leave it running outside Queen while the millionaire runs in and grabs the goods, the steaming white boxes and paper sacks, but no. First, they've got to pass the gauntlet of the backside of their own block, and the other Dean Street boy feels it coming in the prickle of sweat on his neck, he swears he hears the shouts or feels the fine mist even before they turn the corner of Nevins.

His own block has been turned into a time machine. The Dean Street side, it houses the present or maybe the future. It houses the millionaire.

The Bergen Street side, it now appears, is a portal into his own past, the false oasis.

Against his will, as a passenger in this car, he's entering the time machine now.

Everyone knows that those who employ time machines eventually go mad.

Somebody's uncle or one of the stoop sitters from the rooming house possesses the wrench, the holy object. The day is hot enough, the afternoon ripening toward evening with no relief, and that person has gone and brought forth the holy object and to wide acclaim and approval of all stoop sitters wrenched open the hydrant. The result is a geyser, a Niagara, and the kids cavort under the water, splash it at one another, and use it to menace passing cars. This is the hydrant the kids love best, on Bergen, middle of the block. The cops never come and shut it down, it's too deep in the block. Just don't attack the bus, that'll draw trouble. Let the bus go by. All others, beware.

The water forms a river in the gutter, flowing between the parked cars, racing toward Nevins. Yet the millionaire's oblivious. He's playing air guitar on his steering wheel. The millionaire's son is oblivious too. He's either in fantasyland himself, in outer space, hypnotized as he often seems to be by his own gravity knife, his own vicarious street life, or he's maliciously fascinated to see what will occur to his father's automobile.

The other Dean Street boy was once one of the kids in the hydrant, way back when. It was him there, shirtless and barefooted and writhing in the hydrant's gush. He feels if he examined the crowd of bodies at the hydrant now, he'd see his own, the whitest among them. Had he been that kid who scraped the bottom end off a tin can to make a tool for directing the flow? Had he been the one pressing the can to the forceful stream once it had been opened at both ends? Maybe not quite. But he'd been something like a second-in-command. Or maybe third. He'd been, anyway, one of those in the soaked anarchic gaggle at the side of the water-gunner, rooting hard for the result. He knows what's about to happen to the millionaire's automobile.

"Roll up the windows," he says.

"Eh?"

"Roll up the windows."

Maybe he's snapped the millionaire out of his trance, maybe it's just that the millionaire's seeing what's before his eyes as he nears. Miraculously, the windows rise, all four seemingly on the same control button, right as the first drops spatter and sizzle on the BMW's hood. Then the firehose gush batters the car on the hydrant side. Someone's an expert with that can. A mist settles through the open sunroof, but the water-gunner doesn't know to arc the water upward, the water-gunner isn't perhaps familiar with the design of this particular vehicle, so they're spared.

The millionaire's son cackles and dances in his seat.

Then comes the single word that burns the day into the other Dean Street boy's brain forever.

Is it that the word is unthinkable? Can't really be that.

More like something recognized from another plane of reality, something you hadn't realized could come home to your street.

"*Animals,*" mutters the millionaire.

The way he says it, he isn't trying to shock anyone, isn't seeking a particular impression, ironic or otherwise.

Just pushing a given feeling out of his body, into the air.

IV.
The Dance

"**ONE OF THE POTENTIAL PITFALLS** of phenomenology, Annemarie Moi remarks, is that one person's self-ethnography can be elevated to grandiose proportions."

—Rita Felski, *Hooked*

"**I WISHED** to let the child speak, stepping back, not interfering in any way—and instead I exploited him, robbed him, emptied his pockets, notebooks, drawers, to boast to the adults what promise he showed, and how even his little faults were virtues in embryo. I turned my theft into a road sign, practically into a whole highway . . . and spoke of secrets and toys that were not mine—for I no longer have secrets and toys—and I built a tomb for that young boy and placed him in it, a meticulous, calm, factual tomb, as if I were writing about someone made up, someone who never lived, and who with will and planning could be fashioned according to the rule of aesthetics. It was not playing fair. You do not treat a child that way."

—Stanislaw Lem, *Highcastle*

93.
Lovecraft Basement, Part 2
(1985)

The shops on Jay Street shine him on a while, the old guys sensing he desires it too keenly: the identity of the shop with the Lovecraft papers in the basement. He'd endeared himself to them as a scout, bringing in cherry items they made instantly vanish into the collections of buyers they adeptly prevented him from meeting. After a few months of this, he signed on to work at the first of them for peanuts, moving stock around, playing good cop with the customers to their lasting mockery.

"You thought they were buying? I made those tourists a mile off."

These Jay Street guys might be sharks, but they were tired. It was almost like they preferred the two shops unpopulated, as storefront hangouts. Rest homes for books and sharks.

He wore them down. In him, they saw their younger selves, whether they wished this vision or not. Eventually they were fond enough to admit to him that neither had the Lovecraft Basement.

Was it in Brooklyn? Did it exist?

The tired sharks had a theory, actually. Emporium Books, on Livingston Street, between Bond and Nevins. It might not look like much anymore, but the store's continuity went back further than you'd think, further even than theirs. A schlepper from Long Island had purchased the place, not a bookman in any respect. Yet the conjunction of the bus stop and his total willingness to sell any kind of crap that came between two covers meant he ekes a living. There's a copious basement, stock from the previous owner. If such a thing as the Lovecraft Basement exists, well—who knew?

Two weeks later the kid quits and talks himself into a job at Emporium.

The Long Island schlepper, the owner, hires him despite unmistakable reservations. He needs but deeply loathes clerks who know books better than he does. So, he lays down the rules. Rule One: No employee can purchase and take home more than one book a week. The owner isn't going to let his own clerks scout the shop and plunder value he isn't capable of recognizing himself. No sir, you took your pay home in a check, not in books.

Rule Two, which is axiomatic from Rule One: No friends in the bookstore. If you have some proxy come in and buy the good stuff, then it's as bad as if you plunder it directly.

Rule Three is the intriguing one. If the owner sends you down into the basement to get something, no lingering, no looking around. Come back upstairs, pronto.

What's he hiding down there?

Emporium is a mess, the stock collapsing in on itself, most of it handled and rejected a hundred times and still on the shelves. The place is *shopped out,* in the parlance. Yet the owner's suspicions aren't wholly ungrounded. The twelve-foot-high cases need to be browsed on ladders and are shelved two deep. With so much material, going back so far, there are destined to be lost gems in the upper shelves. Let alone in that sacrosanct basement.

The shop's viability has nothing to do with antiquarian books, however. As predicted by the Jay Street bookmen, the owner pays his rent thanks to the lucky conjunction of the Livingston Street bus, which stops right in front, and the materials selected for the clientele who, standing waiting for buses that never come on time, are his captive audience.

What the Long Island schlepper sells is a deep unnerving X-ray into what use Downtown Brooklyn has for things in the shape of books.

He sells bibles, cheap gold-embossed leather jackets, pocket editions, zippered editions, red-letter editions. A whole three-shelf case of options for the bible browser.

He sells "Dream Books," which are basically just cheaply produced pamphlets, frequently updated, which translate dream imagery from the reader's previous night's sleeping into numerical equivalents.

Using these, you could take your revelation to a numbers bookie and bet on your own dream.

He sells porn, new and used. Slick magazines and paperbacks.

Most profitably, he sells Arco brand test prep books for the civil service tests. You want to get into police work? You need to take a test. So, you need the test prep book. Same for housing authority, same for garbageman, and so on. A whole wall of such books, behind the counter, to be produced on request rather than browsed. The clerks have the job of keeping these shelves replenished. The owner throws a little fit if a gap opens up, and a given test book isn't available. Since they sell like hotcakes, whatever hotcakes are, this is one of the more difficult pieces of the job.

The owner has rules, too, for what you tell customers. Never admit you didn't have a book, always say you did. Send them into the deep chaotic stock and they'd forget the original mission and find something they wanted instead. Never mind that this rarely works out, and the staff has to suffer endless complaints that things aren't to be found where they'd sent people to find them.

The owner also scripts his staff on verbal routines for the Arco test books: If a guy comes in and bought the police book and returns to say he'd failed, buy the book back at half price and gently steer him to the fire department test, much easier to pass. A good career. If you fail fire department, well, have you looked into corrections officer?

Fail corrections, there wasn't much anyone could do for you.

Every chance down the Emporium basement stairs, into that dank storage, usually sent in pursuit of more paper bags or rolls of stickers from the bottomless supply, the kid tries to rifle through some corners, to ascertain the presence of an older stratum of material. The owner, from his side, seems obsessed with the basement too. He stands at the top and shouts for the kid if he lingers too long.

"What are you doing down there?"

"Nothing."

"Do less nothing on my dime."

"Why don't you let me organize it sometime?"

"I don't need it organized. I need you up here selling."

Not on my dime is the clue. The kid, having been entrusted with the keys for opening the shop, only has to set his alarm clock for five-thirty in the morning, and get to Livingston Street two hours before the shop's opening. No one can prevent him inventorying the Emporium basement on his own time, his own dime, in this manner. By the point when the owner shows up, ordinarily twenty minutes or a half hour after the eight o'clock opening of the doors, the kid will have tabulated the secret holdings. The owner won't know the difference.

So, he descends those stairs alone, six A.M., trembling in anticipation. To find what? Nothing, mostly. Old books rotting, worse in condition even than those on the shelves in the store above. Titles dusted in irrelevance, superseded histories of subjects dull to begin with. Then, in one corner, a number of twine-knotted, paper-wrapped bundles, seemingly stashed en masse, labelled by one hand with a grease pencil: H.O. PLISTOR.

Plistor?

A code name? Anagram? Those initials can't help but intrigue. He tugs at the twine on the first package. The rigid knot is shrouded in dust, immovable as a sculpture of a knot. He tears the paper at one corner. Inside, a bulging stack of identical perfect-bound pamphlets, horrific hand-drawn claws on some sort of evil human hand visible beneath dripping font that promises to REVEAL—what?

In a fever of discovery, the kid discards all caution, pulls out his ring of keys, to employ one as a blunt serrated knife blade to shred the ancient twine.

With a few rough strokes of the key, the bundle uncovers itself. The claws are those of a monstrously caricatured Chinese man in robes, looming with dripping fangs over a tiny globe.

HEATHEN TERRORS REVEALED.

THE YELLOW PERIL IN ACTION, A POSSIBLE CHAPTER IN HISTORY.

AMERICAN MANHOOD VS. ASIATIC COOLIEDOM: WHICH SHALL PREVAIL?

The kid goes three bundles deeper before he's decisively repelled.

H. O. Plistor's archive is sheer vomit of xenophobic panic, race hatred, eugenicist tracts, all the way to a sheaf of caricatures of Irish immigrants called THE POOR HOUSE FROM GALWAY. A rare and vile assembly, echo of a true collector's obsession, audible through the murk of years.

Antiquarianism itself seems called into doubt.

Everywhere you look, Brooklyn's a fucking sandwich of what's dubious. In the basement, it proves itself to be a four-dimensional object, a sandwich of centuries.

Emporium of *what*, that's the real question.

The kid shoves the bundles back into the dusty recesses and never returns to the basement, apart from when the boss asks him to re-up the supply of bags or stickers or find a fresh roll of receipts for the register.

94.
Williamsburg Savings Bank
(1985)

Before putting the Emporium Bookshop out of its misery, before zooming out again from the antiquarian kid, let's trail him, on one of his regular duties: the two-and-a-half block journey with the cash deposit to a teller window in the lobby of the Williamsburg Savings Bank tower.

Possibly you know that tower, One Hanson Place, the great erection or middle finger of Flatbush Avenue. The Tallest Building in Brooklyn, until suddenly it wasn't, simply because they built all that other hideous looming shit, and swarmed its height in boxy high-rises. Flatbush slowly turning into a mock Broadway, a corridor of mediocre towers, only more Brooklyn because interspersed with ineradicable older funk, the low ugly Department of Health building, the gaudy Junior's Restaurant, home of famous cheesecake, Long

Island University, the wretchedness of Metrotech. But in this era, the Williamsburg Savings Bank Tower stands alone and tall, even as it stands mostly empty, apart from a scattering of dentists' suites. In the ground level, the institution giving it its name still functions, so the tower enunciates something, maybe. A bank with a grand lobby, and a tower above, and a name that isn't "Citi" or "Chase," let alone "Barclays."

But we digress.

The Emporium Bookstore's owner, the Long Island schlepper, fearful of keeping cash on the premises in such a neighborhood, sends his clerk with a deposit every single afternoon, around four, before the bank closes, before the day shift ends.

This is a quarter mile walk in broad daylight, down Livingston Street and then across Flatbush Avenue at Third, past the florist on the traffic island and the Brooklyn Academy of Music.

For a former Dean Street boy, however, there is something almost psychedelic in moving through these Downtown Brooklyn crowds carrying two, three, sometimes four or five grand in cash receipts bundled with a deposit slip in a cloth shoulder bag, ushering the bookstore's daily haul down these particular oft-walked streets.

Dream books, porn, bibles, and Arco test prep guides are a damn good cash business.

At twenty-one, and having grown to a reasonable height and with the increasing onset of a hunched and grungy aspect attracting no particular interest, the antiquarian kid on these occasions moves with reliable invisibility, from Emporium to the Williamsburg Savings Bank lobby, pushing along the sidewalk in throngs of people but alone.

He's come miles from those days, almost without noticing.

Still, he feels it.

The residue of the dance. The hands frisking in his pockets, the routinized demand for him to hand over what he had and they didn't, the wild possibility of a quick holy shit score of a lifetime for anyone who succeeded in removing the cloth shoulder bag from him and discovering the cash deposit.

And what would he do if they tried?

Plenty of times walking in the neighborhood, and at least a handful of times during these Emporium bank deposit runs, the antiquarian kid passed some guy he'd known from I.S. 293 or even earlier, some kid from schooldays whose name could still pop into your head unwelcomed.

Which set of eyes dropped to the pavement soonest? This was the opposite of a staring contest, a game of shame you couldn't know whether you'd won.

And what if they'd said *fuck you looking at?*

And what if they'd said *yo, let me see what you got?*

Broad daylight and crowds of witnesses never used to stop it from happening.

And what would he do in that situation?

It was sheerly mind-boggling.

95.
Guy Who Stuffs Flyers into His Bag and Says Keep Walking
(1991)

Soon we'll quit stalling and say what we mean by *the dance*. It's incredible we've gone this far without doing so.

My discomfort might be the only thing I've made obvious at this point.

Let's stall once more. We'll hold our focus on the antiquarian kid. Trail him down one farther street, a few years since quitting the Emporium Bookshop.

Now he works the night shift at Potpourri, a fussy little first editions place on Broadway and 78th Street. During the day, he prowls the Manhattan thrift stores, uptown and downtown, trying to salt away stock for an eventual store of his own. The closets of his tiny apartment on Mott Street are filling with books. The kitchen cabinets too, since he lives mainly on street meals, slices from Joe's on Carmine, knishes from Yonah Schimmel. Salad passes his lips solely when home to see his parents on Dean Street, maybe twice a month. He's never lived anywhere but New York City. The Mott Street place will have been his one stab at Manhattan before he's destined to sag back to his native borough. Give him this, though, he's trying to bust out.

At twenty-seven, he chain-smokes Camels, walks with a hunched urgent gait, pushes stringy hair back from his rising forehead, resembles the owners in whose shops he suffers employment more than you'd think possible at this age. Maybe in this way he's moving in the direction of his goal. He's replaced his default green army surplus jacket, purchased at Canal Jeans, with a heavy tweed smoker with leather elbows and collar, like some English Midlands gamekeeper. If you listen close enough, he's begun to mutter to himself.

Since those days on Livingston Street, ferrying the cash deposit from Emporium to the Williamsburg Savings Bank, he's grown more and more positive he's attained invisibility on these streets when it suits him to employ it.

It would be easy for someone who'd known him just ten years before, another public school kid, one he'd seen maybe only in gym class, say, or even one he'd larked around with on his own street a certain amount, to pass him on a crowded Manhattan street and not recognize him.

(He told me I once walked by him in this way. I have no idea whether it's true.)

For gathering up the books he scouts from the thrift shops, the antiquarian kid has adopted a wide canvas shoulder-strap saddlebag, of a type associated with bike messengers. Useful for its capacity to expand to hold ten or fifteen hardcovers if needed, yet to lie flat and unobtrusive on his hip when empty. Perhaps it is this bag which has attracted Guy Who Stuffs Flyers to the kid, him alone out of all those teeming on the sidewalk at Broadway and 36th, on the day in question. Perhaps Guy Who just happens to spot the distinctive saddlebag and knows it will suit his purpose.

Right, sure.

Who are we kidding?

What pulls Guy Who's focus on the antiquarian kid is the kid's old scent, that of eligibility for the dance. A residue, which lingers on him still. It's this knowledge which catalyzes the special flush of shame in the kid's cheeks. That makes this episode meaningful to recount here in the first place.

Guy Who Stuffs Flyers singles him out, and it is as though all those years collapse. As though the antiquarian's fear, on Livingston Street, has come true at last, and he is about to be relieved of a three- or four-thousand-dollar bundle, the entirety of a cash deposit from Emporium. A kid-mugging with grown-up stakes.

Only no. It isn't six years earlier, this isn't Livingston Street or Brooklyn at all, and the kid carries nothing worth stealing, much less a cash deposit. What happens today is, anyway, anomalous. The stakes? Nonexistent.

Here's how it goes down:

On the crowded block, New Yorkers all hustling to their various somewheres, antiquarian kid scuffling along at the moment, drifting between urgencies, unsure whether to loop around to a couple of thrift shops to see if there's new stock, or maybe duck into the IRT, be two hours early for his shift uptown, grab a hot bagel at H&H, take a walk to Central Park since the day's pretty nice, when Guy Who zooms on him from apparently nowhere. Black guy. Younger, actually, than the antiquarian kid. Though full grown. Maybe twenty or twenty-one, maybe twenty-two, hard to be sure. Yet, crucially, younger. This is part of the weird sting of this encounter. As if Guy Who is specially equipped to strip off the antiquarian kid's age disguise. Sees him as he doesn't want to see himself, perennially twelve and frozen on the pavement, submitting to frisking and humiliation.

"Yo, come here a second."

The kid looks around, but there's no recipient aside from himself, this much is unmistakable. As on so many earlier days, the surplus human beings in the scene have become pure negative space.

"What?" he says dumbly, numbly.

"Nothing, I ain't gonna do nothing to you, just come here."

"I'm going—"

"Don't say nothing." Guy Who, after a few quick glances up and down the block as if he's being pursued, snags the saddlebag's shoulder strap, and tugs the kid nearer. "Open it, quick."

"There's nothing there."

"I ain't want your shit." Guy Who thrusts a package *into* the saddlebag, something dense and thick, bundled within wrinkled brown paper. Then zips it up. "Keep walking, don't look at me. Go."

"What?"

"Don't stop for five blocks. Don't turn around. Throw it away when you get home. In a dumpster."

The kid looks at him, shocked. Then, shocked at himself, complies. For a block at least, he goes into the crowd, crosses 37th before pausing. A glance back can't hurt, at least he doesn't think so. No one could see half a block in this crowd, let alone two blocks. Nothing to see, no sign of Guy Who. Frozen, idiotic, the kid has to dare himself to wonder: What's in the bag? What's he been made to carry? Drugs? A bundle of money, awaiting some recipient? A recently fired gun, a hot piece of iron? The kid's temples sweat as he unzips the bag.

The paper shrouding conceals a thick wad of flyers. GRAND OPENING, ARCHIE'S DISCOUNT ELECTRONICS. Hundreds of them, glossy, full color, expensively produced, not just some photocopied circular. The flyer is also a coupon. This is someone's big retail play. Archie, if there is an Archie, must have hired Guy Who to press the flyers on passersby, trying to drum up a result. Guy Who, sick of trying and failing to make a dent in the gigantic supply of flyers, had hit on this solution. Probably he raced back to Archie to show he was empty-handed, and collect his reward.

The kid shoves the wad of flyers into the nearest trash can. Some even sticking out of the paper wrapping now, but who gives a shit? He laughs sharply to himself at the idiocy of the episode, but there's something passing through his body as well, a shudder beneath the guffaws. The old fears restored and refurbished in an instant. His willingness to oblige, his tongue like a damp washcloth stuffed into his mouth, the whole transaction between himself and Guy Who: it all had depended on a body of secret operations known only to previous participants. For instance, how many times had the kid been told "keep walking, don't look back at me?" How many times had he been given some absurd number to count off—five blocks, ten? The entire episode was a belated entry in a series, history repeating itself as farce.

Two former children, two men, in an instant of street theater. Two men enacting a pretend version of a former life, one in which children pretended to be old enough to mug or be mugged by one another.

The entire episode of Guy Who Stuffs Flyers, a version of the dance.

96.
The Dance, Part 1
(forever)

Let the antiquarian kid go now. Poor bastard. He's just one in a crowd, watch him melt back into the streets.

He is not we and we is not I.

(We'll meet him again. Though, spoiler alert, there is no Lovecraft Basement.)

It's time to make reckoning with the dance, that which may be the heart of the heart of the matter.

THE DANCE OCCURS between the white kids and the Black kids, not that there aren't exceptions. But mainly.

The dance occurs on the sidewalk. It might seem as simple as a transaction, like that at a toll booth.

By the conclusion of the transaction, what the white kid held in his pocket has been surrendered.

As at a toll booth, this result is expected by both parties.

So, what's complicated about that? What makes it a dance?

Such a simple moment, we could stare at it forever.

THE DANCE IS a dance because no one can tell you in words. The dance is a dance because you have to do it to learn how to do it.

The dance is a dance because it is an elastic ritual, one with blank spaces, intervals, for improvisation. Yet you can certainly get it wrong.

The dance is a dance because it is embarrassing.

The dance is a dance because it defies language.

THAT IS NOT to say that the scene of the dance is one *bereft* of language. We could write its lexicon. A phrasebook, in the tongue of the foreign country just beyond the door of one's house:

"Let me see it a second."

(To see a thing is to hold a thing. To hold a thing is to possess a thing and be free to exit with it in one's possession.)

(What can never be taken from you is the thing unseen.)

(But what is the thing unseen?)

"All I finds, all I keeps."

(One dancer has lied to another and claimed that his pockets are empty. Now, subject to frisking, he consents to this ethical contract. If money is nothing to you, it belongs to anyone to whom it means more.)

"Don't tell nobody. I'll know if you tell."

(Though the dance is invisible to all but the dancers, the dancers have X-ray vision and are alert to one another through walls and time.)

"I'm just messing with you."

(The dance is nothing if not held in ironic parentheses. It is always not-happening while it happens. The dancers are all in on the joke.)

"Fuck you looking at?"

(Nothing.)

"Why you look scared? You scared of me? I didn't even touch you."

(Fair enough.)

"What are you, racist, man?"

(Here it is, the four-dimensional puzzle, the impossible object the dance lives inside. Don't try to solve this at home.)

"You don't have to worry about it, whiteboy. You know it don't mean nothing."

(The dance, ironically, relies on paralysis. Paralysis induced by all the meaning that is being called up but left unnamed.)

There's more, always. But that's enough.

ONCE UPON A time, one of the Dean Street boys wrote a novel about the block, called *Take Me to the Bridge*. The novel had good and bad in it. Many of us others, we experienced a lot of feelings. In other quarters, the novel was forgotten, like most. On our block, it was harder to put out of mind.

A subject for another time.

The point is the writer of the novel wrote about the dance. Though he didn't use that word for it. He used another of the local names for it.

In his examination of the dance, the novelist put a lot of focus on the encounter's intimacy. The nearness of the bodies, the energies that might disclose themselves in the exchange. His great interest was in the way boys make themselves familiar to one another, even in enmity.

Two bodies in conjunction in broad daylight.

One with hands frisking the other's pockets.

One demanding the other roll down socks or roll up sleeves, to reveal what's hidden.

One exercising humiliating dominion over the other.

One sometimes actually stealing the other's *clothes*.

All the while saying reassuring words, using a beguiling tone, to say, "you know I like you. You know this doesn't mean anything. You know this is just what I do to you sometimes. You don't have to tell anyone what happens here."

This is interesting stuff. I'm interested in it myself. I recognize it.

In conducting our inquiry into the dance, however, it may be preferable to stay a little more zoomed out, so to speak.

Maybe we should rise up from the scene on the sidewalk, as if flying. View the dance more like a system of relations, a flow chart of arrows moving here and there, or iron filings polarizing around magnets.

Maybe we should follow the money.

MONEY IN A sock. Money in a sleeve. Money in a shoe.

Other money, fifty cents or a dollar, left in a pants pocket to be found as a decoy, to divert from the hidden dollars.

In this way, you'll remember, the white children dress themselves for the dance.

"Mugging money."

"Take along some mugging money."

"Don't forget the mugging money."

"This is for your sock, and this is for your pocket."

The parents, who purport to be oblivious, and whom the children prefer to believe they're keeping in the dark, will, as we've seen, break cover. From time to time, they'll advise the children openly:

"Just hand it over."

This isn't so original. It draws on the stock wisdom of the dangerous city. The parents, after all, aren't immune. They've been mugged themselves, many of them. They'll rehearse the same advice to one another, to themselves.

What did they expect? They've moved their families to Brooklyn, borough of the stick-up kids. *Manhattan makes, Brooklyn takes.*

"They won't hurt you if you give them the money."

The mugging money is appeasement. It is meant to bring a dance to its conclusion.

Good luck with that.

97.
I
(reluctantly)

I notice I've been increasingly using *I* instead of *we*. I'm guessing you noticed it too. This was always inevitable. We are together in this, but I'm not fooling myself: you are not I.

I knew I'd have to come out of hiding eventually.

But only partway.

It isn't that my privacy is such a precious thing. More it's that I'm just not keenly interested in myself, *per se*. I'm one of the Dean Street boys, yes. But not one of those whose personal person needs center stage. The whole point is that there were a lot of us, after all.

I'd rather just remain the voice of our inquiry.

It isn't like I'm demanding to learn anything about *you*.

98.
White Space
(hiding in plain sight)

I also notice I've resorted to the use of white space in composing these pages.

Like this.

I learned that when sending a manuscript to a typesetter, the way to indicate the wish for a white space between paragraphs is to insert a pound sign between the lines. Otherwise, the typesetter will assume it is an error and simply close up the space. Here, we'll leave this next one visible:

...

What is the white space doing? Regulating the flow of the thoughts, I suppose. Providing a soothing respite. Heightening attention to that which has been islanded. Spotlit.

At the same time, the white space is meant for skipping over, like the white gutters between the panels in a comic book. It is supposed to be invisible, implicit, assumed. It is beyond accusation. If you've got a problem, the white space seems to insist, your problem is with what's *there*, not with what's *not there*.

THE OTHER THING suggested by the white spaces in a manuscript—especially when, as in this manuscript, they are on the rise—is of gaps in coherence. They can be used to depict a mind unravelling. They may indicate unreliability in a narrator, or suggest a tale faltering, coming unstrung in the face of doubts.

Good grief, the lies you have to tell to make the world into stories.

We'll get back to the inquiry soon, I swear to you. To stories. I want to tell you about what happened to the spoiled boy, to the younger brother, to the nemesis, and the millionaire's son. First, I have to finish talking about the dance. And before that, the whiteness.

99.
The Whiteness of the Whiteboy
(Boerum Hill era)

We've done our damnedest, in the course of this pursuit, to widen the aperture, to let in more: more streets, more crimes, more faces, more glances at the periphery of the scene, and at the periphery of our comprehension. To make no preliminary exclusions. To not understand ourselves too quickly, to do even the police in different voices.

Yet.

Let's not kid ourselves.

Despite the relief at knowing life outside goes on all around them, a panoply of other manifestations of the human, we're stuck with this clot at the center, the white contingent among the Dean Street boys.

The white boys. The whiteboys.

The unbearable whiteness of their being.

This elusive quality it is, which causes the thought of whiteness, when divorced from more kindly associations, and coupled with any object terrible in itself, to heighten that terror to the furthest bounds. Witness the white bear of the poles, and the white shark of the tropics; what but their smooth, flaky whiteness it is which imparts such an abhorrent mildness, even more loathsome than terrific, to the dumb gloating of their aspect.

Yeah, okay, I typed that last bit out of *Moby-Dick*, I'm stalling for time.

ABHORRENT MILDNESS? SOME of the Dean Street boys go for an abhorrent mildness. They've mastered an art of being elsewhere than they are, especially while moving down the Brooklyn sidewalk. When they get back to their parlor and crack open the Board Games of Empire, they can breathe again. Turn off their power of invisibility. They're stalling too.

They're stalling until they're older, until they're taller, until summer camp in Pennsylvania when they can pretend they're not from where they're from, until they get into Stuyvesant or go off to college. Culturally, they're inclined to work the margins. Sustaining themselves on *Mad Magazine* and Frank Zappa and Wacky Packages, sardonic attitudes to keep from having to regard anything, most particularly their own emotional reality, from an unironic point of view.

Weather out your childhood. Go deeper into whiteness, don't take the bait. You'll likely be a winner in the end.

In the meantime, hold out for punk rock, destined to help you save face, put a good solid reason behind all the awkwardness and rage.

What about *dumb gloating of their aspect?* Sure, that's another approach. Identify with the street even if it doesn't identify with you, try to wear it down with your sick emulations of graffiti and breakdancing, reverse-token yourself into some group of motley bozos. Be that white kid who stuffs his backpack with Krylon at Pearl Paint while the Black kids run the decoy. Be the goofball, be bigger than life, work a comedy routine with a lot of "yo" and "dang" and "snap" in it. If you stay relentlessly frontal, you might filibuster anyone from shaming you out of this angle. Or maybe just prevent yourself noticing how you're tolerated largely as a joke.

Hey, there's only about a thousand ways this can go wrong, but maybe you'll be the big exception.

AM I BEING unfair? Probably.

Most of the whiteboys of Brooklyn land somewhere between these two extremes. Uneasily between. Always uneasily.

They navigate pain and confusion on a daily basis. So, we should try to be kind. Considered one at a time, we may indeed feel kindly toward them. Yet in this survey of the general condition of their whiteness, we should notice that at all times these boys dwell in the feeling that they've got options, avenues, routes *out*. The whole universe has been sending them this memo: just make it through, and you'll leave all this in the dust.

Life is elsewhere, and you hold a ticket for entry.

Whiteness knows this and it doesn't know it knows this. That is its magic act.

The boys, born into the condition of Brooklyn, could never have enunciated the least of this, not at the time. Here, where they tremble often even to go out of doors and proceed down the sidewalk, it may be difficult to believe the world's your oyster. They are feeling sorry for themselves, and we ought to understand this.

Still, they also get the memo.

They cling to it like a life raft.

BUT WE'RE LEAVING too much out.

We're leaving out the parents and what they believe and impart. What they fervently hope is true: that they're those who came along and marched and sang and made a better world. They're young themselves. It's the middle of the sixties when they commit to this place, the earliest of them. The word *gentrification*, remember, barely coined. Unknown to most.

These are the Jane Jacobs people.

The reverse–White Flight people.

The Gowanus Liberation Front.

They're going to save these row houses and the world.

There are differences. They'll wind up on more than one side of this gentrification. Still, they're all believers, even if they don't agree on what exactly they believe.

Civil rights, neighborhood, community.

Vague enough containers to bear all their perplexities.

They tell others and tell themselves that their kids will go to the local public schools. Some even keep to this. In the schools, in the kindergartens, they hold hands and sing *you-know-what*.

And then go home, a portion of them, to the projects.

And even some of the white kids, the aforementioned Jews, go home to the projects.

Others, to the glamorously protracted renovations on Dean Street.

This world, it existed. If we fail to grant its reality, our inquiry will also fail.

THE PARENTS WHO aren't white, what might they be saying?

Are they idealistic too? Might they be wary of the promises lately made to themselves, to their children?

We'll stay wary, anyhow, of incautious generalizations.

Most people are just trying to live in the house they live in, take care of the humans standing right in front of them. When the old lady coined the name "Boerum Hill" and drew the line down the middle of Bergen Street, did anyone even care that the people on the south side of the street, on the blocks that rounded to the projects, weren't included?

Staring across the street now, from Gowanus, or South Brooklyn, or what have you, at Boerum Hill. Your immediate neighbors to the north.

Same damn block, yo.

Why should anyone *need* to care? That ought to be the point. Life is too much. Life is enough.

SO, SEE ALL the children who are heir to this conundrum, shoved out of doors. Children of all varieties, children from every kind of home. Shooed out from their houses, their apartments, their housing blocks, to occupy the streets, to walk to and fro from the entrances to their schools, to enact their legendarily unsupervised '70s childhoods in the legendarily dangerous and unpatrolled city, the city wreathed in unquenched flame. Left to figure out what it all meant for themselves, to gape at one another and measure the distances in their bodies.

The distance between themselves and the *other* bodies, those standing gaping at them in turn.

The distance between their faces and a knuckle sandwich.

The distance along a block patrolled by one set of men on milk crates at one corner and another set of men on milk crates at the other.

The distance between immediate existence and anything they've been told.

Commence the dance!

100.
The Dance, Part 2
(telling)

See them moving on the sidewalk there.

Two boys meeting two boys and taking up the dance.

Three meeting three. Three meeting two.

One meeting one for a quiet shuffle.

You can't hear the music from here. But they know it by heart.

SHOW DON'T TELL, or so I've been told. Yet at this moment this injunction, only to show, never to tell, it affronts me twice over.

First, it raises my old shame at the dance. It resembles too much the injunction to keep walking, hold your tongue. Never to speak of what's transpired, what your body's absorbed. The implication being that if you tell, you'll be mocked, at best. At worst, accused of something.

As well, it resembles too much the white spaces, the lacunae, the gutters, where everything is artfully unsaid. In its assertion that meaning is better left implicit, show-don't-tell invites no meaning at all. It offers blissful ignorance, benighted passage out from difficulty.

Look over here! Isn't THIS a weird scene? Wonder what it means?

Too bad we'll never know.

If telling fucks up this novel, fair enough. Someone else can make a novel out of this stuff.

SO, LET ME tell.

Brooklyn was territorial. Maybe all of New York City was this way. The territories were often minuscule. They changed block by block. The limits where one territory gave way to another, those were detectable only by the apparatus of the bodies of those territorialized. The children of the sidewalks. The boundaries might be totally invisible otherwise.

The Italians and the Irish and the black-clad Jews had the simple self-respect of their territories. A Black or Puerto Rican kid not wise enough to recognize a natural limit would be referred back to their own territory, often with chains and sticks.

Referred back unharmed, if fortunate.

The white kids in our inquiry, the children of Boerum Hill, of the Brownstoners, they bear the fundamental shame of no territory.

At best they have a claim to Brooklyn Heights. That is, if their parents had the wits and dollars to send them to Friends, Packer, Saint Ann's.

Still, good luck getting from *here* to *there*.

These white boys are the very same ones whose dress and manner stinks of weird privilege, of Manhattan, of elsewhere. They do things like appear on the streets with their indoor possessions, like idiots. Things like go away to the countryside in the summer. Their parents have not the first notion of how to protect them.

They might *feel* poor, but there's poor and poor.

After all, the families are hiring all those plasterers and welders. They're planting all those foolish trees, opening all those foolish stores on Atlantic Avenue. They even volunteer for causes.

That's got to mean money. Even if they think they're hippies.

And they've been told by their parents to play with everyone as if they are all the same. Because, as we all know, civil rights just happened. What a relief, to have the misunderstanding cleared up at last! We are all the same.

Kumbaya, muthafucka.

HERE, FINALLY, IS the dance, then.

Anyone can get robbed. Everyone does. We know this.

But not just anyone can be in a dance. Because the dance is a puzzle and an assertion, the dance is dialectical, the dance is racialized. The dance is call-and-response: you were placed here by civil rights, in the name of your parents' beliefs. The dance dares you to look it in the eye—the gulf between that assertion and this pavement-level reality.

While the DIY renovations are going on inside the houses, the DIY reparations are transpiring on the sidewalks out front.

A THEORY FOR today, then:

When it dawns on the parents, if it dawns on the parents, the nature of this experience in which they have immersed their children, they're driven half-insane.

And remember, some of them were pretty crazy to begin with.

They respond with a gesture typical of those crazed by guilt: bargaining.

If you give the kid money for his sock and money for his pocket, then maybe you can allay this guilt sensation. Just hand it over! It might be a system of taxation, one specially typical of this land of dismay to which you've moved your family, with the intention of renovating a house.

Instructions: just hand it over. Don't fight over a few quarters, for heaven's sake.

Then: smother the whole area in smirking irony.

Call it mugging money.

I SEE WE have a question from the balcony. The balcony being, by definition, that vantage from which one can see the whole dance floor.

If everybody knows what everybody knows, the voice from the balcony asks, then why don't they check for the money in the sock?

Good question. First answer: every once in a while, they do check the sock. This leads, therefore, to the shifting of the money into the heel of the sneaker between the sock and the insole. Which is very stinky money indeed.

But mostly, they do not. Why not?

The answer is only partly the duration and conspicuousness of the operation that would result. Frisking somebody's sock. It's a little riskier. But that's not the main explanation.

The fact is that if money is suspected in the sock, it is grudgingly permitted to remain in the sock. The dance simply doesn't require it changing hands. It would be too humiliating, on both sides. The dance has reached an exact and sustainable level of mutual moral uneasiness at the frisking of the pockets. To go further, especially in the direction of undressing, would be to risk it tipping over into theater of excruciation.

Of course, this tipping-over, beyond even the point of the sock, is in some particular cases precisely what will be sought.

Excruciation. Worse.

We'll go there when I'm ready.

IT OCCURRED TO me to google the term *fair enough*. From *Collins Online Dictionary*: "You use fair enough when you want to say that a statement, decision, or action seems reasonable to a certain extent, but that perhaps there is more to be said or done."

THE GENERAL PARENTAL recommendation, that of passivity in the face of the demand to have one's pockets frisked, flies into the teeth of another typical parental wish: to see their children, their boys, specifically, stick up for themselves. To stand up to bullies.

So, at times, the parents become incoherent. Some of them at least might from time to time reverse course, and suggest to their (boy) children that there isn't anything wrong with popping some other kid in the jaw. This isn't placed in a racial context, no. It's just good old American street corner boyhood.

The boys trained into the dance, they can only shake their head at this suggestion, which anyway is offered passingly, diffidently, in bad faith. The boys know the rules here are different. No one on the street here acts in obedience to some quaint old rulebook, by which one establishes one's fitness for the streets with a single magnificent punch, and thus tested, earns the respect of the boys for blocks around, in fact becomes respected, admired, and never again needs to demonstrate a capacity for violence.

Like in a comic book, when the superheroes always have to misunderstand and fight each other before they become lasting friends.

The children of the dance, they obey a different rulebook. One beyond explanation to their parents. They are born to that special paralysis induced by the combination of hidden weaponry and overwhelming numbers of foes, many significantly older than themselves. And by the entrancing, guilt-inducing language rituals of the dance.

Silence, passivity, self-torment, shame, these are the teachers.

They are such good students.

BY THEIR SILENT acceptance of the terms, the white boys school their parents in turn. Don't ask what goes on out there. Just supply the extra dollar.

Remember, in this inquiry we are following the money. The money is taking a lively path, for sure.

So, what is it purchasing?

This arrangement might be like a toll booth. A magical toll booth, appearing without warning out of the mists, only this is a toll booth giving passage not to magical enchanted lands, but to continuance in your beetle-like procedure down the sidewalk of your own street.

Fair enough?

No. Toll booths don't have feelings. Toll booths, they're satisfied by quarters. Toll booths aren't trying to work their own shit out, on the streets, in the dance.

In the melting pot city, the drop dead city.

In the post–civil rights era.

In the what-the-fuck-is-it era that follows.

In this attempt by the parents to strike a guilty bargain, there's no certification. No receipts for the toll they wish to pay to alleviate their remorse.

You may have to take my word for this. For if my theory is right, no one would ever confirm it. All such bargaining, to exist at all, needs to be drowned in silence. All the participants are, in their different ways, driven inside themselves by the bargains unnamed, by the promises unkept.

Is this a system? Can a system run on shame? At best, it's a highly unstable one.

Can such a thing be relied upon to work the same way each time? Unlikely. Why should it?

It's *not fair enough.*

101.
Quarters, Part 4
(1978)

The two boys with the sawed-off coins in their pockets. They've gone into overtime, into freefall, drift. If this day had any purpose, it's forgotten. From Columbus Park, they've meandered past the entrance stairs to the Brooklyn Bridge walkway, into the cobblestone streets and Mafia warehouses, under the industrial shadows and the faint slap of water on pilings. Down Under the Manhattan Bridge.

(Actual people will later actually believe DUMBO is the actual name of an actual neighborhood. Could there be any simpler measure of the age of Brooklynite you are than how dumb DUMBO sounds to you? I mean, buying into the leafy fiction of Boerum Hill is one thing, but *come on.*)

(I'm old.)

Here, the vacancy of the streets meets the vacancy of the afternoon meets the vacancy of their brains. They've more or less guaranteed zero encounters for themselves. Which, despite the fact that today was perversely predicated on their wish for an encounter of a specific kind, can't help but free up the goofy candor in their bodies. Hoo-hah, we've entered the neutral zone, Nobody's Neighborhood, and we're free and looney as birds! They begin swinging their arms

and singing inane songs. To the tune of the latest hit by The Police—
how ironic of the band, calling themselves that—they shout in unison:

I turned this thing every possible way
I guess I'll have to throw the damn thing away
I can't, I can't, I can't solve Rubik's
I can't, I can't, I can't solve Rubik's
I can't, I can't, I can't solve Rubik's cu-uu-ube!

Their shouts echo and clatter in the canyon of warehouses. And
now, as if specifically beckoned, here come two Black teenagers down
the middle of Plymouth Street's cobblestone. Two utter unfamiliars,
not two we've met before. Today they are two white boys' perfect
counterparts. Like them, they've ranged loose from their ordinary turf,
in their cases, their homes in the Farragut Houses project.

Both of these Farragut boys are in a "left back" contingent at Mark
Hopkins Intermediate School 33 ("There was a time when the American people believed pretty devoutly that a log of wood with a boy
at one end and Mark Hopkins at the other represented the highest
ideal of human training"—W. E. B. Du Bois), otherwise they'd be
off to high school already. To the two white boys, these Black boys
approaching are unknowns. These aren't kids the white boys were in
first grade with. Not kids whose moms have some truck with their
moms. Let alone kids from their own school.

Still, everyone here knows the rules of the dance, don't they?

(If it's always the same, why should each instance remain so electric in memory?)

"Yo, yo, wait up, slow down a minute. Where you going in such a
hurry?" This one, he's the talker for both of them. He's got a nervous
physicality, a need to run that nearly breaks into his walking sometimes. Exercising his mouth partly alleviates this surplus.

"What?" The white boys swallow hard. They can hardly believe
the horrible wonderful putrid elegance of their luck, of their fates,
of their position on this earth. Yet their voices will enter them into
this task automatically, they've barely got to lift a finger.

"Why you look afraid?" the talker asks. Then, rather than requiring them to navigate his question, he half answers it himself, letting them off the hook. "You don't got to be afraid of us."

"I wasn't afraid."

"Nah, course not. You just got that look about you, like you was afraid of folks like us."

"Sorry." It doesn't matter which white boy lets this fall from his mouth, he speaks for both, he speaks for them all.

"Where you going down here? You got lost?"

"Just walking around."

"Aaiiight, I can see that. Going nowhere 'ticular." The talker wonders if he's just invented this, it sounds so curious in his mouth. He says again: "Nowhere 'tic-u-lar."

The quieter of the Farragut boys squares himself in front of the second white boy, the one who's not talking. They'll be counterparts this way, silent dance partners. The quieter has learned at some point that he could almost effortlessly put on the mean face (as his cousin Bobby calls it). He's learned that he could just about cause a white kid to shit his pants with a scowl. He puts on the mean face now.

"Y'all should be careful out here, you know," riffs the talker. "You pretty near Farragut, they's some hard boys up there."

"Thanks for the advice."

"Lucky you ran into us instead."

"Thanks."

"You want to loan a dollar? We forgot to bring a dollar for soda. We'll pay you back."

"How could you pay us back?" This, a piece of sardonic logic-making, pops helplessly out of the mouth of the talking white boy. Having said it, he winces. Sarcasm isn't really in his interests here. Not as part of a conventional dance, nor as a part of the unique tableau the two white boys have fashioned today, the one involving a hacksaw and a vise.

Sarcasm could get his face slapped, both know this. The dance requires otherwise, the dance requires his compliance.

"We'll pay you back, I told you." With this, the talker slips the exchange back onto its track. He reminds his partner of the moves. "What man, you think I'm messing with you?"

"No, I didn't say that."

"Call me a liar?"

"No, sorry."

"Nah, that's cool, I can see you didn't mean nothing. So lemme get a dollar."

"I don't have a dollar." This is the case, this is the truth, but it's also a dance move *par excellence*. They're fully back on script.

The talker scowls and crosses his arms. "Don't *make* me have to check you." The tone is almost joshing now, the threat no longer implied, instead so blatant it's silly, in quote marks, in neon. The blazing incoherence in this is, as we know, the watermark, the identifying signature of this kind of encounter.

"I swear."

"Aaiiight, let me just check you." The talker shakes his head in mock exasperation. "Looks like you got something in your pockets, man, let me just check it."

Meanwhile, the quieter one has already reached for the pockets of the silent white boy, who obligingly raises his hands. Now the talking one does the same thing. This couldn't have gone better, because it couldn't have gone worse. Or couldn't have gone worse, because it couldn't have gone better. Or something.

"What's this shit?"

The two Farragut boys simultaneously draw forth the bait, the surrealist anti-money that has been made ready for them, so many hours previous. The half-quarters, the quarter-quarters. These sit, glinting in their palms, before the shocked eyes of all four boys. The ploy, it has come to fruition. They've attained it, the white boys. The splendid result of their idiot invention.

Yet the white boys are voiceless, reduced to shrugging, wide-eyed mimes. As if knowing nothing of the origin of these mutilated coins.

"Fuck you think you doin'?"

The talker's tone is of authentic revulsion. The dance is in tatters. How disrespectful.

The two white boys produce only sickly smiles, of the *Mad Magazine* "What, Me Worry?" variety.

"Fuck this shit," says the quieter one, tossing the ruined coins at the feet of the white boys, into the cobblestone ruts.

"This how you do it, where you come from?" says the talker. Now it as though they have journeyed to this special zone expunged of all context, the future DUMBO, for a comparison of folkways from two remote realms. "Fuck up your money just for giggles?"

"Well, I guess, yeah," says one of the white boys. There's no defiance in it, just self-amazement.

"Dang." The Farragut boys turn from the scene, over which hangs an air of exhaustion now, and remorse. They stalk off, back up Plymouth Street, and exit the stage in their disgust.

DID IT WORK?

To say, one way or another, you'd first have to know what it was. This little farce, this tiny sunstruck calamity, this barren dance.

The two white boys, they have all along been laboriously attempting to manufacture a Funny Mugging.

There's something poignant in this attempt, sure. But it's also squalid.

With voices they don't possess, in words they'd never be able to locate, the white boys are trying to say: you can't take from me anything that matters, of those things that I have that you want. The money my parents hand me as I go to the door, the money for the pocket and the money for the sock? That isn't anything at all. It's shit.

And though I am terrified to fight you and all of your cousins, I don't have the steel in my spirit. I am instead screwed up like a pretzel when I walk down the street, you can't actually shame me worse than I can shame you.

Not in the long run.

Is it funny? Is it a Funny Mugging?

Let's leave this alone now. We've said enough. We're turning into the Screamer.

102.
Not Even the Big Denominations

(1975)

A Black Dean Street girl is home, reading and listening to records at the same time. She is listening to her mom's Nina Simone *Here Comes the Sun* LP, side one again. (She is in it, really, for "O-o-h Child.") She is reading Agatha Christie's *And Then There Were None*, though she has read it before and she knows who the murderer is. Her mother is in the kitchen. Her younger brother comes home crying. He's eight. The girl is eleven.

"What's the matter?" the girl asks.

"They took my money," says the boy, between fiercely angry sobs.

"Who took your money?" says the mother, who has overheard.

"Them, down on the schoolyard." He means P.S. 38, the school-yard where he has been playing, where they all play.

"Boys your age?"

"Maybe, I don't know."

"You know their names?"

He shakes his head.

"They still there?"

"Maybe."

"Go with your brother," says the mother. "Go get his money back for him."

This is not what the sister wants to do, but she wants less to dis-obey. She puts down her paperback and escorts her brother, who has stilled his weeping, back to the P.S. 38 schoolyard.

A swirl of kids there, the usual. Black and Puerto Rican and Do-minican, some teenagers playing basketball but obviously not attuned to the dealings of the youngers.

"Which one took your money?"

Her brother points to a kid. A little wild and toothy, a hint chaotic. She's seen him before. Barely older or taller than her brother.

She stalks up to him on a straight line though he is careening in circles. Not an evasive maneuver just a body that can't move in straight lines. He's got something in his fist, not trying to hide it.

She grabs his arm, easily too. But the fist is clenched.

"Let me see."

He grins. "No!"

"Let me see." She begins prying his fingers, one at a time. He doesn't admit defeat, makes her pry them all.

"What?" he says defiantly, as though the evidence is not right there in his palm.

Everybody's shrugging and grinning, everybody's going *"oooh, oooh, oooh,"* except her brother.

"Is this your money?"

Her brother nods glumly.

The stuff in the thief's pried-open fist, it's play money, Monopoly money, from the set his parents keep on the shelf with the backgammon set and the Parcheesi and the Po-Kee-No, all the games they played just once or twice and then neglected. Toy money, not the real thing. And it is not even the big denominations, she finds herself thinking later, when she's home, trying to explain to her mother. Not the hundreds or five hundreds. Just the fives and ones.

103.
A Theory of the Wheeze's
(typical)

The Wheeze and I are two or three pints into a quiet night at the Brazen Head when he offers one of his theories. "You realize, don't you, that the Communist witch hunts, the whole blacklisting era, the Rosenberg trial, it's all the result of one man's homosexual panic?" The Wheeze mumbles this first proposition directly into his lager, such that it takes a moment or two for me to believe it is intended to be heard.

"How's that?" I ask.

"Think for a minute."

The temptation is to say nothing, to see how long he'd endure my saying nothing—thinking, that is. It would undoubtedly be less than a minute. Instead, I say "tell me."

"So, J. Edgar Hoover's in the closet, right?"

I agree. I know this fact, we all do now.

"And the mob has the goods on him, right? They're blackmailing him."

"Is that actually true?"

"Common fact."

I open my palm, indicating surrender to common fact.

"The F.B.I. is this gigantic *machine* for ferreting out interstate criminal networks, tracing conspiracies, infiltrating cabals. Prohibition, white slavery, the Mann Act, bank robberies—the Mafia is their natural target. Right?"

In the grip of a theory, the Wheeze is like a conjurer producing a sequence of linked scarves from his sleeve—you can only nod.

"So, imagine Hoover. He's got this machine at his disposal. His whole vibe—"

Here, the Wheeze wiggles his bitten nails before his eyes, to suggest mesmerism or ESP transmission.

"His whole vibe is that the nation is lousy with unimaginable menace. But the actually existing mob he can't pursue, or they'll popularize whatever they were dangling over his head, photos of Hoover in a little pink dress, whatever. So, he redirects the whole material and ideological *apparatus*"—the Wheeze's pronunciation of this word is like a sneeze—"to sniffing out reds. Meanwhile the Mafia flourishes."

"That's—tragic."

"Sure," the Wheeze says. Though he seems in fact electrified.

I mime at the bartender, wishing to close out the tab. But the Wheeze isn't satisfied. He needs me to feel more implication, more complicity, more *something*.

"Shamed longing curdles into violence."

"Is that a—saying?"

His disdain is severe. "I *suppose* it is, since I just said it. Then again, it could be a palindrome. Try spelling it backward."

"I don't get it," I said. We're drunk. I can't follow the Wheeze when we're sober, or when he's drunk and I'm not.

"Like when we were growing up." The direct reference startles me. The Wheeze lifts a hand, flaps it around, indicating *all of this, everything.* What we never speak of, what we always mean. "Shamed. Furtive, denied, displaced, etcetera and so forth."

I blink at him for a moment, say nothing.

Then he lifts his hand again, breezing implication from the room no sooner than he's invited it in. "I mean, all I'm saying is it was a *factor.*"

"Understood."

"One *ingredient* in the smorgasbord."

"Sure," I say. "Thanks." This last, addressed to the bartender, as I scribble on the debit slip. The Wheeze, I see now, introduced his allusion only once he'd observed my fading patience, knew the evening was over, that he'd be able to make his escape.

As if escape exists.

104.
The Wheeze's Implication
(examples)

It's worth pausing to gather examples of the Wheeze's implication.

Boys wanting boys. Or wondering or dreaming of wanting.

Bodies seeking covert sustenance from proximities, from scuffling contact. Brains and voices, meanwhile, wild with panic jokes, a cover on boiling stuff, all that's denied or shamed.

On the one hand, queer Pacific, or the Brooklyn Heights Promenade, the near-to-hand examples, while hardly being Christopher Street, are pretty comfortable in themselves. On the other hand, this is still a time of deep stigma, deep closet, and all types of resultant catastrophes.

The very mayor of the fucking city for starters: he exiles his boyfriend and won't deal with AIDS. Pete Buttigieg, he ain't.

Examples?

We're not talking about those two Dean Street boys who are lovers now, the two who slipped shame's noose. We're talking about nearly anything else.

COULD BE MERE curiosity. Could be life destiny. How to know which (let alone any shadings between) if you're terrified? If the merest curiosity carries risk of self-demolition, self-catastrophe?

To actually be the word everybody tosses so casually.

The word, a grenade with no pin to pull, a joke grenade—unless you put the pin in it yourself.

WHO?

Well, guess who got their hands on a copy of *The Joy of Sex*?

It was right there in the parlor all along, shelved high over the Board Games of Empire, its tan spine disguised in an airless run of bound theses on Hume.

Not *The Joy of Gay Sex*! Forget about grenades—for these two, that would have been like touching a rattlesnake. No, this is the original.

One day shortly following this discovery, after a wearisome re-enactment of the Panzer Battle of Prokhorovka, the parlor's host oh-so-casually mentions that he's been browsing in a *rather* amusing volume. The drawings alone provide hours of fascination. The hair. The beards and beardlike formations elsewhere.

They "peruse" it together.

And because, despite all efforts to experience themselves merely as disembodied brains in jars, brains rehearsing foreign wars, the two are, in the end, teenage boys with working parts, the atmosphere gets flushed and steamy. Their talk evolves through a series of exclusions.

"I wouldn't even want to touch anything wet or with hair, necessarily."

"I don't even need to *see* that, to be perfectly honest."

"The situation is that it's just the breasts I want to touch, or maybe just see. The round part, not the nipple, which seems like it's mainly for baby nutritional purposes or something."

"Nothing wet comes out."

"Well, not ordinarily."

The book is usefully propped between them, blocking any action of the hands beyond its horizon, as they slump side by side on the seldom-used late-Victorian green velvet settee.

"I saw breasts in *The Man Who Would Be King*. I found the nipple part in no way disturbing, but it was the round part that compelled my interest, no question."

"I just truthfully mostly imagine the panties on. A large red brassiere quite gradually removed, that sort of thing." After a moment of sheer breathing in tandem, their talk shifts to early masturbation techniques, the slap, the roller, the pullback, all discarded now in favor of the inevitable fist slide. "Only behold, if one restricts to a single looped finger, this brings out the resemblance to a set of lips."

"Albeit with nothing behind them."

"Well sure. No lips or tongue."

"That's a moisture I can approve of. No association with childbirth or excretory functions."

Both lick their palms.

"Saliva evaporates almost instantly. If you could invent a paint that dries as fast, you'd make a million dollars overnight."

"Not in the cave of the mouth, it doesn't."

"Well obviously."

"The holy grail."

"You can walk around with it in your brain all day and it gets no closer."

"Yet some people are actually experiencing it. Like, *right now*. At least, say, a hundred people in Brooklyn at this very instant. Statistically that has to be likely."

"At four in the afternoon?"

"Any hour."

"We could provide this for one another. A mouth is after all a mouth."

"I can't believe you said that."

"In our hour of need."

"Soldiers in a foxhole?"

"Exactly. My guess is, actually, that you want to."

"You've got the more womanly lips, I'd say. I think you should be the one."

A truth appears: one's nerd companion, sour grapes consolation for entire worlds you've quit, is more than a pulsing, tormented body beside you—he's himself become a world, whose entrancing aspect you study through all five senses.

"It's true, you've got barely any lips at all."

"It's the way I hold my mouth. A habit formed by hiding my braces, but it's become an attitude or posture of the mouth. Like a signature, I can't change it."

"I never thought of that."

"Speaking of which, don't let your teeth become involved."

"It won't go that far, trust me. I want absolutely nothing to do with the peehole. I'm just going to kiss the edge."

Nothing happens. It's as if they'd both been expecting some kind of electricity to jump out, from the mere contact, mouth and penis. Nope.

Then, shocking them both, he gives suck, with an avidity suggesting *baby nutritional purposes*. Or something.

THE CRAZY SUCK isn't reciprocated. It never happens again. It's just too much—I don't mean for you, or me, we'll presume nothing about one another's preferences—but for these two, here and now. Later, in college maybe. For them, now, like one of the rejected board games, it goes back in the box, back on the shelf.

Why on earth would they experiment here, in this place, with being the name everyone calls them already? Better wait until they're where no one would dream of using the word. They feel the clock ticking on their exit from their situation, it isn't far off.

Does this *shamed longing* between them *curdle into violence?*

Not out on the street. Not in this case.

The violence of their shamed longing is instead exercised in wrath at Rommel's Panzer divisions in Tobruk, Georg Stumme's Panzer divisions in Kursk, Hasso von Manteuffel's Panzer divisions in the Battle of France, and so forth.

LET THIS EXAMPLE serve, among the white boys of Dean Street. Are there others? Sure. We can wonder about the Wheeze himself, the decades of solitude. Did he always love—who? Could it have been the boy called C.? Not that we'd raise the topic with him. Plenty of us were a little in love with C.

But no, on this topic we'd better glance at a pair we've barely glimpsed before, two Black boys. They've only had a walk-on, to this point, in a Funny Mugging. They'll play a bigger part.

105.
Idol and Smaller Friend
(1976)

These guys are together all the time. One is fourteen and taller, and his friend who is almost the same age, he'll turn fourteen in a couple of months, but is smaller. Don't call us Batman and Robin! I'm no sidekick. Just friends, leave it at that.

But it's more than that. This taller friend, he's basically the smaller one's idol. He's good at everything. He walks great. He keeps his jeans in the right place on his hips. His sneakers always look bright. He's really funny in a way only you seem to understand.

Try to explain his jokes to someone else, they're not even funny. It's a language of two.

The smaller friend's idol can make the smaller friend do nearly anything.

Hold that thought: nearly.

The smaller friend's idol is great, I mean *great,* at the dance. (This is not their word for it, of course, but what this book is calling it.) The idol is as casual at this form of encounter as if he were merely pausing in his progress down the street to retie his shoelaces. It's a gestural thing, like falling out of bed: shave and a haircut, two bits!

His idol conjures up the mean face like it isn't anything. You might think he's enraged but he's not; he goes away grinning. He enjoins the smaller friend into the encounter and makes him strong by example, by proximity; he makes a mean face mean enough for both of them.

Then just stands there, says to the smaller friend "check his pockets," and though the smaller friend would never have the nerve to do this, he somehow does it. He just goes and does it. The white boys let him. The white boys fall right in line, they don't know what hit them. When it occurs like this, it is always astonishing. A sole piece of perfection in an imperfect world. What might later be called a life hack. Quarters and dollar bills leap from their pockets into your own. Then move on down the street, everyone knows the drill.

You couldn't imagine doing this on your own or with any other person, though you know it is practiced by others.

It takes the idol to activate the smaller friend in this way.

One time he even tried to make him take a fresh-bought slice of pizza, though that was not the triumph it might have been. A rare fumble.

These are not Dean Street boys.

They live outside the lines drawn by the old lady.

They're Gowanus Houses boys.

If somehow presented with the notion of the false oasis they would react with, let's say, a fairly violent unsentimentality. Not only is that shit *false,* it never existed to begin with!

There is a theory propagated by a few of their parents that the white people are not all bad. That some of them marched for freedom. This makes little sense, but then the world makes little sense. Whose freedom? His mother's, to serve slop at the cafeteria of I.S. 293? Thinking on such matters can fuck with your sense of what is real.

The white boys on the street are real. Nobody can tell you they needed to march for the freedom they enjoy. The freedom to act like they don't know they've come to the wrong street, the wrong precinct. That unconscious freedom which you have found it amusing to vandalize, to decorate with dread and shame.

You either let this kind of shit mess with you, or you mess with it first.

This, above all, is what his idol is expert at.

The smaller friend has a teacher from his school who has noticed him on the street in his idol's company and thought to question the arrangement.

"You seem like a kind young man," says the teacher, when she has him to herself for a moment.

"Uh-huh," the smaller friend says back, suspicious of falling into a trap.

"But you don't act kind when you're with him."

The smaller friend is uncompelled. His idol has a magnetism, and the less it makes sense to others the more certain the smaller friend is that it has been assigned to him to be magnetized. To walk down the street in the company of his idol is like moving to music that only he can hear. It feels as if it shows him who he is or could be. It feels right.

Besides, he is a little afraid of him.

ONE FURTHER THING binds him to his idol, though it is a thing that goes unnamed and unspoken, a further thing to make the smaller friend afraid.

Both of their fathers are inside the jail on Atlantic Avenue. A handful of times, early on, the two boys encountered each other in the congregation of children stranded, by the restrictions on visitors, out on the sidewalk. The smaller friend has also been taken inside a few times to see his father. Though he has no idea whether his idol has been inside as well, he supposes it is likely.

For the smaller friend, this speculation migrates toward an area of the deliberately avoided. He works to avoid thinking of the inside of the jail, prefers his diminishing recollection of his father from an earlier time, in a different setting.

A related effect is how the smaller friend flinches when he hears the word heroin.

He just doesn't like the word.

During the brief interval where he allows himself to be placed in the Newgate Program, the smaller friend never sees his idol there. That unaccountable interval in the Quaker rec room, with all those white people watching him, and the scattering of white children who plainly don't belong in the Program. That humiliating interval of small bribes accepted, the apple juice in tiny paper cups, the graham crackers on a napkin. A relief, obviously, not ever to have to discuss that particular situation. Not that it was likely his idol would ever have let himself be placed there! It's a perfect example of his idol's clarity and keenness that it is impossible to imagine it.

The younger friend, too, soon refuses going, saying he'd be happy to stay away, to stay out on the streets. Often at the very moment his mom is up at the jail, the younger friend will be in the company of his idol, with whom he prowls around never mentioning what anyone might or might not just then be doing up at the House of D.

They have plenty of other things to discuss.

SO, HIS IDOL has this one problem, this one bug in his ear. It is very specific. He doesn't want to talk about it, except for those moments when suddenly he does. He talks about cocksuckers. The subject seems to irk him for no reason.

They talk about it in weird bursts. "I heard if you go to the park you could find yourself a proper cocksucker."

"Isn't that a faggot?"

"What you call me?"

"I didn't call you anything."

"That's right, you know you didn't."

"What about those girls on Pacific? You have to pay them, then they do it." They're not actually girls on Pacific, of course. Grown women. Prostitutes. But his idol knows what he means, or he thinks his idol should.

"Nah, man. That isn't what they do."

The smaller friend is confused. Isn't that *exactly* what they do?

But his idol is sure. "They give a blow job."

"Isn't that the same thing?"

"Nah man, are you trying to be stupid? In a blow job they just blow. It takes a proper cocksucker to suck a dick. You remember about Sylvia?"

There was, the smaller friend knows, some humorous story about Sylvia. It was a story that took place on the beach. At night, on Coney Island. That's all he's sure of. "What about it?" he says, to dissemble.

"That's why all those boys was laughing about her. She took it out, but she wouldn't suck on it. Bobby was waiting, but all she did was blow on it. Like she was blowing out a birthday cake."

"*That's* a blow job?"

"That's right. That's all you get. Find a proper cocksucker, you got to go to the park at night."

"What park?"

"A certain park," his idol says, in aggravation. "One part of it. Or down by the docks."

The idol's information seems flawed. Or, at least, incomplete. Yet his idol treats it as absolute. Obviously, some received talk, some unnamed influence, has filtered into this topic. Why does his idol keep using the word proper? Yet here, between them, walking down the street, there is no one to triangulate. To fix what's in error. Therefore, these speculations usually tail off, into shrugging. A change of subject.

And then the topic bursts into the light again, turned in a slightly different direction. "What I heard is, you got to *make* a proper cocksucker, they don't want to do it at first."

"You make them?"

"That's how they get started. They learn to like it."

"When do they go to the park?" asks the smaller friend. "Before or after you make them?"

The idol seems annoyed by this question.

"I mean, why would they go to this park?"

"They know what they want, even if they don't know it," says his idol conclusively. "They feel it in their bones."

The smaller friend knows when to quit asking questions. His idol may be going about things backward. Yet it endears the idol to him even more deeply. This one perfect person, isn't. He's goofy on this one particular subject. And his smaller friend is glad that his idol knows he'd never rat him out, never hold it over him. That makes the smaller friend proud.

One day they are alone, and his idol says, out of nowhere, "I'm gonna find a white boy to suck it proper." It is a hugely satisfactory pronouncement even if it is destined to amount to nothing, as the smaller friend supposes it surely must be. It follows, since his idol is so alert to power relations, that he's conceived this mysterious exchange along those lines. Over whom else has the idol exhibited power, beside white boys?

Just the smaller friend.

106.
Hicksville
(1981)

But while we're here, what about a glance at those other two? The Black kid and the white kid with their secret fondness, their idle afternoons, their predilections hiding in plain sight.

Well, not hiding from C., or the one kid's dad, who walked in.

Maybe tons of people know at a glance but say nothing.

Maybe they go together on a routine basis to get sandwiches at the premature gentrification delicatessen and are suffused in an air of knowing. Maybe they even go there for sandwiches just to feel it. Some forecast of a life that's chosen them.

The things that coincide and coexist around here are truly beyond tabulation.

But—they don't have to fly under Dean Street's radar anymore. Alas.

Many things coincide and coexist around here, but not these two.

Because the white kid's dad got a new job and moved his family to Hicksville, Long Island.

An hour on the Long Island Railroad and a thousand worlds away.

ONE EVENING, THE Black kid's dad hears them talking on the phone, murmuring behind a door, second or third time that week. He doesn't interrupt, just waits it out. What do they have to say that takes an hour on the telephone? Only one thing takes an hour like that. Love talk.

Dad has a smoke at the kitchen table and waits. His boy's sure to circle out again, go fishing in the pantry for a midnight snack—it's like clockwork. No need to go busting through doors. When the boy appears, dad tosses down a twenty on the table beside the bowl of goldfish crackers the boy has poured himself.

"What's that for?"

"Go see your boy."

"What are you talking about?"

"You know what I'm talking about. You're old enough to take the A train. You can figure out the Long Island Railroad by yourself. Check a damn map. Train leaves from Atlantic Terminal, probably take you an hour. Go on the weekend."

So, he goes. Around the station, Hicksville looks no different from deep-ass Queens—low industrial buildings, overpasses, crappy houses, gas stations, nothing to speak of. His white friend and his white friend's mom meet him at the station, which he wasn't expecting but is cool enough. He likes his friend's mom, and the feeling has always been mutual. Any worries, she keeps to herself.

"Take us to the park, mom."

"Maybe he's hungry. Are you hungry?"

"We're going to White Castle later, mom. Drop us at the park." They're silent in the car, waiting for release. "This is good, right here."

His white friend walks a little ahead, tour guiding. Away from the station things have opened out, gotten greener. The park isn't bad, but it's no Van Cortlandt, not even Prospect.

At the outset, something in the white kid seems brisk, bottled, a far cry from their outpourings on the phone. It is as though first duty is to show his Black friend this world he's come to. What it looks like and perhaps what it requires of him.

"Hey, Brooklyn!"

The crowd of white teenagers with mitts and bats is all indistin-guishable in T-shirts and cuffed jeans and feathered hair, like an over-populated audition for a role as Fonzie's cousin. They're jocular and grabby. Up close, the faces are beefy and Irish or long and Jewish or Italianate with long eyelashes, but they dress and behave as if to defeat any hope of distinguishing one from the other for more than an instant.

"We need outfield, we need third base! C'mon, Brooklyn, bring your homeboy!" The slang might be wrong in at least two ways; it is perilously near to *homo*. But it is produced with no shade of anything but dumbbell jubilation.

His white friend shrugs, looks at him helplessly.

"Sure, let's get in for an inning. I haven't hit in a while."

The Black kid takes third, knowing his friend can't handle grounders. He can. He digs frustrating these congenital pull hitters, all accustomed to curling it around the bag and running home, while fielders chase it through the unfenced grass. At the plate, he three times in a row lines it up the middle for singles, scores all three times on home runs.

"Line drives, line drives, this guy hits nothing but line drives."

"Brooklyn's the same way," says another. "It's the streetball dis-ease. These guys think if they pull the ball, they'll break a car window."

"Yeah, well, he's gonna take the pitcher's head off."

"What can you do."

"Ghetto thinking."

"Ghetto's gonna win the game for us, way he's scooping at the hot corner."

His white friend is *Brooklyn,* he's *Ghetto,* it never occurs to the Long Islanders to explore the question of his actual name. The atmosphere's stinky, sarcastic, and totally embracing, albeit on a one-time basis. He's taken up as a pet, unthreatening, an adjunct phenomenon to his urban-weird whiteboy friend.

None of the daily intricacies of the home block, navigations in a shifting mosaic. Here, these guys—whatever they are, Irish, Jew, Italian or unspecified within the local uniformity—here they rule, and can afford munificence.

Nice place to visit, wouldn't want to live here.

And, in this company, the deeper secret between the Dean Street boys, the former and present, is utterly concealed behind the designation of them as freakish cosmopolitans, emissaries from the impossible city.

A FEW INNINGS and things, and a couple of the Hicksville guys need to be somewhere else and the game falls apart. They make their good-byes, and he follows his white friend home out of the public avenues to a quiet suburban street, some trees and lawns, more like Long Island as advertised. The walk to his house is as mute as before but they've restored to each other's wavelength, and they go through the front door and straight upstairs without any tours or hellos.

His friend's mom shouts upstairs at the closing door, "You're back!"

"Yes."

"You ate something?"

"I told you we went to White Castle," his friend, his lover, lies.

"Good, but there's a plate of sandwiches in the fridge, it's there if you need it."

"Okay."

"And cookies."

"Okay."

The bedroom door is locked, the needle dropped on side one of the Alan Parsons Project's *Turn of a Friendly Card*—his white friend's parental payoff for accepting the move to Hicksville is an awesome quadrophonic system—and Brooklyn and Ghetto get right back at it, pick up where they left off, and it really doesn't matter all that much where they are. His dad was right, as usual, Hicksville's no big deal, it's nothing more than an hour on the Long Island Railroad.

107.
Street Book Vendor
(1997)

Say a guy, a former Dean Street boy, now resident of an apartment above a bar on Columbia Street, the far side of the BQE—say that guy has been visiting his aging mom in her apartment near the Brooklyn Academy of Music. Say it's a cooling mid-October Friday evening, one of those magic ones, and he wants to walk that distance across his homeland—now, which street should he choose?

On Flatbush or Fulton or Schermerhorn, he'll be dodging the sidewalk hawkers. Bootleg reggae CDs on a blanket, essential oils and beads, table full of pamphlets manned by stern brothers from the Nation of Islam. In the long tail of the crack and squeegee era, in the year of Abner Louima, with the Disney cleanup still just a Times Square rumor, those streets boil. Still, walking them is an option. What once awed and frightened him now aches of familiarity, yearning even. He could go and saturate in that feeling, of identifying with what doesn't identify with him. The old puzzle takes the form of new faces, new songs, new teenagers and streetcorner types, a scene of false recognitions, not real ones. Walk Schermerhorn or Fulton, there's little danger of being beckoned to by some voice out of the past. The ghosts are only in his head. Outwardly, he's just some white guy, might as well have moved here yesterday.

To walk Dean or Bergen or Pacific, that prospect is another thing entirely. Should he opt for the row-house blocks, should he walk the length of Boerum Hill drunk, not only on one too many glasses of his mom's cold white wine, but on the mythic light eking through leaf shroud to paint the cornices, he'll surely be flinching at hallucinatory Spaldeen ghosts, as if he might have to stick up his hand at any second if someone yells "catch, man!" On these blocks, he's all too likely to be hailed by a body sprawled out on a stoop with a tallboy in a paper bag. Like the last time he walked Dean Street. Not a ghost at all, but a living being addressing him by his right name as though they'd last talked a day or a week ago.

"Yo, how's it going? It's Baby Hector!"

And it surely was. It was Baby Hector. Has he seen him since I.S. 293? How in god's name did the man endure all these decades on the street with that family nickname? Why hadn't the other kids questioned it, replaced it for him, since they all liked the guy perfectly well? Baby Hector weighs three or four times what he did when he was a twiggy outline scrambling along the sidewalk in a game of Running Bases, but it was him.

"Haven't seen you in a while, man!"

Baby Hector had spoken to him out of the ancient certainties of this place. The fact that so far as Baby Hector can judge, the two of them had been born and would die within a block or two of each other. Talk about Running Bases! Venture off one square of slate and dare to advance about fifteen or twenty steps before taking safe harbor. And then, at the next interval, you dash back. From here to there, your whole world.

No. Not today, not after soaking in his mother's wine and decline. Today's not a day for Baby Hector. Or for Big Hector, if he is still alive, or for Eric Fedder or for Marilla and Teeny, or for Mr. Welish and his stoop crowd, or for Milt the Vigilante, or for one of any number of people's moms whose name you forgot or barely even knew to begin with. Just Richie's mom. Tamara's mom. Today's not a day, most of all, for that risk of some deeper encounter, for instance C.—imagine the feelings that would ensue!—maybe having swung around the block again on such a dreamy night. He just isn't up for that.

So, he walks Atlantic Avenue instead. Less chance of confusion there. Atlantic's got wide sidewalks and room to breathe. If the former Dean Street boy is hoping to dodge locked-in memories, he should, once past the Nevins Street Daycare Center, be home free. Just survey the homely aspirations of the shops rapidly turning over, now a bakery or boutique or copy shop, the entrepreneurial miscalculations still possible thirty years into this gentrification. Oh look, now somebody's trying a Vietnamese sandwich joint in the same storefront, that's one to root for.

Or conversely, there are those shops that never budge, businesses that might as well be like a mural painted on a cliff. In Days of Old Ltd., the anchor of the antiques row. Kalfaian Carpets. Steve's, Sahadi's, Montero's, the Brooklyn House of Detention itself, if you want to put it in that framework. A going concern, anyhow. The soul food restaurant, that's been hanging on a good while.

Just past the bail bonds joint, at the mouth of Smith Street, the former Dean Street boy's head is turned by a vendor with a table loaded with books. Dude is grizzled and possibly drunk, seems a little wobbly on his pins, and wearing sunglasses though the evening's begun. The merchandise is surprisingly interesting, though, some beautiful older editions, a few wrapped in plastic like in a real shop. Presumably the guy has set up here to take advantage of the new hipster traffic on Smith, headed to the French restaurant, the newer bars, this weird boomlet that's pushing the Puerto Ricans out after so long.

In no hurry, still relishing the evening, the former Dean Street boy peruses the tables, lifts up a curiosity, a pocket-sized paperback of Melville's *Redburn* with an evocative sketch of a sailor.

"I just collected on a wager with myself, that you'd go for that one." The street vendor's voice confirms all guesses: a drinker's mutter, prematurely aged by cigarettes, then stretched to a drawl with defensive irony. "Now I owe myself a dollar. Double or nothing says you'll set it down when you see the price."

Booksellers who loathe their clientele: a known type. Taking the bait, the former Dean Street boy flips to the first page. The crabbed pencil markings read 10.00. More than he could have guessed, even with the needling remark. Are young French-foodies paying ten dollars for cute yellowing paperbacks, or is this whole setup a lost cause? Is he a fool for being the one person who stopped to browse?

But he shuts the cover on the price and keeps the book in his hand. "I like the drawing."

"Sure, you do. Edward Gorey. He's no Gil Kane or Frank Frazetta, but he's got something."

Is the vendor crazy or just mistaken? Then, a closer look: it *does* look like an Edward Gorey. Score one for the vendor. "I had no idea he drew book covers!"

"There's more where that came from."

"Must have been early work, from the look of it." Now they're making small talk. This threatens to become a pleasant encounter.

"Yeaaaaaah. Before he did his own thing, or designed the sets for *Dracula*, or gift-store coffee mugs, Gorey was a humble commercial hack, much like Andy Warhol before him."

That archly strangled locution, the ceaseless scorn: this vendor's voice nags at the former Dean Street boy. It calls him out, as though from some well of ancient authority. So, he reaches into his pocket to prove the crank wrong. Mercifully, he's got a ten-spot. It falls into his hand, and he pushes it across the table.

"That's all you want? Not one glance at the rest?"

"I've, uhhhhhh, got to go."

"Melville's still all you care for? Or are you still cultivating that childish fondness for Vonnegut too?"

"What?"

"You don't recognize me, you dolt, do you?" The vendor plucks the ten-dollar bill from his grasp.

The former Dean Street boy gapes. Soon, the grizzled features resolve, into something pitiable and arresting, a bleak mirror. They're the same age, of course. This means the Dean Street boy may be, unknown to himself, also a ruined child. The street book vendor is his schoolmate, the one-time searcher for the Lovecraft Basement. The antiquarian kid.

"It's you."

"Only approximately."

With relief, the former Dean Street boy is now able to retranslate the vendor's ambient hostility as the sad devolution of a familiar personality. It's personal, in other words, but nothing to take personally. Time has not been kind. Was it a decade ago? More?—when, having wandered into Emporium Books, he'd last seen him? Good lord.

"I always thought you'd have a shop of your own someday." This is out of the former Dean Street boy's mouth before he sees how cruel it sounds. Needling begets needling, it's like they're instantly back in the I.S. 293 gym, in a contest for who'll be picked dead last for punchball.

"You're looking at it," seethes the vendor. Then mutters to himself, turning gnomic. "I keep my seashell collection scattered on the beaches of the earth."

"Sorry?"

"The whole world's my oyster, not to be eaten in months containing the letter R."

"I think I get it."

"I'm just saying, this is my bookstore. We own the city, you and I, by dint of seniority. You're free to use the restroom, even without a purchase."

A hobbit once, he's Gollum now. He appears dust poisoned, corrupted by the toxin of his interests, much like one of those do-it-yourself renovators who vanished into the lathe and plaster, and emerged ten years later to a world that no longer considered him young.

"You've been doing this, uh, selling on the street, a while?" The former Dean Street boy works to soften his tone. Not all who dish it out can take it.

"I usually work the Village. Sixth, across from the Waverly. Fucking Giuliani gestapo have started chasing me off, so I thought I'd see what the new Left Bank had going for it. My storage space is on Hoyt and Union, so it was a cheap thrill. But these cryptobohemians don't read, they eat and fuck. They rarely even hesitate long enough for me to bum a cigarette."

"What's that trendy restaurant? Patois?"

"Patois." They both savor the dorky syllables, the jokes that make themselves.

"The new Hubert's," suggests the former Dean Street kid.

"That's right, that's right, the new Hubert's." This actually draws a smile from the street vendor. The schoolmate. The madman. His teeth are awful.

Now the former Dean Street kid assesses the folding wheeled cart, the bungee cords, the plastic milk crates shoved beneath the table. The whole economical and squalid air of enterprise, just this side of a derelict's bindle.

There's only one way to salvage this encounter, short of running shamefully for cover. "Probably got a pretty fair wine list."

"I'd like to shove it up their ass."

"How long does it take you to pack this kit up, anyway?"

"Not more than a minute or two. Just watch."

"You think they'll seat us at the bar? My treat."

"Now you're talking," grins the antiquarian kid. Or whatever we should call him now. It's too early to call him the Brazen Head Wheeze, or even the Brooklyn Inn Wheeze, but he's well on his way.

Antiquarianism, a mask that eats into the face.

108.
Hard-boiled
(self-styled)

Many of the white boys of Dean Street will over the years be drawn, in one way or another, to the hard-boiled style.

What is meant by "the hard-boiled style"?

A big question. Maybe a rabbit hole. But let's agree for now that it consists of a language tendency—urbane, jaded, sardonic, reduced— that encodes within it a certain attitude toward conflict and violence.

A stoical and amused attitude.

A certain bravado.

A certain flinty romanticism about masculinity.

For many of the white boys, this is no big deal. Nor do they think themselves particularly distinctive for this leaning. Nor are they particularly distinctive for this leaning.

They respond to film noir and Humphrey Bogart movies, novels by Dashiell Hammett and Raymond Chandler, things like that. And at this point you are thinking, *what white boy doesn't?* It's part of the American vernacular. It doesn't belong to anyone in particular.

Even if later this appetite deepens or expands, and the boys become aficionados of the style, it still isn't that remarkable. Maybe they read Walter Mosley or James Ellroy or Richard Price. Maybe they connect this interest with, say, their pleasure in early Godard films, or early Paul Auster novels, or the way they identify with *The Singing Detective* or *Miller's Crossing*. None of these are such rare or telling appetites.

What's telling is the way they take it so personally.

The way they connect it to their New York City outer borough childhoods. Their sense of having come from, or through, something not everyone understands. The pleasure they take in recognizing certain lineages in street dialect, and connecting those to attitudes they encountered on their own street.

Like when a guy gets shot near an ice-cream truck in daylight and his landlord laughs it off by saying he was a "known con artist."

The boys of Dean Street take the hard-boiled style as their personal legacy, their franchise, their special inheritance.

It may be a way of overestimating their own credibility to themselves.

You can hear it in the way the Brazen Head Wheeze and I talk with each other.

Is it embarrassing? Probably.

The thing is, the hard-boiled style does originate in encounters with authentic violence. With authentic trauma.

Chandler and Hammett, veterans of World War I. Hemingway, whose writing is lurking under the skin of the style.

The war that invented shell shock.

The lost generation.

Trench coat, trench warfare.

Humphrey Bogart and Edward G. Robinson both served during World War I.

Yet, by the time the Dean Street boys absorb it, the hard-boiled style is pretty far from these roots.

Most of them, they learn the voices of Humphrey Bogart and Edward G. Robinson in paraphrase, coming from the mouths of animated cartoon characters. Frogs, rabbits. Or the mouths of comedians, doing impersonations. Rich Little. Woody Allen's *Play it Again, Sam*.

Bugs Bunny didn't serve in World War I.

Neither did Woody Allen.

The Bugs Bunny style is hard-boiled, but ironically. In scare quotes. It brandishes the sarcastic bravado, while retaining none of the courage or stoicism of the authentically hard-boiled. What it provides is a form of mock cowardice to cover real cowardice. Manic tap-dancing, hand-waving distraction. Bugs Bunny and Woody Allen, if you put them under real pressure, are always about to run away, or break the fourth wall and make an appeal directly to the camera.

For the white boys of Dean Street, the Bugs Bunny style performs an end run around the self-loathing of the white boy's position in the dance.

Sawing those coins in half, there's a real Bugs Bunny move for you.

Telling all these stories so I don't have to tell you other stories: Bugs Bunny all the way.

YET THE REAL question might be, what lies beneath the hard-boiled style? This shitty carpet, so tight to the corners of the house in which we dwell—if we pry out the staples and peel it up, might we find a parquet floor?

The risk is that there would be no floor. Just a falling, into something oceanic. Might it be pain? Trauma?

Might it be—love?

109.
Before and After
(increasingly)

We try to resist generalizations, easy binaries, but face it, this one is irresistible: most things involve some degree of before and after.

Childhood in New York City, for instance. For the white people, this tends to have a definite before and after: the abduction of Etan Patz. It is never the same after his parents send that six-year-old on a two block walk to school. After those flyers go up. Such a beautiful kid. It hurts to type his name.

After that, they are like *what were we thinking?*

OTHER DIVIDING LINES may be more secret. Yet decisive to aspects of our inquiry.

For instance, there must have been a before and after to when the banks decide to begin providing loans to the homebuyers, the Brownstoners. When did it happen, exactly? And how? Someone flipped the switch. Someone talked to someone, the long effort of petitioning the cops, the mayor's office, the Jane Jacobs people, and it happened. A neighborhood of nonwhites, a neighborhood zoned for light industry—a neighborhood fated, in some plans, for demolition and clearance in favor of a throughway—now, by force of will, exists. The fiction of Boerum Hill is made real, that day. The old lady's dream comes true.

They don't give it a landmark designation instantly, but that's coming too, just a few years later.

Now, walk those storied streets. The trees they planted, and resolutely replanted, the trees they forged ironwork to protect, all grown tall. The brick they repointed. The high fences that conceal the gaps in the rows, where the houses fell. How could this have been anything but a sacred place? Abandoned, derelict, slated for demolition? Now you're like, *what could they have been thinking?*

SOME PEOPLE WILL prefer the before-parts of this inquiry to the after-parts.

Listen, I understand. The before is honey colored. It glows. If you go far enough back, you might reach the false oasis. Maybe you can live there.

Even short of reaching the oasis, you might, for instance, find the antiquarian kid more beguiling, more sympathetic, than the Wheeze. His quest for the Lovecraft Basement, it had a certain innocent charm. I wish he'd found what he was looking for.

He had better teeth, then. Better breath.

As I write these words, I can see him, nursing a beer, chortling, saying, "Yeah, it's a pity you turned into yourself, too."

THOUGH WE'RE MOSTLY in the *after* part, now, we'll have to return to the *before* a few times more. I know I've been avoiding what I have to tell you. I've held back crimes.

Like held-back children, made to repeat a grade, they've gone on growing anyhow. They're curdling back there.

ANYWAY, THE DISTINCTION breaks down. Just because a thing happens in 2004 or 2019, it doesn't mean it isn't part of the before. This is what the better crime novels know. The hard-boiled detective writer Ross Macdonald, he perfected this, he made it systematic. The crime is always in the before *and* the after.

Some things, like a gentrification, or a trauma, can't be so simply placed in time. They exasperate *before* and *after*. They dwell instead in a null space, a long between. Distrust anyone who tries to pin them to the pages of a book.

THIS INQUIRY ISN'T, finally, about what *nobody knows,* or what *everybody knows.* It is about what a small number of people remember, even if they avert their eyes when passing on the sidewalk. It is about the knowledge that is locked up inside their bodies and how it wishes and doesn't wish to come out.

110.
Sword
(1978)

In the lives of the boys there are before and after situations, of course. Many of these vivid in feeling, but difficult to name.

Others are specific to a fault, like the afternoon of the sword.

The afternoon of the sword results in the *before and after* of C.'s protection—stewardship, chaperoning, whatever—of the millionaire's son.

Has our inquiry reached a before and after of its own? We may have noticed ourselves in pursuit of a crime unfolding in slow motion. A boy and his nemesis. Attention must be paid.

Dueling pistols, mantelpiece. Some crimes you see coming for three hundred pages. Maybe it's time to get on with it?

The afternoon of the sword is part of this story.

WHAT IS IT that day that makes C. suppose it is a good idea to ring the doorbell?

The nemesis, Little Man, may have spooked C., by means of his eerie vigil.

Of course, the vigil was intended to throw fear and confusion. Even if not in this particular direction.

The vigil is simple. It hides in plain sight. The nemesis sits on the stoop of the abandoned house. There is no dog shit stick, but there no longer needs to be. It would be redundant. At this point, the shit is of the mind.

The nemesis has gone unconfronted by any authority since the day of the shit stick. He finds himself deep in an invisibility pocket.

The more totally a nemesis's energies concentrate on their sole client, the more the nemesis benefits from the cloaking device of his victim's shame.

The boy with the gravity knife, the boy whose father drives the BMW with the moon roof open, the boy with the ethereal mother who so rarely leaves the house—he can't know that the force field of denial he projects benefits only his foe. How could he? It's nemesis magic.

Only C. observes this. He's beguiled into the error of this day by self-appointment. Only a self-appointed protector could make it. He strolls along the street and finds the nemesis coolly staking out the millionaire's door from the stoop of the abandoned house and he reads the situation instantly.

Sympathies divide him.

Or, if he is more honest with himself, antipathies.

The nemesis and the millionaire's son, both strike C. as wretched. Yet a greater law pertains. If each of the wretched boys are unimportant in themselves, each are nonetheless part of a world he seeks to reconcile inside his person, the street he attempts to salve and soothe by his powers alone.

He pitches his intervention in the nemesis's own style, one of coming at things sideways.

"Sit there any longer you apt to turn to stone."

"Stone deaf to your jive already."

"You want to see someone, maybe just ring their bell, that's all I'm talking about."

"I might have to fuck a kid up."

"Why be like that?"

"He showed you that knife?"

C. shrugs.

"That's what I thought. He give you his daddy's drugs from the refrigerator, too, don't lie."

"He's cool, man."

"He's cool to you. Since he talks like you, or think he do. When you not around I see him trying to *walk* like you. To me, he's just a dumbass white boy I might have to fuck up."

C. just says, "That ain't right."

Nemesis shrugs. "His mama's real nice to you?"

The remark is equivocal, maybe doesn't even know what it intended to mean. C. shrugs it off in turn: "She's okay."

"Shit."

"Let's pay a call."

Nemesis looks off into the distance but there's no distance to look off into, unless he wants to pretend to be craning his neck to see the bus coming.

"You're so curious about this and that, but all you're doing is staring at a door."

Nemesis surrenders his perch only grudgingly. Yet he does surrender it. A captive of C.'s effusiveness, his charisma. They cross together to ascend the millionaire's stoop. The nemesis hangs a step below as C. rings the bell. Not that he's intimidated, no.

Who'll it be?

The BMW is gone from the block today, if they're checking.

But she never leaves the house. C. is likely relying on this, the cowing presence of an adult female, anywhere.

It is the millionaire's son who opens the door.

His eyes light first only on C., long enough that a brazenly awkward "yo!" comes from his mouth. Then, as he registers the presence of the nemesis, his features pinch in an insectoid way, his cheeks burning instantly red.

"What are you doing?"

"Just coming around."

"Nobody's home, you can't come in." The millionaire's son's voice is stiff and flat. He tries to shut the door. It is at this moment that C. makes what might be his consummate error of the day. Such a small and casual thing. He stops the door with the flat of his hand. He's underestimated the rate of the conversion of the millionaire's son's shame into rage, into panic. Attempting peacemaking where no peace exists.

"Get out!"

"We just want to talk."

"OHMYGODYOUBROUGHTHIMINSIDEMYHOUSE!"

"Ain't inside," says the nemesis. "On your goddamn stoop."

C. only speaks the name of the millionaire's son, his ostensible friend, really his burden.

"OHMYGODYOU'REBREAKINGIN!"

"That's some comical shit now," mutters the nemesis. "We was breaking in, wouldn't go ringing no doorbell."

But the millionaire's son is no longer present to absorb his nemesis's disdain. He's split, booked up the stairs two at a time, vanished into the upper regions of the house. In ceding the doorway, he's converted them into housebreakers.

"Let's get out of here," says the nemesis. He's the practical one now. C.? He's plunged into a dream of his own devising, a passage between irreconcilable zones. He holds up his hands, directing traffic in outer space, bewildered.

"Wait a minute, I hear him, he's coming back down," he says. In C.'s dream-space, the millionaire's son will come downstairs and present the gravity knife and something will be reconciled. All these wretched energies, sufficiently dispelled. He's not fool enough to picture these two as actual friends. They're unsuitable friends. They're unsuitable humans, perhaps. Only C. himself could ever have been friends with either of them, and today the effort is costing him his soul.

"YAAAAAAAAGHHHHHHHHHHHHHHHHHHHHHHHH!"

This sound accompanies sight of the millionaire's son swinging from the newel post and leaping off the bottom steps of his interior stair and charging the two visitors where they stand wallowing at the door. The millionaire's son wears a grinning hideous red-painted mask with arched black eyebrows and leering lips, and horns, and fangs. A ceremonial Japanese Noh artifact, if anyone could identify it. He waves above his head a long, curved, flat blade. An antique samurai katana sword, if anyone etc. These things, mask and sword, have been retrieved from the coffin nook, that special indentation in the wall at the bend at the top of the stairs. Quite possibly they've been placed there by the millionaire's son in anticipation of such use. The speed with which he's made them appear suggests this is the case.

"Oh shit!" says the nemesis, backing off the threshold, and down the stoop. "Your boy gone crazy."

The millionaire's son makes as if to sweep before him with the blade but on his readying backswing C. places his own hand very easily over the swordbearer's wrist, then reaches in and plucks the weapon away.

"Don't come at me with no sword," he says sternly.

"I'm calling the police," says the millionaire's son, through tears misting hotly behind his mask. His voice rasps and falters, vocal cords already shredding by screaming.

"White boy tried to cut your head off for ringing his bell," marvels the nemesis.

"SERIOUSLYIAMCALLINGTHEM!" howls the millionaire's son.

C. chucks the sword down into the foyer. "You do what you like," he says, with disgust. He retreats down the stoop, but not by stepping backward, like the nemesis. He turns his back.

He has returned from distant space.

It's the last time they'll speak, C. and millionaire's son.

Crime?

We're just getting started.

111.
The Whisper of Undercrime
(subliminal)

Sword, nemesis, gravity knife, you see it coming. We all do.

Yet beneath this crime is another. Call this thing an undercrime.

It's that which the parents don't want to talk about. The whispered thing, the overheard thing on the phone calls. By the time of the day of the sword, it's nearly two years old.

The more they don't talk about it, the deeper it slides beneath the skin of their days.

An unutterable undercrime setting the conditions for the over-crime.

Both, undercrime and overcrime, will be obscured into puzzle or myth in the minds of the children. Even the minds of the best remem-berers among them. The two events are connected only obliquely. But they have this in common: the manner in which both occurrences will be smothered together, concealed. Twin shames.

One difference, though, is that overcrimes happen to persons. Might even be committed by persons. People you would never be able to claim you never knew, never hung out with, never called a friend.

Undercrimes often involve unpersons. Those who can be denied, shunted aside.

Picture him now, playing in his room, the spoiled boy.

Understandably, this may be a challenge to do.

His manic public moments, the brief infatuations on the slate, in his concrete yard, or the moments when he buttonholes another kid coming home from school: These are the exception. Between them, he seems to lapse into obscurity, like some kind of erratically flower-ing plant.

But there's gotta be a there there.

Somebody he is when he looks in the mirror.

A row of books and toys.

Thoughts, wishes, dreams, masturbation.

The way he is with a book, it's like he's coring an apple with his eyes. He reads the same ones over and over again, trying to solve them like a trick or a puzzle, a Zeno's paradox. Like every single book he ever read might as well be *The Monster at The End of This Book*, star-ring Grover, the furry puppet from Sesame Street. Grover, who pleads with the reader not to turn the pages, in fear of the promised monster. Grover, who turns out to be the monster he's pleading with the reader not to confront.

If he's going to be involved in something terrible, that's probably because he was born for it.

So, look at him there, curled around the pages, licking his fingers, and ask yourself: Would you even know if this moment, this glimpse, was of *before* or *after*? Is the spoiled boy reading the book backward or forward?

112.
C., Part 4
(1979)

In the year of the sword, C. told himself he was done with them.

Though in truth you never quit a thing, not all the way, not in one instant. It's too much to ask.

What was he still trying to prove? Nothing.

He never had been. It had been somebody's else game, somebody else's fight, somebody else's dream.

Whose? His parents? Their parents?

Who gives a shit?

He'd only taken it for his own. Mis-taken it.

He eased himself out of the scene, off the block, by degrees. It isn't that hard. Everyone's dispersing anyhow, the white boys his age taking the subway every day to wherever—Hunter, Murrow, Music & Art, Stuyvesant. In total indifference, he's taken no test, therefore lands at the school where he's districted, Sarah J. Hale High School. The place offers a continuity with Intermediate School 293 that was near-absolute, all the familiar Gowanus Houses and Wyckoff Gardens boys, with one glaring exception. It is as if they'd gone through the 293 yearbook and scratched out those eight or fifteen white faces.

This simple maneuver reworks his map. The neighborhood is hinged at Nevins Street. It turns out there exists another world just a stone's throw away, in the basement of the Colony South Brooklyn Houses center, on Dean near Third Avenue, Black and Puerto Rican and Dominican teenagers without a white boy to be seen. Only one block east, but astounding how crossing Nevins weeded them out. You might not think he'd be drawn to the social worker vibe of the Colony South Brooklyn joint, but hey. Nobody hassled or preached to the crowd that took over the basement, as though the goal had just been to shift them indoors and call it a win. The scene was actually like an open house, one where some guys with turntables and microphone were up to some solid shit. One famous Saturday night they even managed to recruit Grandmaster Flowers to run a show in the adjacent P.S. 38 schoolyard.

Another world, another world, another world.

C.'S FINAL WHITE boy is an impoverished affair, a sad joke. From his later perspective, an afterthought. If C. didn't stop to think of it from time to time, shaking his head, no one on the block would probably even remember that the white boy in question had even arrived on the block.

Well, one person would. The childless white woman in the tall, lonely house who'd had the bright idea that she could suddenly handle a foster kid at her age of 40-whatever. Her husband an obvious disinterested absentee, she'd maybe been driven half-insane seeing the Dean Street mob play on the block until dusk and not having one to stand on the stoop and call home to dinner for herself. So why not dial in for takeout? The kid is scrappy and suspicious eyed. He's previously been bounced from an Irish-Catholic household in a poorer quarter of Bay Ridge. C. reads him like a book. He'd wager this kid has never previously been in a situation where the Blacks and whites did anything but sporadically beat on one another, and figures he can ease the poor sucker's entrée to the special mixed-up block onto which he'd parachuted.

Why?

C. can ask himself a hundred times and not find an answer. This was an operation of pure muscle memory. Old habits die hard. C. catches the foster kid on a hot afternoon sitting on his stoop in a blob of protective leaf shade, turning the pages of a thick brown hardcover album, looked like an antique photo album maybe, with his face expressing maximum irritation and perplexity.

"What you got there?"

"Fucking stamp collection. Her brother sent it to me."

"Whose brother?"

"My mother, the lady who lives here, maybe you know her."

"So, you mean your uncle sent it to you?"

The white kid sneers, finding this apparently humorous. "I had a mother or two, but I never had no uncle."

"Lemme see."

The white foster kid shoves it at him.

"She said it was a world-class collection. Just looks like a bunch of stamps to me."

They examine it together, the early pages filled in with rows of engraved George Washingtons and little government buildings, all monotone green or purple or blue.

"Dang."

"What?"

"They didn't leave you much to do."

"You think it's worth something?"

C. catches the scent of deal to be struck here. The album is typical white antique shit, always cherishing what smelled of dust and royalty. But it might bring a few dollars. The childless woman's name, C. knows, is something like Pierrepont or Witherspoon. Just like people like that to toss some valuable shit at a foster boy. "I know a place we could find out. Worth a visit just for the air-conditioning. Show you if you split it with me."

"Deal."

He leads the kid and his album up Hoyt Street, to Livingston, the back entrance of the time-lost wonderland that was Abraham & Straus. The department store has solid-gold elevators, distinguished by the smell of the oil that kept them running, run by dapper elderly Black men who clank the gate shut and whirl them upstairs with a smooth-running golden cranking device. Like some kind of ascent to air-cooled heaven, you just have to have the audacity to act like you know where you're going. In their case, the eighth floor, which is, really, the only floor worth mentioning. The record store, the board games, and two separate counters for coin and stamp collectors. That this exists anywhere would be a rumor or a dream. That it exists in their neighborhood is a strange fucking magic indeed.

"Where'd you come by this?"

He's coached the kid on a story on the way up: be firm that your uncle died and left it to you. Not foster uncle, real uncle. Death being that which ended talk. C. suspects that if the stamps are legit, the clerk's avarice would do the rest. Why work at something as preposterous as a stamp counter in a department store in downtown Brooklyn unless you dug the shit yourself?

In fact, any offer they receive will be a fraction of the real value. C. is certain of this as well. But it will be found money.

The stamp counter clerk hands over forty dollars, as though he's guessed he should offer an amount easily split between the boys. C. tries to persuade the foster kid to browse the record store, but no chance. The foster kid seems to feel he's gotten away with something and wants to depart from Abraham & Straus pronto. Fair enough. They go downstairs by escalators instead of the elevator, for cover. Back out into the blaze of day.

"You hungry?"

"Sure."

"C'mon, we can afford something good for a change."

The air-conditioning at Junior's Cheesecake is as good as that at the department store. They get a table upstairs and wolf bacon and eggs and cheesecake and leave a fat fuck-you tip for their skeptical waitress. That leaves them with money in their pockets still. Heading back to the block, the foster kid says "you know where I can score some cheeba?"

So, C. takes him to the pot store on Bergen Street.

An all-around satisfying first encounter. The foster kid might seem like an already half-completed project, ready in all respects to accept the imprint of C.'s tutelage. Too bad he is destined to have his local education nipped in the bud, in the stupidest possible circumstance.

HOW DO YOU bring authority down on your head in a virtually authority-free zone?

Easy. Bring a gun to school.

The foster kid, though he is C.'s age, has managed to be left back a year or two, so he attends 7th grade at Brooklyn Friends, the destination chosen by his foster mom.

He is caught with the gun within the first two weeks, because he is idiot enough to be showing it around at recess.

How do you make such an incident even more damningly stupid?

The gun isn't really a gun, or not a functional one anyhow. Just a chunk of metal, the handle and barrel and chamber of some old ironwork street piece, with several crucial elements missing entirely including a firing pin.

A cherished artifact smuggled from who-knows-where, from the foster institution most likely, kept stuffed down at the bottom of a bag of hand-me-down laundry. The kid transfers it to his brand-new Jansport backpack, and brings it every day to school as a fetish or security blanket and then one day waves it around and has his precious object confiscated and that is that. Next day, the childless woman returns him to the foster agency.

He is officially forgotten by the block.

It is an echo of the gravity knife, and equally foolish. When white boys aren't helpless, they are chaos. C. is done now, done with featuring himself as their emblem of possibility. Let them cross over on their own steam, let them find someone else to show them how to lace their shoes and how to walk down the street. He is out.

113.
Movie Star
(2005)

A movie star is moving onto Dean Street.

He's a verifiable star. He played a half-Martian warrior king in a special effects movie. In his credibility mode, he was nominated for an Oscar for something seriously boring about a person who is dying. He wears a baseball cap underneath a hoodie, and he wears sweatpants and walks his Boston terrier at night even in the rain. Not looking at him is a full-time job. Everyone in the neighborhood works together on this project, that of not looking at the movie star.

The movie star bought the former abandoned house. Yes. The same one.

Into the early '90s, long after the tide had turned, and the last rooming house was gone, the abandoned house sported cinderblock windows and looked like it might need to be demolished. Then, abruptly, it was gutted and stabilized and repointed by a developer. By this time, it was impossible to claim that the neighborhood's gentrification was premature. Or that it wasn't a gentrification, that it was instead a rescue or rebirth, a Cinderella or Phoenix.

So many idle footnotes, so many locked-in memories. Why should the movie star know he is living in the abandoned house? Outwardly, it looks the same as all the others. Only a little nicer.

Those who revered and feared the abandoned house as an object of mystery, a dead zone in their midst, are old and bitter and confused.

Our inquiry may be considered lazy, and possibly even cruel, if we let the movie star stand in for so much else that has come to pass. For instance, the stupid glamor of the Smith Street restaurants. He's not to blame for that.

Nor is he to blame for the galling towers rising up on Flatbush, or the ludicrous expansion of the notion of "Park Slope" to encompass, now, everything southward to the cemetery, and westward to the dead land of tire outlets and gas stations.

He has nothing personally to do with the kitschy commercial travesties, the T-shirts and baseball caps, the restaurant names and band names made out of the signifiers of local grit, like the toxic canal and the fading industries, the powdered cheese factory on Bergen, the coffin wholesaler on Union.

The movie star is not answerable for the bar named "Wino" on the corner where there used to be a guy lying on the sidewalk who you had to step over to get to the subway.

It would be strange to imagine the movie star to be the cause rather than merely a curious symptom of the whole phenomenon, that of the dollar signs that have taken command, the sheer fucking money of it all. The swollen numbers, the zeroes stacking up.

This place is changed.

Even the changers have changed and been replaced.

The displacers, now, often, displaced.

The broken-down Brownstoners, whether hippies or squares, pot-heads or drunks, they now sit on their stoops and take glares from the newer residents, just as they once gave out glares to those sitting on stoops, those who made them afraid, who alienated them from their decision to live here. Now it's their turn to be the ones who look a little bedraggled, to seem a little too unkempt, to live in houses that need repainting, to drag down the property values. Or to give up, be priced out, be bought out, be embittered.

These are their just deserts, you say?

Maybe.

The procedure, that of waves of succession and replacement, is perhaps beyond our scope to incriminate.

It's all too much, give it a rest.

It's not a crime to want to wear a GOWANUS or 718 or TAKE ME TO THE BRIDGE T-shirt.

Who cares which white rapper went to public school and which went to Saint Ann's? Get your head out of the ass of the past.

Young French and Dutch and German people are very nice. They can travel where they like and spend money where they like.

Street cred is not actually a thing. A line of credit, that is much better.

The cabs will actually take you to the bridge now, and across it, late at night. Farther, they'll find riders hailing them on the Brooklyn side, on the sidewalks of Smith Street, and they'll cross the bridge in the other direction full, rather than empty. This is a good thing.

That it makes your jaw sore not being able to start to explain how it was different before isn't a crime either, or even a thing.

And oh, the novelists. The plague of Brooklyn novelists.

If you are the Brazen Head Wheeze, it is the novelists that stick in your craw. How funny, really. Out of all the possible things to object to!

Well, to be fair, he does object to all of the things, actually. The aforementioned, and much, much more.

You name it, he objects.

He just doesn't happen to know who the movie star is, and if you explain it to him, the name doesn't seem to register. The most recent movie star the Wheeze would certify as legitimate and impressive to him is Marlon Brando. If you like, he will explain to you why there has been no real movie star since Brando. Brando was the final one, the end of the line.

This current movie star is okay. He really obviously loves his dog. He also, truth be told, nods in a very human and humble way from beneath his hoodie if you do venture to meet his eye. He is on the record as being in favor of many good causes, and he has the taste not to jam with his rock star friends though he is purportedly a fairly dedicated musician.

Say it with me: no crime, no crime, no crime.

There is no crime here.

Movie stars need places to live like anyone else. Why not Dean Street?

It's a very nice place to live.

Audacious hipsters of all genders make a show of leaning down and making cooing sounds and reaching in for a quick caress of the Boston terrier's ears, without acknowledging the dog's owner in any way, a kind of anti-flirtation. The dog accepts this wild surplus of attention eagerly, gratefully, without suspicion.

A dog doesn't know that a movie star is a movie star, and that is why it is likable of the movie star to keep a dog around.

It does seem funny, though, to one tired witness, on one particular night, to see the movie star standing in his hoodie in the rain with his dog on the corner of Pacific and Nevins. He really cuts a strangely passive figure, the movie star. He is stopped, staring at his phone, his articulate brow furrowed. Not calling someone, no. Staring as if waiting for someone to call. His dog stares up at him.

A poignant scene. It stirs the thought that this was once the famous corner of the tolerated prostitutes, the cop-sanctioned truck women. And what, in a sense, is a movie star if not a kind of flesh peddler? No, really—isn't there supposedly some kind of lineage there, the painted courtesans, the backstage assignations with wealthy patrons? Wasn't that in a book the tired witness once read, or a movie?

It's enough to make him want to shout, "how much for the dog?" A punctuation through the decades. But it wouldn't make any sense to do it, and he doesn't, and goes home.

114.
Real People
(an uncanny condition of our inquiry)

They're all real people, that's the strange thing. Now that I'm attempting this writing, I have to confess I had no idea how confusing it would be.

Anyone I mention here, I made them up. They're inside a novel. And yet, in order for that to need doing, for it to be possible, they had also to exist. The movie star, for instance. He's my invention. But a real movie star came to Dean Street. Several, actually. That had to happen for me to be driven to my invention.

The couple who left the neighborhood, just for instance. Those who only rented on Wyckoff for a year or so. I don't know them, by definition. They left! But needless to say, they existed, which is why I had to make them up. They existed, and so did those they did and didn't meet at the party in 1970: a blockbuster, a redliner, a real estate broker, and their own evicting landlord, who had his car set on fire. The people who set his car on fire. All real, inside the fiction. If they weren't, then the fiction that constitutes this inquiry wouldn't matter at all.

The children, the parents, the policemen. The Screamer, the Wheeze, the old lady.

You think I would make up that an old lady named the neighborhood? You know better. Dean Street's novelist, he made her resemble Miss Havisham, from Dickens. He made her very "novelistic." I don't have the capacity, or the time, really. And this inquiry doesn't require it. So, I just made her like a flat cutout, like a shadow moving through our inquiry, one with the words "old lady" attached to it.

Is that more or less useful than the Dickens thing the novelist did? You decide. I'm just doing the best I can to advance the cause here. If anything, I've had to tone it down, to make you stay with me, to keep us in the hunt. Everything, all of it, really happened. But more so.

Me? I'm just a character in this novel, the one who happens to be writing it. But someone like me surely existed, let me assure you of that. If such a person hadn't existed, I wouldn't have been obliged to make myself up.

As someone once said, if you gaze long enough into the disclaimer, the disclaimer also gazes into you.

115.
Rememberers
(then and now)

Two old friends sit in a garden. She's Black, he's white.

The garden is in the backyard of the house where one of them grew up. Her parents never left, never sold.

There's a plate of bagels, gravlax, capers, lemon wedges.

On all sides, the new owners. The high backyard fences, for privacy, for sound insulation, where once there was an alley that ran through all these backyards. Low or broken-down fencing, later. Cyclone. Ailanthus trees growing like weeds. Now, those have been rooted out in favor of more elegant shade trees.

From where they sit, they can see at least four houses currently building out into their backyards, extensions with new all-glass sitting rooms or breakfast nooks, and new patios above. Easy to hate on the new construction, but what did you spend all that money on if you don't have the right to punch out into your own back lot for a little more space?

Still, this backyard is a kind of sanctuary, a little timeless zone.

These two, they're telling stories they've told before, burnishing tokens. Updating the Rolodex of the past, the fate of all those children they were once children among.

Yet also surfacing new feelings and thoughts.

Contrasted to the way this street once had them at its mercy, there's something—let's not say complacent—but *luxuriant* in their contemplations now.

She says "it seems like every kid from the neighborhood either went to jail, or became a cop."

They laugh and shake their heads. The remark does something to their feeling about being from this place. Opens it up, into a figurative panorama. Like they're flying overhead, seeing around the edges, the bend of time. Her remark's an exaggeration, but not wrong. It cuts close enough to home: His brother spent time at Rikers and also upstate, in Spofford, and Watertown. Her brother's a prosecuting attorney.

Or consider those two sisters they knew of, on Bergen Street. One sister a uniformed beat cop, then a lieutenant, solid career in blue. And the other sister, who got heavy into crack, was lately spotted on 14th Street by someone reporting things not looking so good. A miracle possibly that she still walks the earth.

Now he says to her "so what are we? Criminals or cops?"

They laugh, a little uncomfortable.

They're writers.

They're rememberers.

Rememberers are the ones who remember. Who consider the before and after too much. They don't have to be writers. Many rememberers are those who are still around, who never left. But it can also happen to those who ran away, who've spent their adult lives in

Thailand or Nova Scotia. One day they might think they are going about their usual business, and then suddenly they start with the remembering. A little fissure opens up in the combination of time and self. The past comes flooding through.

Despite themselves, these helpless rememberers are hard at work. They're trying to figure something out. Irked by what they don't know but heavily suspect, they're unwilling detectives, along on our inquiry.

HERE'S A REMEMBERER STORY:

On a day in the early 1990s, two Dean Street boys, one Black, one white, sit in a coffee shop on Shattuck Avenue in Berkeley.

Their journeys to this meetup are divergent ones. One of them is passing through Berkeley because his father, the former actor, has moved here from Brooklyn, having taken a job in the office of the Berkeley Repertory Theater. He's nothing like his father. He finds Berkeley an obnoxious, undisciplined, indulgent place. He's an unusual product of his environment. Or should we consider him the product of an environment *refused*? Having excelled in computer science and Farsi language study in college, he found himself quietly recruited for a post-college training program in CIA analytics.

Well, somebody's got to do those jobs. He's a desk worker, an analyst. It isn't as though he murders people.

Yes, it's the Slipper.

The other guy careened in a different direction. He worked as a high-end bike messenger in Manhattan, early '80s. In the company of Rastafarians and speed-heads and wannabe triathletes, he excelled, was a star of the profession. He made such a good living at it that he never went to college, indeed, barely graduated high school. When his interests elaborated to carbon-frame bikes, harsh vertical climbs, and the importing of Thai Sinsemilla, the Bay Area beckoned, as an outpost of things outdoorsy, and doorway to the Pacific Rim drug trade. His money-losing bicycle boutique is a superb front for the flow of cash.

Though they attended Brooklyn Friends School together, it's not clear these two ever actually liked each other. Their parents stayed in touch, or they'd have no chance of this meetup, one conducted in a mutual atmosphere of perverse curiosity and genial hostility.

Perhaps the only thing they clearly have in common is the unresolved feeling for that zone of origin which, though denied, still helplessly defines them. The confusions of Dean Street are therefore projected by each onto the other, deepening the antipathy.

A drug smuggler and a spook? Is this some version of *every kid from the neighborhood either went to jail, or became a cop?* Maybe. Though it doesn't feel exactly like what the two writers in the backyard had in mind. Too far from Brooklyn.

Neither of them have been clear with the other about their actual profession.

We'll skip the niceties, which between these two aren't so nice, and jump to the point where one of them introduces an abrupt act of remembering.

"When I think of you as a kid," says the drug smuggler to the Slipper, "I picture this one movie in my head. I play it all the time. I wonder if you can see yourself this way—probably not. You used to do this thing."

"What thing?"

"We'd be out on Jay Street, after school, trying to get home across Fulton. Some guy would be threatening to hit you. Put you in a headlock, browse in your pants, whatever. But you'd fall down before they could touch you. It was like a *routine*. You'd be on the ground flattened and whining like you were hurt already. Keening. That's the word for it. I can see you forever on the pavement in my mind's eye, preemptively keening."

"No," says the Slipper.

"You don't recall it, do you?"

"Wasn't me. You're confused."

"Kind of thing you probably sublimate."

"I remember other people under duress, when I think of it at all."

"Duress?"

"Other people?"

"Other kids, yeah."

"Well, I picture you with your unique approach, which was very vocal and, as I said, triggered by as little as a sidelong glance."

"Thanks for the gift of the image, now let's move on."

With that, they quit the bout of remembering—or, at least, of remembering in a way that pertains to our inquiry. The terse and disagreeable reunion is put behind them, quickly enough. What were their parents thinking, shoving them together like this? Some friendships, or so-called friendships, are better left to wither and be forgotten.

HERE'S THE THING, though.

The image—the descriptive offering—stays in the mind of the Slipper. Not just for days, or weeks, but for years. He gives it grudging audition in his mind's theater, his private recovery room for suppressed and deleted information about himself. Was that really him, on the ground, whimpering? *Keening?*

Nothing like this is ever encompassed in his old teenage ledgers, all of which he has tucked deep in storage.

With all his codes and cryptograms, there was never one for ME, KEENING.

Yet the keening scenario is too compelling, too persuasive to entirely dismiss. Can it be that he has conveniently Slipped from his own memory of himself?

The Slipper has to grant that even he was once known and seen. Witnessed, inside attitudes and situations not of his devising or control—basically, that is, pre- and early adolescence. Jay Street, Fulton, Schermerhorn.

The place of no-control: that was the place he'd come from. Come through. Neither of the two, sitting there, had needed to describe that world by which they were both formed.

Perhaps the description was, in fact, a portrait of a form of Slipping. Who wouldn't opt not to be injured, if the outcome was to be the same? Humiliation, the toll of passage. Playing possum, mugging money, whatever. The longest judo move in the entire martial art:

knowing you're going to win in the end, because you're going to get out intact.

He might even conclude he admired the tactic. Not every picture is pretty from the outside.

His father had called it *helping out your fellow man*.

Yeaaaaaah, not quite.

BUT THIS ISN'T the end of the story.

Twenty years later, the Slipper—still in analytics, never implicated, so far as he knows, in the Agency's dirtiest work—finds himself sitting with another long-lost former Dean Street boy, another Brooklyn Friends School kid, in Tokyo, Japan.

Some have gone a long way out of their way to be elsewhere, and this guy is one. A true expatriate, having moved to Japan after college, never once again living in the United States, let alone Brooklyn.

Yet mellowed by age, and willing now to be a rememberer. They're at a ramen joint, seated side by side. Real hole-in-the-wall place, inside knowledge required, the sole *gaijins* in the joint. The cold sake is flowing. The evocation of those boyhood times settles into their bodies, at such distance now in both time and space, to become a mellowness, a fondness, a wonder. We once were alive, we remain alive, fifty-something men showing no sign of injury. Neither speaks in a Brooklyn patois, or an accent either earned or assumed. The names they mention—streets, schools, teachers, bodegas, a nemesis or two—are all ticked off aloud as if according to some rote system, perhaps a religious catechism.

They even mention he-who-goes-never-mentioned, that one formerly known as the millionaire's son.

Last anyone knows, that sick dude was chief lawyer for a major entertainment agency.

Very possibly unlike his father an actual millionaire. Which, from their current vantage, doesn't mean anything so remarkable.

These two are glad enough not to know more.

Then the expatriate brings up the case of the Berkeley guy, the drug smuggler. For the Slipper, in the two decades since their sole grown-up encounter, he's kept tabs in only the loosest way. Word through his dad, who still lives in Berkeley, is that their old acquaintance's high-end bicycle shop had evolved into a fortune in commercial property. That he'd gobbled up a few empty storefronts on the Shattuck end of town, near the Bart stop, and seen their value mushroom as Telegraph Avenue stopped being a place where Berkeley's aging middle class wished to spend their money.

Another day, another gentrification.

"Though I'm unclear how bicycles turns into real estate," says the Slipper.

The expat laughs. "He'd stop in Tokyo going back from Saam Liam Thong Kham. He was into something more than bicycles. Remember Reefer Delivery Man?"

"No shit."

"No shit."

At this opportunity, having found himself deep in his cups, the Slipper spills forth that upon which he has ruminated for twenty years: the picture of himself on the pavement, untouched, whining for mercy. *Keening.* The picture painted by the drug smuggler. Here, in the company of his old friend, in this foreign land, has come the chance to triangulate that intel. The description of himself cringing on the sidewalk has remained lodged awkwardly on the bottom shelf of his self-knowledge.

The Slipper describes it. The keening. But the expat only shakes his head.

"That's him, not you."

"What?"

"It's a total projection. He whatchamacallit, he snowed you, one hundred percent. He gaslit you. I remember *him* like that, not you. Him on the pavement mewing like a kitten. Him the one who folded like an accordion before he was even touched."

"Interesting."

"Seriously. He externalized his trait. Believe me, I was the one who had to try to cross Schermerhorn Street in his company. I saw it all. He was the last to develop."

"Develop?"

"Anything. Height, shoulders, a deeper voice. All he had was this strategy."

"Tactic. I think the right term is tactic."

"With him, I'd call it a strategy. A life-pursuit, to fall before touched. He'd have been cooking it up nights, lying awake staring at the ceiling."

"He became such a hipster. The bike thing, the drug thing."

"He was sulking. The bike thing was all about reinventing himself in Manhattan, covering his tracks. Another strategy. Listen, telling you it was your behavior, your trait—twenty years later he's still figuring out how to get out from under it. Like ventriloquism, throwing his voice."

"Astounding. I'm astounded."

"I remember once, I'll never forget the voice, he said *I . . . only . . . have . . . one . . . coat.*"

"Meaning?"

A shrug. "They wanted his coat—someone didn't have even one. He'd grasped that under the circumstances he could embarrass his tormentor if he went there rapidly enough, to a place beneath human dignity."

"We none of us had any. Dignity, I mean."

"He had less."

They gesture for another sake. The cups are filled, and they drink. At this juncture, it remains incredible to recall such things, acts lacking clear analogue in the regular index of human situations. The Slipper feels almost that he has been robbed of something. The description had entered his body. It now shifts to the status of an excised portion, a phantom limb. He's never considered himself empathic to any unusual degree, but he'd taken the stigma aboard easily.

Then again, maybe this wasn't personal. Wasn't even individual.

Perhaps it was the case that under what the drug smuggler had called "duress" they had all, essentially, shared one body. This would include the Slipper and the expat too. Maybe they'd adopted the denied behavior in turn, modeled one from the next.

Perhaps they all bore the trait. Hence embraced it naturally, upon hearing.

If so, shoving it back and forth among themselves would be a futile exercise indeed.

BUT ENOUGH WITH these far-flung rememberers. This inquiry, this book, features a couple of rememberers much closer to hand. The Brazen Head Wheeze, for one. Me, for another.

Him and me, unlike the Slipper and the expatriate and the drug smuggler, we never ran. We stayed in the neighborhood. We didn't go to jail or become policemen.

We didn't become writers, either, not really.

We're the ones who have to do the next work here. Now it can be told.

But first I have to tell you about the novelist.

116.
He's Holding Court
(2019)

This particular night, the Brazen Head Wheeze startles me with an unattributed pronoun. (I know, I know, I'm a fine one to talk.) The Wheeze is seated at his usual stool at his usual bar, curled like a savage question mark around a beer I'd just bought him, as though daring me to impound it. He speaks without meeting my eye. "He's back, you know."

"He is?" I blurt. Since I know the Wheeze, I know who he means. He means the novelist.

The Wheeze issues a grunt of confirmation. It is a sound full of pained indictment of my innocence, as if I should have known.

"You saw him?" I ask.

"He's at the Brooklyn Inn. He's holding court."

"You went in?"

"Oh, I wobbled through, on my way here." The Wheeze's voice shrinks, to something resembling that of a mole overheard in its burrow. "He didn't recognize me." In him, injured dignity is nearly indistinguishable from pride. The Wheeze's degeneration is his license, his credential.

"Holding court to who?"

"Whom."

"Whom."

"I could hardly make out individual faces. They formed a frieze of sycophancy, like wallpaper made from a George Grosz painting. One of them held a pad, for jotting the pearls that fell from his lips. I suppose the Times Art Section has commissioned another profile. You know, the kind of piece accompanied by a photograph of him standing thoughtfully contemplating a Spaldeen, in front of a graffitied wall."

"Where would they find one, these days?"

"Which, the Spaldeen, or the wall?"

"They could photoshop in the graffiti. I suppose the Spaldeen is harder."

This type of banter isn't difficult for me to maintain, at least in the Wheeze's company. His atmosphere is infectious. Truthfully, it is well-trod ground for us. Tonight, he surprises me, though, by saying, "Let's go over there."

"You hate that place. You hate that guy."

He smiles, peeling back the grizzled lips with which he ordinarily veils the chaos of his teeth. "We're the oldest of friends," he says. "You and me and him, we go way back. Besides, he owes a round."

"He does?"

"Sure, he does. We're his characters, he owes everything he has to us. Without us, he's nothing."

"I don't know if he'd see it that way."

"We'll set him straight, then. It'll be just like your old favorite,

Breakfast of Champions. Don't Vonnegut's characters all surround him and tell him what they think of him?"

"Something like that." As I recall, it is more the opposite, truthfully. At the end of that novel, Kurt Vonnegut surprises his characters by showing them that he controls them, that he's the god in their universe. But I don't wish to further exhibit my familiarity with Vonnegut in front of the Wheeze, because he's already had so much fun at my expense about it, over the years.

It's unfair. The Wheeze himself gave me the book, when he was sixteen, and I was fourteen. Before he was the Wheeze, back when he was still the antiquarian kid. He'd pressed it on me. And it had had the desired effect. It blew my little mind.

Ever since, he's needled me for my allegiance to it, and to that other talismanic book, *Moby-Dick.* The Wheeze is very disappointed by the limitations in my reading sensibility. He has lots of other, more grown-up literary favorites he believes I should have developed an interest in.

Helplessly, sitting here now, I begin to view the Wheeze very much as if he is a character in Vonnegut's novel, one gently mocked by his author for his pretenses of independence and free will.

"We'll go over there and do an intervention," he declares. "We'll set ourselves free of that damned book."

IT WOULD BE fatuous to list among the crimes of this book the fact that a kid we grew up with, one of the Dean Street boys, wrote a novel. There's nothing so remarkable, anyway, in the act of writing a novel. Anyone can do it.

Lots of people in lots of places must at some point have to deal with the fact that someone they once knew has written about the time and place that they remember from their own coming-of-age.

And left a lot of things out.

It isn't the novelist's fault, is it, what he recalls or doesn't, what seemed important to him or not?

Maybe.

It isn't the novelist's fault that he glazed it all in the amber of his self-pity, is it?

Maybe, maybe not. Artistic privilege.

It really can't be held against him that *whiteboy Brooklyn novelist* became such an unbearable thing, so shortly thereafter.

Crime of taste, at best.

What's aggravating to the Wheeze, and I suppose it irks me as well, is how the novelist agglomerated so many different white boys into the outline of one body. He drank our milkshake; he sucked us dry. We others were at once everywhere in his pages, and nowhere. The novelist hogged all the glorious conundrums for himself.

And he claimed C. as his defender, alone. As if. I don't know if C. even particularly *liked* the novelist. If I could, I'd ask him.

WORSE THAN THE novel, if you ask the Wheeze, is the fact that, years after *Take Me to The Bridge* had been happily forgotten, no longer read, it became the famous T-shirt, sold from one particular boutique on Smith Street. Those of us who'd stayed, the semi-voluntary rememberers, we were forced to pass on the sidewalk young white hipsters with the words *Take Me to The Bridge* emblazoned on their chests in a graffiti font that was plainly ersatz, over a silhouette of a kid dancing in the spray of a hydrant. It was a weird phenomenon. The T-shirt became a thing you'd see worn by members of Japanese boy bands in a photo shoot, as the fake-gritty "Brooklyn" brand slowly colonized the glossy pages of the world.

IT IS AN uncommonly beautiful night and the streets between, the old paths we walk that bring us from the Brazen Head to the Brooklyn Inn—Atlantic to Hoyt, Hoyt to Bergen, past the now-silent upper window of the Screamer—are vibrant with young people, scurrying in gaggles or couples. If they walk singly, it is sloped forward in a texting frenzy, as if against a stiff wind, their faces lit and flushed.

It occurs to me that the Wheeze and I know nothing, really, of the present life of the neighborhood. We only see a past city, cluttered with ghosts so vivid they completely obliterate our view of the present. That the Wheeze detests the present shouldn't fool anyone into thinking he knows what it is.

Tonight, though, he doesn't trouble to harangue anyone as we make our way from one bar to the other. He doesn't even denounce them to me. He's flushed too, buzzed on his higher purpose. That being: to drop some kind of piercing truth, in the form of himself, at the feet of the novelist, like a hunting dog with a kill. *You fired the gun,* he might wish to say, *and here is the cadaver.*

The Brooklyn Inn is beautiful, as ever, despite being throttled with the same crowd that fills the streets. The long bar, the high ornate mirror, the corner windows. The no-television. Much more beautiful than the Brazen Head, really. It's absurd that the Wheeze has pitted himself against it, as though he lives in monkish denial of that for which he most hungers, that which would make him complete. He ought to be the Brooklyn Inn Wheeze, we all feel this, don't we? He's in exile.

So, perhaps he isn't a hunting dog, tonight. Perhaps he's an exiled king, come to claim his place. He rushes the door. I can barely keep up.

Yet, on entry, he only skulks past the scene at the corner of the bar, the babble of heads and voices, the knot of attention within which presumably lurks the novelist. The Wheeze is hardened to his role, his type, his furtive, needling, marginal style. He's no insurgent king. It's too late for that. I follow him to the bar's far corner, where he squeezes in, placing his back to the wall, much to the annoyance of a couple who scowl at him but give way.

In this company, he resembles a homeless person. It hits me like a bolt. This fact is better disguised at the Brazen Head, which is nearer to the big avenues, the bridge on-ramp. The light there is harsher and therefore more forgiving, averaging the Wheeze's own harshness into the decor. There, he's the fly in the ointment. Here, in the light of the restored residential blocks, the brownstone glow, he's a dead cockroach in the butter.

"Aren't you going to talk to him?" I ask.

The Wheeze's look is poison. He waves his hand at me, disgusted.

"I'll get us beers," I say. "I'll say it's on his tab."

This draws a snicker, at least.

I see him now, the novelist. He's the same, the kid we knew. He's only a bigger kid. It's true in the author photographs, and now in person. His aura of self-fascination has pickled him in youthfulness. Though I feel the same is true when I see any of us, all the former boys. Even the Wheeze, unrecognizable though he may be at a first glance, as when I found him selling books on the corner of Smith and Atlantic. We're all the same. Boys who wear the names and the outlines of men.

The crowd thins, both the ambient bodies and the courtiers around the novelist. Now it is just a faithful two or three conversing with him, no one I recognize. No sign of a journalist, either. Perhaps the Wheeze hallucinated the presence of a journalist. Who'd ever need to read another profile of the novelist, at this late date?

The Wheeze, in his insinuating way, has put himself in the line of sight. He sits glowering over his beer, letting the moment find him, his usual method. And it does.

"This used to be a French restaurant, actually," says the novelist. The words leap out, as if he's baiting the room. "Called Hubert's. Got a star or two from the Times, in the '70s."

"King's Pawn," growls the Wheeze, quite loudly.

"Sorry?" It may in fact be the novelist who's taken the bait. It only took patience.

"King's Pawn, that's the notable precursor." The Wheeze lifts his pint glass to his shoulder, without turning, to toast them, and to confirm that yes, it's the novelist's group he's addressing, though he won't meet their eyes. "Hubert's was a blip, an historical anomaly. It belonged in Manhattan and found its way there soon enough. This place was known eternally as *The King's Pawn*, a classic Brooklyn drinking establishment, and it shows the thinness of your sense of provenance and accountability that you dddddddon't apparently even recognize the nnnnnname."

I hadn't heard the Wheeze stuck on a consonant in a long while.

Perhaps it is this that causes the novelist to look from the Wheeze to the Wheeze's silent companion—me, that is—and then back, and then leap up and exclaim his proper name. As for me, I'm recognizable, but the name isn't coming to his lips. The novelist and the Wheeze were truly friends, long ago. I was only an onlooker to their friendship.

"Is it really you?" asks the novelist.

"The question raises ontological difficulties," says the Wheeze. "Before we address it, we have to establish whether the questioner is really who they bbbbbbelieve themselves to be."

"Fucking hell. You're still here."

"Of that much, we can be sure."

"Unchanged!"

The Wheeze grins fakely, offering a wordless demolition of this untruth.

"Damn, brother." The novelist fishes for his street voice. Under the circumstances, his endearment seems more a pronouncement on the shocking state of the Wheeze's teeth. The Wheeze, savoring the effect, has frozen his falsified smile, and his next words issue from between clenched teeth.

"I . . . *read* . . . your . . . *book*."

"Oh, thanks." This is automatic, but awkward.

The Wheeze, mercifully, loosens the rictus. "You did it. You really did it." His eyes are moist, but I can hear him rounding into form. I'm not worried about his consonants anymore. "You're our prodigal collective mouthpiece. Our *bard,* if I may."

"I tried my best."

"You're our tuning fork. Our percussive resonator. The book is so very full of . . . *music*. It's like a great pop song. There's a hook on every page, I found myself helplessly wishing to sing along. You can quote me on that, feel free."

"Okay."

"*Let me take you to the bridge,* you said, and you did. You took me to the bridge, and from that soaring span I beheld the city whole and entire."

"Right, that's enough." The novelist's voice has dropped. He's not without defenses, surely.

"You lifted us up in your song."

"Uncle," says the novelist, who then looks at me. "Tell him to quit."

I lift my eyebrows to express my powerlessness.

"I've been hoarding your clippings. I have a great big collection. The albums are stacked practically to the ceiling."

"No, you don't."

"I watched you on Charlie *Rose*. I heard you on Terry *Gross*. I saw your *TED Talk*." *Rose, Gross, TED*—these syllables, hissed. "And now you're back, to that same old place that you laughed about. You're among your *people*! The little characters in your head, they never really *ever* quit talking to you, do they? All you have to do is write down what they say."

What can the novelist do? Ask the Wheeze to step outside?

No.

But in his pride, the novelist tries to thread a needle, that between cowering and keening beneath the Wheeze's attack, and mounting an attack of his own. (Never pick a fight with someone uglier than yourself—I heard that once.) Locating a sulky defiance he says, "I did what I could with what I had, old friend."

"You did more than that! You did what you could with what *I* had, and what *he* had, too." The Wheeze salutes with his pint in my direction.

"Go write your own version, if you think I got it wrong."

"Oh, no, I couldn't possibly."

"Why not?"

"The revolution is in the history books now, comrade. And better than that. It's spelled out on a famous T-shirt."

"What is it you think I did?"

"You know what you did."

"Why don't you tell me."

"You *gentrified gentrification*."

V.
Brooklyn
Crime Novel

"TO BE BORN IN THE street means to wander all your life, to
be free. It means accident, incident, drama, movement. It
means above all dream. A harmony of irrelevant facts which
gives to your wandering a metaphysical certitude. In the
street you learn what human beings really are; otherwise, or
afterwards, you invent them. What is not in the open street
is false, derived, that is to say, literature. Nothing of what is
called 'adventure' ever approaches the flavor of the street. It
doesn't matter whether you fly to the Pole, whether you sit
on the floor of the ocean with a pad in your hand, whether
you pull up nine cities one after the other, or whether, like
Kurtz, you sail up the river and go mad. No matter how
exciting, how intolerable the situation, there are always exits,
always ameliorations, comforts, compensations, newspaper,
religions. But once there was none of this. Once you were
free, wild, murderous . . ."

—HENRY MILLER, *Black Spring*

117.
The Big Bus
(1976)

The inquiry needs to find an end. We're near our limit. We can't endure more.

A conclusion? Hard to say. It may be merely an exit door. Another deferral, another disclaimer.

Whatever.

Last call.

Time to divulge the worst things we know. The worst we rememberers can remember. Here's one.

THE YOUNGER BROTHER has seen the advertisement on television, and he's heard his older brother talking about it and it becomes one of those obsessions: *The Big Bus*. He doesn't have any way of knowing why it seems so urgent to him. Maybe it's the way it obviously means nothing to any of their parents but isn't explicitly for kids, one of those radar signals sent out.

A movie about a bus, what's the big deal.

An atomic-powered bus, a comedy that's also a disaster movie. Or something like that.

Star-studded with people no one has ever heard of.

There hasn't yet been *Airplane!* or any other movie of this sort. It has a kind of *Mad Magazine* vibe, possibly.

It sticks in the mind, but information is scarce and you're pretty sure it'll be out of theaters in two weeks, so panic is setting in.

The summer after *Jaws*, the summer before *Star Wars,* and the only other movie with any vibe at all is *Logan's Run,* the plot of which you memorized from the Marvel Comics adaptation. So, late June 1976 is a Death Valley area, basically.

He corners his older brother about it to the point of being banished from said older brother's bedroom.

"It's really good?"

"It's funny. I didn't say it was good."

"Would I like it?"

"You would like it." Almost an insult in this.

"You want to see it again?"

"No, I don't want to see it again. Quit asking. Go with your friends. You're old enough. It's right on Fulton Street." His brother names a couple of kids.

"They're at camp."

"Then I can't help you. Get mom to take you."

This is totally unsatisfactory.

So, next afternoon, he resorts to the spoiled boy.

He knows he can get the spoiled boy excited about it. This beats going alone, which he anyway wouldn't do in a million years.

"The Big *Bust*?"

"What?"

"You want to see a movie called *The Big Bust*?"

The spoiled boy blinks at his mother in confusion. "Big Bust?" he repeats.

"It's a private part of a woman's body."

"Bus, mom. It's about a *bus*. Tell her."

The younger brother has been invited inside, escorted upstairs, in order to persuade the spoiled boy's mom directly of the reasonableness of this journey downtown to see the movie. This home, the apartment the mother and son occupy together, never a place he felt he actually needed to lay eyes upon. The covered armchairs and heavy drapes and carpeting, the bookshelves full of dark volumes, not one single comic book or toy visible, suggests that the curse of this house is that the spoiled boy's mother is secretly somehow a grandmother.

"It's a comedy movie," says the younger brother lamely. "It's playing at the Duffield. Walking distance." He's never been inside the Duffield.

"Your parents approve of this?"

"Sure," the younger brother half lies. On the one hand, his parents haven't actually given approval. On the other, they'd surely not comprehend why approval was being sought. The summer-stranded boys were at the start of a long crawl of sweltering days. The money was his own allowance. Against their recommendation, he'd refused day camp in Cobble Hill, in exchange for the promise of never saying to them "I'm bored"—*so why are you even asking me this?*

"The matinee's just a dollar-fifty," the younger brother continues. "We'll be out before it gets dark." *Even if we stay and watch it twice.* He's done that, with movies he likes, at the Heights Cinema and the Rex on Court Street. In the dark, with the air-conditioning, why not? That's if he can convince the spoiled boy to stay. They never kick you out.

"You need more than that. For popcorn." She hands the spoiled boy a five-dollar bill. The younger brother's protest rises to his lips: the five's not divisible, into one for the pocket and four for the sock, or perhaps even two for the sock and two for the heel of the shoe. A single bank note is an all or nothing proposition. And they're headed up past Fulton Street. Yet he remains silent. He'll instruct the spoiled boy to put it in his sock. The younger brother's own mugging money should be sufficient.

Dance, dance, dance.

THE DUFFIELD, THOUGH blessedly cool, is too big inside. Dizzying in its dim spaciousness, like staring at the night sky. The younger brother much prefers the shallower Rex, or the pokey rooms of the Heights Cinema. Amid what seem a hundred rows of busted seats only a few bodies are visible, already slid down in the chairs, heads mere shadowy bumps. A few with knees up across the row in front. Still, to sit at the back seems absurd, though it would feel better to be closer to the ticket sellers and candy vendors in the lobby. To the bathrooms and exits. But you'd come to see a movie on a big screen, not shrink it to a distant billboard framed by dark. So, they move down, find seats in the center of a row a third of the way from the front.

At the instant the curtain bunches upward and the house lights fully dim, a repeated *chuff* sound is heard as selected patrons discreetly pull tabs on cans of beer.

Barely through the trailer, a few minutes into the ostensible hilarity (hot dog vendor, experimental nuclear facility), the two appear suddenly in the seats directly behind, all too easily.

Can't turn and look directly, but enough is obvious even in peripheral vision.

Black kids, taller, older, no chance.

The two reach over the seats and easefully cradle necks in elbow joints, just because the necks are there.

"Let me check your pockets," says one, not bothering to whisper, relying on the on-screen roar and the cavernous indifference of the Duffield. His tone is bored. An in-theater dance. Which to him is, seemingly, no novelty.

The spoiled boy is silent. The younger brother too, of course. He'd had no way of predicting his companion's likely response, has never been to the dance with the spoiled boy, but then again, yeah, sure, of course he did. Even in this freaky framework, who doesn't know the script?

Folding money is extracted, quarters bounce out to the sticky floor. Nobody's blaming anyone else for the sloppiness in this, and nobody's groping down there to find them. It's over in a few seconds.

"Watch your movie, now," whispers the one. "You know we just messing with you, right?"

The younger brother hears himself issue some inarticulate hiccup or grunt of assent, just to end it. He feels in charge, responsible. He's eight or ten months older than the spoiled boy, technically speaking. Yet with his older brother, his partial access to C., his savvier parents, he's advantaged a thousand ways.

And this was all his suggestion. The Duffield Theater, walking distance.

Over in a few seconds, yet they sit afterward gelled in total silence, the movie washing over them like a broadcast in an alien tongue, like an art installation flickering on rocks on the moon. Do either of them laugh out loud a single time? Not that the younger brother can recall.

But recollection's a tricky thing. Neither of them will ever mention the movie to anyone, ever again, nor can the younger brother recall anything that transpires in it. He'd have succeeded in making himself forget the title, he later thinks, if it wasn't for the spoiled boy's mother asking "the big *bust*?"

Thank god, it isn't a movie anyone would ever mention to him for any reason, anytime, under any circumstances. Thank god, it isn't *Star Wars* or *Jaws*.

JUST AN ORDINARY dance in an unusual setting?

No.

They're waiting outside the theater, all that time.

Nothing better to do? Sinister agenda?

Like so much, this could be in the eye of the beholder.

The younger brother and the spoiled boy, they freeze together on the pavement. Tongues turned to stone. It's like they're still inside, their throats resting in the crooks of the older boys' elbows. Like it turns out it never ended, the movie just unspooled in time's void. Out here in the glare, three-thirty in the afternoon, Duffield Street seems a long way from the crowds on Fulton. All ordinary worlds appear suspended. Maybe picking up the spoiled boy instigated a curse on reality, maybe it gummed up the clocks.

The younger brother and the spoiled boy, not meeting each other's eyes.

It is at this juncture that a knife is possibly displayed, though it is never seen again. Perhaps it is only mentioned.

"YOU WANT TO stay and watch it again?" he'd asked the spoiled boy, when the lights came up. He was certain of only that much, that he'd said that.

The spoiled boy had only looked at him like he might be crazy.

"Okay, never mind I said anything."

Had the younger brother also said, at any point "don't talk back, let them take what they want"? Had he also said "don't do anything to make them angry, and they'll go away"? Or had he merely thought those things, radiating them from his brain into the spoiled boy's? Had the spoiled boy even needed to be instructed in total and utter compliance? Probably not. And probably therefore he'd not said them, though he felt liable for them as commandments, given how they stood carved in stone in his mind.

Staying through the second show, even halfway through, that might have changed things. At least he could know he'd suggested it.

THE HOYT-SCHERMERHORN SUBWAY station. The older boys march them down Bond Street and into the reeking stairwell. They use the Dean Street boys' own money, confiscated inside the movie theater, to purchase four tokens. Then downstairs. Onto a groaning GG train, which sits waiting for the CC like a spider in its nest, one crouching beneath the daily world.

Out of daylight again, into the theater of the tunnels.

Yet like the Duffield Theater, this auditorium is becalmed. No one sees them.

In later accounts this would be the source of second guessing. Would-haves and could-haves. Why not tug on the sleeve of nearly anyone? A motorman or conductor or just the nearest human?

Well, the nearest human is passed out in his shitted pants.

The four aren't occupying the motorman's car, nor the conductor's.

Eight years before Goetz, far from Manhattan, there's nothing controversial in the four youths sitting together, apparently. Maybe they're friends. They sit so quietly.

The spoiled boy had spoken, once, as they entered the station.

"I never rode the subway alone."

"You're not alone, you're with us. Now shut up."

At Bedford-Nostrand, they exit. A station four stops from the homes of the two white boys—walking distance, really—but a place they've never seen. From the station, just another block's walk to the wrecked storefront, to which the older Black boys have earlier found access, and find it again, easily. Many years later, a Dunkin Donuts will occupy the site. This day, this year, so many such storefronts await demolition. The children have found themselves a way inside this one. They're all children. They go in.

THE BRIGHT WHITE gutters between panels; the empty spaces of imagination's failure; the gaps in which the locked-in, locked-out memories are blown out by flare; the pitiless sun toward which one shouldn't gaze; the expunged or obliterated moments that can find no purchase in the self; the details over which the machine that knits consciousness into a seeming whole jumps over, gratefully; those facts which the prosecuting attorney will affirm never need to be spoken aloud in the courtroom, in the cause of not further traumatizing the children, and to the omission of which the boys' parents consent; those facts which need therefore never appear in the official records of those other children, those whose crimes will be judged sufficient, even with these redactions, for maximum sentencing under the very newest law, that permitting them to be tried, essentially, as adults.

ANYWAY, NO ONE needs a court transcript, let alone the prosecution's sealed depositions and police files. Anyone who happened to read the first accounts in the newspapers learned enough. Too much. What was described there was enough. The two white boys left naked in the abandoned building, left to cry for help. When the other two had—as the newspapers described it, "finished with their fun," they'd confiscated their victims' clothing and tossed it in a dumpster, then gone home to their own homes, their own families. To dinner.

The Black man who heard them shouting for help and looked inside, the Black man who ushered the unclothed, terrified children from Nostrand Avenue and covered them in borrowed coats and deposited them at the police station hadn't stayed long enough to make a statement of his own, or even to be identified. He knew to steer clear of the police. He wanted no part of what had and was about to go down.

THE WINDOWS ARE boarded, the signage wrenched down, the outside of the building revealing nothing. Inside, the moldering rooms feature some sort of smashed showcases. Glass littered on a linoleum floor that is itself shattered, cracked shards and dried glue. In the showcases, teeth? Mouths? Can this have been some sort of dentist's office, or oral surgeon's? Dentures. Models of dentures, demonstration models, plaster models of sections of jaws and bridgework.

It smells like cat piss.

Probably cat piss.

Nothing to do with the former dentures showroom.

At first there is some stalling and pleading, some chokeholds and arm wrenching. There is also some jocularity. Assertions that "everybody's cool." The usual implication, that to say or even think anything except that they were all playing together in a knowing way, a special secret way, secret from the uncomprehending adults, was to be racist.

Standard dance stuff, in a nonstandard venue.

Then, it is as if the nonstandard venue asserts itself. Its special aspects, of risk and possibility. A dance is a thing of the streets, it concerns the chance of bystanders as much as it concerns the participants. These four are off the streets now, in some bracketed, untested reality, a Negative Zone. Alone with the terror of one another and of themselves.

Within the wrecked offices are two spaces—a fitting room? Would that make sense? Or a supply room, and the other the public front? Doesn't matter. Two rooms, distinct from each other. The taller of the two captors and the spoiled boy go into one.

The taller boy has reserved the spoiled boy for himself.

But what happens to the younger brother?

The second of the two Black children—the one who has been

placed in charge of the younger brother, the sidekick, who is smaller than his idol—he pretends. He delivers a mock-assault, rather than a real one. His heart isn't in it.

Before even beginning, this boy, the smaller friend, he leans in and whispers to the younger brother.

"I've seen you before."

"What?"

"Newgate, man."

The younger brother blinks at this, trying to understand. "You're in the Newgate Program?"

"That's right. I know you, you came around with your moms."

What is there to say to this? The young brother says nothing.

The smaller friend announces his plan, his little piece of triage. "Act like I'm messing with you."

"What?"

"Act hurt. Be crying, man."

The younger brother is not so slow that he fails to accept this gift. He's been in this sort of dance before, where one of the participants isn't truly enthused. The younger brother obliges instantly. He mimics crying.

A talent of the schoolyard, the art of keening on command.

In contrast to the copious, undisguisable tears he'd wept just two months before, on the day of the thwarted street hockey show-down, when they'd found themselves stranded on the wrong side of the BQE, boxed in by the four Italian teens, as the younger brother recalls it, he never authentically wept a tear the day he led the spoiled boy to see *The Big Bus*.

"Act like I made you suck my dick."

What would this even consist of?

"Don't say I didn't."

The younger brother nods.

"I'll fuck you up," his nominal captor says, throwing it in for good measure, though now it is clear they are afraid not of each other, but of the same other person, the smaller friend's idol. Afraid of him and of the universe into which they've fallen.

"Make some noise," his captor says. "Or I got to make you."

The younger brother again obliges. They've become allied, performers together. Soon, though, it is clear from the noises that come to them that no one is listening. And so, they become dumb spectators, attending the more earnest show taking place. They fall silent, for more than a moment. Doomed witnesses, sunk in disaster.

THAT QUIET BETWEEN them, the strangest secret of all. For all subsequent obliterations of memory, knowledge of this uncanny interval will never exit the younger brother's body. For all he must endure, there is this further guilt.

The clue that will bring the police to the houses of the two abductors is the obvious one: the Newgate Program. The Quaker rec room. The mention of this connection between the boys narrows the list of suspects to a scant few. A few descriptions, a knock on a few doors, a sorrowful shake of the head. I know that boy, yeah. Could have seen it coming. Not because he's a bad one, but he had no selectivity. It's his friend, the idol, who is the piece of work. His friend the idol who had been a widely noticed ticking bomb. Only a question of when.

Act like I made you suck my dick. Under initial questioning by police and parents, the younger brother obliges this demand. He gives obedience to the script. It isn't difficult to do, no specificity is required. All evidence will be sealed. No one wishes to hear his report a second time. They barely wish to hear it a first. The ostensible center of the tale goes unexamined. *Of course* these boys were both raped. Didn't they take their clothes? The tale burnished is one of abduction, kidnapping, a journey in broad daylight and under the ground, the boarding of a train, that unsummoned motorman or conductor, the utilization of the shamefully neglected property, the fragmentation and neglect of community and human value, threats with a knife that either did or did not exist. The induced passivity in the children sent unprepared into the world. These are the materials of the parents' burning phone-tree for weeks and months afterward.

Then all the talk is hastily buried. Too much had been said.

Who's the younger brother protecting? From whom? The one Black kid from the other? Better that both should go into the system, go to Elmira, as both do, to be boys destroyed in the manner of men, as both will be, than he betray his promise?

Protecting the spoiled boy's mom? How?

Protecting himself?

It was no effort. They'd all been schooled by one another in silence. In the keeping of the facts of the street from their parents, who plainly couldn't handle them.

THE SOCK—AT THE catastrophe's conclusion, when the two white boys found themselves commanded to disrobe and surrender their clothes—the sock the younger brother unpeeled from his damp foot still had folding money in it. Three dollars, curled to his shin. These flaked off to the floor of the ruined storefront and were overlooked.

118.
Sparkle Stoop
(1978)

Methods fail. The rhetorical money we've kept clenched in our fists will buy nothing—not time, not forgiveness, not distraction. It's funny money, Monopoly money. Not even the big denominations, just the fives and ones.

We are turning in our badge here. We would like to quit these streets.

Yet we can't shirk this one last story. Even if we're without our tools now, our sardonic distancing maneuvers. Our Bugs Bunny shit.

THE OTHER WORST thing, the legendary unnamable event occurs on Halloween. A day of disguises. When the rememberers try to reconstruct it later, the events have disguised themselves within the disguises, they've gone to hide inside the general atmosphere of unreality, the impossibility. That must have been a horror movie we all saw later, right? That didn't happen on the block.

The holiday always a horror movie to begin with, raw eggs hurled with great force across the schoolyard. How the fuck can they not make it a school holiday and give a kid a fair chance to hide indoors all day?

By the time of the trick or treating, the candy handed out at the top of the stoops, there's an hour or two of relief, the parents all out for a walk with the little ones, you can actually breathe for an hour or two before night falls.

Then be in hiding if you're not a fool.

It is at the twilight transition moment that the nemesis of the millionaire's son slides down the sidewalk with a group of his boys from Gowanus Houses. They're half-assing their way around the white blocks with paper bags, gathering candy because who could say no? They're kids, right? *Right?* And it's Halloween, the rules apply equally. A couple of them wear something passing as costumes, one a skull mask, another with a Spider-Man barely fitting on the head, surely meant for a four-year-old.

Hey, the white people put a decoration out, or a carved pumpkin on the top of the stoop, advertising they've spent money on a bag of miniature Mr. Goodbars or Almond Joys or 100 Grands. Advertising that they know the script. So, what's the problem? It's another version of the unspoken deal: hand something over, make us go away, choose other battles. In this way the nemesis and his group could farm enough candy to fill a barrel, if they didn't eat half, more than half, on the spot.

Into this vortex of chaos, the parents of the youngers trying to scurry home, to persuade them they've hit all their friends' houses and to settle, to call it a full score and go home, the streets falling to darkness and some hooting from up Nevins and Bond Streets, a lone figure in a plastic Nixon mask breaks from the shadows of the abandoned house and crosses the street to trail the nemesis and his group at an eerie distance.

Two presidents ago and probably none of these kids even know what that face is supposed to mean. Just looks like a kind of melted face.

It all happens in a second, and those who saw it and those who heard it described and created for themselves the feeling that they must have actually seen it will debate the details in whispers for decades.

But really, there are no details.

It happens too fast for details. The moment is opportune and the boy in the Nixon mask just runs up and does it.

Or maybe this scene is flooded by that most blinding light, the moment into which one cannot ever entirely see, the activated desire of the whole body of one human being to leap the limit and to destroy the life of another, to wipe it from the planet, to transform another person into a corpse to rot in the soil that presumably waits beneath these slates everywhere.

LITTLE MAN ISN'T at the top of a stoop, he's in a cluster of guys crowding at a basement entrance beneath a stoop, which puts him a step below his attacker.

Jostling in to collect some candy.

Which puts him with his back turned and a step down and oblivious to the millionaire's son in the Nixon mask.

Who brings the opened gravity knife down on the skull of his nemesis with all the force he can muster, which mercifully isn't enough to break the skull, especially since he hits at an angle, not dead on. So, he doesn't actually *stab his nemesis in the brain*. Close but no cigar.

He rakes off sideways and just plows loose an amount of scalp and hair, which seemingly instantly seeps blood like rain into his victim's eyes and soaks the neck of his white Adidas T-shirt.

Little Man, on reflex, reaches for his head, and also turns to see his attacker—to behold the crazed Nixon face. The millionaire's son, incompletely satisfied by his result, the skidding of his blade where he'd hope to drive it into something to the hilt, swings down again.

The tip pierces Little Man's cheek just beneath the cheekbone and cracks two of his upper molars. Again, a less than pleasing result, a sensation less like a plunging in, more like stubbing a toe. Little Man may seem to be made entirely of bones and stones, his covering of flesh a mere costume. Then again, there is starting to be a lot of blood, an amazing amount. This stills the attacker's hand. The white shirt has begun to be a red shirt.

For an instant they both hear their own adrenaline breath, against the layered tapestry of Halloween effects, the shrieks of tiny children, the tumult and babble of distant police actions, though none close.

You wanted me to show you the gravity knife. Well, there you go.

And then the attacker is gone, run mad off into the streets, to hide elsewhere in the immediate aftermath. He's still clutching his knife until he notices and wipes it on his jeans cuff and closes it into itself and shoves it in his back pocket. He can't run home, since they all know, don't they, where he lives? But it's Halloween, and if he goes into Cobble Hill or Brooklyn Heights he can be lost in the scene, the milling white parents and kids, for hours still.

Just another Nixon in the night.

THAT ISN'T THE whole story. It might be half.

The boys around Little Man try to convince him to go to the hospital. Just down Dean Street, yo, we'll walk you there man, you look *bad*.

Somebody with half their sense has put a rag up on his head and pressed the flap down and maybe it's already not bleeding quite so much. The knife-tip's hole in his cheek swells shut, the second blow barely even an afterthought to those tending him, though the rasp of broken teeth against the wound's interior is as hot and fierce and grievous a pain to Little Man as the sensations emanating from his skull. There's a lot of loud voices shouting a lot of different things, but the outcome isn't really in doubt. Little Man's going to the hospital, it's just a question of when. Of how quickly they can convince him.

But first, yes, the nemesis knows where that dude lives. The injured party's wailing voice comes out on top. He wants to go there. It isn't far.

Okay, but then we're taking you to the hospital. Holy Family, man, it's just down the block. Those nuns will stitch you up and they won't even make you pay.

Don't worry, man. We'll kick that dude's ass for you later.

Don't worry, man. We got your bag of candy right here.

Let us suppose, for a moment, that you are Little Man.

Your career as nemesis has been poised from the start on a sense, a certainty, of unspecified injury. Injury and howling injustice. A howling only you can hear.

Now your injury has been bloodily specified and the howling is coming from your mouth, from your body.

Your howling wants ears. Your injuries want witness. It wants to say "see?" Perhaps this is nearly all it has ever wanted, though we shouldn't presume. What's certain is that it wants it now, much more than it wants the crushing defeat of the hospital and the stitches, the mothering of the nuns. More even than it craves revenge. Just witness.

So it is that the nemesis determines that this time it will be him who ascends the stoop and rings the bell, that no one will have to ring it for him. And so it is that he proceeds, fighting those who attempt either to console or dissuade him, to make his appearance at the famous millionaire's house, to present the results of injustice now that they have at last become unmistakable, now that they are streaming down his temples and into his eyes and ears.

This blood must be beheld, before anything is stitched and bandaged and managed away, before it can be dismissed. And so it is that Little Man begins his legendary ascent to ring the bell.

His companions fall away at the top, easily. Or maybe it is uneasily. Possibly the story of the samurai sword has gotten around a bit by now. The efficacy of blades, the superhuman attack with no warning, none of these elements can be wholly lost on the boys of the street, and so at the top it is only Little Man himself there to ring the bell and present himself for restitution and witness.

SPARKLE OPENS THE door. She's wearing a blouse and capri pants and tennis shoes, and she shivers when she feels the cool touch her. Her eyes take in the street, and she shivers again. Her eyes fail to focus on what's before her.

"Look!" The nemesis holds out his palm, the palm that has been pressed to his forehead. "Look what he did, ma'am." He calls her *ma'am*. Only with the bloody seepage in his mouth and the brokenness of his teeth and the swollenness of his interior cheek his words are uncommonly muffled and useless. They seem not to reach her ears.

Instead Sparkle says: "We have no pumpkin."

"Your son did this to me, look, he knifed me in the head."

"We have no pumpkin and yet you come."

Has she even glanced at him?

"He tried to kill me with a knife and you're talking about your pumpkin."

"There is no pumpkin, that's what I've tried to tell you." It wouldn't matter if Little Man had the enunciation of Rex Harrison, her favorite actor, he'd never be understood. Sparkle is drunk. She speaks as if to herself. It is as if she's moved to the lip of a stage in a scene set in a lonely bedroom, to speak a monologue audible only to a hushed and invisible audience at the footlights. In fact, her voice is nearly drowned in the distant shrieks of Halloween. The sirens that are always coming, though never exactly for you. The ladder trucks racing to unquenchable fires. "They promised me if I had no pumpkin, and the lights were kept low, the bell wouldn't ring yet it continues to ring."

"Your boy tried to kill me, woman," says Little Man, in a low howl adjusted to the woman's comportment, her drunken maundering.

"I don't understand."

"Look, he murdered me in the head."

"That makes no sense."

Little Man falls to hands and knees on the stoop before her. His body is in shock and pain and he is also seeking to deepen the eloquence of his petition to her, the picture of his distress, since the blood seeping through his ears and to his soaked collar is apparently insufficient to move her. So Little Man collapses at her feet.

"Get off my steps," says Sparkle.

And she begins kicking at Little Man's fingers.

WHAT CAN WE say about Sparkle? What can we know?

She's drunk.

Her marriage, probably, is a joke.

Her marriage to the man who calls the children who dance in the hydrant spray animals.

Well, sure, they are animals. We're *all* animals.

Before her crawls a damaged animal. Does Sparkle even understand, or does she somehow mistake what she sees for a more ghoulish Halloween costume than she has ever understood could exist?

We might call them two damaged animals, even.

One of whom is kicking the other down the brownstone stoop.

We're not here to cut any slack.

Little Man recoils his stinging fingers, injury added to injuries, and half tumbles, half stumbles downward, making clumsy retreat to the slates below. From there, he is tenderly guided along the sidewalk, across Bond Street, to the doors of Holy Family, for repair of his scalp and his cheek by the nuns.

Sparkle? She shuts the door.

A few of the Dean Street kids, rememberers, will argue about who among them truly saw this happen, and who only heard it described, for the rest of their lives. The rest may prefer never to believe it happened at all. Nor will they be challenged to recall it by their parents, nor by outside accounts. It isn't a thing involving the police, because the nuns who stitch the wound don't invoke the police.

Kid on kid stuff. Halloween. Maybe not quite a crime. Nothing that would make the papers. Nothing that would get anyone labeled a predator. Nothing that would change laws. Just a fucked thing happening in a fucked time.

THE BRIGHT WHITE gutters between panels; the empty spaces of imagination's failure; the gaps in which the locked-in, locked-out memories are blown out by flare; the pitiless sun toward which one shouldn't gaze; the expunged or obliterated moments that can find no purchase in the self; the details over which the machine that knits consciousness into a seeming whole jumps over, gratefully; those actions which will go unmentioned in a boy's intake interview with a new psychiatrist, a genial man on the Upper West Side of Manhattan, recommended by their Brooklyn Heights pediatrician—and why on earth did they not move to the Heights, or to the Upper West Side, in the first place, what could they have been thinking?—occurrences that go recorded nowhere but move instead into blurred half rumor, unless it is the case that the one kid in the costume of a mercenary ninja, the one who never grouped or thronged with the others and who in fact never trick-or-treated, didn't want any candy, just was out on his own strange patrol and practicing going unseen by the others, scurries home and chronicles the event in a ledger on his desk full of *Soldier of Fortune* magazines, using his own strange system of shorthand which renders the episode thus: $ x lm.

119.
Show Don't Tell
(an American thing)

It is such an American thing, isn't it? That injunction. The admonitory miming of the zipping of the lips.

Never apologize, never explain.

Don't ask, don't tell.

Move along now, get off the stoop, no mouth from you. Tell your story walking!

Fuggeddaboudit! If I hear one more word outta you, Alice, pow! To the moon!

Loose lips sink novels.

As I believe I may have asserted once previously, fuck that shit. If you don't care to know what I think, skip the chapter.

If there was a deal, the deal was broken.

If there was a deal, when did it break?

If it broke, who broke it?

The Brownstoners—we'll risk repeating ourselves on this point— they didn't think with one mind. Some were communists, some real estate speculators (though their moustaches might not tell you the difference), and everything in-between. They weren't even all white. Some intermarried or adopted children of a different skin tone than their own. Some sent their children to the local public schools; some wouldn't dream of it. "I wouldn't put my kid on the front line of a so-cial experiment," they might say. So, their kids were made to walk to Pierrepont Street, to Remsen Street, to Saint Ann's or Packer. Or to Jay Street, to Brooklyn Friends School.

They can join the public school ranks when they get into Stuyves-ant or Music & Art. Or pass the test for Hunter College High School, you hotshot. For high school, for those four years, they'll be true city kids.

Then off to private college.

Here, the terms of the deal may be visible.

We'll be in the neighborhood, but not the schools.

They'll be public school kids, but just for four years. A fourteen-year-old can handle the subway.

We'd buy on Bergen, but not on Wyckoff. You don't need me to say why.

You can have what's in the pocket, but let the kid keep walking after, leave him unharmed.

You can even have what's in the sock.

But no missing persons, no milk cartons.

JUST AS THERE were back-to-the-land people, there were back-to-the-city people, the Jane Jacobs army. They introduced themselves to their neighbors. They started community centers and community gardens. They had tree-planting days to which all were invited. They'd arrived, the Gowanus Liberation Front.

Utopia? It's the show which always closes on opening night. The Brownstoner parents, they had a false oasis too. One that thrived even more briefly, before being exhausted, extinguished. In their secret hearts, the deal was broken. You'd marched for freedom, sure. But you moved into a house on the edge of the old white enclaves, the Italians in Carroll Gardens, the Irish in Park Slope.

Generalizations are slippery. Different people hold differing views. We all know this.

Did most Brownstoners hear the word "animals" come out of their own mouths? No. They never would have uttered that word. That wasn't them.

They didn't have to say it.

They had the old enclaves to say it for them. They had Milt the Vigilante to say it for them. They had the city and the police and the banks, they had the *New York Times* and *Time Magazine* to say it for them. They had the mayor and the cops to say it for them. They had their fear, and in their fear, they bathed, and told themselves they'd done their best.

They only had to not say *no*.

"I WOULDN'T PUT my kid on the front lines of a social experiment," they'd bragged, not seeing that the social experiment was themselves, was in themselves. That there was no "control" in the experiment, no outside to the laboratory.

We are all just children playing in the street, even before we exit the doors to our houses.

THE WHEEZE, HE spends long hours at the Grand Army Plaza branch of the Brooklyn Public Library; he is an absolute wizard with the microfiche. The results, he sends me, in enigmatic bursts, as attachments to emails. He is "working on something."

> *The Amsterdam News*, Brooklyn Edition, Saturday, March 12, 1966:
> *NEGROES IN PARK SLOPE ATTACKED BY WHITES*
> *Bombings, Beatings Reported: A white youth gang bombed a Negro*
> *home in the Park Slope section of Brooklyn Sunday night, about*
> *24 hours after white youths broke windows of another Negro home*
> *and allegedly fired shots at the door . . .*

> *Brooklyn World-Telegram*, Monday, April 23, 1963: *ARE*
> *BLOCKBUSTERS WINNING E. NEW YORK? White residents*
> *have been reported selling their homes and leaving the community*
> *in large numbers . . . A rising number of clashes have taken place*
> *between minority group teenagers who have recently moved into the*
> *community and white youths from older East New York families . . .*

> *Brooklyn World-Telegram*, Thursday, April 7, 1966: *MORTGAGE*
> *SQUEEZE IN INTEGRATED NEIGHBORHOODS Young*
> *white couples from outside the borough face delay, if not denial,*
> *of mortgage money to buy decayed brownstones in the integrated*
> *areas of Cobble Hill, downtown, and Red Hook, a survey revealed*
> *today . . . The bankers admit they don't want to risk mortgage*
> *money on decayed houses in deteriorating neighborhoods . . .*
> *What's more the arty young couples found that their hunt*
> *for homes had been preceded by at least 20 years by another*
> *tremendous migration, the arrival of Puerto Ricans, Southern*
> *Negroes and West Indians from Jamaica and Antigua, to Cobble*
> *Hill, downtown, and Red Hook. "Some of the Negro families in the*

DARE area have been here for 100 years," Miss Killeen said. The big wave, of course, in the last 15 or 20 years, since World War II. A fair percentage of non-whites have been tenants here for 30 to 35 years. Negroes and Puerto Ricans have bought the brownstones for 10 to 15 years. Mrs. Rose Segretto, now 80, bought her house at 191 Dean St., 15 years ago. Mrs. Edward Early, an Iroquois Indian from Canada, has owned 186 Dean St. for 28 years.

The cover story of *Time Magazine*, Monday July 11, 1977: THE YOUTH CRIME PLAGUE . . . *Across the U.S., a pattern of crime has emerged that is both perplexing and appalling. Many youngsters appear to be robbing and raping, maiming and murdering as casually as they go to a movie or join a pickup baseball game. A new, remorseless, mutant juvenile seems to have been born, and there is no more terrifying figure in America today . . . most are nonwhite kids whose resentments are honed and hardened in the slums.* The issue of *TIME* is dated the week before the 1977 blackout.

A month later, a second cover reads *MINORITY WITHIN A MINORITY: THE AMERICAN UNDERCLASS: "The awareness that many Blacks have been successful means that the underclass is more resentful and more defiant because its alibi isn't there." Others echo those sentiments in gutsier language. Says Naomi Chambers, a Detroit social worker, who is Black: "Now that some Black people have cars, dresses and shoes, there is jealousy. Jealousy can make me hate you and take what you have." Indeed, the Blacks who looted during the New York blackout were totally nondiscriminatory, emptying out stores owned by Blacks and whites alike.*

In the same email as the links to *TIME*, the Wheeze attaches something I suspect has been less simple for him to find. *Analysis of National Crime Survey Victimization Data to Study Serious Delinquent Behavior: Phase II: Trends in Juvenile Criminal Behavior in the United*

*States, 1973–1981, A Summary of the Major Findings. John H. Laub,
Project Director.* A poor, blurry photocopy from the records of the U.S.
Department of Justice.

In the period from 1973 to 1981, the rate of juvenile offending in
personal crimes in the United States and in urban areas showed a
stable pattern.

The PDF was unenticing, the language dry. I found myself
skimming to the last pages, where a series of conclusions were laid
out in numbered paragraphs.

In summary, the NCS data do not support the contention that,
for the personal crimes of rape, robbery, assault, and personal larceny,
juvenile crime has risen dramatically over the last nine years . . .
The NCS data also do not support the notion that, for the personal
crimes of rape, robbery, assault and personal larceny, juvenile crime
is currently more serious than it was nine years ago. Based on a
variety of indicators such as the percentage of injured victims, the
use of weapons, and the proportion of completed theft, the overall
seriousness of personal victimization committed by juvenile offenders
showed little substantial or systematic variation between 1973 and
1981 in the United States. Here again popular conceptions were, for
the most part, not supported by the NCS data.

The rate of Black juvenile offending in total personal crimes,
violent crimes, and theft crimes <u>declined</u> over the 1973 to 1981
period. The overall decline in juvenile rates of offending was
attributable in large part to the decline in rates of offending among
Black juveniles.

The rate of white juvenile offending in total personal crimes
and violent crimes revealed <u>little change</u> over the 1973 to 1981
period. However the rate of white juvenile offending in theft crimes
<u>increased</u> for this time period.

In the 1973 to 1981 period, for offenders age 12 to 17, Black
males, white females, and Black females all exhibited substantial
<u>declines</u> in their rate of offending in total personal crimes. The only

group to reveal an <u>increase</u> in total personal offending for this time period was 12-to-17-year-old white males.

The instances of underlining in the document seemed to reveal a certain voice, the presence of an author, impatience deepening as they rolled the carriage of their typewriter back to under-strike the words or phrases in question.

Blacks in the United States are on the average victim of more serious personal crimes than are whites for all three offender age groups.

Over the last decade serious criminal behavior by juveniles has been portrayed by the media as increasingly common, particularly in urban areas, and possessing a malicious, violent character . . . furthermore, law enforcement officials have expressed similar views; for instance, Deputy Police Commissioner of New York City Kenneth Conboy recently stated that the crimes for which these youngsters are being arrested are "more ruthless and remorseless and criminally sophisticated than ever before" . . . the past decade has also been characterized by a growing public concern with crime along with legislative action, some of which has resulted in potentially more severe penalties for juveniles who commit serious crimes . . . in many ways this investigation fails to support empirically the popular presentations of the media and the public, and, perhaps more importantly, seems to contradict current legislative policies and trends. Numerous state legislatures have passed or are contemplating legislation that would in effect dramatically change juvenile justice systems as they are presently constituted . . . include lowering the maximum jurisdictional age . . . making waiver to adult court less restrictive . . . redesigning sentencing schemes in juvenile court to allow for the possibility of longer sentences . . .

The Wheeze sends these along without comment. If I understand him, he is making an attempt, perhaps a futile one, to discern whether the special nature of the old lady's dream—*The Little Gentrification That Could*—functioned as a start-up lab or beta test for a wider project. Was it too eccentric to be relevant? Too cute or queer to be culpable?

Was Dean Street "scalable"?

Possibly we had our own Etan Patz, years early, wandering around alive in broad daylight, the ruined spoiled boy.

Possibly our own Bernhard Goetz, the millionaire's son, the avenger.

Does it matter that we were all, once, most of us, friends?

I do my best to read whatever the Wheeze sends me. I think in a way he *has* discovered his Lovecraft Basement there, at last, in the microfiche viewing room at Grand Army branch of the Brooklyn Public Library. Though it may not have been the one he thought he was looking to find.

VI.
No Music

"WHO'S WRITING THIS BOOK?"

—FRANK B. WILDERSON III, *Afropessimism*

120.
Together

(2005)

Say a guy, a former Dean Street white boy, walks into a bar called Boat on Smith Street and sees them there, together.

This guy fled Brooklyn nearly a quarter century earlier, for college in San Francisco. By doing so, he'd placed in the rearview mirror not only these impossible streets, but his two alcoholic and dysfunctional parents. Plus, two younger siblings he could never have rescued from that house, however much survivor's guilt to this day plagues him.

Out of college, he'd mastered computer graphic design. Taken a job with ground floor stock bonus on what was to become one of the world's most absurd fortunes. Just a handful of stock, thrown his way during the start-up phase, which he sold at the exact right instant, allowing a permanent luxury. Around the same time, he began too regularly populating San Francisco's hipster bars, cultivating a taste for retro cocktail culture—the highball, the gimlet, above all the Manhattan. Manhattan! Island to which they'd all aspired! With their help he numbed, then pickled, his guilt. Then spent five years unpickling. Worked, with a sequence of shrinks and sponsors to unmake his compulsion, his addiction. It is only after drying out, and also making a painful extrication (and expensive divorce) from a woman unready to journey with him into sobriety, that this guy, now in his forties, has been drawn back.

To Brooklyn. Where he never needed to return.

His mom died. Finally. Not a nice scene. Her body discovered after the mail piles up. Neither younger sibling wants anything to do with this, though they're eager enough for their share of the sale. His sister, she's in Florida, three kids and a day job—why should she have to visit Brooklyn to meet with the realtor? Just sell it, for fuck's sake! His brother, in Alaska, which says maybe all that needs saying. He's sworn off cities generally. The former Dean Street boy—the recovery-web-designer-elder-brother—knows: It's his to handle. No one's going to do it for him.

All's worse even than his worst imagining. The house is ruined. Who knew it was possible? His mother lived in a stupor of denial, dwelled in the basement solely, never going upstairs. Her quarters are a warren, a hovel. A floor above, the parlor is sealed in dust, his father's stereo albums and typewriter still unmoved from where they'd been when his father died a decade earlier. But that's the good news. Above this waits disaster. He'd heard vaguely the roof needed repairs, a decade earlier. Well, it hadn't had any. Along the back edge, it's half-collapsed. The tar dried and baked and finally dissolved, into black fragments which then had pooled and seeped, a kind of toxic soup invading the upper story. His room. Not that he cares. It's the realtor's advice to him, to delay and oversee a cleanup and repair—this constitutes his nightmare.

Needless to say, he can afford to take a hotel "downtown," a Marriott—they had those, now—and wait it out.

Needless to say, he falls off the wagon.

His abject survey of the new bars on Smith lands on a favorite named *Boat*. He finds perverse amazement in the air of fake provenance exhibited by the bar's regulars. What if he opened his mouth and regaled them with what Smith Street was thirty years earlier, how it once functioned in his life? Not a chance. The bartender makes a killer Manhattan, that's the point.

He'll dry out again once home. Sleepy Sausalito, safe distance from San Francisco's bars. Even more from Brooklyn, from his drowned childhood bedroom, from this unwelcome task of return.

THE WHITE KID and the Black kid, still *together*. The word is there, waiting for him. Not that he'd ever consciously grasped what they'd been to each other as children. The only name being those atrocious syllables they'd all thrown at one another—and had had thrown at them—so regularly that they meant nothing at all.

Faggot, the way they'd used it, wasn't a literal thing anyhow.

Not like what the whispers said about these two.

He's three sheets to the wind by the time he realizes who he's staring at. They sit at a high top together, over beers, and smile at him like he's gone nowhere in the past thirty years, like they're hardly surprised. It's a hot night, they're wearing dress shirts rolled halfway up their forearms, not a drop of perspiration visible. They exude a kindliness, a benevolence, as well as a kind of ease and elegance that—all of it—utterly shames him. Yet he feels the glistening mask of his face lighting up when they speak his name. *You fucking pathetic drunk.* He bellows theirs back. Never forgotten, how could he forget any of their names, the block's kids? My god, he's been lonely. Like a knife through him the instant they invite him to their table.

He nearly trips coming over to join them.

Three rounds later they're still clean, upright, and alert enough to catch him by the elbows as he slides off the high stool.

He staggers, turns it into a pratfall curtsey, *where'd that shit come from?* Pulls a hundred from his wallet and tosses it on the high top before they can stop him, then reels out the door and up Smith, turns the corner to Dean, and passes out in his clothes on his mother's deathbed.

HAD HE LET them get a word in? Barely. Instead, it had all geysered forth—his mom, the ruined roof, the odyssey through recovery, the enigma of his marriage and divorce. They'd listened fondly, though it could hardly have been the night out they'd been envisioning. All of it some kind of dismal filibuster, beyond his control to halt. Perhaps also to keep from questioning or remarking explicitly on what was before him. What he had no language for, let alone for how it seemed to gut him, to demolish defenses against a strain of homesickness he'd had no inkling he endured.

Did he ask them one direct question about themselves or their lives? Nope. In their kindly curiosity and solicitude to his drunken need, they'd let him go on about himself all night. Had he even learned whether they'd been together continuously, all these years? Was such a thing possible? Was that how they'd survived the slaughter that had effaced all memory of queer Pacific Street, the population of young men there? Or had the two of them gone separate ways for a while, then bumped into each other—perhaps at this very bar!—and serendipitously relocated this well of feeling?

Oh, there might have been one direct question he could recall. He'd been railing about the changes in the neighborhood—as if he knew, as if he really understood anything, in contrast to those who'd stayed, all these years—and then he'd asked, "so, what, would you two just like, go into any of these bars along here? They're all like this?" He knew what he meant by the question, and maybe they did too.

His old childhood acquaintances had looked at each other and shrugged.

"Pretty much, sure," said the white guy.

"You see other people we knew?"

"Not so often," said the Black guy.

"There's that one place," said the white guy. "It's a little more old school. Not actually old, I mean, it's only been there for, like, ten years. But remember we saw Salvador in there?"

"Sure," said the Black guy. "I see Salvador, he's still around." He seemed to want to keep it vague. Then, as if he'd caught himself avoiding the topic, he smiled, and said, "what he means by old school is that it's actually sort of a cop bar. Cops and firemen. We just happened to try it one night and there was Salvador. Sal. Funny to see him. I wouldn't say we'd be much inclined to stop in there again, though."

The white guy smiled too. "Probably not our first choice. Fewer yuppies than in here, though!"

"Yes," agreed the Black guy. "Fewer yuppies."

Any number of implications were left lying on the table, too obvious or elaborate to explain. The former Dean Street boy hadn't located the courage to press for more. Yet, could it be that he'd glimpsed one fraction of discord between them, evidence that their positions weren't, couldn't be, aligned in *every* respect?

Maybe it is a thing too elusive for him, in this moment, to pursue. The former Dean Street boy is only certain of the implacable togetherness of the white guy and the Black guy. Certain of how it leaves him, by contrast, eternally excluded.

Yet this hint of discord? Perhaps, after all, it wasn't equally simple for the white guy and the Black guy to go into their neighborhood's cop bar. As on that first day in Hicksville, when the white softball-playing teenagers had dubbed them Brooklyn and Ghetto, or again, in so many spaces the two have entered together, select clubs or parties on Fire Island or in Sydney, Australia, spaces where the novelty of their pairing raises a minute stir not only of fascination but of discomfort, or even rage—perhaps after half a lifetime of this, it isn't, for the two of them, *equally* simple. No.

But the former Dean Street boy is in no position to press. Anyway, the discomfort between the two now vanishes. It had only been a glint.

DID HE ENVY them their intimacy? Sure, but not in that way. He'd had chances to know. In San Francisco it represented a sort of epic failure, not to volunteer or be recruited to the cool kids' team. He'd had a queer sponsor. This charitable person, this more-than-friend, had even offered the suggestion to the former Dean Street boy, one day. Had asked if he knew about the Kinsey Scale. "Everyone's a little of both, you know that, right?"

"Sure," he'd said, surprising himself with the ease of acknowledgment. Many things came easily with this confidante.

"So, what if *that's* what you're running from?" his sponsor had said, with the absolute selfless clarity that was his gift—that what he'd thrown wasn't a pass, but what he thought might be a lifeline.

The former Dean Street boy had considered it. Challenged his inhibitions, even to the extent of finding a man to make out with, through the pants, someone not his sponsor. He didn't want to fuck that up. But alas, no. There wasn't anything wrong with it, but there wasn't enough for him there. It was to be women, for him. He told his sponsor, who laughed knowingly. And who believed him—another part of this man's gift.

"Why are you laughing?"

"I feel sorry for you," his sponsor said, so gently.

"Why?"

"Straight men are the loneliest creatures on the planet. They've got no one to talk to."

WHAT HE ENVIED in these two, then, was their intimacy with that lost world of days. The living archeology of the slates, daily rumors of a quadrant different over there from the one here, the secret life of another kid's house, the ailanthus and fig tree shadow-fathoms of the backyards. The physical graze of friends or even enemies, the weird tenderness even, even, of the dance.

Tonight, he might be the loneliest creature on the planet, beyond even that generic condition his sponsor had ascribed to straight men. What was it, to be bereft of a childhood you couldn't consider without flinching? To pine for things you couldn't explain to another without tangling in defensive confusion? Wasn't it enough that he, that all of them, were divorced in time from that refuge? Why should it also be impossible to name?

How could it be tolerable, okay, maybe even perfectly wonderful, just to stay? Never to have run from this place?

How could it be fine to be—*together*?

Just having a nice night out with your boyhood friend from the block. Black kid and white, now in their forties, like him.

Taking an hour out of their evening to buy a local drunk a beer.

Like they'd never stepped outside the false oasis. Like for them it *wasn't* false.

He'd have gone home with them, if they'd asked. But how foolish, this thought. They had no use for him.

A week later he is back on the plane, the roof adequately repaired. Three weeks after that he is dry again and there is an offer on the house. He lets his brother and sister split it fifty-fifty.

121.
Who's Writing This Book?
(an abyss)

Who's writing this book?

It didn't spring from the Slipper's ledgers. Accurate though they might have been.

The novelist? I can hear the Wheeze sneering. "You can't grasp reality from within a fiction," he once said to me. "That's why Boerum Hill is impossible to think about. We're all stuck inside the old lady's fiction."

Is it C.?

C. handed out the nicknames. C. picked the teams and positioned the players. C. wrote the street for us.

But who's writing C.?

I'm trying, and surely failing.

122.
C., Part 5
(1994, 2008, 2019)

Decades on, out of these wreckages of the past, C. troubles over few. Each day trails a flotilla of unburied corpses. If he's learned anything, it is not to cultivate more than the necessary allotment.

So far as Brooklyn goes, he lives and works in New Jersey.

Sure, the neighborhood's still there if he goes around. A few slouchers on stoops, a few who'd answer the door if you knock. And sure, if he moves in those ancient orbits, he's offered news. The varied ascents and falls. C. nods, takes it in, but asks no questions. Fifty years of reports of his own demise and resurrection, he might well be someone else's unburied corpse to shrug over. He knows this and doesn't hold a grudge.

He goes less and less.

When his father reverse-mortgages the house, the fool, he ends up at the Bishop Mugavero Senior Center on Dean and Hoyt. His room, third floor, looks out across to the window of the former Screamer. She's silent now, only a voice in C.'s head. A silent screamer.

His father, never the talker, is silent now too, curled in himself, bewildered survivor into a new century. On any temperate day, he gets parked in a wheelchair out on the patio of the former Holy Family hospital. That's where the two of them visit, if it can really be called visiting. Right overlooking the ramp where C. and the Slipper and their whiteboys ran their feeble skateboards that hour before they were stolen, that day they abandoned skateboards forever.

Father's voice in his head.

Screamer's voice in his head.

The voice of the white boys of Dean Street in his head.

He almost never goes back, once his father passes.

WHAT DOES HE owe to the white boys of Dean Street?

A ninety-day stint at Rikers, that's what he owes.

In the first year of the Giuliani squeegee man purges, the Giuliani-Disney reboot, the racist Giuliani stop-and-frisks, C. owes to the white boys of Dean Street the last, the stupidest, and the most consequential of his three arrests.

He has been scraping by in those days by working as a mover, taking things on and off a truck, in a crew that moved offices in Manhattan. Files, filing cabinets, truckloads full of papers it is hard to believe anyone will ever look at a second time, papers it is hard to believe need hauling anywhere but to Fresh Kills.

Don't ask, just move these boxes, five to a teetering hand truck, into the elevator.

The job puts money in his pocket for going out at night, and at this time going out at night is what he likes to do.

The episode, the arrest, is one he prefers not to recollect, not least because of his own costume on the night in question.

It is a party night, and a balmy night in June, and he is a freak in those days. He is arrested while wearing a feather and beaded vest over his bare chest and belly like some member of the Village People. Additionally, he features at that time a white and purple streak dyed into his hair.

(There comes a day two decades later when his then-new wife shows him how in their early days, she managed to dial up his mugshot on the internet, just checking out his precursor life, due diligence on a man who talked too little of where he'd come from or been since. "Laughed my ass off, too," she says.)

He's been making a run, no doubt of that. The night in question he's already been at Webster Hall, Limelight, and Wetlands, dancing here, snorting there, not finding what he's looking for and unsure whether he'll recognize it if he does, yet unable to go home. The drug has filled him with a pacing energy—perhaps the Manhattan streets are the nightclub he seeks, the entire constellation of faces on the hoof.

It is his odd misfortune to be rounding the corner of University Place at two in the morning just as the *Rocky Horror Picture Show* crowd spills out of the Movieland 8th Street.

And there, in the mad costumed throng on the sidewalk appears a former Dean Street white boy.

Not a major one, just part of the crowd. C. has to struggle to pull up his name. He's not one of the Beatles, name-wise. Just one of the apostles.

But this apostle now stands on the Eighth Street sidewalk in an ill-fitting black butler's outfit, with a gold lamé vest under a black jacket, no shirt underneath—they're both facing each other on the Manhattan sidewalk in vests with no shirt. Of course, the former whiteboy's also got white face paint, red lipstick, and black eyeliner, plus fingerless leather gloves, and his hair slicked back to a fringe at his neck.

And this apostle stands pointing in wonderment at what's before him, as if he's the one seeing an apparition. Or like a child who's just seen a clown.

This will be the last night C. ever dresses loud for clubbing, plus he's dyeing the stripes back out of his hair first chance he gets. For any number of reasons.

Now the former Dean Street boy says C.'s name aloud in a tone of questioning, then adds, "What are you dressed as?"

"I ain't dressed *as*, man. I'm just dressed."

"Well, I'm Riff Raff. I didn't know you were into this!"

"I don't even know what this is." He's lying, actually. He knows. He thought this ritual midnight shit died around the time he was out of high school, thought it was native only to the 8th Street Playhouse, now long gone. But he knows.

Can this be what he was looking for, tonight?

No.

But it's sure what he couldn't have predicted, he'll give it that.

Half an hour later, as the costumed revelers thin out despite the warm night, white kids sending the scant-dressed girls out to hail the cabs and then jumping in five to the back seat, he and Riff Raff remain in front of the marquee, shooting the shit, sharing a joint.

That's when Giuliani's shock troops roll up. The new format you've been hearing so much about lately, but it isn't quite real until it happens to you. And at that point it's *too* lately.

They call themselves, what, the "anti-crime unit"? What does that make the regular cops, then—pro-crime? Four beefy New Jersey types, technically plainclothes though they're all unmistakable, not trying to fool anyone. These are cop uniforms, too, in their own way: three in oversized starter jackets, one in a Rangers jersey, all with moustaches and their badges on chains around their necks. They come out shouting, slapping cuffs on right away, completely into the show for all and any who might be watching.

This is the beginning of the cop-happy time.

It is their city.

Everything, public urination, graffiti, open container, all of it treated like a violent felony interrupted. Like a bank robbery.

Once they've frisked you, found nothing much, they relax, begin with their asshole bantering. But make no mistake. There's no way you're talking yourself out of this bust. Though god knows Riff Raff is giving it a go, tonight, talking about how people used to be able to smoke on the street in Greenwich Village, local tradition.

Sure, people used to.

White people.

How could C. have been so stupid? The costume he was in wasn't helping with anything either.

There's no talking the cuffs off your hands and so you're down for the full ride, off to the Tombs. It's a Friday night and you won't even see a judge for a preliminary hearing until Monday morning.

Nine times out of ten such a judge will call it even on a beef like this one. The sentence, so long as you cop the plea, will be "time served" for the weekend in jail. R.O.R.—"released on recognizance." Don't let me see you in my court again, next. But don't try and point this likelihood out to the arresting officer. It gets you nowhere, or possibly worse than nowhere, might draw some special attention.

C. is more or less flying under the radar here, because Riff Raff is making so much noise on both their behalf.

The point isn't that you'll serve serious time on just one of these pickups.

The point, as he has carefully explained to him by his Rikers cellmate, is that each bust gets you in the system, and then the clock is ticking. Then the counting begins.

They're into their broken windows theory now, their cumulative game. Three felonies is three strikes, the new law. But what about misdemeanors? Though not writ in law, these are subject to a rule of three as well: three misdemeanors and you're up for a bid at Rikers. No more warnings or lectures from the bench, no release, no recognizance. Word has come down.

Lock them up.

Get them in the system and start counting.

C., before this arrest, sits on one open container pleadout, and a second on possession of graffiti materials.

Open container?

Sitting on a stoop. A way of life. If the anti-crime unit had been patrolling Dean Street in 1972, they could have swept up a dozen rooming house men for open container on a daily basis.

Graffiti materials?

That's legal stuff, art supplies you can purchase at Canal Paint, but not to be carried around in a backpack by a Black man.

In the Giuliani anti-crime regime, in the cop-happy city, C. has entered the system for the third time. All three times on bullshit beefs.

He's awarded a ninety-day bid at Rikers.

Free entry to the Rocky Horror Picture Show.

HE DOES, HOWEVER, owe the refuge of his present career, the stability of his life here in New Jersey, to another kid from the neighborhood. A Colony South Brooklyn Houses basement acquaintance, a tall break-dancer he'd previously last seen spinning on his head on a chunk of cardboard at Albee Square Mall. Two weeks after C.'s release from Rikers, he runs into this guy in a three-piece suit at Washington Square Park. Financial advice, investments, cold-call sales, that's his line. Seeing C. down on his luck, he goes avuncular. All that exists between them is the tether in time and space, but that's plenty. Why not help a brother? White folks help their own, that's how it works.

C. has been released without parole. Given the courtesy of a fifteen-minute conversation with a social worker about do you have a place to go to and what are your plans? The social worker hands him a folder full of pamphlets about BOCES and Re-Rout, The Fortune Society, vocational training. Stuff he chucks in the trash on the Queensboro Plaza subway platform.

He hasn't gone back around to ask about his old job with the office movers, whether out of injured pride or just not feeling like it, he can't quite say.

Now here's this former breakdancer from Albee Square telling him he can work on the telephone?

Wouldn't he need a broker's license?

Hell no, he could be on the phone pushing packages tomorrow.

When you get a client near to commitment, hand the receiver to a broker. Meaning his friend, the former breakdancer in the three-piece suit. Who is nonetheless down at Washington Square for purposes perhaps better left unquestioned.

The former breakdancer touts his "shop"—the back half of a storefront in Spanish Harlem. C. should come around. He explains, too, that he's got another protégé, someone much like himself. Guy from the old neighborhood, a former Gowanus Houses boy, also with a record, who sits and makes calls and is soon to get a broker's license of his own. That's how far this protégé has come. C., the former breakdancer explains, should come up and see how it works. Watch a call or two, sit in.

Why not? Has he got something better cooking?

IN THE SHOP in Spanish Harlem the next day, C. discovers the identity of the other protégé. A kid he knew only passingly, but famous in an unspoken way.

The protégé is the smaller friend, whose bullying idol drew him into catastrophe.

The two who captured the two white boys and made the newspapers.

That story talked of everywhere at once and then covered in silence so thick it was almost religious.

C. can still recall his mother's angry clucking at him when he made the mistake of asking what she knew about what happened to those two.

Later, on the street, C. learned they'd disappeared up to Elmira. A thing you didn't want to think about. But here he is, in the shop in Spanish Harlem, selling financial services on cold calls.

Talking sweetly, sympathetically, to the old people on the other end of the line.

C. remembers this about this kid now: his ineradicable sweetness and impressionability, his air of merely wanting to assist his chaotic friend in whatever was needed: steal a slice of pizza, get his dick sucked, scoop up a white boy. Unfortunately, white boys come in pairs, or they did that day.

Next thing you know your picture is in the *Daily News* and your story is told in a whisper to frighten younger children.

Next thing you know your story is told in Albany, to help change laws allowing minors to be tried as adults.

Mutual recognition passes between them now.

"Pick up the other extension," the former smaller friend says. "Listen how it's done."

C. picks up the extension and listens.

The former smaller friend has got a good way of switching up his voice, emphasizing all in it that's nerdish and unthreatening to a white ear—and now C. recalls this too: how teachers liked this kid, once, because he had that nice voice when he wanted, because he really ever only wished to please.

C. listens in as the client is moved close to commitment, and then, at the moment of closure, is switched to the phone of the former breakdancer. They are always to be called clients, the former smaller friend explains, after he's switched the call. Always spoken of respectfully.

Is this who C. is now? Apprentice to one who could not be helped? What does that make *him*?

He shuts up and learns.

On a smoke break down on the sidewalk, C. casually ventures the name of the smaller friend's disastrous idol: How did it go for him?

The idol's former smaller friend just shakes his head.

"It didn't go easy," is all he says.

IT TURNS OUT that at this new game C. is as much a natural as he was at stickball, at stoopball, at wallball. His old gregariousness, now this becomes his stock in trade. He monetizes his talent for palaver, for drawing a listener over a line, into his confidence. Into their own confidence, that's how he prefers to view the procedure. He instills confidence, or reveals it. Clears an area, like a campground, which the client might not have glimpsed in the weeds of their own financial yearning and distress. The fear that they're missing out on what everyone else knows, secrets of solvency, adequate retirement, affordable European vacations.

Ten years later, C. has his own license, his own tiny office and landline, his own compass for navigating the gray zones inherent in the profession. The investments he sells on the telephone, they don't always lose money, though as in all matters you can only help people up to a certain point. He skirts the pyramid-formed opportunities, though these present themselves to him everywhere, ground floors onto which you'd best hurriedly seduce enough clientele not to be trapped there yourself.

He's got nothing to apologize for.

He is not specially inclined to apology. Money flies up and down— that's what it does. You catch it as it flies.

When relations or heirs of some of his older clients call him with their grievances he explains it to them patiently—again, up to a certain point.

His number is easy to find. His office location? That he has worked meticulously not to advertise.

ON THIS DAY, however, on return to his office after stepping out for a sandwich and smokes, he finds a card jutting from the seam of the door. It is the card of a real estate broker from White Plains, one who's taken the time on a weekday to journey out here and seek him in his secret office—what's up with that? Not a name he recognizes, but the number is circled and underlined, and accompanied by an emphatic CALL ME.

After eating his sandwich, C. calls. Sure enough, on the phone the guy starts in all incensed, something about targeting his mother's nest egg.

"Listen, all I do is put opportunity in front of people, they make their own decisions."

"Why her? That's my question."

"Why anybody? I talk to who answers the phone."

"You're trying to claim this is some kind of coincidence?"

C. feels a heat rising in his neck. First the unannounced visit, the card in the door. Now this weird implication.

"Coincidence? What are you talking about, man?"

"I'm still in the area, would you mind if I stopped by?"

Whatever this is, it doesn't resemble the approach of a fraud investigator, or even some jumped-up lawyer or cop. C. tells the mystery man sure, to come on by. The mystery man appears at his door in twenty minutes. It is the spoiled boy.

SHOULD HE HAVE recognized the woman's name, or her voice? Unlikely, with the volume of calls he initiates. Even the large number who entertain some portion of his pitch, who invite a callback, or purchase a financial instrument or two. Had he heard her voice more than a time or two? That was decades ago. And neither she nor her son, frankly, have distinctive and memorable names.

Just more white people.

What might have grabbed his attention, now that he pulls the line up on his sheet, is the 624 prefix. He notes these when they appear: the 624s and 625s and 852s. Boerum Hill prefixes, numbers he'll never get out of his head. Has he thought of the Brownstoners when he dials the phone? The aging renovators, fearful empty nesters, living on the rent from the duplex, watching their real estate taxes soar, bewildered by the appearance of storefronts with names bragging of notions they'd fought to erase, like the Gowanus Canal Supper Club, or Cheese Factory, or Plaster & Lathe? Hell, next they'd have a bed-and-breakfast on Dean called Rooming House. Or a boutique called Prostitute on the corner of Nevins and Pacific.

Has he envisioned them when he cold-calls those prefixes? Their desperation and bewilderment? Their readiness for his pitch? Of course he has.

Now the son, the former boy, stands at his desk. The indulged and protected one, the one for whom protection failed totally. Soft features and sloped shoulders like a collapsed building, elbows held near his sides like a bargain with the indignities of his fate, like he's always just trying to slide into a crowded A train car without bumping anyone.

This effect, the extent to which the spoiled boy still resembles himself, is one C. has no doubt he provides in return.

We all look like ourselves forever, that's the funny part. Just worn down.

"I'm not asking why," the fifty-year-old spoiled boy says. "I'd just ask you to quit, okay? Lay off, pick another target."

C. forms and abandons his defense in one instant. This isn't a courtroom. "I can do better than lay off. Let me make her some bread." He catches himself even as he says it. Charity? Bragging? Call it sport.

But no. The spoiled boy shakes his head. "Scratch her off your list, okay?"

C. shrugs. "As you wish."

It's the end of it. Also the last time he'll lay eyes on one of the white boys of Dean Street, at least to the best of his knowledge. As well, and for what it's worth, consider it the last time he dials a 624 or 625 or 852 prefix. Fuck 'em.

It means nothing.

Nada, zilch, zero.

Nothing at all.

It wasn't as though they'd struck some deal requiring they all go through life thinking about the block forever.

123.
Allegory
(erotic)

There was once a boy who fell in love with rows of houses.

Call him the Allegorical Kid. Don't bother trying to conjugate him to the preceding pages. He exists in a different space, all his own.

The Allegorical Kid was a freak. The love of these houses was the only form of eroticism that really touched him.

Just one house wouldn't do the trick, though he could appreciate a single one. The repointed brick or freshly resurfaced brownstone, the lintels of brownstone, the cornices of black painted cast iron. He'd run his eye over a good example, and feel a delight shudder through him. A tease or flicker of a fulfillment yet to come. One house was like a kiss.

But what the Allegorical Kid really needed to achieve ecstasy was a fully refurbished row of such houses. He knew this sensation, felt it throbbing deep in him, at a cellular level, tasted it in dreams. Yet he had barely known it in actuality.

His own block was a crude disaster. There might be ten or fifteen row houses on the entire street that struck him as rightly appointed, as crisply and correctly restored. There were, in one case, three in a row that felt right, a little mini-burst of gratification—if he could only lop off the dismaying, imperfect houses bracketing those three. But he couldn't.

His heart rose at the appearance of scaffolds, at the sight of the men in white T-shirts and painters' caps and with their dungarees and shoes caked with brownstone globs, at the sight of their trowels and mixing tubs. A perfected block, a perfected street, this was the coming thing, he felt. All of the logic of the heart pointed in this direction. Who wouldn't thrill to see the restorations?

Who wouldn't, sure, maybe. But for him, an obsession.

THE DREAMS HE had were flying dreams, though he rarely rose higher above the slate sidewalks than he would if simply running along them. He ran to achieve takeoff, then soared skippingly at the same level, his sneakers breaking contact with the ground, his legs lifting behind him as if swimming. He might be flying only at the speed of running, too. But effortlessly, carried as if in some jet stream. He'd rise to the height of the parlors, the top of the stoops, no farther. Then weave downward, so if he'd chosen, he could drop his feet slightly and graze the slates, or resume running.

Though he was never conscious of his penis while still in the dream, it was always rigid when he woke. Plank-like, numb, uncanny. In this embodied form, the dream carried itself into his waking hours.

ONE DAY THE Allegorical Kid sat with a friend on the friend's stoop and talked as they stared, absently, at the doings of the block. The different groups passing by. The clattering bus, the windless trees, the lazy silence punctuated by a dot of merengue or the ice cream truck's mad looping jingle. Across and up the street, two men on a scaffold with putty knives scraped the aging pale pea-green paint from the brick of a housefront.

"They're gonna make 'em all look the same," said his friend.

"They're restoring them," the Kid said.

"I like the colors. It's boring, all the same."

This came as a shock. It was true, in some earlier phase neither of decline nor refurbishment, in the name of upkeep but without regard for the cause of historical treatment, many of the brick fronts had been painted gaily. Eggshell white, or weird toothpasty pastels. One was even lavender. It was chaos. The boy had never considered how anyone could be drawn to it. His friend seemed absolutely crazy to him. Yet maybe it was something less than craziness. An absence. His friend lacked a certain nerve or receptor, one the boy not only possessed but which centered in his psyche, in his body, in his lusts.

Otherwise, why not enjoy the candy colors, even if they tended to flake and peel? If one was a child, one should enjoy colorful things! Not drool after repointed brick, or stone the color of malt, or of ex-lax, the chocolated laxative.

How did he become such a fetishist?

WAS HIS A defensive response to the trials of the streets? Maybe so. If so, a preconscious one. The Allegorical Kid was unaware of turning from the life of the children, the life of his own childhood, toward the renovator's art. The plasterwork, the wrought iron, the soupy brownstone facing that gelled into an edifice. Unaware of when he'd begun lingering around sidewalks in front of the antiques shops on Atlantic, marveling at the power of the lye and turpentine, used to strip seven layers of paint from a marble mantelpiece. Unaware of when he first viewed the men who rubbed the marble pieces with the ferocious solvents as heroes in some kind of enterprise of conquest or reclamation, some kind of war. He only knew that by the time his sexuality might have developed along other lines, it was too late.

Of course, he knew his own house was one of the problem ones. His father had vowed to do the interior himself, had surrounded himself with the right information and materials, all the special knowledge, but had left before completing it. At least the front was passable. It had been when his parents bought it. The brick and brownstone were their true colors and intact, the metalwork and lighting and painted address numbers unruined by any of those erroneous or anachronistic flourishes that sometimes crept into the more cursory renovations.

HE COULD NEVER attain satisfaction on his own street. It remained a dream. For satisfaction he had to resort to certain glowing, leaf-shaded blocks of Cobble Hill or Brooklyn Heights or Park Slope, where a long-enough sequence of the right kind of row houses had been preserved or restored to the ancient standard, made to exemplify their fullest selves. The easiest to find were the short blocks: Clinton and Henry Streets in Cobble Hill, 6th Avenue in the Slope. There, a run of perfect brownstones could go from corner to corner. Far more elusive was a long block of comparable beauty. That remained his ideal, a block long like his own, long enough to resemble the run-flying slate sidewalk of his dreams. There was one block of Sackett he adored, between Hoyt and Smith, though those weren't all the grandest houses; he could sometimes get off there. Anytime he stumbled onto a good row, with nothing to impede his joy, nothing painted wrong, no blighted brick face or stucco, no fake gas jet lamps, he'd grow excited, whether he'd been searching or not. Once or twice rapture had taken him completely by surprise, a waking dream, a diurnal emission.

Yet rapture remained elusive. This part of his life was largely thwarted. His eroticism left dying on the vine.

The block on which he'd grown up, that would forever elude him.

Ironically, though the desirability of the houses on his block continued to escalate, and many of the weakest links in the past were snapped up by wealthy buyers, more than capable of bringing a brownstone to perfection, the standard by which his sensibility had formed was slipping away, into the past. The new buyers, those who displaced the original renovators of his parents' generation, they didn't actually care that much for the heavy ornate parlor ceilings, the sworls of plaster and marble, the intricate moldings and chess-piece banisters. They often purchased the buildings to gut them, to create open plans, install metalwork spiral staircases, two-story ceilings that smashed through the basement level up to the second floor. They were impatient with the limited space of even the most commanding four-story row houses, and plopped extra penthouses onto the ceilings, or built decks out over sun rooms into the backyards, expanding the footprints, destroying the original outlines. Sometimes what they ripped out were precisely those hand-restored details the first Brownstoners had so painstakingly labored over and cherished.

Even when the exterior resembled the old style, the Allegorical Kid knew too much, he saw too much, had been inside too many of the houses on his own street and seen the travesties, to find himself erotically entranced as he needed to be.

At least in some other neighborhood he could pretend the interiors had been handled correctly. And in the Slope and Cobble Hill there hadn't been quite such a mad rush of the wealthiest hipsters, the dot-com and pharmaceutical fortunes, the film stars. Ironically, the slowness of the original gentrification had made it possible for the last and gaudiest of the gentrifications to land on his own street, in the end. And with that gaudiness came a wreckage to his erotic endeavor.

Ironically, the proximity of the housing projects, Gowanus Houses and Wyckoff Gardens—that which had checked the progress for so long, that which had kept the bankers from believing these streets could ever be the Slope or the Heights, or even Cobble Hill—it was this which had left the door open for the late madness, the culmination, the crisis, the speculation and turnover, the European and Russian money, the weirdest and hippest of the restaurants—a Montreal smoked meat and bagel shop!—and the ruin of the precise and careful restoration he'd grown up hungering for.

Had the old lady's dream come true?

Hard to say.

Had hers too been an erotic fixation?

Ridiculous question. Withdrawn.

His fixation, at least, had soured in the air of new money, and even newer money after that, and it had never come true.

The Allegorical Kid, now in his fifties, was an erotic fugitive.

124.
No Music
(an ending)

We swore at the outset: no music, no honeyed light. Let this inquiry be pure, be flayed of that stuff, the ooze of nostalgia. No special lexicons of forgotten street games. No time for that now.

If the boys get no names, why should the songs? Who cares? You can't hear songs from this distance. This isn't a playlist. This isn't a dance party. Just count the crimes. Trace the deals, the broken bargain.

Yet the light, the music, it snuck in anyhow. Inevitable, I guess. Our poor inquiry? In the end, it amounted to little. The account of crime was just a medium, a language loom. Suspended in it, absolute loss, the junk of the past, a few Yoo-hoo bottlecaps flooded with candle wax, a *Penthouse* stolen from a parking lot watchman's booth. So, sure, some music crept in too. That old hard-boiled style, so difficult to shake, another music. The corny vernacular: put an egg in your shoe and beat it, tell your story walking. All the swears, the oaths, the motherfucking cocksucking fuck fuck fuck, fuck you and this whole goddamn remorseful nostalgic pile of shit you're always trying to hand me, the shit on your shoes when you walked in the door, the shit of the past that will never wipe off, and, above all, the unspeakable word hiding in plain sight everywhere, always passing on the pavement whenever you glanced up from your own shoelaces.

But you know the phrase: I'm rubber, you're glue, whatever you say bounces off me and sticks to you.

We were all rubber, all glue, on those streets. Sometimes I think I am nothing but the accumulation of the names I was awarded on the pavement.

I, you ask?

Who was I?

I was one of them, the children of Dean Street, specifically between Nevins and Bond. I could be coy, and suggest to you that I was one of the girls, but I'd really be asking you to humor me. Asking you to pretend to think it. I could also claim to be Black. See me there: just a lonely Black man, walking down the street. But no. Obviously no. I was a white boy.

Am a former white boy still.

There were those who ran away and those who stayed; I was one of those who stayed. Beyond that, let me decline to specify. I would prefer not to narrow it down. Let us just say that I am among them always. Black, brown, white, boy, girl. The rememberers and the forgetters. I am in their company. I love them too much to want to say more.

Acknowledgments

In this writing I've been reliant on help to an unusual degree. It may be impossible to express the depth of my gratitude to this wealth of carers, thinkers, and rememberers. Nuar Alsadir. Mirene Arsanios. Helen Atsma. Daniel Aukin. Tamosin Bardsley. Miles Bellamy. Brian Berger. Celia Bever. Jessie Black. Wade Black. Joseph Brooker. Arielle Cooper-Lethem. Jeremy Davis. Kevin Dettmar. Eliot Duhan. Tony Gerber. James Hannaham. Sean Howe. Julia Jacquette. Luke Jaeger. Peter Jaeger. Donna V. Jones. Jarett Kobek. Matthew Lanes. Julie Langsam. Pat Lee. Rich Lee. Blake Lethem. Mara Lethem. Eugene Lim. Maureen Linker. Diane Martel. Eliza Martin. Neil Martinson. Celia Mattison. Frederick McKindra. Sean Meyer. Criss Moon. Anna Moschovakis. Alexander Nazaryan. Sarah Neilson. Aaron Nottage. Lynn Nottage. Julie Orringer. James Peacock. Tim Pierce. Ivy Pochoda. Claudia Rankine. Jess Row. Dione Ruffin. Earl Rusnak. Karl Rusnak. Anne Sanderson. David Shapiro. Alissa Simon. Joel Simon. Eric Simonoff. Adam Snyder. Christopher Sorrentino. Sam Sousa. Dana Spiotta. Clifford Thompson. Kyla Walker. Kyla Wazana Tompkins. Elvia Wilk. Ben Willett. Stacie Williams. Gavin Wilson. The mistakes are mine.